FC-10.

Orphan Train

Previous Books
by James Magnuson

The Rundown
Without Barbarians

James Magnuson
&

Dorothea G. Petrie

Orphan Train

The Dial Press

New York

Published by
The Dial Press
1 Dag Hammarskjold Plaza
New York, New York 10017

Manufactured in the United States of America

Second Printing—1978

Design by Francesca Belanger

Library of Congress Cataloging in Publication Data

Magnuson, Jim.
Orphan train.

I. Petrie, Dorothea, joint author II. Title.
PZ4. M1876or.   [PS3563A352]   813'. 5'4
78-5820
ISBN 0-8037-7375

Acknowledgments

I would like to thank Hester Ferris and Richard Snow for invaluable aid, and our editor, Joyce Johnson, for her outstanding guidance.

J.M.

Many were helpful in the development of this story, among them: Virgene Bollens, Maggie Field, Jerome Kass, Candace Lake, Phoebe Larmore, Nigel McKeand, Marcia Nasatir, Seth Nasatir, Carol Roper, and Joe Wizan.

My gratitude to my husband, Daniel Petrie, and son, Daniel Petrie, Jr., for their time, encouragement, and support.

D.G.P.

Historical Note

The summer of 1973 I took my mother, June Leo Grundy, to the centennial of Dysart, Iowa, the small town where she was born. There I met her old friend, Ben Pippert, whose personal history was highly unusual. He had been one of a group of very young children who had arrived in Dysart by train on a wintry day in 1894. They had been herded off the train and into the town hall to be put up for adoption by anyone who would have them. He was one of the ones chosen. The remaining children were put back on the train to try again in another town along the route.

I was fascinated by his story and in particular by the phenomenon of the "orphan train." Two years of research followed, during which the little known, remarkable story of the Children's Aid Society came to light. Over a fifty-year period, between the years 1854 and 1904, the society sent out more than 100,000 homeless New York street children by train to towns and farms in rural areas across America.

D.G.P.

Orphan Train

*T*he poor jammed Sixth Avenue waiting for President Pierce that July 14th in 1853, but the president was late. They had stood through the rainstorm, and now the sun had come out. The bands in the doorways were playing again and the hawkers were back at work, selling hot corn, apples, and tiny American flags. The police kept pushing the crowd back, trying to keep the avenue clear, but with little success. Ragged children darted and ducked past them to wave up at the Crystal Palace that rose high above Bryant Park, the delicate dome of glass brilliant in the sudden sunshine.

A girl, no more than ten or eleven, danced for money in the street. She had short red boots, grimy ribbons in her curly hair, and a filmy red scarf that she raised and lowered coyly in front of her as she danced and sang, dropping a shoulder, sliding a leg out and back, teasing, suggesting . . .

I'm Pierre de Bon Bon de Paree, de Paree,
I drink the eau de vie, eau de vie . . .

Her audience of sailors and fire laddies and Bowery Boys in their plaid trousers applauded and hooted and sniggered and threw coins. As the coins bounced and rolled along the stones, a large, fierce-looking woman with wispy red hair bent down, quick as a cat, and retrieved them, dropping them into a small leather bag.

When she wasn't busy retrieving coins the woman stood with her arms folded, eyes moving constantly over the crowd. The butt end of a knife protruded from her belt. She looked to be in her late forties, with a great, square face, and when she adjusted her blue kerchief it only partially covered the livid scar on her neck.

Next to her stood a blind beggar, dressed in layer upon layer of rust-colored tatters and rags, his long, stained fingers wrapped around a cane. His head was twisted to one side, like a bird listening intently for any movement in the earth. He smiled constantly, but both he and the woman were on the alert in the holiday crowd.

As the girl danced she kept looking back at the woman, but the woman gave no sign of recognition.

When I ride out each day in my little coupé
I tell you I'm something to see . . .

The girl put her hands on the top of her curly head, rolled her hips, and batted her eyes at the fire laddies.

Coins chimed on the street and went rolling. The woman scrambled for the coins, reaching here and there, under people's feet.

The blind beggar, head still twisted to the side, suddenly flicked his cane and swatted down a rolling coin.

"One more over here for you," he said. "One more for Lizzie the Dove. Under my cane."

Lizzie retrieved the coin, dropped it in her bag, pulled the drawstring tight. She looked at the blind beggar, then patted him on the arm.

The blind man reached out and jangled the leather bag with his long, stained fingers. "J.P.'s doin' a nice bit of dancin' today, I see, Lizzie."

"Ahh," Lizzie said. "It's the Crystal Palace openin'. We always do better on holidays."

"No, Lizzie, it ain't that, sailors don't throw away their money on glass palaces. J.P.'s a good girl. You hold on to her, Lizzie. You treat her right. A couple more years, she'll be worth a lot more to you, Lizzie the Dove."

The girl's dance was beginning to slow down, she was tired. She looked to Lizzie, appealing to her, but Lizzie only nodded sternly for her to go on. A trio of policemen were headed down the avenue toward them. A couple of the Bowery Boys began to drift back through the crowd, pushing aside an organ grinder.

Then, suddenly, a man burst out of the crowd. He was an older man, not a gentleman, but not a pauper either; a clerk or a scrivener, most likely. He wore a snuff-colored jacket, and he was a bit lame in one leg and supported himself with a stout stick. His kerchief was askew, his face flushed, and he seemed quite drunk.

He wriggled in time to J.P.'s song, trying to imitate her, then bowed to the crowd. Some fire laddies sent up a raucous cheer. He moved toward the girl, lifting his feet as if he wanted to dance. J.P. moved back, but the man in the snuff-colored coat kept limping toward her, lifting his stick, holding it close to him with both hands, swaying with it as if it were his dance partner. A group of canal boys slapped their knees and punched each other in the shoulders, roaring with laughter.

For a moment J.P. tried to play along, shaking the scarf in

front of him, then pulling it away. He lunged for the scarf and missed. A couple of coins rolled by them.

"Let's see you catch her, old feller!" someone shouted.

"Let's see what you can do!"

More coins sailed through the air. A half-eaten ear of corn skidded past.

"That's for your dancin', you old cripple!"

Egged on by the crowd, the man in the snuff-colored jacket pursued J.P., his face flushed, swiping at her with his free hand.

J.P. looked toward Lizzie, but Lizzie was down on her knees, scooping up coins. The blind beggar leaned forward, swinging his head from side to side, trying to follow the cat-calls of the crowd.

J.P. was deftly avoiding her pursuer, but she was rattled now, confused by the ugly shouts of the crowd and the lurching man; suddenly she had become a frightened child. She dodged behind a sailor, skipped through the canal boys, and ran for Lizzie.

The old man in the snuff-colored coat still pursued her, never sensing danger until it was too late. As J.P. dashed past, the blind beggar stuck out his cane, caught the stick of the man, and, with a deft flick of the wrist, sent it flying into the air. The man would have fallen flat on his face except for the fact that his fall was broken by the butt end of a knife catching him in the chest.

He straightened up and stared at Lizzie the Dove.

"What in Sam Hill . . ."

"That's enough," Lizzie said. "You leave the girl alone."

"Leave the girl alone? I never touched the girl. This beggar struck at me. . . ."

"All in fun," Lizzie said. The beggar stood motionless, smiling, head cocked, leaning into their conversation. Lizzie pulled tight the drawstrings of her leather pouch.

The man was confused now. "The girl is . . . she's yours?"
"More mine than yours," Lizzie said. J.P. stood behind Lizzie, still breathing hard, the red scarf balled up tightly in her hand. The blind beggar stroked her hair. The canal boys had turned their attentions to a vendor of sweetmeats.

The man looked around for support. There was none. "All the same, the man didn't have to knock me down."

"All in fun," Lizzie said. "It's the holiday." Lizzie smiled for the first time, and raised her hands, pressed together as if in prayer, so that only the man in the snuff-colored jacket could see the knife concealed between her palms. His eyes grew wide.

"I didn't mean anything," he said. "It was just with the opening of the Crystal Palace. . . . Well, a man's got to celebrate the best he can, right? And none of us can get a ticket, not today. . . ."

"That's right," Lizzie said.

"I didn't want to hurt her. She's a beautiful little girl. I had a little girl like that once. . . ."

"All right, mister, why don't you go over and take a look at the exhibition? Maybe if you stand around outside long enough, one of them philanthropists will give you a free ticket, maybe John Jacob Astor himself . . ."

The blind beggar reached out and handed the man's stick back to him.

"Why, yes," the man said. "Yes, I think I'll do that." He nodded to J.P., who didn't smile, just pulled closer behind Lizzie. The man in the snuff-colored coat limped off into the crowd.

A shout went up and then another. At first few knew what it meant, but the police were swinging their clubs now, trying to force the crowd back. People tried to get out of the way, buffeting against one another. "Horses! Get back! Look out for the horses!"

Far down the avenue came the mounted guard, ten abreast, their horses clattering and shying, tossing their manes in impatience. Panic ran through the crowd, as people began to shove and stumble, trying to get back to the sidewalk. A woman went down, got up, and went down again, knocked off balance by a stocky man running behind her. A vendor tripped, ears of hot corn were trampled underfoot, more people slipped and fell.

Lizzie gave the drawstrings of her leather bag a final jerk, then dropped the bag down the front of her shirt. When she looked up, she didn't see J.P.

"J.P.!" She craned her neck, looking right and left. "J.P.!" Her voice was angry, then alarmed. Muttering a string of oaths, she darted through the crowd, shoving one person aside, sending another sprawling, until she spied the curly head bobbing in front of her.

"J.P.!" She reached out and clamped the girl by the wrist. J.P. looked up at her, flinching as if afraid of being hit. "What's wrong with you? Are you daft?" Lizzie stared at her, J.P. couldn't speak. "You just stay here. By me, love. Where you'll be safe. Come on now. . . ." She yanked J.P. toward the sidewalk.

The horses cantered nearer. The soldiers were brilliant in their uniforms, their buttons shone. Some of the crowd applauded, others still scrambled, trying to get out of the way. A young boy darted, barefoot, out into the street, fell, then rolled out of the way of the horses.

The blind beggar still stood in the street. He had been spun around a dozen times by the surging crowd, and he tapped wildly with his cane, rapping people's legs, trying to get his bearings. "Lizzie!" he shouted. "Lizzie the Dove!" He screamed in terror now, his long, stained fingers reaching up.

J.P. saw him and pulled back against Lizzie. Lizzie turned

and growled something at J.P. The girl pointed at the beggar, and, although Lizzie grumbled, she allowed J.P. to drag her back. J.P. reached up, taking hold of the fumbling, frantic stained fingers of the blind man. Lizzie gave J.P. a jerk, yanking them back toward the sidewalk, the three of them lurching and stumbling in a chain, scuttling out of the path of the prancing, high-spirited horses.

*T*hey were late and it was Emma's fault. She stood behind her uncle, the Reverend Edward Symns, who fumbled through his pockets looking for the tickets. Over his shoulder Emma could see the packed hall, the mammoth equestrian statue of Washington, the bunting draped from the balconies, and then, looking higher still, the slender ribs of iron arching overhead and the great glass dome of the Crystal Palace that had the appearance of a majestic balloon about to ascend. Inside, the band had just struck up "Yankee Doodle."

Emma felt her heart beat just a bit faster. She reached up under her rose-colored bonnet to be sure her combs were still holding her hair in place.

Her uncle found the tickets and handed them to the attendant.

There was nothing her uncle hated more than being late.

Emma knew that, and yet she had taken all morning getting ready. Emma was not a vain person, but today it mattered that she look well. Looking well could be a complicated affair; there were corsets and petticoats and hoops and the new gray satin gown that Emma had bought specially for the occasion. Then there was the biggest challenge of all, her hair.

Emma's thick, lustrous, and unruly auburn hair was her great pride, but her greatest trial as well. It seemed to have a life of its own; brushes and curling irons could only tame it temporarily before it began to escape, springing free into ringlets and curls of its own devising. Emma had spent the last hour of the morning working on it. She had coiled it and looped it, smoothing and tightening, jabbing it with combs until she was sure that it was secured.

This was not usual behavior for Emma, but the circumstances were not usual either. The opening of the Crystal Palace and World's Fair was the great social event of the year. Everyone was going to be there and, as Emma was particularly aware, they were all going to be there in couples. It being only three days after her twenty-eighth birthday, Emma was perfectly attuned to how the coupled world looked at twenty-eight-year-old unmarried women escorted by their uncles. Phillips would probably be there, with his new wife no doubt, and Emma did not want to look as if she needed sympathetic glances from an old fiancé.

"You may go right in, Reverend Symns." The attendant handed the light blue tickets back to Emma's uncle.

Reverend Symns offered his arm, Emma took it, and in they went. Entering the Crystal Palace was utterly dazzling, the great hall packed with men in cutaways, ruffled shirts, and black top hats, the women floating in clouds of satin and lace.

Emma's uncle thought the whole thing was wonderful. He

pointed out all the luminaries on the great stage to Emma. There was Jeff Davis, the secretary of war, and next to him, the governor of New York, and wasn't that Winfield Scott, didn't Emma recognize him?

A young man with a mustache and a slim European cane under his arm bumped into them, then skittered past without apology.

Reverend Symns spied an old friend, Mr. Goelet, sitting down in the front in one of the choice seats; the two men raised their hats in greeting to one another. A little farther on Emma's uncle spotted Horace Greeley, the newspaper owner, in a vigorous conversation with Carstensen, the architect who'd received so many jeers for the many delays in the opening of the Crystal Palace.

A fresh-faced attendant took Reverend Symns by the elbow. "Could I see your tickets, sir?"

"Why, of course," Reverend Symns said. "The president hasn't arrived yet, has he?"

"No, sir," the attendant said. "He's expected in just a few minutes."

Reverend Symns turned and smiled at his niece. "Well, Emma, it didn't turn out so badly after all. I suppose all can be forgiven." He winked at her.

The attendant returned the tickets to Reverend Symns. "Sir, if you'll go to the back of the floor here, another of the attendants will help you."

"Fine, fine." Reverend Symns tipped his hat to a dazed-looking young man in the crowd. "Do you remember him, Emma? The inventor we had dinner with, terribly intelligent fellow . . ."

Emma and her uncle moved down the aisle, jostled on one side by a stout gentleman in white waistcoat, bumped by a woman in a purple bombazine gown on the other. Reverend Symns was in too excellent a humor to take offense at any of it. His ordinarily stern and somewhat forbidding profile somehow seemed softer to Emma. He strode along, coattails flopping, greeting old friends in the crowd.

"Hello, Mrs. Webb. How are you? Mr. Webb . . ."

"Oh, Reverend Symns, what a delight . . ." Mrs. Webb virtually sang out, the ostrich feather on her hat shaking with her enthusiasm. Mr. Webb leaned over, nodded politely. Mrs. Webb turned her attentions to Emma. "Oh, Emma, my dear, you've never looked better!"

Another fresh-faced attendant rushed up, anxious to clear the aisle. "Your tickets, please."

Reverend Symns handed over the tickets without looking. "Mrs. Webb, I must say, this is a pleasure . . ."

"Oh, Reverend Symns, we miss you so much at Trinity. Why, Mrs. Gardner and I were talking just the other day, how it doesn't seem right, not to have you there."

"We all move on to other things, don't we, Mrs. Webb? Tell me, how is Mrs. Gardner?"

Emma scanned the crowd, keeping an alert eye out for Phillips. It was not that she was afraid of seeing him; there was nothing for either of them to be ashamed of, not really. Emma touched her hair, making sure it was still in place.

Offering up the tickets, the young attendant smiled apologetically. "Excuse me, sir, but that will be up the stairs."

"Up the stairs?" Reverend Symns said.

"In the west balcony," the young attendant said.

"The balcony," Reverend Symns said.

Mrs. Webb protested. "There must be some mistake . . ."

"No, no," Reverend Symns said. "It's perfectly all right. Mrs. Webb, perhaps we'll see you a bit later. Mr. Webb . . ."

As they made their way to the stairs Emma regarded her uncle with amazement. Did he really not care? The slight had been blatant. He gave no indication that he was aware of it. The light blue tickets in his fist, he pointed out the exhibits to his niece. "There, Emma, look at that, isn't it wonderful? Who do you suppose is the sculptor? Not that Danish fellow? You know about these things, Emma, I don't."

Her uncle had been insulted, Emma felt it even if he didn't. Reverend Symns had been one of the most prominent clergymen in the city for fifty years. He deserved a place on the platform; none of the dignitaries there had done anything more for the progress of New York than he had. For him to be shunted back to the balcony was outrageous. Just because he had retired from Trinity Church and wasn't in the public eye in the same way . . . or at least not this public.

"Emma, look, steam engines! Now isn't that something! You're too young to remember, Emma. . . . Oh, but it's all very grand, isn't it?"

By the time they reached the top of the long stairs Reverend Symns, his face suddenly white, had to stop to catch his breath.

"Are you all right, Uncle Edward?"

He reached out and patted Emma's arm. "I'm fine, Emma. Just give me a moment."

Yet another young attendant came and took them to their assigned places, far back in the balcony. Reverend Symns stood on tiptoe, craning his neck to see what was going on down on the floor. Several seats away a man in a white suit and a Panama hat, a New Orleans planter no doubt, clapped his hands to the band music and sang along. "Stuck a feather in his hat and called it macaroni . . ."

Emma turned and stared out through the glass dome, down onto Sixth Avenue. The street still thronged with people, with hurdy-gurdy men and hawkers and beggars, with the poor who hadn't been able to get in, yet displayed their tiny American flags like the most fervent of patriots. Some waved up at the Crystal Palace as if expecting the president to magically appear and bestow some blessing on them. A young girl danced at the edge of the street, then disappeared behind some pushcarts.

Emma watched intently from her high perch. There was something in the restless movement of the crowds of the poor that frightened Emma, and yet she knew that her uncle had made his work among these people, that he was honored among those outside the Crystal Palace if not by those within, and perhaps that was what had freed him from slights and insults, knowing where his true place was.

There was a discreet tap at Emma's elbow. "He's coming in now, Emma. The president's coming in."

Emma stared down at the sea of bobbing black hats. Under one of those was the president of the United States. Which one, she could only guess.

The band played "Hail Columbia" and this was followed by a very long prayer and the "Old Hundredth" followed by an even longer address, during which Emma's uncle pointed at William Backhouse Astor, followed by an extraordinarily brief speech by President Pierce. The president welcomed everyone, even those "who came to us from the gray old nations of Europe." He spoke of the science and technology that would sweep away ancient privilege and usher in a new age of brotherhood and freedom, of the railroad that would unite them all like hooks of steel, of the exhibition as a brilliant sunburst heralding a brighter future. The exhibition was officially open.

Emma and her uncle wandered through the exhibition halls, through what seemed like endless displays of reapers and mowers, clocks and cotton gins. In front of the exhibit of the new Colt revolver her uncle exchanged a few words with Henry Ward Beecher before the crowd bore them away in different directions.

Emma and her uncle were in the French wing, bending down to examine a new Fresnel lamp for lighthouses when a woman's voice rang out behind them.

"Reverend Symns! Reverend Symns!"

Emma's uncle rose to his full height. Mrs. Gardner, a handsome darked-haired woman of fifty, swept toward them and grasped both of Reverend Symns's hands. "Why, Reverend, you're looking just wonderfully. Mrs. Webb told me you were hiding yourself back here."

Reverend Symns was smiling warmly. He was never a man, Emma thought, to be indifferent to female admiration. "You know my niece Emma, don't you?"

"Why of course!" Mrs. Gardner thrust a gloved hand toward Emma. "How are you?"

"Just fine, thank you," Emma said, just warmly enough. Mrs. Gardner didn't notice; she returned her attentions to Emma's uncle, and Emma went back to her examination of the Fresnel lamp. Her uncle had never lacked for the attentions of women when he was at Trinity Church, and it was something he had missed since his retirement. Emma was not going to begrudge him his indulgence; he had few enough of them.

"I hope you're enjoying the exhibition," her uncle said, his voice taking on a new vibrancy.

"Oh, very much," Mrs. Gardner said. "I wouldn't have missed it for the world. Why, just everyone is here, aren't they?"

"Not quite everyone," Emma said. Mrs. Gardner looked mildly disconcerted. "Tell me, which is your favorite exhibit?"

"Oh yes, why . . . Kiss's *Amazon*. It's quite spectacular. I hope you've seen it."

Reverend Symns looked at Emma. "I don't think we have, have we, Emma?"

"Oh, then you must. It's very powerful, very emotional. It's right outside here. Let me take you." Mrs. Gardner took Emma's uncle by the elbow and began leading him off. "Now you must tell me why we never see you."

"It's my new work, Mrs. Gardner."

"Now this is your work with the homeless children, isn't it? Yes, I think Mr. Gardner told me. Why, I think that's wonderful . . . those poor little creatures . . ."

Emma followed her uncle and Mrs. Gardner, staying a few paces back. This was not a conversation she wanted to become involved in. Emma ordinarily had good manners, but she had been in conversations with Mrs. Gardner before and had little patience for Mrs. Gardner's highly predictable prejudices.

Kiss's *Amazon* was gigantic and, Emma thought, terrible. A mounted woman warrior, her arm drawn back, her ample bronze breasts exposed, was poised to plunge her spear into the tiger that had already sunk its teeth into the neck of the rearing horse. The sculpture had attracted a circle of murmuring admirers. Emma found everything about it excessive; its size, its sentiments, and its symmetries.

Her uncle hadn't noticed the sculpture at all. He was doggedly at work with Mrs. Gardner.

"We have to be able to provide these children with hope in this world before we can offer them hope for the next," he was saying. How many times had Emma heard her uncle try to convince people with these very words. Mrs. Gardner blinked, touched her face with her gloved fingertips, looking concerned and beginning to look uncomfortable. "There are thousands of these children in the Fourth Ward alone, living in residences where the police are afraid to go unless they're in squads . . ." Emma almost had the words memorized. ". . . as many liquor shops as houses, and the worst dens of vice. The dance saloons where prostitution exists in its most brazen form."

Mrs. Gardner looked down, pulling absently at the fingers of one of her gloves. "Yes, I've read about it in Mr. Greeley's columns . . ."

Reverend Symns was not about to let her off the hook. "If you could see it with your own eyes, Mrs. Gardner, these ragged, wild girls with their baskets and pokers gathering rags. Come down to the mission, meet these children. . . . Without the Christian enthusiasm of people like yourself there would be no hope at all."

"But where have these children come from, Reverend Symns?" Mrs. Gardner was uncomfortable and embarrassed now. She tried to make a joke. "I take it it's not spontaneous generation?"

Emma glanced at Mrs. Gardner. She forgot her vow to stay out of the conversation. "I think, Mrs. Gardner," Emma said, "that the Lavoisier experiments have proven that there is no such thing as spontaneous generation."

Mrs. Gardner looked alarmed. "Oh, well, my dear, I wouldn't know about biology, I was only making a joke."

"I believe that the experiments showed that the flies and maggots, rather than springing out of the air, had actually hatched from eggs planted in open wounds and rotting meat. . . ."

"Emma," Reverend Symns said.

"I'm sorry, uncle."

"Your niece seems to know a great deal about science for a young lady," Mrs. Gardner said. "No doubt she's one of your converts?"

"Convert to what?" Reverend Symns asked.

"Oh, to the work with the children. Certainly, Reverend, if you can't convince your own niece, how can you expect the rest of us . . ."

"Emma has been a great help," Reverend Symns said, a bit coldly. It was a sore point.

Emma decided that she didn't like Mrs. Gardner at all.

There was nothing that Emma disliked more than ignorance passing as wit. Spontaneous generation! Perhaps it was only inane when referring to maggots and flies, but it became a very nasty joke when applied to vagrant children.

In the past year more than three hundred thousand immigrants had come through the port of New York, jamming into a city of half a million. In the lower wards of New York, three, four, and five families lived together in single rooms. The vagrant children came from these homes, from families destroyed by poverty or disease; others were deserted, lost, or abandoned.

No one knew quite how many homeless children there were in New York. The chief of police had estimated ten thousand; others said more, but any one who walked the streets of New York had seen them, walking rag-bundles of children, dirty, foulmouthed, begging, selling papers or apples. Several times Emma, returning home at night, had looked out of her carriage to catch a glimpse of a child curled up asleep over a warm grating.

There were stories in the press now almost daily about the gangs of thieving children, embryo courtesans, a swelling army of child criminals. There were the dark stories, too shocking for polite conversations, that Emma's uncle had come home with, stories he wouldn't be sharing with Mrs. Gardner. An eleven-year-old girl Uncle Edward had visited in prison had made her living for more than a year by posing as a seller of toothpicks and fruit. After making her way into the offices of the counting houses, and after the turn of the key, the girl would sell herself for practices that no one in polite society dared speak of.

One of the things that Emma admired most about her uncle was that once he saw a problem he never flinched from it. Even when he was at Trinity it had been his habit on Sunday afternoon, after preaching the morning sermon, to visit the poor on Blackwell's Island. Emma, as a young girl, had always been impressed by the effect those visits had upon her uncle. Often he wouldn't speak of them at all, or, if he did, it was only in the briefest, most cryptic way. It frightened Emma to see her uncle, a man who usually had something to say about everything, struck silent for hours at a time. His silence made Emma press him with questions, and one of the answers he gave her had stuck, reverberating in her young imagination for months afterward: in response to her question of where he had been, he replied that he had spent the afternoon standing among the wrecks of the soul.

Reverend Symns had been retired for two years, and since then he had devoted almost all of his time to work with the vagrant children. He wasn't alone. There were a growing number of ministers who had joined him in the hard, Sisyphus-like work. They established industrial schools and Sunday meetings, lodging houses and reading rooms, and now, under the leadership of a young minister named Charles Loring Brace, they were charting the most daring plan yet to deal with the multitudes of poor children.

Her uncle was engaged in a great work, Emma knew that, and she knew, too, that he was disappointed that she hadn't joined him in it more fully. There was no entirely satisfactory explanation for why she hadn't.

In part, she had kept her distance out of a fear of becoming a professional church woman. Emma had been around church work and church women for all of her twenty-eight years and she felt in need of a little fresh air.

In spite of that, she had tried to help her uncle, more than a few times, and every time she came back feeling that she was a failure. She'd always returned disappointed in herself, disappointed at her awkwardness with the children. No matter what she told herself rationally, there was a part of her that was repelled by their dirt, their smell, their casual obscenities.

Once she'd accepted an invitation to present a magic-lantern show of the Holy Land at one of the Sunday meetings. The boys had taken advantage of the darkened room to roll marbles on the floor, toss spit wads, and exchange cuffs to the backs of each other's heads. By the time the lights were turned back on, Emma had a full-fledged brawl on her hands, one that she was helpless to control. Reverend Brace and a passing policeman had to be called in to quell the uprising. Emma never went to another Sunday meeting. No one, no matter how high their ideals, can be expected to look forward to the opportunity of being ineffectual.

Emma's contribution now was reduced to two afternoons a week spent at the society answering correspondence. The response to the society's work had been immediate, overwhelming, and often heartbreaking. Emma opened letters from parents who felt they could no longer raise their children, letters from prisons and hospitals, letters of children driven out of drunkards' homes, boys cast out by stepmothers or stepfathers, tales of suffering, loneliness, and temptation.

Emma had been touched and shaken by many of the letters, and she answered them thoroughly and conscientiously in the fine, even hand she had learned at the Hartford Female Seminary, but on those occasions when one of those ragged, dirty children, having actually found its way into the building, would poke its head in the door to ask for directions to the reverend's office or the loo, Emma found herself stiff and wary, as if she were face to face with some wild, untamed creature.

Mrs. Gardner was proving a difficult convert. "But tell me honestly, now, Reverend Symns, do you really think that reading rooms will have much of an effect? I mean, these poor dears with no place to lay their heads, one can sympathize, and I do—my, but you do present the case so well— but Mr. Gardner was telling me, just the other morning over breakfast, that the docks are absolutely overrun with these poor creatures. Why, the amount of theft from Mr. Gardner's warehouses alone . . ."

Emma bit her tongue and decided against making any remark about the warehouses of Mr. Gardner. Her uncle handled these women so much better than she ever could.

"Yes, I know," Reverend Symns said, nodding, as if to acknowledge that a point had been made, though perhaps the wrong one. Emma had seen that nod before.

People were knocking all about them, craning their necks, exclaiming over the spear-carrying Amazon. When Reverend Symns spoke again, there was a new edge to his voice. "I'm aware that these children need more than reading rooms, and so is Reverend Brace. They need Christian homes and decent work and a chance to make something of themselves. . . ."

Mrs. Gardner looked a bit frightened.

"Don't you agree, Mrs. Gardner?" Reverend Symns asked, more softly.

"Well, of course. But Christian homes don't grow on trees, do they? But perhaps your Reverend Brace has arranged to furnish all that?"

"We are making that effort," Emma's uncle said. "We've been in communication with farmers and manufacturers and churches in the Middle West . . . places where an extra mouth to feed is also an extra hand . . . where good clean air and hard work could make something of these children."

"But the Middle West?" Mrs. Gardner couldn't have sounded more shocked if Reverend Symns had suggested the Sahara.

"We've written to people in Indiana, Ohio, Michigan, as far west as Illinois."

"Illinois? My dear Reverend Symns, you must be mad, you're sending these poor children into Indian territory."

"Now Mrs. Gardner . . ."

"I know perfectly well, Reverend Symns, that there aren't any more Indians out there, or wild ones, at any rate, and I'm sure these buckskin-and-calico people are all full of hearty democratic virtues, but, truly, Reverend Symns, I've never understood why milking cows or collecting eggs or getting up at dawn makes any one more virtuous than the rest of us. Come now, Reverend, are we city dwellers all that wicked?"

Emma could hold herself back no longer. "I don't think my uncle is as concerned with your wickedness, Mrs. Gardner, as he is with finding these children homes."

"Yes, of course." Mrs. Gardner straightened, again taken aback by Emma's abrupt entrance into the conversation. "And I suppose you would know, wouldn't you, Emma?"

"I've read some of their letters, Mrs. Gardner. Many of them have lost children of their own. And from what I know from those letters, I would sooner trust them with a child than anyone I've met at the exhibition."

"Emma!"

"I'm sorry, uncle."

"I want you to apologize to Mrs. Gardner. I'm sure you didn't mean . . ."

"All I meant, Mrs. Gardner, is that the letters I've read are quite generous . . . open-hearted . . ."

"I'm sure they are," Mrs. Gardner said, trying to smooth her ruffles.

"Excuse me, uncle, I believe I'll go look at the daguerreotype exhibit. I'm sure you and Mrs. Gardner have many things you'd like to discuss."

"Of course, Emma," Reverend Symns said. "Of course."

"It was very nice seeing you again, Mrs. Gardner."

"Very nice seeing you, Emma," Mrs. Gardner said. "Mr. Gardner and I will have to have you over to the house. So we can have a chance to visit in a more relaxed setting."

Emma moved through the crowd, her face burning. She knew that she had behaved badly, but Mrs. Gardner's snobbishness was more than Emma could let pass. The society had received a letter from one of what Mrs. Gardner would have called the buckskin-and-calico people, and the pain in those careful lines was still fresh in Emma's mind. The letter had thanked the society for sending their circular. The town had lost a dozen children to the fever the winter before, the minister and his wife had lost both their little boy and little girl. They would welcome any children who needed homes, the letter said, and the day after they received the society's circular the minister's wife began preparing a room in the hope that they might be so fortunate as to find a child themselves. . . .

Mrs. Gardner was a silly, smug woman, and her uncle was foolish to put up with her. No doubt he would have said in his own defense that people can be changed, must be changed, but Emma just didn't see the shining possibilities in Mrs. Gardner. No doubt that indicated that her uncle was a better person than Emma, but it was exasperating. Her uncle always saw possibilities in everyone; he was the only one who had thought that Phillips was the eminently possible mate for Emma, and Emma had been slow to forgive her uncle for that.

Emma again scanned the crowd. She was sure that Phillips was here somewhere, with his new wife on his arm, no doubt; Emma's friend Martha had said that they had tickets. Emma hadn't spoken to Phillips for months; their last communication had been the note that Emma had sent him on the occasion of his wedding—a kind note, Emma thought, but she had never gotten a reply.

There was no reason for Emma to be anxious about the meeting. If she ran into Phillips, she would be perfectly pleasant; neither of them had anything to be ashamed of. She and Phillips were not meant for one another, and the only reason she'd agreed to the ill-fated engagement was that it seemed a chance for independence and a full, adult life. Her uncle, ever a believer in possibilities, had encouraged her.

Her uncle thought him perfect—educated, attentive, Christian, as well as a dry-goods-store heir. And he *was* perfect, as Emma soon discovered, perfectly self-assured. A large-headed young man with a round, placid face, Phillips combined a certain slowness of comprehension with a strong reliance on his own opinions. He had opinions about everything. His opinions were like a great, smothering blanket that could render the flickering, smoldering stuff of life into a safe, gray bed of ashes.

As soon as she made this discovery Emma canceled the engagement, as tactfully as she could, blaming herself and her coldness. She told Phillips that she, like Mr. Emerson, in his essay on friendship, could not suffer people to come too near, and, again like Mr. Emerson, was unsure whether this was a fault or an ideal. Emma did such an excellent job with this sort of talk that Phillips ended up simultaneously impressed, confused, and full of pity, but his male pride was spared.

Emma's friends were horrified at her breaking off the engagement; beggars and twenty-eight-year-old single women were not supposed to be choosers. Emma gave her friends a variety of explanations, but in her heart of hearts she knew that it was her unshakable and perhaps childish belief that better things were in store for her.

Standing without an escort in the milling crowds of the Crystal Palace, Emma felt herself something of an adventuress. Her anger toward Mrs. Gardner dissipated quickly—there were too many people and things worth looking at to waste time being angry. Pushing ahead boldly on her own, Emma made her way into the daguerreotype exhibit.

The pictures were interesting. There were many too many of variety actresses and soldiers for Emma's taste, but there was a marvelous one of the Cincinnati waterfront, another of Sam Houston in an enormous plaid bow tie, one of Harriet Beecher Stowe sitting next to a sickly plant, and a shocking picture of Lola Montez, the notorious actress, leaning over a chair, a cigar dangling from her fingers. Emma would have spent some time examining Lola Montez if her attention hadn't been diverted by two men arguing, quite loudly, in the middle of the aisle.

One of the men was an artist, there could be no doubt. He wore a cape, his hair was long, his profile striking, in a way that suggested vegetarianism or other dietary experiment.

His opponent was even more striking to Emma, though in an altogether different way. He had dark good looks, white teeth, curly black hair, and now, with his face flushed with anger and his legs spread wide in the stance of a soldier, he exuded an alarming sense of energy, nearly tangible and not the least genteel.

The artistic gentleman was carrying the debate, numbering his points emphatically on his fingers. The broad-chested young man sighed, smiled, shook his head, and interrupted the orderly argument with some emphatic gestures of his own. Their voices rose in unison.

The point of the gentleman's argument was that whatever the daguerreotype was, it certainly wasn't art, and that daguerreotypists couldn't be considered artists. Artists had visions, artists had morals, they weren't mere mechanics, the true artist was present in his work. How could there be art without an artist?

It became clear now, from the nature of the artistic gentleman's remarks, that the sturdy young man with the astonishingly dark curls was a daguerreotypist. It also became clear to Emma, who had attended more than her share of lyceums, that the artistic young man was using a number of specious arguments.

There was a small crowd gathered around the two men— perhaps this gave Emma a sense of protection in numbers— even so, when ideas were involved, Emma tended to forget herself. A remark occurred to Emma, a right remark, quite to the point, and a right remark is something almost impossible to hold back, even for a properly brought-up young woman. Emma suddenly found herself stepping forward in a most unladylike way and saying, "Excuse me, but wasn't it Mr. Emerson who said, 'I am nothing, I see all'?"

The two men stopped, astonished, and stared at her.

The artistic gentleman recovered first. "I believe once again I've missed Mr. Emerson's point."

The young daguerreotypist laughed. "I believe you have."

The artistic gentleman bowed out gracefully. "Excuse me, won't you? I'm meeting friends over at the French painting exhibit." With that he turned on his heels and disappeared into the crowd.

"Thank you, miss," the young daguerreotypist said. "I was wondering what it was going to take to get rid of that fellow. I just never thought of Emerson."

"I should be getting back to my uncle," Emma said. She looked around her in a daze, searching for an escape.

"Oh, but you haven't seen my pictures," the daguerreotypist said. "They're right over here."

He pointed to the cases almost directly in front of her. They were the pictures of the variety actresses in an array of antic poses, some in costumes, others in little more than tights.

"You take a lot of pictures of women," Emma said.

"Oh, yes, I like women. I'm sympathetic to their cause." Emma couldn't quite be sure if he was ironic or not.

"I should be going," Emma said.

He smiled steadily. He was very sure of himself and his charms. "By the way, I'm Frank Carlin."

Emma didn't say anything. She may have made a social blunder, but she hadn't lost all sense of propriety. There was no way he was going to get her name out of her.

He reached into his back pocket and came up with a small packet of white cards. "I have a gallery down on Broadway. Let me give you my card. You'd be welcome any time." He held out one of the cards. She didn't take it.

"I've always thought of having one's picture taken as something of an indulgence," Emma said.

"Oh, don't worry about that," Carlin grinned. "I'll take you for free. I usually don't get a chance to take pictures of women of your type."

Emma glared at Carlin, but he didn't seem to notice. "And what type would that be, Mr. Carlin?" she asked in the coldest tone she could muster.

"Oh, I don't know. The way you're dressed, I'd guess, charity lady, something like that."

"Well, you've guessed wrong, Mr. Carlin!" Emma turned to go.

"I didn't mean it as an insult," he said. "Here, take my card. It's a perfectly respectable place, and I've just brought in some new rosewood furniture."

The card was again thrust at her. Taking it softened her exit—in fact, it canceled her exit altogether, because the next thing that happened was that Emma heard her name being called behind her.

Emma turned, the daguerreotypist's card still in her hand, to confront Phillips with his new wife on his arm.

"I thought that was you, Emma," Phillips said, in a puzzled voice.

"Hello, Phillips," Emma said, hiding the card in her hand. She couldn't think of one other thing to say. Everyone stood silent, smiling at one another. The daguerreotypist was not disappearing.

It was the ever-reliable Phillips who knew what to do next, introducing his wife and his former fiancée.

Lydia had perfect little features set like raisins in a tea-cake. "I've heard so much about you," she said.

"And I about you," Emma replied. She reached up to her bonnet. A wisp of hair had escaped; she tucked it back in.

The daguerreotypist had not removed himself.

He smiled at Phillips. "Frank Carlin," he said.

"Phillips Davies." Phillips smiled remotely.

"You're all old friends?" Carlin said.

"Very much," Phillips said. "And you?"

"Oh, no, we just met." Carlin smiled. "I'm showing my pictures here at the exhibition. These are mine right over here."

"Oh, say!" Phillips's eyebrows rose. "These are delightful." Phillips bent over the case to scrutinize one of the pictures, then straightened up again. "You know, it's my opinion that Americans do this sort of thing better than anyone . . ."

Emma hated them both. She knew exactly what Phillips was thinking: Poor Emma, lonely and single, so lost without me that she's reduced to taking up with strange daguerreotypists.

"Perhaps I can give you my card," Carlin was saying to Phillips.

Lydia smiled steadily at Emma.

The whole intolerable situation was relieved by a familiar voice.

"Emma!"

Her uncle was striding toward her. He never looked at Phillips or the wife or the daguerreotypist. "Emma, I think we should be going. I have a meeting at the society at four."

"Of course, uncle."

"Hello, Reverend Symns," Phillips said.

Emma's uncle looked dimly at the young man, taking a second or two to remember who he was. "Oh, hello, Phillips. How are you?"

"Fine, sir, fine. Surely you're not going yet? There are so many exhibits, you can't have seen them all."

"Exhibits are all very well, Phillips, but there is real work to be done. Isn't that right, Emma?"

"Yes, uncle," Emma said.

Farewells were exchanged. Emma was relieved when Carlin did not offer her uncle a card. As her uncle drew her away, Emma was aware that the young daguerreotypist was watching her leave. She found it unsettling. She tightened her grip on her uncle's arm.

Outside in the street her uncle tried to find them a free carriage, drawing Emma through a tangle of revelers and souvenir hawkers. He was so anxious about being late for his meeting that he was nearly oblivious of her. Emma was filled with gratitude all the same. He was right, there was work to be done, good work. Emma could breathe again, she felt relief at being freed of an awkward, stifling situation. She didn't belong in places like that, any more than her uncle did.

Once in the carriage, Reverend Symns settled down to his papers. Emma leaned forward, discreetly examining her reflection in the glass of the carriage door. She was all too familiar with her face and its faults—even framed by the rose-colored bonnet, the cheekbones were too sharp, the nose a bit too prominent—but did she really look like a charity lady?

A sudden movement caught her eye and she looked up, beyond her reflection and out into the street, at the jostling, shouting crowd, at the gaunt, hard faces of the poor.

*T*here was something crawling on her neck, and it woke J.P. She reached up and squeezed it without looking at it, felt it pop between her fingers. She flicked it away with her thumbnail.

She threw back her blanket. She clung to her pillow for a second, the goosebumps rising quickly on her arm. It was October, and every day it seemed to be getting colder. It was eighteen fifty-four—more than a year had passed since the opening of the Crystal Palace; for more than a year J.P. had stayed alive in the streets by dancing for coins.

She rolled over and stared out at the huge room. Tiers of bunks covered all four slimy walls. A streak of light shone through a crack in the far wall, but so far the girl was the only one awake in the Den of Thieves.

Perched perilously on their ten-cents-a-night bunks, the sleepers seemed as harmless and gentle as lambs. Jack the

Baggage Smasher hugged his pillow, One-Eyed Harry lay on his back, one burly arm thrown up over his eyes, Fred the Assassin muttered softly in his dreams. Even Lizzie the Dove, in the bunk next to the girl's, was curled up tight against the cold like a baby, only the butt of her knife showing under her pillow. It was peaceful now, but it would start again in another hour, the grumbling, the bickering, then the drinking and the terrible fights. . . .

She stepped out onto the straw and mud floor, pulled on a jersey and then a pair of trousers, jerked the belt tight. Lizzie the Dove moaned in her sleep. J.P. stood motionless for a second, afraid to breathe. Lizzie rolled over, and the girl could see the puffy livid scar on her neck. Lizzie's broad back rose and fell, rose and fell.

J.P.'s gaze was intent, not once did she take her eyes off the sleeping woman. For over a year Lizzie had bullied and worked and used her—protected her was what Lizzie would have said—but no more.

Lizzie's head was off the pillow now, the knife lay exposed.

J.P. took a step forward. Lizzie shuddered, as if in the grip of a bad dream. J.P. waited until Lizzie was still again, then reached forward quickly and grabbed the knife.

She stared down at the blade, her hands trembling, then looked again around the huge room. One-Eyed Harry had rolled over on his stomach. J.P. looked back at Lizzie, the sleeping woman's mouth had just opened.

J.P. reached up behind her own neck and took a handful of hair, hacked at it with the knife. She worked quickly, the dull blade pulling and catching, making the tears come to her eyes. Lock after lock of curly hair fell away. Some catching on her jersey, she brushed them away. Silently she chopped and cut until she was completely shorn.

She slipped the knife back under Lizzie's pillow. She had to move fast now. J.P. leaned over her bunk, and with her fingertips gently pried loose one of the bricks. She reached deep into the hollowed-out space and lifted out her treasures, laid them on her blanket. There was a man's watch, minus the hour hand, a red silk scarf, a coin with a Crystal Palace commemorative stamp, a painted doll's head, a soiled lace bow. She stuffed the red silk scarf deep into her pocket, found a newsboy cap under her blanket, and out of the newsboy cap took a well-folded piece of yellow paper. She stared at the paper for a second, then pulled the cap tight on her head. She hitched up her belt. She could pass.

Silently J.P. slipped into the alley, Murderer's Alley, quiet now so early in the morning. She moved quickly along the walls decorated with the rough drawings of ships, flags, and eagles. She felt her heart leap up. She'd made it. She began to run.

A cane flicked suddenly cross her path. She sprawled headlong in the dirt, and, before she could scramble back to her feet, long, stained fingers had her by the throat, pulling her up. J.P. stared into the face of the blind beggar.

"Now, there, J.P., what are you in such a big hurry for? What's the rush?" J.P. clutched the yellow piece of paper and didn't say anything. "I heard you comin' along so quicklike and I wondered . . ."

Still holding her tight with one hand, he ran the fingers of the other hand softly over her face, ran them over her short, jagged hair. He knocked off her newsboy cap, then reached down and picked it up. He crumpled it in his fingers, and a smile spread across his face. "Now what's this, J.P.? What sort of get-up do you have here? Tryin' to pass yourself off as somethin' you're not? Tryin' to give ol' Lizzie the slip?"

His rich, alcoholic breath was right in J.P.'s face; it nearly made her choke. "Lizzie would be mighty insulted if she knew, J.P. She'd think you didn't care about her. Maybe she'd even think you felt like we weren't good enough for ya

. . . not like your high-class actress mother, wherever she may be." He laughed, and the long, stained fingers relaxed. J.P. stood free.

The beggar frowned, his blind eyes blinking at her. "Well, we're not good enough for you, J.P. We're not good enough for anyone." He reached out and put the newsboy cap back on J.P.'s head, pulled it down tight. "Go on. Get out of here, before she wakes up." J.P. stepped back. He groped for his cane, found it, swung it impatiently in her direction and missed. He laughed.

"Sing 'Pierre de Bon Bon' for me, J.P., one last time. Let's see if you still remember it."

J.P. started to walk away. She was leaving Five Points. The blind beggar began to clap his long, stained fingers, awkwardly, like a child. "I'm Pierre de Bon Bon, de Paree, de Paree . . ." He was singing, in a high, crackly voice. She started to run. "I drink the eau de vie, eau de vie . . ." She was never coming back to Five Points, never, never. . . .

The ancient horse jerked the ragpicker's wagon slowly through the streets. A pig reared up, afraid of being trampled in the mud, and trotted down an alley. Mr. Delaney cooed and clucked to encourage the old horse, then pulled the animal up short in front of a decaying tenement.

Mr. Delaney shouted toward a small shed that rested against the side of the building. "Hello, lads! Anything today?"

Two small children crawled out of the shed, a black-eyed nine-year-old and his skinny six-year-old brother. Together they pulled a bundle of rags toward Mr. Delaney.

"How's this, Mr. Delaney?" the bigger boy said. "Me and Ben been up all night pickin'."

"Not bad, lad, for this time of year. But not that good either." Mr. Delaney climbed down from the wagon and picked up the bundle, shaking it down with a judicial air. "Packed a little loose, isn't she, Tony? You're not trying to short-change your ol' friend, are you?"

"No, sir, Mr. Delaney. Times are hard."

While his big brother did the bargaining, Ben patted the horse.

Mr. Delaney threw the bundle into the back of the wagon. "Well, I'll go for three cents, seeing that times are hard." He reached into his pocket for his purse.

"Can't you make it a little more, Mr. Delaney? Me and Ben, we're leavin' today. We're going out west on the railroad."

"So you'll be goin' out west, will you now? And what will your father say when he comes lookin' for ya?"

"He won't be gettin' out of jail. It's him that's fixed it. We're goin' out west to live with a family."

"What family is that?"

"Don't know yet."

The pig had come back around the corner of the building to reclaim its spot in the mud. Ben faced the animal, stamped his foot at it. The pig raised his head, sniffing, then grunted, not giving ground. Ben picked up a stick, readying himself. The boy and the pig had reached an uneasy truce.

"I thought so," Mr. Delaney said. "And where is this charitable family supposed to be?"

"Don't know that, neither. But it's the God's Truth: we's goin', ain't it so, Ben?"

The ever-wary Ben never took his eye off the pig.

Tony pulled out a dirty, much-folded piece of yellow paper and handed it to Mr. Delaney. "It's all wrote out here and printed too."

Delaney unfolded the paper and stared at it. It read: WANTED: HOMES FOR CHILDREN: CHILDREN'S AID SOCIETY. Delaney stared at the small, mysterious symbols that marched across the page in such neat rows, stared at them as long as he estimated it would have taken someone who knew how to read. Delaney patted the flank of his horse, nodded sagely, and handed the piece of paper back to Tony.

"Very nice, lads, very nice." The printing had impressed Delaney and perhaps it made him generous. "Here we go. A whole nickel, seein' as it's a special occasion."

Tony beamed at the nickel. Ben put down his stick to come have a look. Delaney climbed back up in his wagon.

"Thank you, Mr. Delaney."

"I hope you find homes, boys. They've got to be better than this. God save you, boys, the Lord watch over you . . ."

He picked up the reins and slapped the hind quarters of the horse. The ancient animal shook itself awake and then plodded blindly forward.

It had gotten down to choosing between very small things, and Emma was finding it difficult. Emma sat on her bed, her jewelry box open beside her. Uncle Edward was downstairs at breakfast, drumming his fingers, no doubt, but that didn't make it any easier. Emma had never been on a railroad trip before, and there was no one to tell her what to wear or how much she could bring: *Godey's Lady's Book* was without advice for what to do when you were traveling with a carload of orphans.

The sunlight warmed the bright, cheerful room. There was a lovely October light; outside the window, the bright leaves trembled in the autumn wind. It was Emma's favorite season in New York. She felt a small twinge of fear. If she went down now and told her uncle that she'd had second thoughts. . . . No, it wouldn't do, she saw that, second thoughts wouldn't do at all.

It was still hard for Emma to believe that she was making

this trip. For the longest time there hadn't been the merest suggestion that she should be the one to accompany her uncle in the first placing out of children. She had suffered with her uncle through the controversy leading up to the journey: the protests of the Catholic Church, the attacks in the press where the Children's Aid Society was accused of everything from trying to turn New York's thieves, liars, and vagabonds loose in the West without supervision to trying to sell the children as slaves to line their own pockets.

The year had been a difficult one for Emma's uncle, and he needed her more than ever. She had stood by him, comforting him when he was most upset, sharing his indignation, ministering to his needs without much thought of being ministered unto.

She became more directly involved with the work. She accompanied her uncle to the schools and the Children's Aid Society board meetings, and when her uncle and Reverend Brace began to interview men who might assist her uncle on the trip west, Emma was invited to sit in and give her opinion.

Sitting in on these interviews as one after another of the candidates was found unacceptable, Emma felt herself oddly disconcerted by the two men. They listened to her opinions, they appreciated her feminine influence, but it wasn't enough. With her new interest and vision of what was to be done, Emma found being relegated to the sphere of feminine influence highly dissatisfying.

Her relationship with Reverend Brace did not make things any better.

Emma was aware that her uncle would not have been displeased if she and Reverend Brace had developed a more intimate relationship. It wasn't something he advocated openly—after Phillips, he had learned his lesson—but Reverend Symns had a habit of dropping remarks about what a

courageous young man Reverend Brace was, what a principled young man, and attractive to women too, didn't
Emma think? He made these remarks just often enough to
make things awkward for Emma. The remarks were accu-
rate enough. Reverend Brace was courageous, principled,
and attractive to women, but at this point he was throwing
his full energy into the work with the children, and besides,
Emma felt that he still viewed her as the ineffectual young
lady who had let a magic-lantern show for boys turn willy-
nilly into a riot.

For a period of months her discontent mounted steadily as
steam in a kettle. After the finish of what must have been the
tenth of these interviews the two men were commiserating
about the difficulty of finding the right person: someone
strong, yet gentle, resilient, but understanding, someone
Reverend Symns felt he could work with, yet someone who
would be good with the children. Without warning, Emma
volunteered.

The two men stared at her. Was she serious? Emma spent
a half-hour convincing them she was. Emma was tired of
being an influence, she wanted to be a force "in her own
right." Wouldn't a woman be a help in supervising the girls?
Reverend Brace, ever polite, listened and said nothing. The
two men glanced at one another. The society's secretary
came into the room, very sorry that she had to interrupt, but
there was another man outside, waiting to be interviewed.
Emma's uncle stood up, stretched, and smiled. Tell the man
we're sorry, her uncle said, but the interviews are over.

Emma's room was in perfect order. Her books stood in
neat rows, the stacks of *Putnam's Weekly*s piled carefully in
the corner. Her little cast-iron horse and surrey sat on the
nightstand, her painted china doll perched on her desk,
smiling serenely back at her. Her uncle had never approved
of that doll. He didn't approve of any doll, for theological
reasons—it was sacrilege to reproduce the human form—but

Emma's mother had given it to her and Uncle Edward could scarcely object.

Emma stared at her books. There wouldn't be much time to read on the trip, she knew that, but she couldn't go without taking something. In her entire life Emma hadn't been without reading matter for more than twenty-four hours. Surely one book wasn't asking too much. . . . She scanned the row of books trying to decide. There were the Emerson essays, Washington Irving, the Longfellow, and then—oh, but she would have to hide it from her high-minded uncle— *Retribution* by Mrs. E.D.E.N. Southworth . . .

Emma stood up when she heard a carriage pull up outside. A man in livery tied the horse to the hitching post and strode toward the house.

She had to decide now. She looked back toward the bed. The objects were not very many: a small gold cross on a chain, the pendant Phillips had given her the night they were engaged, a brooch, a locket. Emma picked up the locket and opened it.

She stared at the miniature portrait inside it, her mother's picture. She had not really known her mother or her father. They were only as real as her Uncle Edward's stories had made them: a handsome young couple; he was a minister, just out of seminary, she knew three languages; he had a mustache, she had a beautiful singing voice; they had spent a year in Europe before coming back to New York where he was to take a church, where Emma was born, and they were totally devoted to one another right up to the day that they drowned when a rowboat overturned on a Saturday outing. There was one emotion, at least, that Emma felt she shared with the children on the trip: that ineradicable sense of abandonment that comes with the loss of one's parents. Emma closed the locket and put it in her bag.

As she came down the stairs she could see her uncle sitting erect at the table. He stood up as she entered the room.

"Good morning, Emma."

"Good morning, Uncle Edward. I'm sorry I'm late getting down. There are so many things you don't think of till the last moment."

It seemed to Emma that her uncle's face looked a bit sharper and older. "Of course," he said. They both sat down and Reverend Symns bowed his head for prayer. Emma did the same.

"Dear Lord . . ."

A loud bang made Emma look up. The butler was bouncing Emma's trunk down the stairs. Reverend Symns glanced at him. That was enough. The butler put down the luggage and bowed his head.

"Dear Lord, bless this food, that it may sustain us on our journey . . ."

Emma tried to listen to her uncle's words, but her own feelings were in too great a confusion. Part of her was exalted by the absolute daring of what they were trying, to do—the two of them, a sixty-seven-year-old retired minister and his spinster niece, well, it was a fact, she could say it out loud now, taking twenty-six New York street Arabs and orphans on a train and finding them homes in the West. Part of her was afraid that she would be discovered to be the ineffectual young woman that she suspected Brace thought she was. Part of her—Emma was now ready to admit to herself—was filled with a selfish excitement, excited by the simple fact that she was going somewhere, finally; her life was going to change. She knew that once she got on that train her life was not going to be the same—and she welcomed that. Emma added a silent Thank You, Lord, to her uncle's prayer.

There was a swill-gatherer singing "Old Dog Tray" as his dog jerked the swill car through the muddy paths of Dutch

Hill. When he saw the well-dressed young man with the broad shoulders coming toward him, picking his way carefully around the puddles, the swill-gatherer stopped singing, and when the man came closer, the swill-gatherer pulled off his cloth hat.

"Mornin', Reverend Brace."

"Morning, Charles, how's your wife getting on?"

"Oh, she's better, thank you."

"And your work?"

"What can you say about swill, Reverend? It's steady. That's the nice thing about bones, rags, and swill, you don't have to worry about the supply."

A hunchbacked child sitting in front of a chicken coop got up and came down to stare at Reverend Brace.

"Charles, I'm looking for Mrs. Slater's place."

Charles grimaced. The dog raised a hind leg to scratch at his harness. "Mrs. Slater? She's in the third shanty down on the right there, but I don't know why you'd want that nasty ol' . . ."

"Thank you, Charles."

Brace ducked his head as he entered the small shanty. A couple of chickens flew up ahead of him, beating their wings wildly in the air, circling, then settled under a small table. A woman sat sewing in a rocking chair, and a young girl sat on the floor, sewing with her. Three more children, half-clothed, sat on the bed staring at Reverend Brace. Under the bed a dog lay gnawing a bone. In the far corner of the room was a jungle of old wooden boxes, wheels, rags, and matresses.

"Mrs. Slater?"

The jungle of refuse jangled slightly. Reverend Brace stared at it. He could just make out the boy's eyes staring out at him.

Mrs. Slater looked up, unperturbed. "That's right."

"I'm Reverend Brace of the Children's Aid Society."

Mrs. Slater tied off the thread she was working on and stood up. "Patches, come out here."

"I ain't goin', can't make me." The voice came from the jungle of refuse.

"He's been hidin' in that corner all night," the woman said.

Brace peered into the tangle, smiling. When he put his hand on the piled-up boxes to take a better look, the tangle shifted, something clattered to the floor, the uneasy chickens took briefly to flight, and the boy wedged himself still farther behind his barricade.

"Where do you live, son?" Reverend Brace said.

"Here," came the answer from behind the boxes.

"He don't live here," Mrs. Slater said. "He don't live nowhere." Brace could hear the dog crunching on his bone. "His mother died two months ago and I said he could stay here for the night, not forever. I've got enough of my own. I can't keep him. He don't even have a real name. Just Patches. Get out here, Patches." Mrs. Slater reached suddenly back into the lattices of metal and wood and Patches bit down on her fingers. Mrs. Slater screamed in pain, the chickens flew up in Reverend Brace's face and he knocked them away with his arm, the dog barked and one of the children on the bed jumped down and ran out the door.

"Damn you, Patches, you're a child of the devil, a child of the devil. . . ."

Brace leaned forward against the latticework. "Don't be afraid, son. I'm not going to hurt you. We're going to send you to the country, to a good home."

"I ain't goin'. Gonna stay here."

"He can't stay here." Mrs. Slater sucked on her fingers. "That devil-child ain't stayin' one day longer. I have trouble enough of my own."

Reverend Brace took a form out of his pocket. "I'll need you to sign for him, Mrs. Slater."

Mrs. Slater wiped her hands on the front of her dress, then reached for the form.

From behind the jungle of boxes came the boy's voice. "What are you signin' me for?"

Mrs. Slater looked closely at the form, holding it to the light.

Patches came tumbling out into the room. "What are you signin' me for?" He threw himself against Mrs. Slater. The woman pushed the boy away.

"I'll make my mark," she said.

There was one stop they had to make, her Uncle Edward said, before they went to Clinton Hall. Emma scarcely heard him, her attention diffused by the clopping of the horse's hooves on the cobbled streets, the swaying of the carriage, the bright fall leaves, and the vague, fleeting thoughts that come at the start of any journey. It wasn't until the dark, dirty archways were in view that Emma realized that the one stop was the Tombs.

Her uncle got out of the carriage, looked up at her.

"Do you want me to wait?" Emma said.

"No, I want you to come with me. This is something we should do together." He extended his hand to help her down.

A matron led them to an interview room where they waited. The room was windowless and damp. Emma felt the weight of the gray walls pressing in on her.

A girl was brought in. She was perhaps fourteen, thin and pretty, brown curls framing her face; her eyes were intelligent and old for her years. Emma felt those eyes upon them both, assessing them.

"Could you tell me your name?" Reverend Symns said.

The girl didn't speak until she was prodded by the matron. "Sarah, sir," she said, pushing back her hair.

"Have you been here long, Sarah?"

The matron prodded the girl again. "Only two days, sir." She spoke with a slight German accent.

"And why are you here?"

"I do not know."

"She knows perfectly well," the matron said. "Don't let her try to play the innocent with you, sir."

"I think the girl can answer on her own," Reverend Symns said. The girl looked at him more closely. Reverend Symns addressed the girl himself. "Why are you here?"

"I will tell you, Reverend. I was working out with a lady. I had to get up early and go to bed late and I never had any rest. She worked me always, and, finally, because I could not do everything, she beat me. She beat me like a dog and I ran away. I could not bear it."

Emma stared at her lap, distressed, escaping the girl's sharp gaze. Emma wondered what those sharp eyes had seen. She tried to imagine it. . . .

Reverend Symns moved uneasily in his chair. "But I thought you were arrested for being near a place of bad character," he said.

"I am going to tell you that, sir. The next day my father and I went to get some clothes I left there, and the lady wouldn't give them up. And what could we do? What can the poor do? My father is a poor man who picks rags in the street and I have never picked rags yet. He said, 'I don't want you to be a ragpicker. You are not a child now. People will look at you. You will come to harm.' And I said, 'No, father, I will help you. We must do something now that I am out of place.' So I went out. I picked all day and didn't make much and I was cold and hungry. Toward night a gentleman met me, a very fine, well-dressed gentleman, an American, and he said, 'Will you go home with me?' And I said no. He said, 'I will give you one dollar.' . . ."

Emma glanced at her uncle. He never looked away from the girl's face and Emma could see the anger rising in him, could see the tightness in his chest and face.

"And I told him I would go. The next morning I was taken up outside by the officer."

"Poor girl!" Reverend Symns cried out at last, not able to contain himself any longer. "Had you forgotten your mother? And what a sin it was?"

It was as if Reverend Symns had slapped her across the face; the tears welled to her eyes. The matron shifted her weight from one leg to the other, frowned, folded her large arms. Emma looked angrily at her uncle. He was wrong to have said that, Emma thought, it was cruel.

"No, sir, I did remember her. I remembered that she had no clothes or shoes and that she died alone with no doctor to tend her. And I had no shoes and only this . . ." She plucked at her thin dress. Emma felt herself wanting to defend the girl. No one had the right to be asking these questions. Emma wanted to tell the girl to stop, that she didn't have to answer anything more, but Sarah went on. "I know what making money is, Reverend. I am only fourteen, but I am old enough. I have had to take care of myself ever since I was ten years old and I have never had a cent given me. It may be a sin, Reverend . . ." The tears were raining down her face now and she made no effort to stop them.

"I do not ask you to forgive it. Men cannot forgive, but God will forgive." Her body shook with emotion. "I know about men. The rich do such things and worse and no one says anything against them. But I, sir, I am poor. I have never had anyone to take care of me. Many days I have gone hungry from morning till night because I did not dare to spend a cent or two, the only ones I had. Oh, I have wished sometimes so to die. Why does God not kill me!"

She choked on her sobs. Emma's uncle waited for a minute, then began to speak quietly. There were homes and work, places where Sarah could make an honest living.

Sarah was mistrustful. "I will tell you, Reverend, I know men, and I do not believe anyone, I have been cheated so often. I do not trust anyone."

"But you are a child," Reverend Symns said. "You need a home."

"I am not a child. I have lived as long as people twice as old."

"But you don't want to stay in prison."

"Oh, God, no! There is such a weight on my heart here. I would kill myself if I had to stay here!"

"Then come with us," Reverend Symns said gently. "Come west with us and we'll find you a home, away from here."

"No. I will not go with any man. No."

"You see?" the matron said. "You see what these troublemakers are like, Reverend? You can't reason with 'em. You try to do 'em good, they don't even know what it is."

"I will not go with a man!" Sarah said.

Emma looked angrily at the matron and then at her uncle. She looked at Sarah.

"Would you go with me?" Emma said. Sarah looked at Emma and didn't say anything. "Could you trust me?" The girl's lip was trembling. Emma turned to her uncle. "Could I talk to Sarah alone for a minute?"

"Are you sure, Emma . . ."

"Beg your pardon, miss," the matron said, "but these bad girls learn how to play on your weakness, when you're not used to 'em."

"It will only be a couple of minutes," Emma said.

Reverend Symns rose slowly from his chair. As he left the

room, he looked back over his shoulder at Emma. He did not look displeased.

A half-hour later the carriage was swaying through the cobbled streets, Sarah sitting between Emma and her Uncle Edward. The girl was exhausted, and her head rested lightly against Emma's shoulder.

Whatever words Emma and the girl had exchanged were already forgotten. All Emma could remember was the almost numbing rush of emotion, the girl's hunger for comfort, for sympathy, the crying out, the clinging, shivering embrace.

"Have you taken a look at the maples in the park here, Emma?" her uncle said. "They're really quite lovely."

"Yes, Uncle Edward," Emma said, though she really hadn't seen anything for the last few minutes. She touched the sleeping girl's arm, this girl who was not a child. The journey had changed.

A crowd had gathered outside Clinton Hall when they arrived. The Children's Aid Society sign that hung over the entrance to the gothic building was spattered with tomatoes.

Emma and Reverend Symns got out of the carriage, taking Sarah by the arms, keeping her between them as they pushed through the crowd.

They did not go unnoticed. A man with a white whisk broom of a beard who was haranguing the demonstrators spied them almost immediately and pointed them out.

"There! You see? They are taking a child before your very eyes. They are taking these children from the only place they have ever known to be bound out to servitude for the rest of their lives." Reverend Symns's face was set, his lips tight and angry. "These innocent boys and girls are being sent into slavery with no rights at all."

"Let the girl go!" someone in the crowd shouted.

Emma walked faster.

A woman plucked at Sarah's sleeve. "You don't have to go with them, girl, come away, now. This is your only chance."

"Let her go! Let her go!" people were chanting in the crowd now.

A large man stepped out in front of her uncle, blocking the way. Uncle Edward tried to step around him. The woman was pulling on Sarah's arm. They were at the steps now and they began to run, dodging the angry, shouting people. The door opened and they rushed inside. The door was slammed shut behind them.

Sarah stared wildly about her, suspicious suddenly. "What they were saying? Was that true?"

"No, Sarah," Reverend Symns said. "There are people who oppose us, people who don't understand and don't want to understand . . ."

Two Roman Catholic priests were coming down the stairs. They nodded abruptly to Reverend Symns.

"Good morning, Reverend Symns," the older of the two priests said.

"Good morning, Father McQuade," Emma's uncle said. The three clerics bristled at one another for a second. Reverend Symns found the first missile. "I take it those are your demonstrators outside, Father?"

"They are no more my demonstrators than these are your children, Reverend."

"Did I ever say they were my children, Father?"

"But they will be your children soon, won't they, Reverend Symns? By the time you've completed your would-be errand of mercy. You can scarcely expect it to remain a secret, the fact that you are taking Catholic children and making them into Protestants . . ."

"No Catholic child has ever been brought to us, Father. A poor child is brought and we care for it."

Sarah's eyes darted uneasily from one cleric to the next.

"It sounds very charitable, Reverend, but both of us are old enough to know what evils have been committed under the name of charity. The fact remains that you are placing children of one religion in homes of another, destroying every trace of their faith and filial attachments and sending them into some indefinite region . . ."

Reverend Symns's face was red with anger. "We are sending them to the West, Father. Where they will find homes with people who will care for them better than any ignorant . . ." Emma saw her uncle stop himself just in time.

"Better than any ignorant what, Reverend? Better than any ignorant Romanist?" Father McQuade said. "What about these children's faith, Reverend?"

Reverend Symns spoke slowly, trying to control his words. "I do not know. Here is a child. Take her and make her a good Baptist, or Methodist, or Christian of any sect. Love her for herself. Can't that be enough, Father?"

"I'm afraid not, Reverend. I'm afraid not."

The two priests nodded abruptly and whisked past and out the door.

Above them, on the second floor, was the sound of children's voices. Reverend Symns started up the stairs, then stopped and looked back at Sarah. "It's all right, Sarah. I'm not selling you into slavery, you have to believe me." He stretched out his hand to her. She took it.

The second floor was in a state of bedlam. Boys were everywhere, in all stages of undress. Small mounds of old shoes and dirty socks and clothes were scattered like islands across the slippery wet floor. Splashes and howls came from behind a broad screen, and women carried great steaming tubs of scalding hot water back behind the screen to replenish the bathtubs. Naked boys leaped out of the women's way, skittering and darting as if they were avoiding the steamy torrents of Hell itself.

From the other side of a closed door marked GIRLS came more howls and screams, more highly pitched.

Emma led Sarah through the door and introduced her to one of the matrons. When Emma returned, a slight, red-haired man with trembling hands was talking animatedly to Reverend Brace. Two small children, a boy and a girl, cowered behind him.

"I can't keep them," the man said. "Their mother's dead. I want them away from here. They'll end up as drunkards or thieves in this city, I know it. Take my children away from this . . ." His eyes shut tightly. He was sweating heavily in the steamy room, and he reached up and wiped his brow.

"But surely, you've raised these children so far," Brace said.

The man turned and grabbed the boy by the wrist. The boy seemed terrorized by his father. "I can't raise them. I can't afford to have someone raise them. . . ."

"Watch your back!" A woman with a tub of steaming water was steering her way across the floor. The two children jumped back behind their father's legs.

"Take them west. Make something out of them." The man turned to appeal to Emma and Reverend Brace. "I can't raise two kids in this hellhole, they'll come to no good here."

"You have to be sure," Reverend Brace said. "If there are any other choices . . ."

The man's hand shot out, pushed against Brace's chest. "I'm goin' now. You take 'em. I've done all I could." The man turned suddenly and knelt down on the wet floor, jerked his two children to him. "These people will take care of you. You, Timmy, you watch over your sister. Eileen,

don't . . . you're going to be all right. You're going to grow
up big and strong and you'll ride horses all your own. . . ."
The sweat rolled down the man's face. "These are nice people. They're going to find you a home, a real one."

The man stumbled to his feet. The two children were too
terrorized by their father's violent movements to give any
sign of sorrow. The man stood blinking at them for a second, reached down and squeezed the wet knees of his trousers, then turned and ran down the stairs.

Brace knelt and put his arms around the two children.
The oldest one pulled away, staring down the long, empty
hallway.

A boy raced across the slippery floor and threw open the
door to the girls' room, revealing a naked twelve-year-old.
The girl screamed at him and threw a bar of soap, a matron
set down a tub of water and swung a towel at the fleeing boy.
"Liverpool, get out of there!"

Patches came running by and Brace reached out and
grabbed him by the wrist, pulling him up short. The boy
struggled, protesting, but all that the young minister did was
slip the bar of soap into Patches's hand, squeeze it firmly so
he knew the boy had it, and let him go. Patches, surprised,
stood for a second, staring at the bar of soap, then grinned
and ran off.

Brace bent down and scooped a pile of wet, dirty clothes
from the floor and tossed them at the large laundry basket
in the corner. The stench was still in the air. Emma tried to
smile; she was still too finicky, she knew it; there were going
to be a number of things to get used to.

A small boy in a newsboy cap stood in the doorway clutching his yellow piece of paper and blinking at them. He took
a deep breath, pulled his cap down tighter on his head,
hitched up his trousers, then sneaked past the wash area,
grabbed fresh clothing, and ducked behind the screen.

Emma stared at the rough, wild children. Two boys were having a tug of war over a blue shirt. One of the matrons tried to pull a comb through another boy's hair, and he yelped and kicked, tears coming to his eyes, and she held him with one arm around his thin waist. Another matron was being held at bay by a towel-snapping boy with a withered arm. They snarled and barked at one another, their voices echoing in the high-ceilinged room. Emma felt a chill, suddenly, as if these were not children she was watching, not children as she had known them, but wild animals or some savage tribe whose language she'd never been taught. These small fierce creatures had survived carelessness, brutality, and ignorance, and the marks were still on them; it would take more than a few tubs of steaming water to erase them. Emma felt the stirrings of panic.

"Emma?"

She turned. It was Reverend Brace, watching her with a look of concern.

"Are you going to be able to handle all this?"

"Of course," Emma said. She straightened up. She wasn't going to have anyone take her for less than she thought her due. The boy with the withered arm was still snapping the towel at the matron. "Young man!" Emma said, her voice ringing with a new-found authority. It worked. The boy stopped, the towel still stretched tight, the matron cowering with her hands in front of her face. The boy stared at Emma. "Come over here, please," Emma said.

The boy threw his towel over his shoulder and came to Emma.

"Tell me your name, please," Emma said, trying to maintain her firm tone.

"Mouse," the boy said, rubbing his shoulder with his chin. Emma's heart was beating fast. She was very aware of Brace still watching her.

"Tell me, Mouse, why were you snapping your towel at that lady?"

"Don't like her."

"Why not?"

Mouse was examining Emma closely, looking her up and down, fascinated by her hoop skirts. He was not more than nine years old, and he was very small.

"She wanted me to take a bath."

"And you don't want to take a bath?"

"No." Mouse looked up at Brace. "Who's he?"

"His name is Reverend Brace."

"Don't like him either."

"Mouse, why don't you want to take a bath?"

"I'll just get dirty again, miss."

"Tell me, Mouse, would you like it if somebody snapped a towel at you?"

"No, miss, I'd punch 'em all up."

"What are towels for, Mouse? Can you tell me that?"

Mouse was silent. "You gonna towel-snap me, miss?"

"No, I'm not, Mouse. And do you know why I'm not?"

"No. Why, miss?"

"Because you're going to need that towel, Mouse. Because, right now, you're going to go over and tell the lady that you're sorry, and after that you're going to march back and take yourself a bath, and when you're finished you're going to dry yourself off . . . with that towel. Isn't that right?"

Mouse stared at her. Then smiled. "I never had a lady boss me before," he said, and with that, he marched off.

Emma turned to Reverend Brace. "Now, Reverend Brace, you can just tell me how I can help."

Reverend Brace took Emma by the arm and led her to a table near the door on which were piled papers, tags, blankets, lunch boxes, and Bibles. Reverend Brace picked up a piece of paper.

"This is a list of the children with as much information as we could get. Once the children are clean they will be sent here. What we want you to do, Emma, is to provide them with a tag giving name, date of birth, religion, if they have one, parents, living or dead . . . and make sure it's securely attached," Reverend Brace said. "We don't want to be losing anybody; we've got enough problems already." He smiled. "After that you can give each child a blanket and a box lunch."

The wild-haired boy who had opened the door to the girls' bathroom was being dragged into the bath area.

"I ain't got fleas. Come on, guv . . ."

"In you go, Liverpool." Behind the screen he went. There was a loud splash.

Patches ran out from behind the screen, naked and wet, came to a skidding halt when he realized the way was blocked. A worker grabbed him and pulled him back. Water splashed across the room.

The door opened and a police officer appeared, shoving two boys in ahead of him. The older boy was broad-shouldered and surly, the younger was thin and nervous, his eyes flitting about the room. The officer looked at the orders in his hand.

"Mr. Charles Brace?" the officer said.

"I'm Reverend Brace." Emma noted with approval that Brace was not above asserting his position when he thought it necessary. "We don't need those cuffs in here, do we, officer?"

The officer stared at Brace, sizing him up. "Maybe so, maybe not."

"In that case, I say not."

The officer stared at Brace a little longer, waiting for some great retort to come to him. It didn't come, and he bent down and undid the cuffs. "Whatever you say, reverend. My orders were just to deliver these two thieves to you." The officer spun the empty cuffs on his finger. "I guess they're yours now, you can do with 'em what you want."

The two boys rubbed their wrists. The smaller boy fingered one of the blankets on the desk, as if he were unsure of what to do with his hands now that they were free. The bigger boy nodded to him in a curt, disapproving way. The smaller boy let his hands drop to his side. Emma stared at the two boys.

"There's just this release somebody's got to sign," the officer said. The bigger boy became aware of Emma's looking at them. He returned her stare, defiant, issuing a silent challenge. Emma looked away.

"And they've got to be out of the city, you know that, reverend," the officer said. "We see 'em on the streets, they're goin' right back in, no matter how many ministers they got workin' for 'em."

The signed release in his hand, the officer had to content himself with a final contemptuous stare before leaving.

The bigger of the two boys smiled insolently at Brace. "You handled him pretty good," he said.

"You're Bruce?" Reverend Brace said.

"That's right. This here's my friend, Tom. I'll tell you, rev, I could go for some grub."

Brace met his gaze steadily. "First you could go for some baths, fumigating, and fresh clothes. We need to be ready within the half-hour." The two boys didn't move, staring at the minister. The shouts of the other children echoed around them. The smaller boy broke first, turning away, fidgeting with his wrist.

"Or do you prefer prison?" Brace said. "You've been given your choice." Emma was shocked by Brace's sudden hardness. Brace turned to the smaller boy. His tone softened suddenly. "A little soap can't be that bad, can it?"

The boy broke into an embarrassed grin. "Naw, I guess not."

- 58 -

"All right, Bruce and Tom, the baths are over here." The two boys followed Brace across the room.

J.P. joined the line in front of the table where the lady sat filling out tags. The loud-mouthed boy Liverpool was in line behind her. J.P. felt a flutter in her stomach: the lady looked like one of those nice, honest types, easy to fool, but you never knew till you were right up to them. J.P. pulled her newsboy cap down a little tighter.

"Your name, please?" the lady said.

"J.P." The lady looked up at her. J.P. fought back her panic and took the offensive. "What's yours?" J.P. asked. She heard Liverpool snicker behind her.

"My name is Miss Symns," the lady said. Her tone was perfectly even. "What do the initials stand for, J.P.?" the lady asked.

J.P. scratched under her hat. "I forget." Liverpool snickered again. J.P. noticed that the lady's bag was sitting open on the table next to her. She caught the twinkle of something metallic near the top.

"Where were you born?" the lady asked.

How many questions did this lady have, J.P. thought. "New York, I guess," J.P. said. The lady wrote it down in her nice, even hand. I could tell her Timbuktu, J.P. thought, and she'd write that down, I'll bet. That was the problem with these sincere ladies, they weren't too sharp. "Where were you born?" J.P. said.

"New York," the lady said. Miss Symns wasn't going to get mad, J.P. could see that. She was one of those. "Religion?" the lady said. J.P. wasn't listening. The open bag wasn't more than a foot from her left hand, it would be an easy snatch, and the lady deserved it if she was going to be so smarmy and nice . . . "Don't you believe in God?"

"Don't know him," J.P. said. It would be as easy as pie.

The lady smiled. "Perhaps we can introduce you." J.P.

looked at the lady dubiously. If that twinkly object turned out to be silver, it would be worth a couple dollars in a hockshop.

"I heard about him," Liverpool butted in. "My pals tell me it's lucky to say something to him when you're sleepin' out on bad nights."

The other children laughed. Miss Symns stood up. "That's enough!" she said. J.P. was surprised; the lady could get mad after all. The boy with the withered arm couldn't stop giggling. "Mouse, did you hear me?"

"Yes, miss, yes . . ." the boy said.

It was as easy as pie. J.P.'s hand darted across, lifted the bright locket, and slipped it into her pocket before the lady even turned back.

Miss Symns sat down. J.P. stood silently in front of the table as the lady finished filling out the tag. That was too easy, J.P. thought, it wasn't even much fun.

The lady stood up and leaned across the table. J.P. stiffened as the lady fixed the tag to her jacket.

J.P. lifted the tag so she could read it:

NAME: *J.P.?*
BORN: *New York?*
AGE: *Nine or Ten?*
RELIGION: *None?*

"You write with a real even hand, miss," J.P. said.

Emma smiled and handed J.P. a blanket, a Bible, and a box lunch. J.P. did not smile back.

"Are you glad to be going?" the lady asked.

J.P. looked at her suspiciously. "No."

"Then why are you going?" Too nice, J.P. thought, just too nice.

"It's startin' to get cold outside," J.P. said. She turned and walked off to one corner of the room. She sat down, leaned against the wall, looked back at the lady, who was busy now with Liverpool. J.P. reached into her pocket, and, cupping her hand so that no one could see, she lifted out the silver locket. She snapped open her prize, then grimaced in disgust. There was nothing but a picture of some lady, just a worthless picture.

Emma had never imagined her uncle the way he was now, striding at the head of a column of children, coattails flying, leading them through the streets of New York like some Episcopalian version of the Pied Piper. There was no doubt that the sight was odd; it had to be odd to make the hawkers and rag-and-bone men stop and stare, and they did. The parade picked up a variety of hecklers, walking alongside, shouting out at the children.

"You're daft for goin' . . . . They ain't gonna find you no homes."

"You're gonna work and starve, you'll see!"

"Ain't you scairt of gettin' scalped by the Indians?"

"Ain't nobody gonna want you bummers out there."

A Bowery Boy stepped out in the street, resplendent in his Prince Albert cinched frock coat and moldy beaver top hat. "Hey, ain't that Liverpool! I swear it is!"

Liverpool grinned, but kept on walking.

"Where you goin', Liverpool?"

"Going to the country!" Liverpool shouted back.

"The country! What can you pinch in the country, Liverpool?" the Bowery Boy shouted.

"Country apples, I guess," Liverpool shot back.

"Country apples! Hey, that's a good one! Country apples!" The Bowery Boy slapped his thighs, spun around, and disappeared into the crowd in search of someone to tell the good one to.

The children moved on down the street, watching the

people on the sidewalk. As they passed a wooden tenement, girls stared out from behind torn curtains.

The South Street Seaport was more than a match for the parade of children, swallowing them up in its own confusion of drays and carts. Everything that could be moved was in motion, barrels and boxes and wheelbarrows a constant threat to crush an inattentive child. Emma and her uncle did their best to herd the children, who seemed overwhelmed by the profusion of delights, the smells of fish and tea and tobacco and spices, the gilded figureheads of the ships, their jib booms thrusting far out over the cobbled streets, the counting houses, the cordage shops, the sail lofts, even the gulls that glided in to fight over scraps of oysters and cod on the wharves.

After a half-hour of patient herding, the group stood before the *Isaac Newton,* a well-seasoned paddle-wheeler tied at one of the farthest docks. The crowded deck buzzed with talk of commerce, merchants striking up deals with peddlers, traders of corn and upstate land speculators exchanging tips, gossip, and high hopes; while down below on the dock, gangs of sweating, tight-muscled men loaded freight, rolling heavy barrels up the gangplank. Their shouts and curses rang out in the air.

Emma, her parasol unfurled, looked back over the children, making yet another count.

Liverpool nudged Bruce. "What's comin' off? We're supposed to take a train. They're putting us on a bloody boat."

"The station's in Albany, idjit!" Bruce said.

"Watch who you're callin' idjit, idjit," Liverpool said.

"I'll call idjits like you what I want," Bruce said.

"Oh yeah?"

"Yeah."

Liverpool gave Bruce a shove, and Bruce returned the favor.

"You two boys!" Emma said. "You stop that, right now . . ."

"Gangway! Watch yourself, lady!" Emma stepped out of the way of two men rolling a barrel up the gangplank.

Emma's uncle conferred with the captain, a barrel-chested man with the knack of doing several things at once: negotiating with Reverend Symns, supervising the loading of freight, greeting his new passengers, and nibbling away at a piece of pie that he held, without benefit of plate or napkin, in his broad hand.

"Sure, I'll let you take 'em on deck, Reverend. But you gotta keep 'em in line. Hello, Harry, how are you?" The captain bent over, nuzzled out a big bite of pie, his eyes darting nervously over the crowd of children. "Didn't know there'd be so many of the little beggars. Same old story, nobody tells me anything. Hey, Dick, don't let those barrels drop like that!"

"Keeping the children together, captain, is not an easy task."

"Know that, Reverend, know that. I'll let you take 'em on deck, but once we're on the water, it's the steerage below. I've got valuable freight on this boat. . . . I'd like to help you out, Reverend, but this is a commercial enterprise. These merchants, they're my meat and potatoes. . . ." The captain licked his hand clean.

"We'll manage, captain," Reverend Symns said.

The captain nodded toward Emma. "The Children's Aid Society didn't mention any lady coming. I'm afraid our accommodations aren't really . . ."

"My niece will stay with us."

The captain grimaced. "But Reverend, she's a real lady, I couldn't do that! Let me make some arrangement."

"My niece will stay with us!" Reverend Symns said.

The captain stared for a second, then shrugged and

started up the gangplank. "Belay that line! Take it right! Dick, watch this, will ya?"

It had to happen. In all the bustle, the loading and hurry and confusion, the little Irish girl, Eileen, was bowled over by a runaway barrel. To add to her indignity, she was dragged, dirty and crying, by one arm by her seven-year-old brother Timmy to Miss Symns. Timmy was outraged at what they had done to his sister, and he wanted Miss Symns to do something about it. Emma had her hands full just trying to pick up the now-hysterical little girl, who felt everyone was leagued against her, and who kicked and scratched and wailed with renewed vigor. There was a tap at Emma's elbow.

"Say, look at that, miss." It was J.P., pointing toward shore.

"Please, J.P., not now," Emma said. "Timmy, help me with your sister."

"Look at him, miss," J.P. said. "He's being so careful with his boxes he must have diamonds or something in 'em."

Emma turned to look and, as she did, Eileen hooked her fingers in Emma's bonnet and pulled it askew. Standing on the wharf, his back to the ship, a broad-shouldered young man with curly black hair was supervising the unloading of a number of oddly shaped boxes from a carriage. Even before he turned, Emma realized that it was the young daguerreotypist she had met at the Crystal Palace more than a year before.

One of the deckhands pushed the barrow loaded down with the young man's boxes up the gangplank, the daguerreotypist only a step behind him. J.P. was right; he was guarding his boxes as if they were filled with ivory from Madagascar.

Eileen jerked Emma's bonnet even more radically to the

side of her head. "Eileen, stop it!" Emma said, giving the girl's hand the mildest slap, which only served to redouble her cries.

Her brother stood at Emma's side, swearing vengeance on the man who had knocked his sister down. "When I catch 'im, I'm gonna kick 'im in the shins . . ."

The young daguerreotypist was headed right toward her. With one hand Emma held the dirty crying child, with the other she tried to keep her bonnet from falling off. She turned her back to the deck, stared out over the water, hoping he would just pass right by.

"It is Miss Symns, isn't it?" he said. "You never came to have your picture taken."

Emma tried to look at Eileen, but Eileen had her fingers so entwined in the ribbons of her bonnet, that Emma, trying to turn her head, only succeeded in twisting the brim over her eyes. Emma fought to recover her dignity and her sight. Thinking that perhaps he hadn't been recognized, the young daguerreotypist reintroduced himself: "Frank Carlin. We met at the Crystal Palace. More than a year ago, if you remember."

Furious, Emma set the crying child down at the deck and tucked her hair back under her bonnet. "Yes, I remember," she said.

He was smiling broadly, looking as happy to see her as if she had been his oldest friend. Emma found it disconcerting. "And that's your uncle, isn't it, over there?"

"That's right," Emma said.

Mouse came up and tugged on Emma's sleeve. "Miss Symns, that boy over there took my lunch box." Emma looked across the deck where Tom was leaning against the rail, rifling through a lunch box.

"Tom!" Emma shouted. "You give that back to Mouse. Right away!"

Tom looked up, surprised. He shrugged, set the lunch box down on the deck, spat over the rail, and strolled off in pursuit of Bruce.

"These children, Miss Symns . . ." Carlin started. Emma did not help him out, so he went on. "You and your uncle are taking them to Albany on a day outing?"

Emma stiffened. "No, Mr. Carlin, we are not. We're taking them . . ."

Someone brushing past had knocked the unstable Eileen down again. The little girl sat on the deck bawling, her arms reaching out for Emma to pick her up. Emma picked her up. Carlin stared distastefully at the child.

"Now, what was that, Miss Symns?"

"I said, we're not taking them on a day trip." The child whimpered in Emma's ear. "We're taking them west, to find them homes and, for the older ones, work."

"Really." It was clear that he didn't approve.

"Is there anything wrong with that?" Emma asked.

"No, no."

"Then what is it?"

"It's just that you don't strike me as the sort of person who's lived a life exposed to adventure."

"I don't consider this an adventure, Mr. Carlin. Many of these children have been living on the streets, without anyone to care for them . . ."

Timmy was pulling on his sister Eileen's leg. "I'm gonna beat 'im up, Eileen, no one's gonna hurt you . . ." Eileen gave weak little cries for him to stop.

"Timmy, just leave her alone, she's going to be all right!" Emma said. Eileen rested her head against Emma's shoulder. "And you, Mr. Carlin, I suppose you're off on an adventure?"

Carlin leaped at the opportunity to talk about himself. "I suppose you could call it an adventure, Miss Symns. But hard work, too. It's the biggest stroke of luck in my life . . ."

"I want to get down now, Miss Symns," Eileen sobbed.

"You're better now?" Emma said.

"Yes, Miss Symns," Eileen sniffled.

"All right, then. But I want you to stay right here by the rail where no one can knock you over. You understand?"

"Yes, Miss Symns."

Emma set the child down and looked back at Carlin. He had that I'm-being-patient-and-I-want-everyone-to-know-it look. Men didn't like to be interrupted when they were talking about their work, Emma knew that. "I'm sorry, Mr. Carlin," Emma said.

"No, don't be," he said. "Tell me, Miss Symns, how are you going to be traveling?"

"By train."

"From Albany?" he said.

"That's right," she said. He smiled.

"And you're going as far west as . . ."

"Illinois," Emma said. Carlin laughed. "Is there something funny about Illinois, Mr. Carlin?"

"No," he said. "It's just that we'll be seeing a lot of each other, Miss Symns."

"You're going to Illinois?"

"Farther, Miss Symns. Even farther." Cursed male pride, Emma thought. Just because he was interrupted once, now he was going to be mysterious about his plans, try to get her to drag it out of him.

He said nothing more, but reached out and tousled Eileen's hair. He shook his head skeptically and smiled.

"You have prejudices against these children," Emma said.

He looked quickly at her. "Well, perhaps you can convert me, Miss Symns."

Shouts went up from the far side of the deck. A circle of children opened for a second and Liverpool careened across the deck. He scrambled to his feet as Bruce came at him. Liverpool ducked under Bruce's swing, danced away, parrying and dodging the bigger boy's blows. Shouts of encouragement went up for both fighters.

Passengers shouted to one another to come take a look, grinning and pointing.

Liverpool began to taunt the heavier Bruce, dancing from one foot to the other, hands by his side, bobbing and weaving. The frustrated Bruce flailed the air and some of the onlookers began to whistle and hoot.

Tom suddenly leapt out of the crowd and grabbed Liverpool around the neck. Liverpool, his face white, kicked out to keep Bruce off him, then threw Tom to the deck. The streeters moved in, shoving and hitting, piling on one another.

One of the passengers tried to pull one of the boys off, but the man next to him stopped him. "Hey, don't ruin the fun. This here's better'n a dogfight."

Reverend Symns, coming from below deck, rushed in, but was caught in the melee and spun around and down, his coattails flying.

Emma grabbed one of the children who twisted free. Carlin pushed his way through to Bruce and Liverpool and yanked them to their feet, shook them, and set them down. Bruce wiped his bloody nose on his sleeve; he was still furious.

Carlin looked at his hands and then at his coat; there was blood on both. He looked at the passengers, whose smiles had turned a little uneasy. "Where can I wash this off?"

"There's water below deck," one of the men said.

"Are you all right?" Emma said.

"I'm fine," Carlin said. "Except that you've forced me to the conclusion, Miss Symns, that you've bitten off more than you can chew."

The boat whistle screamed, and the boat began to slide

away from the dock. Patches ran to Emma and hid his face in her dress. Mouse was up on the rail, balanced precariously.

There was the monotonous, lulling clacking of the paddle wheels and the falling of water. Ben, wide-eyed, clutched his brother Tony. Bruce and Tom and another of the boys who'd been in the fight huddled together, whispering furiously. The little girl named Annie refused to look toward the shore and instead played with the tag around her neck. J.P. pulled down her newsboy cap, watching Carlin who was laughing and joking with a group of merchants at the far end of the deck.

Her hands resting on Patches's shoulders, Emma, too, was studying Carlin, though in a less obvious way, she hoped. He was laughing easily, boyishly, and Emma admitted to herself that he had a certain attractiveness. But she didn't like his opinions. The remark about her having bitten off more than she could chew—well, she would show him. . . . She realized that she hadn't actually found out what he was doing on the boat.

Carlin raised his eyes and caught Emma looking at him. He smiled. She looked away, out over the water, at the docks and jumbled buildings growing smaller and smaller. Patches pulled free of her and ran off down the deck to join Reverend Symns. Emma's gloved hands trembled on the rail. She felt a growing sense of exhilaration, she wasn't sure why. . . . It was because she was beginning. Yes, that was it. She was beginning. Emma shivered, drew her cape around her, and watched as the city grew smaller and faded into the distance.

*I*n the evening, after the cracker box and the gingerbread were passed around, some of the older boys sat down on the gangplank and began to sing. They sang "Oh Susanna" and "Way Down in Ca-i-ro" and "My Old Kentucky Home" and "Hard Times Come Again No More," and it wasn't long before they had attracted a full audience of merchants, who, in the flush of after-dinner whiskey and general good spirits, applauded after each song and pitched pennies. The captain said that if the boys would sing "Hard Times Come Again No More" one more time he would invite everybody to the upper saloon for a drink. The boys obliged him, singing with great feeling, and the captain made good his vow, leading the cheering audience up the stairs.

Everyone crowded into the tiny saloon, arranged themselves elbow to elbow along the burnished wooden bar, against the walls under the paintings of the great sea battles, leaving one table free for the boys to stand on as they sang and one after the other told their stories.

The stories came easily. The boys knew they were entertaining, and they played to their slightly drunk but appreciative audience, telling more about themselves than they ever had under the direct questioning of Emma and her uncle.

It was not a situation that Reverend Symns would have approved of, with the drinking and the tossing of coins, but he hadn't been feeling well after dinner and was resting below deck. The situation didn't make Emma feel very comfortable either, but since the boys seemed at ease and were talking about themselves, Emma was not going to give up the chance to hear them.

The biggest show-off of all was Liverpool, who told an incredible story, weaving freely between fact and fiction, depending upon the inspiration of the moment and the coins flying in his direction. Liverpool's parents had died in Liverpool, that's where he'd picked up his name. After they died, he'd signed up as a ten-year-old cabin boy, come to New York, jumped ship, lived with an aunt for a time, then run away from her, and lived by his wits as a snoozer and a leader of the Dutch Hill streeters.

"You ever go to school?" someone shouted out.

"Go to school? Oh, they couldn't keep me in no bloody school. I took the broom to the schoolmaster when he was going to punish me, and that's how I got tossed out. No, I'm a free character." There was a ping, and Liverpool scanned the floor quickly, then bent down and scooped up a coin. "Thank you, sir. I was a snoozer, sleepin' in doorways and around engine houses. I tell you, gentlemen, there isn't a man in New York that can construct the bolt or bars that can hold me in."

The audience laughed. A big, tipsy man, a corn merchant, sang out, "Tis the song, the sigh of the weary . . . Hard Times, Hard Times, come again no more . . ."

"My aunt, she used to lock me in for safe keepin' till she got home, but I kept gettin' out. The captain of the police, he was so tired of havin' me brought in, he and my aunt devised this punishment they thought could frighten me."

"What was that, Liverpool?"

"Many days have you lingered around my cabin door . . ." the corn merchant sang.

"Pardon me, sir, but I've got the stage now," Liverpool shouted at him.

"What punishment was that, Liverpool?"

"Hangin' me."

"Hangin' you?" The audience guffawed. There followed a rain of coins. Liverpool quickly retrieved them. "That's right. And they did it too. Hung me up by my feet to a post till I promised to be better."

"But ya weren't no better, were ya?"

"Nope." Liverpool grinned.

The corn merchant muttered, "Let us pause in life's pleasures and count its many tears. . . ." Liverpool glowered at him, but didn't say anything.

"After that my aunt placed me with the Brothers, who put me in a kind of prison where they chained me by the leg to keep me from scaling the walls." A couple of the passengers hooted; Liverpool grinned at them. "If you don't believe me, there's the leg." Liverpool tapped his left thigh. The audience roared, pennies flew through the air. Liverpool was enjoying himself.

"After that my aunt sent me to Randall's Island where I had it all figgered to swim to shore when one of the other boys ratted on me. Then my aunt tried to place me in a home in Hastings and I was there a month till I got tired of that so I wandered home and my aunt said she didn't want any more of me and she was going to live with a soldier, so I went back to my touring."

Liverpool got a ringing round of applause as he stepped

down from the table. Patches, standing at Emma's side, clapped till his palms were red. He beamed up at Emma.

"He sure can tell a nice story, can't he, Miss Symns?"

"He certainly can, Patches, but I think it's time for us to go below."

"Aww, Miss Symns . . ."

"It's late, Patches, and it's very important that you get your rest. Tomorrow is going to be a very exhausting day."

"But, Miss Symns, can't we stay just a little while? Everybody's havin' such a good time and they'll be so sad if we go."

Emma said nothing. She looked out over the crowd of men. They were all smiling, genial, but Emma didn't trust them. Her instinct was to protect the children from them, from their laughter, their curiosity, but she knew that she had let things go too far: if she tried to pull the children away now, she knew she would have a major revolt on her hands. She didn't see Carlin. She hadn't seen him all evening and she wondered where he was.

Story followed story, tales of drunken fathers and beatings; children piecing together a living by collecting rats for terrier fights, holding horses, collecting rags. A girl named Jane had swept crossings and lived under a stairway, her father had died on Blackwell's Island and her mother was in prison—the merchants loved every one of the stories.

"How about you, little girl?" the drunken corn merchant said, pointing at a bewildered Annie. "That's right, you. You live all alone?"

"Yes, sir," Annie said, frightened.

"And you have no parents?"

"No."

"No one takes care of you?" another, more sympathetic man said.

"No, sir."

"Where is she? We can't see her back here," came a voice from the back.

"Here you go, darlin'," a tall man said, reaching down, taking Annie around the waist, and setting her up on the table.

"So how do you live, little girl?"

Emma stepped forward. "Annie, you come down here with me," Emma said, but it was as if Annie, dazed and frightened by the attention of the men, couldn't hear Emma. She looked out over the crowd with a small, frozen smile.

The drunken corn merchant wasn't paying attention any more. He was humming, "There's a pale drooping maiden who toils her life away."

"I did the ladies favors," Annie said.

"Did the ladies favors, did you? What kind of favors were these?"

"I sold them fruit."

"Fruit? What kind of fruit?" the sympathetic man chuckled.

"I don't remember," Annie said, very serious suddenly. "All I remember is that I sold fruit to the ladies in the fine dresses."

"And where did you do this, little girl?"

"At the Forget-Me-Not," Annie said.

A ripple of knowing laughter went through the room. The corn merchant suddenly perked up. "The Forget-Me-Not! I know that wh-o-o-re house!"

The remark brought the house down, men spilling their drinks, doubling over, turning away to hide their guffaws, coughing and gasping.

"Annie, come here!" Emma strode across the room and took Annie down from the table.

"I know what favors you did, little girl! You were one of

them panel thieves, weren't ya?" Emma started to pull Annie through the crowd, but men bent over, smiling, their sympathies quickened by alcohol, wanting to apologize for their drunken friend, wanting to be helpful, wanting to set it right, but only impeding the way.

The corn merchant was grinning. "I mean, you fellers all know what a panel thief is now, don't ya?"

"Oh, be quiet, George," someone shouted out. "There's a lady in here."

Emma looked up. Carlin was standing in the door of the saloon, looking in, looking puzzled.

"What it is, see, the women get you back in the room, you understand . . ."

"No, it's *you* they get back in the room, George."

Carlin stared at Emma, looking disturbed now. Emma looked away. "Annie, let's go." Liverpool, head down, was counting his pennies in a corner.

The corn merchant waved his hands impatiently. "And there's not much furniture back there, if you take my meaning. . . . Just the bed and this one chair for you to put your clothes on . . ."

A man with a brandy glass bent toward Emma. "Don't pay him any mind, miss. You know how men get . . ."

"Would you please get out of my way!" Emma said, pushing him back.

Carlin strode across the room toward her. "Excuse me, Miss Symns, but what the hell is going on here?"

"So you take off your trousers and you lay 'em over the chair . . ."

"I'm trying to get these children out of here, Mr. Carlin, if you'd just get out of my way."

"And the chair's laid right against the wall, see, so while you and the lady are occupied, the panel thief, this little girl they got hidin' back of the wall . . ."

Annie suddenly pulled free of Emma, tried to push back through the wall of men. "Annie, please . . ." Emma grabbed her hand again.

"No, Miss Symns, no, I sold fruit to the ladies. That's all. He's lying, Miss Symns."

"Jesus Christ!" Carlin muttered.

". . . entombed back there like the Pharaoh's concubines entombed in the Pyramid, and the kid just slips the panel open . . ."

"What's that fellow's name?" Carlin asked the man next to him.

"George," the man said.

". . . and she reaches in, snatches the wallet, takes the big bills and leaves a couple small ones . . ."

Emma gathered Annie up in her arms. "I brought fruit to the ladies, Miss Symns, that's all I remember . . ."

"Hey, George!" Carlin shouted out.

"Yeah?" The corn merchant answered vaguely.

"You getting all worked up there, George?" Carlin said.

"What do ya mean? I'm tellin' a story. Lemme finish my story."

Carlin stood next to the bar. One hand was on a pitcher of ice water.

"But aren't you getting kind of warm, George?" Carlin said. "Come over here, George."

Emma moved through the crowd, carrying Annie. Men stepped aside to let her pass.

"What for?" George said, but he moved a couple of steps toward Carlin.

"Because I thought maybe you could stand some cooling off," Carlin said.

Emma was at the door of the saloon, her back turned. The scorn in Carlin's voice made her look back in time to see Carlin raise high the pitcher of ice water, in time to see water tossed in a soft arc, in time to hear the gasp of surprise from the corn merchant, the hoots of the other men.

It was enough. Holding Annie close to her, Emma marched the children out onto the deck and into the cool night air.

Emma wandered the deck for almost an hour after tucking the children into their hammocks. She walked restlessly up and down, trying to calm her nerves. No one bothered her. The tradesmen, leaning over the rails, talking and laughing among themselves, became quiet as she passed, greeting her only with polite nods.

Emma stood alone, looking down at the churning water as it fell from the paddle wheel, then staring at the dark bluffs along the Hudson, the occasional twinkling lights as they passed a town.

Easy male laughter rang out farther down the deck. Emma did not see what there was to be so genial about. Emma felt that her first day had been an utter failure. She should have stopped the fight between Bruce and Liverpool before it even started, she shouldn't have allowed the children to go up to the saloon at all. Mr. Carlin must think her a complete fool. Not that his boyish heroics had made things any better; she shuddered to think what would happen if he took it into his head to always come and rescue her. Emma was tired and discouraged. Her mind kept coming back to the drunken corn merchant's story, even as every fiber in her body was repelled by it. Annie had denied that it was true, or at least that the little girl was her—but if it wasn't her, it was some other child. No one denied that. None of the men there had been shocked. Not even Carlin, really, Emma thought bitterly. They treated it as a story they already knew. That was what infuriated Emma, their easy recognition of it; it was taken for granted that men just knew this sort of thing. Their only objection was that this sort of thing wasn't to be spoken of in polite company. Was Emma really the only one who didn't know the way things were; and if they all knew, didn't they see the horror of a child existing like that? Emma couldn't think of it any more. She had to try to get to sleep.

In her wide skirt, she maneuvered her way down the ladder into steerage. She held on to the ladder, letting her eyes adjust to the darkness. At the far end of the room she could see her uncle, sitting asleep in a chair. Boys were stretched out on the floor beside him. The place smelled of straw and animals.

Emma knelt and began to pray. As she did, she became aware of whispering. She stood up and peered into the darkness, finally saw dark forms in the hammock against the wall, saw that it was two children locked in an embrace. Emma stepped quickly over the sleeping bodies toward the hammock.

"Young man!"

Emma yanked at the boy's sleeve. The boy's head jerked up; it was Liverpool. Legs flailing, he tumbled out of the hammock and scrambled back to his blanket.

Jane, the crossing-sweeper girl, looked up at Emma, wiping a strand of hair from her mouth.

"Are you all right, child?" Emma said.

"Yes, miss." The girl wormed around in the hammock, straightening her clothes.

"But you mustn't," Emma said.

"Yes, miss," the girl said placidly.

"It's a sin," Emma said. "It's wrong."

"Yes, miss." The girl suppressed a yawn. "Anything else, miss?"

"No, no. Go to sleep, child."

The oil lantern on the ladder cast an eerie light over the sleeping children. Emma dozed fitfully.

Reverend Symns slept upright in his chair, head resting against the wall. Abruptly his eyes opened in shock. There was a sharp pain in his chest. He waited. The pain came again. O Lord, how manifold are thy works, in wisdom Thou hast made them all. . . . Reverend Symns tried to breathe, staring out across the dim space. The boat rocked, the lamp on the ladder swayed. The earth is full of Thy creatures. Yonder is the sea, great and wide, which teems with things innumerable. . . . A small animal noise escaped his throat. He struggled with the words . . . Things innumerable, living things both great and small. He took three short breaths, there was air in his lungs, he was going to be all right.

Emma was awake suddenly, not sure why. She stood up and listened, peering through the darkness. She moved down the row of hammocks. Sarah, murmuring in her sleep, turned over. Relieved, Emma peered over at her uncle and the boys. Everything was still. She lay down again, pulled up her blanket, and closed her eyes.

Reverend Symns leaned back. The pain had subsided, but a sheen of sweat glistened on his forehead. This was to be his great work, God would not let him fail now. It wasn't for his own glory, he was sure it wasn't. It was for these children and for Emma, too. His breath caught suddenly, and he was dizzy, just for a second. He waited. No, he was all right. How he had worried over her, worried that she had been hurt too much by the broken engagement, worried that she would end up as one of those bitter women who always hang on the edges of life, never daring. . . . No, this trip was part of his obligation in raising her. There go the ships, and Leviathan which Thou didst form to sport in the sea. He was there now, in the dark belly of Leviathan, like Jonah, he was fulfilling the call of the Lord, no matter how he resisted. Slowly, his breathing returned to normal and he slept.

In the morning Reverend Symns was the first one out on deck. As the children came straggling and yawning up from steerage, he greeted them heartily, jollying them up, his face filled with a bright expectancy. Emma watched her uncle's new exuberance with uneasiness.

As the boat neared Albany, moving past foundries and coaling stations, the children grew more excited. A great cheer went up when the city came into view, rising up from the western bank in irregular terraces. The hills were covered with fine old houses, towering churches. At the highest point stood the state capitol, nestled in among trees.

When they docked, the streeters were the first ones off, racing down the gangplank with their blankets and lunch boxes under their arms, and Reverend Symns was right in the middle of them. Standing on the dock he looked back at Emma, still on the boat, helping Ben with his buttons.

"Come along now, Emma," he shouted. "Come on."

"I'm coming, Uncle Edward," Emma said. She pushed Ben down the gangplank ahead of her. Her uncle waited for her impatiently. "Uncle Edward, are you sure you know the way?"

"No, but we'll find it," he said.

"Shouldn't we ask?" Emma said.

"I don't see why," her uncle beamed.

"Uncle Edward!" Emma protested. "You don't know this city."

"No. And that's one of the things I like about it."

They marched on foot around the state house, Reverend Symns striding briskly in the lead, turning back to encourage the others and to be sure that fruit wasn't being filched from the sidewalk stands. Emma hurried the stragglers along, picking up dropped blankets and lunch boxes. She was aware of her Uncle Edward's approving smiles.

There were Albany boys lined up along the street, and

they found the ragged little parade a handy target for their wit.

"Hey, boys, what you doing?"

"Here's a penny for ya, boys! Dive for it!"

"Goin' off into slavery, are ya? If it was me I wouldn't be goin' so easy."

Liverpool wasn't one to back down from a challenge. He shouted back at them, "You want to know where we're goin'? I'd be glad to tell you. Glad!"

Reverend Symns put his hand on Liverpool's shoulder. "Don't pay them any mind, son. We've got better things to be doing."

"It just gets my dander up," Liverpool said.

"So tell us where you're goin'," one of the Albany boys shouted. "We're waitin'."

Liverpool turned and faced his taunters. "We're goin' west, where we're goin' to settle down and grow up to be bloody great men."

"You? A great man? What a bag of gas that is!"

"What do you snoozers know? The West's the place for growin' presidents, and that's the truth."

The Albany boys laughed. "You sayin' you're going to be president."

"Don't worry about them, son," Reverend Symns said. "We should be getting to the station." But he was smiling, and it was evident that he was enjoying Liverpool. An audience had begun to gather; carriages and carts and drays were backed up, trying to wend their way through the crowded street.

"I can't say," Liverpool said. "Can't say if I'll be president. But I'll tell you this . . . if you want to be bummers always and shoulder-hitters and timber merchants in a small way by selling matches, then you'll stay right here in Albany."

"And if we don't?"

"Then you'll go out west and become farmers."

"Farmers!" The boys cackled. "Sodbusters?"

"Yes, farmers," Liverpool said. "If you want to be the man who'll make his mark in the country, you will get up and come with us, for there's lots on the prairie a-waitin' for ya." Liverpool's oratory was making its mark; the street was jammed with amused onlookers, and two carriages, in attempting to squeeze through, had locked wheels and the drivers were yelling at one another and the horses were neighing piteously. A policeman was warning people to clear the street, but one of the dirtiest of the Albany streeters, a boy with matted hair and clothes so tattered they looked like layers of rotting autumn leaves, was listening intently to Liverpool, enthralled by every word.

"Come west!" Liverpool declaimed. "You can make your way in the world so you won't have to call no man your boss. Only think of it, fellers, here you're happy to get a whiff of the roast beef and out there, you'll be stuffin' it in your mouth alongside the pumpkin pie till you're sick of it. I want to be somebody, boys, and somebody don't live here, no how. You'll find him on a farm in the West!"

Liverpool's final flourish was greeted by a chorus of cheering and hooting. Coins flew in the air, one of the trapped horses bolted, somehow yanking its carriage free. The driver, who had dismounted to try to dislodge the locked wheels, was left standing in the mud. He ran after the runaway carriage, cursing and waving his arms, finally stepping on a small dog that yelped and ran through the crowd. The policeman shouted at Reverend Symns to move his children along and Reverend Symns shouted back that that was what he was trying to do. Emma reached out for Eileen's hand. Liverpool, his arms raised over his head like a champion prize fighter, was clapped on the back by the New York streeters, and slowly the parade of children moved down the street, followed, at a distance of perhaps fifty yards, by the dirty Albany streeter with the matted hair.

Emma looked at her Uncle Edward. His face was covered with sweat.

"Uncle Edward, are you all right?"

"Yes, Emma, I'm fine." He smiled and wiped his forehead. She saw that his hand was trembling. "It's just a bit warm this morning, don't you think?"

"Yes, Uncle Edward," she said softly, afraid. She could feel a chill breeze blowing from the river; it wasn't warm at all.

As they approached the station they joined a stream of immigrants: Germans, Irishmen, Italians, and Norwegians. There were families, the smaller children hurrying on foot, the babies carried in their mother's arms, gaunt men with all their worldly goods wrapped in great bundles secured by tightly knotted ropes. Reverend Symns halted their march for a second to give instructions; they were to stay together, watch out for one another, hold on to their blankets, wait until they knew what car was theirs before they went climbing into any train. He spoke simply, warmly; Emma thought he was magnificent.

Liverpool's voice came from the back of the crowd of children. "Here's a boy what wants to go to Illinois, sir. Can you take him with us?" Liverpool had his arm around the dirty Albany streeter with the matted hair.

"Well, now, Liverpool, do you know this boy?"

"No, sir. I just met him but he's as hard up as any of us."

"Do you even know his name?"

"No, sir." The boy whispered something in Liverpool's ear. "His name's John, Reverend. And he's no father or mother and nobody to live with and he sleeps out nights."

Reverend Symns looked to Emma. "What do you think, Emma?"

"We don't know the child at all, Uncle Edward," Emma said. "If we take every homeless child we meet it will be impossible."

Emma's uncle was not looking at her, but staring steadfastly at the boy. "If he's left to float here his end is certain, isn't it?"

"Yes, Uncle Edward," Emma said. She was a little angry; one of the things that had always irritated her most about her uncle was his habit of asking her advice when he had no intention of listening to it.

Reverend Symns addressed the boy. "Tell me, John, why do you want to go with us?"

"Well . . ." John looked nervously around at the other children. "I always wanted to go and be a farmer and live in the country . . . and eat pumpkin pie."

Uncle Edward smiled. "I think we must try this boy. John, you can come with us and we'll do our best by you, on one condition."

"Yes, sir."

"I want you washed and scrubbed in a half-hour, because we're going to be leaving very soon. Do you think you can do that?"

"I think so, sir."

"Emma, perhaps you could take him and give the boy a little help. . . . There must be a washroom in the station."

"Of course," Emma said. She looked at the dirty boy, at the matted hair, and took a deep breath. Well, yes, this was what it was going to be like. Steeling herself, she took the boy's hand. "Come along now, John," she said.

Reverend Symns went in search of the conductor, his army of twenty-seven streeters tagging along behind. The immigrants pushed and bumped against him, smelling of garlic and alcohol and tobacco. Reverend Symns was sweating again; he wiped at his face and took a deep breath. It would be all right, he would be sitting down soon.

Nothing seemed to be going right with the immigrants— everyone was insisting that they were in the wrong car, a German with a foghorn voice shouted that his baggage had received the wrong mark and two Irishmen argued about which direction Chicago was and weren't the cars on the wrong track.

Reverend Symns finally made his way through to the conductor, a harried, red-faced man who assured Reverend Symns that, yes, he had gotten their telegram and that the children would have their own car, it was all taken care of. Before Reverend Symns could ask another question the conductor turned his attentions to two Norwegian girls who were traveling without a protector.

Standing in the middle of the railroad yard with the children clustered around him Reverend Symns excited some curiosity among the immigrants. He was a head taller than anyone, well-dressed, with the bearings of a real American, a figure of some authority, though no one could be sure what that authority was, a railway official, perhaps. A German woman who could speak no English came up to him and shoved her ticket in his face, and it took several minutes of gesturing before she could be convinced that he couldn't help her.

Young boys moved through the crowd, hawking sandwiches and apples. An incoming train sounded its whistle. Trainmen, their arms waving, shouted and cursed for the crowd to move back.

Reverend Symns felt as if a weight were being lifted from him. Some things just didn't seem to matter to him any more. It had always been possible to say that they shouldn't have mattered, and yet they had: the petty hurts and imagined slights that accumulate over a lifetime in the church, the wounded pride he'd felt at being passed over for a younger man, the disappointment he'd felt at never having married, never having a child of his own. That didn't matter to him any more. Or even the fact that he probably wasn't the right person at all to be taking these children west; he was old, he had trouble speaking with children, he always had, and these children were even more difficult than most, he knew that, and it didn't matter. He would do the best he could.

Men surged around him, cursing and shouting. Hammers rang out on steel, there was the hiss of steam. Reverend Symns nearly lost his balance as two workmen pushed past him.

He was not afraid. His heart was high and racing, and the only thing that made him sad was the thought that what he had preached for fifty years he only understood now: that when Christ was in you, the old, sinful, envious, resentful man can be shucked off, that man can be free, that all things can be changed through Christ and that there was nothing he had to be afraid of facing.

Not even the most carefully guarded secret of his life; that he had resented having to raise Emma. He had never breathed a word of it to her, never hinted at it to any friend. To those who knew him well, he had always said how providential it was, having no family or children of his own, that he had Emma. But he never felt that. Instead, he felt almost exactly the reverse, that it was a cruel joke; that more than anything else he wanted his own family, a child that was his, that came from his own seed.

He'd felt Emma as a weight on his life, a reminder, a burden. He'd fought against the resentment, he'd prayed for God to open his heart, and yet the resentment had remained. He'd always treated Emma with the greatest kindness—many of the women in the church felt he doted on her—he was attentive to her smallest need, sent her to the finest teachers, and still he could not root out the resentment he felt.

His soul was singing now, because for the first time in his life he believed in miracles, that nothing need be lost, because that obligation he had resented for twenty-five years had become a blessing. When he saw her walking away with the dirty Albany streeter with the matted hair—she had been walking a bit stiffly, making it perfectly clear that she regarded it as a disagreeable task—he felt that he did love her and that this trip was right for both of them. He knew that there would be difficulties, but they were going to work and grow together. All things seemed possible suddenly— through Christ. If he could come to love Emma, so would midwestern farmers, strangers, come to know and love these children, change them and be changed by them. Reverend Symns felt, as if for the first time, the transforming power of God's love.

There was a shout and the crowd surged around him, the immigrants rushed to the boxcars. Reverend Symns twisted around, looking for the conductor, but couldn't spot him. The children, not to be outdone, pushed their way forward, squirming under and around the slower-moving adults. Reverend Symns moved after them, shouting to one and then the other to stay close to him. A woman with a large wicker basket slammed against him, someone stepped on his foot. An old man stepped out of his way with the fearful deference one would show to a prophet. The anxious foreign voices rose around him.

The children had climbed into a car already full. Some stood, some of the very little ones found seats on laps of friendly strangers, some sat on the floor. "Reverend Symns! Reverend Symns!" they shouted down to him.

Standing outside the car, he looked up into the face of

Liverpool. Behind Liverpool huddled a toothless old Italian woman, who blinked down at Reverend Symns. "Here we are, Reverend! We'll make a place for ya," Liverpool said. There was no mockery in the boy's voice. Liverpool stretched out a hand.

The car looked dark and airless; there were no windows and only rough benches for seats. Already there was a stench from so many people being packed in like animals. Reverend Symns felt a twinge of fear. He looked around again for the conductor. The conductor had promised them a separate car, where was he?

"Come on, Reverend, we'll give you a hand up."

The children's hands were reaching out for him. Reverend Symns looked up at them, trying to focus his eyes . . . one does not enter the Kingdom except as a little child . . . Reverend Symns lifted his knee, placed it against the edge of the open door. The children took his hands, there were many hands on his own, they were lifting him up, and once he was up, they all cheered him. Reverend Symns stood up and brushed off the dirty knees of his trousers, a German woman joining in.

"See, Reverend?" Liverpool said. "Didn't I tell ya there was room for ya?"

Reverend Symns tried to reply, but he couldn't. He was gulping for air, all the curious faces staring at him. The toothless Italian woman stood patiently at his side, holding his elbow. Reverend Symns heaved, trying to get air into his lungs. He blinked, but his eyes refused to adjust to the cave-like dark of the boxcar. He wished the woman would let go of his elbow.

The children were asking him questions, but he couldn't see them. He put his hands out toward them, feeling like a blind man. It was growing darker, he felt that the car had started to move, though he knew that it hadn't. He tried desperately to focus his eyes, squinting, trying to find a still point, and he saw a dark woman sitting in the corner on the straw, wrapped in a shawl. She was smiling at him as she nursed her child, her teeth were discolored, and then the light narrowed and he was falling . . .

Carlin had struck up an animated conversation with a traveling phrenologist while waiting in line to get into the passenger car. In front of them was a Quaker couple and behind was a banker from Utica and his red-headed wife. Everyone in line was relaxed and in good humor, in marked contrast to the scene a few cars back, where the frantic mob of immigrants ran back and forth, trying to clamber their way into the already-full boxcars.

Carlin's conversation about the rigors of bringing phrenology to the provinces was interrupted by a busy little man in a paper collar who carried a sheaf of newspapers over one arm, a notebook in the other hand, and a pack of tickets with the strings hanging down secured by an elbow. The little man thrust one of the papers in Carlin's hand.

"No, thank you," Carlin said.

"No, no, absolutely free. No obligation. You owe it to yourself." He turned away to hand a paper to the Quaker couple.

Carlin, with the phrenologist looking over his shoulder, stared at the paper. It was called *The Railway Accident Gazette* and was a record of the principal accidents in the Central States over the last six months. There, in the cheapest print, were all the most frightening cases of passenger cars smashed to pieces, deaths by scalding, derailments, and locomotives blown up in the air.

"Good Lord!" the phrenologist muttered. The little man in the paper collar had just foisted a copy of the *Gazette* onto the banker from Utica.

"Excuse me, sir," Carlin said. "But what is this all about?"

"What is this all about, you say?" the little man repeated. "What do you think it's all about?"

"Frankly, I'm at a loss," Carlin said.

"Let's face facts, sir, journeys are perilous things. Many people aren't aware of it."

"What's your game, mister?" the phrenologist said.

"I happen to be, sir, the agent of the Albany Life Insurance Company."

"Ah-hah! You're trying to terrify us into a suitable frame of mind."

The agent protested. "You think you know what lies in wait for you an hour down that line? No one does, sir, no one, but measures can be taken . . ."

"Balderdash!" the banker said. "Why don't you go sell your insurance to those immigrants, they all seem about to trample one another to death. You could sell them trampling insurance."

Some of the onlookers began to snicker. The agent ignored them. "To be frank, gentlemen, we only deal with the better sort of people." He turned to Carlin. "Take you, sir. What would happen if you should meet with some mishap, a derailment or a boiler explosion, scalded to death, perhaps, or horribly burned, what would happen to your loved ones?"

"Not much, I reckon," Carlin said mildly.

"Do you have a wife?"

"No."

"Mother, father?"

"No."

"Who would there be, then, to handle the arrangements. . . ."

"I guess I'll just leave that to the railroad," Carlin said. His friend the phrenologist cackled appreciatively.

Two ragged children were running toward the passenger

car. Carlin recognized one of them as one of the boys who'd been in the fight on the boat. They ran up to Carlin, breathless.

"Please, sir, he fell! You've got to help us."

"Who fell? What are you talking about?" Carlin said.

"We don't know if he's alive or dead, mister, please . . . it's Reverend Symns."

The banker pulled his wife back out of range of the wild-looking, panic-stricken children. The agent stared, clinging tightly to his papers. Only the phrenologist maintained his good humor.

"Say, Carlin, these children yours? Man says he ain't got a wife and the next thing you know . . ."

"Where is Miss Symns?" Carlin said.

"We don't know. She went off somewheres and we don't know anybody, sir, and you're her friend. . . . Please, mister. They've taken him back into the station house . . ."

Carlin looked around at the shocked, uncomprehending passengers, then stuffed *The Railway Accident Gazette* back into the agent's hand. "All right, let's go," he said.

When Emma came out of the washroom she saw that the passengers had already pushed into the cars.

"Hurry up, John," she said, pulling him by the hand. Poor John's eyes were still smarting from the comb pulling and tearing through his newly cut hair. He was like a shorn spring lamb, his face and ears still pink from scrubbing, and he had to run to keep up with Emma's brisk pace.

A few last passengers were scurrying up and down the length of the train, trying to find the right car; vendors were packing up their goods.

Emma hurried along the cars, looking into each one, until she finally saw the children waving to her from the last boxcar.

"Miss Symns! Miss Symns!"

"Hurry," Emma said. She started to run, dragging the stumbling child after her.

When Emma saw the panic in the children's faces she was sure it was because the train was about to leave. They were all talking at once, but Emma didn't listen. She boosted John up into the boxcar, lifted her skirts, and had her knee up against the open door when Sarah, her face white, leaned down and shook Emma by the shoulders.

"It's your uncle, miss, your uncle . . ."

Emma looked at Sarah. "Where is he?" she cried.

"He is sick, Miss Symns. They have taken him to the stationmaster's office. They have already sent for the doctor."

Emma turned and ran. John jumped out of the car and, like a lamb in fear of being separated from its mother, ran after her.

When Emma opened the door to the stationmaster's office, the roomful of men turned and look solemnly at her, all except her uncle, who lay in back on a table, staring up at the ceiling. The doctor stood over him, threading together the metal tubes that formed his stethoscope. The doctor bent and put the instrument to Reverend Symns's chest. The railway men in their uniforms were looking grave, the conductor ran his fingers nervously around the brim of his official blue cap. Liverpool and Mouse were next to the stationmaster's desk. Mouse, looking as if he was about to cry, was playing with the keys of the telegraph. Carlin was there too, standing stiffly against the wall. Emma didn't understand why, but she didn't have time to wonder about it. Emma stared at her uncle, her face white and drawn.

"Is he going to be all right?" Emma said.

The doctor straightened up and looked at her. "Your uncle has had a heart seizure."

"Oh, Uncle . . ." She moved toward him, but the doctor held her back.

"There's no need for that," the doctor said. John, who'd

followed Emma in, wandered over to the two other boys and they whispered together. "If he lies quietly and does what I tell him he could live another thirty years. Six months of rest and he'll be fine."

Everything in Emma fought against the doctor's words. How dare he tell her uncle what he was going to do, her uncle was too strong-minded a man to accept that. Uncle Edward had never rested in his life, it would be utterly impossible. Emma stared at her uncle, completely still now except for the fingers twitching softly on the edge of the table.

Finally Reverend Symns turned his head and reached out toward Emma. She took his hand. His eyes were soft and glistening. He tried to speak, but couldn't at first. Emma waited, her eyes filling with tears. Emma was vaguely aware of an odd metallic clacking from the corner of the room. Reverend Symns finally spoke. "Emma, you must get the children off the train. Notify the society." He paused to re-catch his breath. The metallic clacking continued, but Emma never took her eyes off her uncle. "They will have to go back to New York." His voice was thick, he cleared his throat. "We'll have to cancel our plans."

There was a sharp slap behind her. Emma turned. Mouse was holding his hand. The stationmaster stood over him, protecting the telegraph keys. "You just keep your dirty little hands off the equipment," the stationmaster said.

Emma passed her hand gently over her uncle's brow, but her eyes were still on the stationmaster and the boy nursing his hand. She felt too weak and overwhelmed to say anything.

"Emma, you must . . ."

Liverpool stared at Emma, looking angry and betrayed.

"Just lie quietly, Uncle Edward," Emma said. "I'll take care of everything." Carlin, standing near the door, opened it for her. Emma nodded to the three boys, who seemed to hang back from her. "Come on, now, you boys are coming with me."

Emma stared up at the desolate children standing in the door of the boxcar. Annie had both hands wrapped tight around its metal handle. Tony held his little brother Ben, his face filled with despair. Sarah, squeezed in between an Irish couple, refused to raise her eyes.

"Is the Reverend all right?" Patches asked.

"He isn't dead, is he, Miss Symns? Bruce was sayin' . . ."

"What are they going to do with us, miss?"

Emma was still for a second. She gazed up at the crowded, smoke-filled car. Filthy, Emma thought, filthy, and the smell was horrible.

"I want you to get down," Emma said. None of them seemed to hear. She spoke again, more angrily. "Get down, please, all of you."

"Why, Miss Symns?"

"Because I said so."

Annie started to cry. "You promised, Miss Symns, you promised. . . ."

"We can't get down now," J.P. said, "or we'll lose our places."

"J.P., please don't make it more difficult."

"I knew it wouldn't work out," Tom said bitterly. "I knew they were just lyin' to us."

More of the children were crying now; tears made tracks down Patches's dirty face. Little Eileen, who scarcely understood what was being said, was inconsolable.

Liverpool, standing next to Emma, kicked at the platform. "I ain't goin' back," he said. "I don't know about the rest of you, but they ain't gonna get me back in that city, no sir."

Emma turned angrily on Liverpool. "Liverpool, if you don't learn to curb that tongue of yours . . ."

"Miss, there's nothin' you can do to me that ain't already been done. I ain't goin' back."

She stared at Liverpool and then back at the others. What her uncle had asked her to do was impossible, she saw that. She couldn't ask them to give up that dirty, smelly boxcar; it was their chance, their hope. She and her uncle had made a covenant with those children and covenants, her uncle had taught her, were not things that you break.

She turned and began walking slowly back toward the station house.

"Where are you going, Miss Symns?"

"You just wait, all of you," she said. "I'll be back."

Her uncle turned his head on the table when Emma entered. "Emma . . ."

"Yes, Uncle Edward."

"You've told the children?" Emma was silent. "Did they take it badly?"

Emma looked around the small office. The railway men had gone. The only men left were the doctor, Carlin, and the conductor, who stood impatiently near the doorway.

"I didn't tell them, Uncle Edward," Emma said. Wordlessly, he pushed himself up on one elbow. "I couldn't," Emma said. "We promised them homes. . . ."

Her uncle sank back upon the table, stared up at the ceiling. "And what do you propose to do?"

Emma stood, her face stinging, feeling like a disobedient child. "I don't know, uncle."

"You can't go alone, Emma."

"I wouldn't be alone, uncle. It was you who taught me that when we do the right we are never alone . . ."

"Miss Symns!" The doctor's voice was as sharp as a rasp. "If you please. . . ." He motioned to her. She took a step toward him and he grasped her firmly by the arm. "Your uncle is a very sick man, he is not in any shape to be arguing with you about a carload of guttersnipes."

"Doctor, this is between me and my uncle. I'm afraid you don't understand what's at issue here."

"What's at issue here, Miss Symns, is your uncle's health. Now . . ."

The conductor chimed in. "I've got a train to run out there, folks. Now I need a decision . . ."

"Gentlemen, excuse me." It was Carlin. "I'd like to speak with the lady for a minute."

"What do you have to do with this?" the conductor said. "I've got a late train, mister."

"I happen to be an acquaintance of the lady and her uncle," Carlin said. He met the gaze of the hostile conductor. "Now don't get me wrong, I'm in favor of trains running on time too, but it seems to me that the lady has suffered a terrible blow and that you're asking her to make up her mind about some important things in very little time." The conductor grimaced, looked down at his feet. "She deserves five minutes, don't you think, gentlemen, to try to think things through? Give her a chance. Let me talk to her." The doctor and the conductor said nothing. "Miss Symns?"

Carlin moved toward the door, and Emma followed him. Together they stepped outside. Carlin shut the door softly behind them. The station yard was still furious with activity. Three porters charged past, clearing their path through the crowds with angry shouts. A train boy sang out at the top of his lungs, "Tobacco . . . candy . . . cigars . . . all the latest newspapers and magazines . . ."

"Thank you, Mr. Carlin," she said.

"I hope you're all right," he said. "I know this must be an awful shock."

She looked keenly at him. "I couldn't ask them to go back, I just couldn't."

"But what about your uncle, Miss Symns?" he said, softly. He waited for a moment, but she didn't answer. "Who will take care of him?"

Now Emma was angry. "The doctor said that he would be fine." Carlin said nothing, but Emma felt his silent disapproval. "You don't know my uncle. He's worked for almost two years to make this journey possible, it would just destroy him if we had to return these children."

"But what did he ask you to do, Miss Symns?"

Her face was burning. "I see now, Mr. Carlin, what side you're on." She yanked open the door and had taken one step into the office when Carlin grabbed her by the arm. The doctor and the conductor looked up, startled.

"I'm not on any side, Miss Symns. It's just that with all this upset I don't want you to go off and do something rash."

The two of them stood in the open doorway. Emma, as angry as she'd ever been in her life, kept her voice low to avoid disturbing her uncle lying, silent on the table, in the middle of the room. "I appreciate your concern, Mr. Carlin. Would you please take your hand off me."

"Miss Symns, you've got thirty children out there in that boxcar and no one to help you."

"Twenty-seven, Mr. Carlin. Would you please keep your voice down."

"All right, twenty-seven."

"This is none of your affair," Emma said.

"I know it's none of my affair, but if I may be frank, Miss Symns, you've had more than your share of problems handling these children already, and you're not always going to be able to count on people being around to help you out."

"I don't intend to, Mr. Carlin. And I don't intend to count on you, in case that's what you're worried about. . . ."

"Miss Symns, please, I'm only trying to help." Once again he took her elbow.

"Would you please not touch me!" she said. "I don't want to be comforted, can't you understand?"

"Emma . . ." It was her uncle's voice. She turned, frightened, and looked at him. "Come here, Emma."

She walked slowly to him, clasped his hand. "Yes, uncle."

"In my coat," he said. "Get the forms and my Bible."

Emma took his coat from the chair, placed the forms and the Bible in her uncle's hands. The minister placed his hands over hers on the Bible.

"The Lord hath said, Be strong and of good courage fear not, nor be afraid, the Lord, thy God, He is with thee; He will not forsake them."

He squeezed her hand, staring at her. Emma was unsure. "What is it, Uncle Edward?"

"Bless you, Emma, bless you."

The doctor moved in to separate them. "He needs his rest, Miss Symns."

"Thank you, Uncle Edward," Emma said.

The conductor was standing at the door, Carlin beside him. "Lady, I'm sorry. . . ." The conductor said.

Her uncle's head rolled back; it was the doctor who held her uncle's hand now.

Emma turned, and, head high, walked out the door.

The sound of the slamming door made Reverend Symns turn and reach out his hand. "God Bless you, Emma," he said. The doctor was silent. The only sound in the room was the irregular ticking of the telegraph sounder.

*I*t did occur to Emma, jammed into a boxcar with fifty immigrants and twenty-seven homeless children from the streets of New York that, perhaps, she had been rash. All afternoon Irishmen passed around bad whiskey and sang bawdy songs, Germans shared smelly pipes with their wives, babies squalled and nursed and left no babies' duties undone. There were no windows in the boxcar, and when the air became too thick to breathe someone would pull open the sliding door, putting the smaller children in constant danger of falling out. Emma shouted to them to be careful, scolded them, and the immigrants watched her and whispered among themselves. Who was this strange American lady and why did she have so many children?

Emma reflected to herself that nothing wore off faster than nobility. As the miles disappeared beneath the clicking rails her decision to go on alone with the children became more and more suspect, perhaps even a bit selfish. She thought of her uncle, alone, stretched out on the stationmaster's table, the words of the doctor. . . . Whatever grand cause she was serving, Emma had left her own.

The point now was to do the best she could. Emma unrolled a map and pointed out to the children the stops they would be making, tried to answer questions.

"We're going all the way out west, right, miss?" Patches asked.

Emma smiled at the freckle-faced boy with the broken tooth. "Not all the way, Patches. To Illinois. Here." Emma pointed out Illinois on the map to Patches.

"Will we see Indians?"

"We might."

"I bet we will," Patches said. "I bet we will."

Emma's eyes scanned the car. John, dirty and sweaty again in spite of all Emma's efforts, squatted patiently in the corner, watching an Italian mother nurse her child. Bruce, standing in the crowded aisle, tried to bully an apple from a disgruntled German. Behind him stood the boy who hung around Bruce constantly, what was his name? Tom, that was it, Tom.

"What's going to happen to us, miss?" Annie asked.

"What do you mean, Annie?"

"When you give us away. What happens?"

"I'm not giving you away," Emma said.

"Do we gotta work?" Tony asked.

"What if they beat us?" asked one of the girls.

"Or starve us?" asked Mouse.

Emma laughed. "They're not going to starve you. Oh, not you." She patted Mouse's round belly.

"But what if we don't get took?" Patches asked.

"You're going to be taken," Emma said firmly.

"How do you know?" Emma looked up in surprise. It was Bruce.

"I beg your pardon?" Emma said.

Bruce persisted. "How do you know?"

"Patches, would you hand me my bag, please?" Emma said. Patches instantly obliged her. After a brief search, Emma pulled a letter from the bottom of her bag.

"What's that, Miss Symns?"

"This is a letter. From a minister in Rock Springs, Illinois."

"Where's Rock Springs, Miss Symns?"

Emma looked steadily at the children. "I would like you all to just listen for a minute, please. Am I asking too much?"

"No, Miss Symns."

As Emma began to read the children grew silent. When she read about the dozen children lost to the winter's fever, about the minister losing both his little boy and little girl, Tony and Ben came over and stood next to Emma and stared at the paper.

" 'We will welcome any children who need homes,' " Emma read. " 'The day after we received your circular my wife began preparing a room in the hope that we might be so fortunate as to find a child ourselves. . . . Yours in Christ, Reverend William Krohn.' " Emma folded the letter, put it back in its envelope, and looked up at the children. "Does anyone have any more questions?"

For the moment they didn't.

The sun began to fade through the slats of the boxcar. The children grew quieter. Three or four of the boys were playing cards in the far corner. These children were a cocky, tough lot. And brave, Emma thought. They waited patiently, knees up, eyes wide open, not missing anything. There were no complaints about the dirt or the noise or the smell. They were waiting.

Night came. At a stop for water and wood the conductor came back to tell them that passengers were to furnish their own lights. Emma protested; if she had only been told before they would have made provisions. The conductor shrugged and walked off.

Darkness had never seemed half so thick to Emma as it did in that stifled car. It was relieved only here and there for a few minutes by a lighted pipe. The German in the corner kept up a constant fire that soon had them all choking with smoke. When Emma asked him to stop he only answered with a grunt and a fresh supply of the weed.

Emma nursed her annoyance in silence. The man seemed to be able to puff even when he was asleep. The curls of smoke were lifting beautifully above the bowl when suddenly the pipe smashed against the side of the car, breaking into a dozen pieces. That woke everyone, and there was a hullabaloo in a half-dozen languages, but no one could settle on the cause. Bruce and Tom leaned back to back, feigning sleep through the entire affair.

In the occasional flickering light, Emma watched as one after the other of the children fell asleep. They were like little old men and women, sharp and tense, with angular shoulders and emaciated frames, but once sleep came the muscles began to relax and they grew children again. Tony and Ben and the little girl, Eileen, curled their bodies close to Emma, reaching up drowsily for a hand or an arm to hold. Emma ran her hands absently over their small bodies. Though she was exhausted she could not sleep. Night only magnified the terrors and uncertainties of what she had taken on. Each time she felt herself slipping toward sleep she was brought alert again by the cry of a child, a breaking bottle, a muttered curse, the lurching of the train. Halfawake, in need of some object of comfort, Emma reached for her bag. In the darkness, she fumbled through it, searching with her fingers for her locket. It was gone. Or perhaps not. Perhaps it had just fallen on the floor, it was too dark to look for it now. Emma felt a painful sense of loss. It was so silly, she thought, to be upset about her locket when her uncle had been struck down, but it was one more link to her past torn away. . . .

Maybe it had fallen out in all the confusion at the station. Or maybe one of the children . . . it was silver, after all. Emma dismissed the thought from her mind. On edge and without solace, she drifted back toward sleep.

It seemed that the train stopped several times, though she was never sure, and then some time in the middle of the night it did stop, screeching to a halt, sleeping bodies rolling against one another, babies wailing, men shouting and screaming.

The door was yanked open and the immigrants shook their children awake, groped for baggage, and, with much shoving and pushing, stumbled out into the night. Frantic, Emma forced her way to the door to keep the orphans from tumbling sleepily after the immigrants. An Italian woman waved to Annie. The train whistle sounded, there was the brief sweet smell of dew and grass, the boxcar door was yanked shut.

The boxcar was theirs alone now.

Patches woke first. He felt terrible. In Dutch Hill he'd at least had some blankets and straw to sleep on. His back was sore from the hard wood floor and he was prickly all over from dirt. He sat up, pulling his nose as if that would take the stench away, and rubbed his teeth with a finger. He looked around but didn't see anybody to complain to; they were all asleep. The only sound was the clacking of the rails. He pulled at his nose. Air was what he needed.

Patches stood up and went to the boxcar door. The first try didn't budge the door at all. The second try he yanked harder and the door budged maybe an inch. Patches backed off a couple of feet, gathering himself up, then went at it with his full sixty pounds. The door gave suddenly, sending Patches somersaulting, nearly pitching him out on the tracks.

Sitting upright, Patches stared in amazement at the biggest, most golden field he'd ever seen.

The light pouring into the boxcar began to wake the children, one after the other. They rubbed their eyes, crawled to the open door to stare and point, their excited talk waking the last of the sleepyheads, till by the time Emma awoke it looked as if all of her charges were in danger of plunging en masse out onto the roadbed.

Emma shouted for them to get back, but no one was listening.

"What's that, miss?"

"Patches, you get back in here!"

"Oh, but, miss, what is it?"

"I think it's a cornfield, Patches."

"Oh, yes, them's what's makes buckwheaters."

"I want that door shut! Liverpool . . ."

"Cows! Look over there! Cows!"

"My mother used to milk cows!"

"Did not!"

"Liverpool!"

"Did so."

"Look! Look there!" They were passing a cornfield spread with ripe yellow pumpkins. "Just look at 'em! What a heap of mushmillons."

"Miss, do they make mushmillons in Illinois?" Liverpool asked.

"Yes, they do," Emma said, "and if you intend to get to Illinois in one piece you'd best stop hanging out the door."

"Ah, fellers, ain't that the country though? Won't we have nice things to eat?"

"Yes, and won't we sell some too?" Tony said.

Liverpool stretched both arms high in the air, calling for attention. "Hip! Hip! Boys! Three cheers for Illinois!"

Their cheering was interrupted by the whistle of the train, and suddenly they were headed through orchards loaded with large, red apples. The children's enthusiasm rose to the highest pitch. Keeping them within doors was almost impossible now. The biggest, most daring boys leaned far out, arms reaching, hats swinging, all whooping and hollering. Two or three times a boy made a lucky swipe and came up with an apple in his hat, but the train was going a little too fast to make it easy and the apples were just a little too far out of reach and kept slapping off the hands and hats of the eager boys and bouncing along the ground, rolling to a stop along the tracks as the train sped onward.

It seemed to Emma that it took forever for the train to pull into the small rural depot. A woman ran across the tracks ahead of the slow-moving train, pulling her bonneted little girl after her. The depot sign read Lockport, New York, and the station was surrounded by buggies, carriages, and wagons, some of them loaded with bags of grain. Two black boys stood on the steps, baskets on their arms, selling fruit.

The conductor led a perspiring minister toward the box-car. With as much ladylike dignity as the situation would permit, Emma let herself down on the platform.

It seemed to Emma that there were an awful lot of people waiting to meet the train. Four or five passengers got down from the passenger car and were greeted by their wives and husbands, mothers and fathers, with a great many embraces and handshakes and tossings of babies into the air, but even after the reunited families made their way through to carriages and wagons, the crowd was not significantly diminished. They all seemed to be squinting through the afternoon sun in Emma's direction. Emma realized with terror that they were waiting for her and the children.

The conductor introduced her to Reverend Archibold, a round young man with soft brown eyes who spoke to Emma in low, confidential tones. She had difficulty focusing on what he was saying, too distracted by the presence of the waiting crowd. They seemed like hard, flinty people, men in overalls and hats, women in calico dresses. Emma nodded a hello in their direction. A tall woman in a simple bonnet wiped back a strand of hair, flickered a smile at Emma. In the street beyond the station the buckboards were drawn up, horses stamped off the flies.

Emma only heard phrases from the murmuring minister . . . "if they actually met the children here . . . most effective . . . you could address them here . . ."

The children moved warily out of the boxcar, shielding their eyes in the sudden light. Two or three came quickly, confidently, like Liverpool. Bruce leaped down, faced the crowd sullenly, hands on hips. Sarah slid down cautiously, like a timid swimmer testing the waters. Mouse jumped down sideways, his withered arm protected from the crowd's view. They struggled out, one after the other, till finally they were all out on the platform, though still hanging back in the shadow of the boxcar.

". . . the hopes of our people, the expectancy . . . so whatever you'd like to say . . . I think I'd best just turn it over to you. . . ." The minister looked at her.

Emma glanced at Reverend Archibold, saw that he had nothing more to say, and took a deep breath. With a small, fixed smile on her face she walked slowly to the center of the platform. People nodded to her.

"Afternoon, ma'am."

"Welcome." People murmured hellos.

"Why thank you," Emma said softly.

Emma was aware of Carlin standing in the door of the depot. He had just bought an apple from one of the small black boys and was rubbing it up, examining it for blemishes. All the same, Emma felt as if he were watching her. That was all she needed, Emma thought, a critic. He thought she couldn't manage it, he was just going to stand back there, eat his apple, and wait for her to fail. Well, she would show him . . .

"Ladies and gentlemen," Emma began. Her voice betrayed her. There was a noticeable quaver. Emma cleared her throat and tried again. "Ladies and gentlemen, my name is Emma Symns of the New York Children's Aid Society, and I can't tell you how heartening it is . . ."

Emma was interrupted by a series of short, jolting bangs and rumbles. She turned to see the train begin to slide down the track.

"Hey!" Liverpool shouted. "They're takin' our bloody train!"

The brakeman, leaning out from the last car, waved gaily. "Don't worry, son, we're not goin' anywhere. We're just puttin' on a new locomotive."

The brakeman was right, the train wasn't going anywhere—it slid down another fifty yards and then came to a stop on a spur track—but by now Emma was thoroughly rattled. She tried to collect her thoughts, but without success. She was angry with herself; she'd seen her uncle handle public situations like this a thousand times, and if he could do it, she could do it. She could begin with the facts. Emma held up a piece of paper for everyone to see.

"You have all seen these circulars that were sent from New York. The instructions are clear. Boys fifteen years and older are expected to work till they are eighteen for their board and clothes. At the end of that time they are at liberty to make their own arrangements." Emma heard the children whispering behind her. Emma ignored them, concentrating instead on the squinting, curious faces of the farmers. She tried to imagine them with children, tried to pick out the kind ones, the harsh ones. The man with the belly and the straw hat, would he drive a child too hard? The short woman with the round brown arms, was she gentle? "Children under the age of twelve are expected to remain till they are eighteen. They must be treated by the applicants as one of their own children in the matters of schooling, clothing, and training . . ."

Again she heard the whispering behind her. This time she turned. Bruce nudged Patches in the ribs. When he saw Emma glaring at him, he quickly straightened up.

Emma cleared her throat. "The society asks the families to report by letter on the progress of the children once a year."

A farmer near the back of the crowd waved his hand in the air. "How do we know they won't run off?"

The man with the belly answered him. "Ever see a cow run from a haystack? Treat her well, she'll stay." Several people laughed.

"If the family finds the child unsatisfactory or if the child is unhappy or mistreated, the society will terminate the agreement and a new home will be found."

The farmer in the back was waving his hand again. "How do you do that? The society's in New York."

"A visitor will be sent to check on each child," Emma said. "If this journey is successful, other children will be sent west. Are there any other questions?"

Standing on the depot platform, Emma looked out over the crowd. They were murmuring, talking to one another. Some of the children sat on the steps, the others were crowded behind her, waiting and watching. Emma couldn't help but glance over at Carlin. He stood at the far end of the platform, leaning against a window jamb, a half-eaten apple in his hand. She had spoken well, she knew she had, and he must know it too.

Emma spoke more urgently. "These are wonderful children. Very special children. I've only known them for two days, but they have shown me a patience that would put any of us to shame. They've come a long way, these children, and it hasn't been an easy way, and they did it because they believed that there were homes here, homes with you, and good, honest work." Under one of the buckboards a squat boy wrestled with a bulldog, raising clouds of dust. Some of the crowd turned to watch.

"If there are no more questions, is there anyone . . . who would like to select a child?"

Patches never heard much of Emma's speech. He was too busy examining the faces of the farmers and storekeepers who confronted them. He liked the way the lady with the fat arms looked, but the man with her looked like a bear and his whiskers went every whichaway, it scared him. The skinny lady with the fan looked kind of serious, but there was a tall, stooped man who laughed easily, maybe Patches would try a joke on him. He just couldn't remember any right now, off the top of his head. . . .

Bruce poked him in the ribs.

"Hey, cut it out!" Patches whispered.

"Who's gonna be the first?"

"First what?" Patches said.

"First to go."

"I don't know."

"Bet it ain't you."

"How come?"

"You're too scrawny."

"Am not."

"Bet they take the girls first. You can guess what they want

— 110 —

them for. Or maybe ol' Tom here, he's the workhorse type."
"Who'd you say?" Tony said.
"I say Tom."
"Naw, I say one of the girls," Liverpool said. "I'll even give odds."
"Bet it's me," Patches said.
"How come?" Bruce said.
"Just feel it," Patches said.
"Bet you a nickel it's not," Bruce said.
"All right," Patches said.
"You don't even have a nickel," Bruce said.
"Do so."
"Let's see it."
Patches reached deep in his pocket and held a nickel up to Bruce. Bruce nodded. Patches turned and saw Emma glaring at him. Patches put the nickel back in his pocket and Emma went on talking. Patches rubbed the nickel in his pocket. Bet it's me, he thought, bet it's me.

For almost a minute no one spoke. The only sound was the snarling of the bulldog as he wrestled this way and that, trying to tear the stick from the hands of his tormentor.
Emma turned back to the children. Tony took his brother Ben's hand. Liverpool rolled his eyes and smiled, looking up at the sky. Emma reached out to straighten J.P.'s collar. J.P. ducked away from her touch.
"Miss?"
Emma turned to face a young farm couple. The woman was square-shouldered and wide-hipped, her bonnet tight around her face. Her husband, long-limbed, had the largest Adam's apple Emma had ever seen. The woman held back, staring, while her husband bent forward, his face inches from the children's faces, then leaned back, scrutinizing them like a man examining horses, then turned back to laugh self-consciously to his friends in the crowd.

He bent over Mouse. "How're your teeth, son?" Before
Mouse could answer, the man reared back and grinned at
his friends as if he'd cracked the best joke in the world.

"Fine, sir, just fine."

"Fine, you say." The man bent down again, his hands on
his knees. The man's face became serious, almost troubled.
Mouse had his arms folded, concealing his withered arm.
"What's your name, son?"

"Mouse."

The long-limbed man reared back wildly, turning back,
hands on hips, to share the laugh with his friends. "Mouse.
He says his name is Mouse." Three or four men laughed;
the boy who'd been wrestling with the bulldog slapped his
thighs. The man's wife did not laugh. Mouse rubbed his
nose. The man did not recover quickly from his amusement.
"Mouse, eh? We got quite a few of them." The man blinked,
pulled at his mustache. He took Mouse by the shoulder,
looked down at the boy's withered arm, then looked back at
his wife. She nodded. "But none like you," he said. "We'd
like you to come home with us, son," the man said.

People started forward, cautiously, self-consciously, at
first, coming up the steps of the platform to the children.
Emma moved among the crowd, introducing children to
adults, giving names, trying to set people at ease. The pudgy
Reverend Archibold, his face shining, helped her, reassuring
townspeople, winking good will.

It began to happen, all too fast. The man who ran the
general store took a boy named Robert that Emma scarcely
knew, an Irish couple took two girls, there was a shy German
boy who went off with a widowed blacksmith, where had
Emma put his papers. . . . Emma answered the same whispered questions over and over again, got into an argument
with a farm couple who wanted to take Ben, but not Tony—
"We like the *little* one"—Emma insisted that brothers would
have to stay together. No, they would not make exceptions.

Patches wandered dejectedly through the crowd and then sat down on the edge of the platform, staring across the tracks and rubbing his nickel in his hand. Emma saw him go and knew that she should go and comfort him, but she couldn't, there wasn't time now. She leafed through the forms. She had placed six, seven, eight children.

A thin, birdlike woman was speaking to Annie. The woman's hands trembled as she touched Annie's hair. Her husband, massive, distrustful, leaned against the station wall watching her.

"You like Annie?" Emma said.

Startled, the woman drew her hand back from Annie's hair. "Yes," she said. "Yes, very much."

"Are you having a good time, Annie?"

Annie nodded shyly.

"Do you like this lady?"

Annie looked up at the woman and nodded again.

Emma spoke to the woman. "Do you think, then, that you'd be in a position . . ."

The woman turned quickly, staring at her husband, her eyes pleading with him. The thick man pushed himself away from the building and started toward the wagons. His great frame lumbered across the dusty road. The woman let out a sharp, high-pitched cry. "No. No," she said. "It's impossible." She turned back to Annie, cupped the girl's face in her trembling hands. "My dear, my dear . . ." She pulled back suddenly and began to run, clutching at her skirts as she went, running after her man.

J.P. had had enough of farmers peering at her, feeling her muscle to see what a rugged little guy she was. J.P.'s mother was an actress, a good one, and if these farmers knew who her mother was, they wouldn't be treating her like this, that's for sure. J.P. tried to imagine what it would be

like if her mother came looking for her and found her living
with some backward dairyman, the scorn her mother would
feel, her laughter. . . .

J.P. pulled down her newsboy cap and kicked at the platform. She had imagined her mother coming back to get her
often enough. Too often. It wasn't much of a comfort any
more. Didn't matter—she didn't want these farmers feeling
her muscle anyway. J.P. found it a cinch, slipping away from
the crowd, around the corner of the depot.

The train sat, looking completely deserted, on the spur
track. J.P. peered back in through the depot window. The
engineer, the fireman, and the Lockport stationmaster were
laughing over their coffee. She looked up and down the
road. There was no one watching her except for a couple of
carriage horses.

One quick dash and she was on the far side of the train—
out of sight of everyone. Her heart was beating fast, her
spirits started to lift. She didn't need any of the others. She
climbed up, tried the baggage-car door. It slid open and J.P.
swung herself inside.

The shadowy interior was a rich jumble of suitcases and
crates, harnesses and saddles, buckets and knotted bundles,
barrels marked molasses and whiskey. For a moment J.P.
was stilled by a condition approximating awe: in all her days
of petty thievery she'd never had such an opportunity. She
could take her pick. The only problem was knowing where
to begin.

Her problem was solved when she spied the neat stack of
odd-shaped boxes in the far corner. She hadn't forgotten
the care Carlin had taken while loading them on the boat.
No one was that careful unless there was something to protect, something valuable.

A couple of minutes of industry and J.P. had the boxes ar-
rayed around her on the floor of the car. Her fingers skill-

fully undid the knotted ropes and with a broken knife she picked away at the locks. Her first finds were disappointing, some square copper plates, bottles of chemicals neatly organized, then a tripod, some tiny brushes, a holly cast-iron pyramid, a black box with wooden knobs and smelling of iodine. . . . She'd just about given up hope of finding anything worthwhile when she pried open a heavy box that turned out to be daguerreotypes in their hinged satin cases.

She picked one up, opened it, and stared in astonishment. It was the picture of an actress in an Indian headdress. She picked up another—again an actress, this time in tights and a tightly laced corset. The third was an actress with long flowing hair, in a gauzy dress holding a rose. J.P. picked up one after the other, picture after picture of actresses, with the mad thought in her head that, sooner or later, by some quirky twist of fate, she might find a picture of her mother.

She was so absorbed in the task that she didn't hear the baggage-car door opening. It wasn't until the shaft of sunlight from the opening door fell across her face that she looked up and saw Carlin standing outside the car.

"What's going on in here?" he demanded.

She dropped the daguerreotype she was holding, heard it crack on the floor.

"Jesus Christ!" Carlin said.

J.P. started for the door, but Carlin was too quick for her, pulling himself up to block her path. J.P. turned and tried to escape over a pile of suitcases, but Carlin grabbed her by the back of her belt and pulled her back.

"Hey, mister," J.P. said. Even as he was pulling her back, she was twisting, and as he tried to grab her with his other hand, she stomped down hard on his foot. He let out a shout, and she was free again.

Around the car they went, J.P. leading him over saddles, hopping through piles of harnesses, weaving in and out between barrels. J.P. threw buckets down behind her to try to trip him up, but she couldn't lose him.

"You dirty little thief. . . ." J.P. heard him kick a bucket away.

"Hey, mister, take it easy. I didn't take none of your stuff . . ."

Carlin shoved over two heavy barrels, cutting off J.P.'s retreat.

"Hey, mister, you're crazy . . . what are you doing?"

He didn't say anything, just stood there, trying to catch his breath. He had her trapped in the corner. He was limping on the foot that J.P. had stepped on. "Come here," he said.

"I'm not coming there," she said.

"I said come over here." Only once or twice before in her life had J.P. ever seen anybody look this mad. He looked as if he were ready to strangle her in the harnesses if he caught her.

The boxful of chemical bottles was on the floor only a couple of feet away. It was worth taking the chance. J.P. kicked open the box, there was the sound of breaking glass, and she tried to run for it.

It almost worked. Fumes of iodine and other, unidentifiable chemicals filled the car. Carlin stepped back, coughing, his hands in front of his face, but as J.P. dashed by him, he turned and lunged for her, caught her by the cuff of her trousers, and she went sprawling headlong on the floor of the car. There was the sound of copper plates falling to the floor. They both scrambled, but this time Carlin had her.

"Let me go! Let me go!" She started to cough because of all the fumes.

He was shaking her by her collar. "Do you know what you've done. Do you have any idea?"

"Get your hands off me, mister!" J.P. made the mistake of trying to stomp his foot again. He was too quick for her this time, jerking her away—then reaching back and slapping her across the face, hard.

J.P. started to cry.

Carlin let her go, ashamed suddenly of what he had done. J.P. sat down on a trunk, her face in her hands, the tears running down her cheeks.

"You hit me! You hit me!"

"I know I hit you. Do you know what you did, you ignorant little . . ."

"You didn't have to hit me that hard, you could have broken my jaw."

"What were you looking for, money?" Carlin was still plenty agitated. "Is that it, money? I'll give you money." His hands trembling, Carlin reached into his pocket, pulled out a dollar and threw it at J.P. He stared glumly at the broken chemical bottles and the copper plates scattered across the floor. "Oh, my God. . . ."

"Why don't you hit somebody your own size?"

"You know what this is, son?" Carlin said, pointing to the debris.

"Sure, I know, it's picture-taking stuff. So? You didn't have to act like a wild man." J.P. reached down and picked up the dollar from the floor.

"You don't know much, do you?" Carlin said.

"I know enough," J.P. said. "I've seen all this stuff before, lots of times. You're probably going to set up a parlor in Chicago or something, right?"

"Wrong."

"Well, what then?"

"I'm going to St. Louis first of all. Where I'm meeting General Douglas. You ever heard of General Douglas?"

"No."

"Well, he's a very important general, a hero, in fact, in the Mexican War. You ever heard of the Mexican War?"

"Course I did."

"The government has asked General Douglas to lead a survey of the Rocky Mountains, look for possible routes for a transcontinental railroad."

"A railroad over the mountains? You're fooling me!"

"That's right. A railroad over the mountains. And he's asked me to come with him. I'm being asked to do things no daguerreotypist has ever done before, take pictures of things nobody's ever seen. The general wants a document, a record . . . it's a chance that doesn't come twice in a lifetime. It's something I've been working and scheming for for years. I've invested every penny I have, bought the best equipment I could find, packed all the plates. Then some miserable little guttersnipe comes along . . ."

"Mister, how was I to know?" Carlin looked at J.P. without saying anything. "You're going to turn me in, aren't you? You're going to tell Miss Symns."

"I don't know yet."

"She'll send me back to New York if you do tell her, you can depend on that. I'll be back in the streets. Probably I'll have to go back to Lizzie . . . that's Lizzie the Dove, but the name's a joke, that's for sure. You just don't know what she's like. . . ." J.P. stared at Carlin. "What are you going to do with me?"

"I haven't decided yet," Carlin said. "I want to ask you something."

"Sure."

"All those other children, they're out there, meeting farmers, trying to get homes. That's what you've come for, right? So what are you doing back here?"

"I didn't like the look of any of them," J.P. said.

"You didn't like the look of them?"

"They're just a bunch of farmers."

"Bunch of farmers!" Carlin laughed. "So how do you expect to find a home?"

"Dunno."

"Well, you're a pretty incorrigible case, aren't you? Bound for no good." There was the faintest trace of a smile on Carlin's face.

"I didn't mean to break your stuff, mister, honest. If I'd have known you were going with a general— I hope it's not all ruined."

Carlin didn't say anything, but bent over and picked up the cracked daguerreotype of the actress. He looked at it for a second, then set it down on a trunk. "I'll just have to see," he said. "If I go to work with a buff brush maybe I can get some of these plates back in shape. If not, I'll just try to pick up some more in Cleveland or St. Louis." He gingerly picked up one of the chemical bottles and put the stopper back in, grimacing. "Phew!" he said. He looked at J.P. "I hit you kind of hard there, didn't I? Sorry. I guess I just flew off the handle."

"Oh, it's all right. I don't mind. I would've done the same thing if somebody had broken into my stuff."

Carlin chewed on the inside of his cheek, sizing her up. "Tell you what. I won't tell Miss Symns about this . . ." He motioned to the broken bottles, the copper plates strewn across the floor. "And you don't mention that I . . . you know . . ." He pointed to the side of her face where he'd hit her. "You know how women are. I wouldn't want her to think . . ."

J.P. looked at him keenly. "I know what you mean," she said.

"So you want to go back out there?" Carlin said.

"No, not right now," J.P. said.

"Well, then, why don't you help me clean up this mess?" He knelt and began to pick up copper plates. He looked back at her. "Just be careful."

"Humph." The farmer's thick strong fingers squeezed into Bruce's arm. "Humph."

The farmer's son, a bull-necked boy of nineteen, reached out and did the same. "Humph." Bruce jerked his arm away, rolled down his sleeves.

The farmer leaned back on his heels, narrowed his eyes, hooked his fingers in his belt. "You afraid of work?"

Bruce didn't answer.

"What'd you say?" the farmer's son asked, cocking his head to hear Bruce's reply.

"Touch me again and I'll knock you into the middle of next week," Bruce said.

The son turned and grinned at his father. "Ain't he a wildcat!" The father didn't say anything, just frowned and scratched the back of his broad, leathery hand.

The two boys faced off, waiting for the other to make the first move.

Tom was at Bruce's side. "Drop the blinker, Bruce."

The father waved his hand in disgust. "Enough of that talk. You two fellers are gonna learn to get on or you'll answer to me . . . an' I can lick the two of ya fallin' down the stairs. Don't worry, I know how to get work outta boys like you."

The man grabbed Bruce by the arm and pulled him toward Emma. Bruce tried to pull away, but the man's grip was too fierce. "We've decided on this boy!" the man shouted out.

Emma looked up from talking to the couple that was taking Mouse. She was tired and dazed. She smiled a tight smile at the farmer holding Bruce.

"Why that's fine, Bruce is a good boy." At first all she noticed was the odd look on Bruce's face. "Bruce?"

Bruce couldn't speak.

"What are you waiting for, boy? The lady's speaking to you."

Bruce tried to pull away, the farmer held him. Still, he couldn't speak. As big and strapping as he was, Bruce was still a child without words; all Emma had to go on was his frightened eyes.

The farmer addressed Emma. "I guess we got ourselves a deal then, huh?"

Emma's mind raced. She said the first thing that she could think of: "Are you a member of the church?"

"What's that?"

"Are you members of the church?"

"Church? Well, we're Christans if that's what you mean. My old lady gets saved twice a year, regular, at the camp meetin', if that helps."

"But are you members of a church?"

The farmer moved uneasily. "No. Is that a requirement?"

"No, it's not. But the society does require that the children have schooling and training."

A small crowd had gathered to watch the debate. The farmer had let go of Bruce's arm.

"You call this here a child?" the farmer said, grinning.

"I do," Emma said.

"Well, I figure we can learn this child what he needs to learn."

"And what is that?" Emma asked.

The man raised his voice. "Now you're startin' to make me mad, miss. We need another good strong boy."

Emma handed him a piece of paper.

The farmer stared at it. "Now what do I need with readin' matter."

"Our instructions are very firm," Emma said. "Boys between the ages of twelve and fifteen are expected to work, but must be sent to school a part of each year. After fifteen it is expected that they receive wages."

The farmer grinned. He looked left and then right, searching for some support. "Oh, that's fine," he said.

"That's fine with you?" Emma said.

"Just fine," the farmer nodded. Emma and the farmer glowered at one another. She did not back down. "No, it ain't fine for me, it's fine for a charity. But I ain't a charity, I'm a farmer. And I need another hand."

"Then, sir, I suggest that you hire one," Emma said.

The farmer raised one fist, trying to summon up some crushing final word. He failed. He crumpled the circular into a ball and handed it to Emma, then turned and shoved his son through the crowd.

Emma turned back. Mouse and his new family were staring at her. Sarah came over and squeezed Emma's hand. No one said anything until the round Reverend Archibold came bustling through the crowd.

"Perhaps I can get you a cold drink, Miss Symns?" She didn't reply. "I think we've done pretty well here, don't you? Rather remarkably well if you ask me. Ten children placed in homes in one afternoon, I think that's pretty splendid work."

"And were they good homes, Reverend Archibold?"

"We can pray that they will be."

"Yes, we can pray," Emma said.

"Don't worry about that ol' man, miss," a woman piped up. "You did right to stand up. Ol' Garrett's about as agreeable as a skunk."

Emma looked down the track where J.P. and Carlin were walking back toward the depot. Emma wondered where they'd been.

"Oh, you're right there," someone added.

"Now, Miss Symns." Reverend Archibold placed a friendly hand on her arm. "There's a husking bee this afternoon at the Wilsons' farm. It'd be good for you to do a little relaxing. And it would be good for the children."

Emma ran her hand over her face. She was suddenly feeling faint. "I think we should stay with the train," she said.

"Now, Miss Symns, the train doesn't leave till tomorrow morning anyway, what's the sense in that? I don't see why you shouldn't have some fun. Do you?"

Emma looked at the quiet faces of the children who hadn't been taken, at Patches, sitting on the edge of the platform, angrily throwing pebbles down on the track.

"No, you're right, Reverend, there's nothing wrong with fun. We will be happy to accept."

*T*hey rode in Reverend Archibold's wagon, the children packed tight in the back, Emma sitting up front with the minister. Clucking the horse along the road, Reverend Archibold kept up a flow of jolly stories, even made an attempt at teaching a song. It didn't go well. Not many of the children were in the mood. Emma felt that somehow they blamed her for their not having been chosen, that she had somehow betrayed them. One or two tried to put the best possible face on things; if that many had found homes in one afternoon, it wouldn't be long for them either—they'd be next.

The rest of the children were quiet, just sat hunched together, holding tight to the sides of the wagon as they hit the rutted, washed-out section of the road, taking in every detail of this strange new land, the bare cornfields and the bright leaves of distant groves.

The Wilsons' yard was a tumult of animals, people, and

corn. Women rushed back and forth from the log house with pots of food; children and dogs tumbled together, men strutted around the ridges of unhusked corn, each man giving his appraisal, passing the jug, having a laugh.

Emma and the children were not the only guests who were outsiders. A group of seven or eight men gathered near the smokehouse, gathered around a black box mounted on a tripod. Sitting in front of the tripod on a split-bottomed chair, waiting patiently for his picture to be taken, was a wrinkled old farmer. Bent over the camera was Frank Carlin.

J.P. raised her hand and waved, and Carlin waved back. He stood there for a second, smiling at Emma, as if he wanted to say something. Emma stiffened. She still felt as if Carlin were watching her, judging her. She still didn't know what to make of him.

Arms raised, Karl Wilson came over to greet them. He was a beaming host, his harvest was in, and he was irrepressible. He lifted the children down from the wagon, whether they wanted to be lifted or not, and he did it with the enthusiasm of a man tossing bales. He insisted on knowing all their names and when they told him, he'd say, "Ben! Now that's a mighty proud name. I had a cousin named Ben."

Karl Wilson led Emma up into the log house. On the wide porch, a quilt was stretched out on a rack. Inside, festoons of dried apples, peaches, peppers, bunches of sage, and pennyroyal hung from the rafters. Everywhere was the smell of food. The women stopped their work when Emma entered. One, tongue-tied, wiped a smudge from her face with an elbow, rushed over, and hugged Emma around the waist. "I heard about your work, miss, and may the Lord bless you! And I know He will! I know He will!"

At the fireplace a woman straightened up slowly and turned. It was the thin woman who had wanted Annie. Her eyes met Emma's, then she wiped her hands on her skirt and walked out the door.

"Miss Symns! Miss Symns!" She recognized Tony's shout. "Come look!" Emma went to the door and stared out. A horse and wagon jostled into the yard. On the driver's side sat a long-necked, grinning farmer, on the far side sat his square wife. Between them sat Mouse, holding on to the reins, looking both scared and excited.

Ben and Patches ran toward the wagon, shouting up at Mouse. The other children joined in, crowding so close that they were in danger of getting stepped on by the horse, till the long-necked farmer finally took the reins and pulled the animal to a complete stop.

Mouse jumped down from the wagon. The children peppered him with questions, and he was happy to answer them. He told them about his room and the dogs and the cats and the food they'd given him. Patches made Mouse go over everything—item by item—and what they said and how they treated him.

"And they gave me a calf."

"A calf!"

"You mean a cow?"

"A calf! They gave me a calf. It's mine to raise."

Bruce was skeptical. "But how do you know it's yours?"

"They gave it to me."

"They say they gave it to you. They could take it back any time. Maybe they just said that so you'd do all the work. You don't have a paper that says it's yours, right?"

"No."

"But they've got a paper that says that you belong to them."

"I don't belong to them. I work for them. I'm part of the family. That's what they said. They gave me the calf so I'd be part of the family."

The other boys were silent. Finally Patches said, "It sounds real good, Mouse. I just wish it'd been me."

At the depot Carlin had fallen into conversation with a farmer, who, when he discovered that Carlin was not only a daguerreotypist, but also had never been to a husking bee, promptly invited him. The farmer dropped a few hints that it might be the hospitable thing to do to take a few pictures. Carlin was feeling pretty miserly about his remaining plates in the wake of J.P.'s assault on them, but he agreed to take a couple of pictures on the condition that he could choose his subjects. Secretly he was pleased; he wasn't shooting variety actresses any more, he was shooting real Americans, people who'd never had a picture taken before. Which wasn't to say they didn't have their vanity too.

"What's happening to ol' Jeems here?"

"Jeems is havin' his likeness made."

"Is he all right? Can he talk? Hey, Jeems!"

Jeems sat in front of the camera, his eyes fixed on the lens, every finger clenched in place, every muscle in his face rigid, his eyebrows contracting with furious resolution.

"He's going mad. His brother got the same look just before he went crazy. . . ."

"Don't blur the picture there, Jeems."

Carlin stood up and waved for Jeems to relax. The picture taking was over. While Carlin put the plate face down over the mercury bath, Jeems staggered away from the chair, looking dazed.

"How you feelin' there, Jeems?"

"Ain't you afraid of breakin' the machine?"

"With a face like that he shoulda charged you double."

Taking a pair of pliers, Carlin held the mercurialized plate over an alcohol lamp. The men all watched as he then poured a thick liquid over it, shaking the plate slowly.

Jeems scratched at his ear, impatient, watching as Carlin

rinsed the plate in clear water and slipped it into a wooden case before presenting it to him. The man craned to have a look. Jeems was transfixed.

"How'd it come out, Jeems?"

"Let us have a look there, Jeems."

"That's me?" Jeems said.

"That's right," Carlin said.

"That ain't me," Jeems said.

"Yes, it is," Carlin said.

"Yeah, I think it caught your meanness real good," one of Jeems's friends pitched in.

"It's the Devil," Jeems muttered He looked suspiciously at Carlin. "How's that contraption work, anyway?"

"Sunshine, Jeems, sunshine pure and simple."

"Ask me, I think it's the Devil."

"Come on, Jeems," another of his friends said. "A man can't quarrel with his own likeness."

"I gotta go show this to Martha," Jeems said. With that he put the daguerreotype case under his arm and lurched toward the house.

"Hey, likeness man, how about takin' me next?"

A man with a limp was to be the judge of the cornhusking, and he circled the heap of unhusked corn shaking his head, squinting critically, making judicious murmuring sounds. Ben was right in his footsteps, shaking his head and squinting too, trying to get the hang of it.

"How's she look?" Tony asked.

The man with the limp looked down at Tony. "What you say, little feller?"

"I say, how's she look?"

"Looks fine, son, looks fine." The man bent down, like a man looking under a bed for a lost shoe. Tony did the same.

"Seems to me the right-hand side of the pile is bigger— That doesn't seem fair," Tony said.

The man with the limp straightened up, hooked his fingers in his overalls. "Well, sonny, you're right." Tony smiled and hooked his fingers in his overalls. "The right-hand side is a mite bigger, but if you'll look close you'll see that that's mostly the long yellow gourd corn." He looked down at Tony. "And you know what that means?"

Tony took a guess. "Easy shuckin'."

The man looked at Tony suspiciously and spat on the ground. "That's right. Over there on the other side you got your little flinty corn that can be mighty hard goin' on the hands. You see what I mean?"

"Yes, sir, I do." Tony spat on the ground.

The man looked at him long and hard before he spoke. "For a kid from New York you ain't so dumb."

Emma stood on the porch, watching. A cheerful woman in a wide bonnet was at Emma's side, furnishing a running commentary. There was a big to-do about choosing captains, with all the young bucks strutting around, shoving each other by the shoulder, throwing in their two-bits' worth, laughing loudly at jokes that were incomprehensible to Emma. One side was to be headed by Tip, a muscular young man named for Tippecanoe, the woman said. The captain of the other side was a short, intense fellow named Bud. The picking of sides went on, the cheerful woman second-guessing each pick—"Oh, not Burt, why he can't husk corn for beans—" till everyone was chosen but the old man named Jeems—"Had the shakes for about a year, Jeems did, but he's lot better now—" Jeems looked around the yard with the hangdog look of the unchosen.

Tip spoke up. "Tell you what, Bud, how about you take Jeems and I'll take the likeness man."

"The slicker? You'll take the slicker? Well, I don't know . . ."

"Mr. Carlin, how about it? You ever husked corn?"

"Husk it? Why I never even eat the stuff. But I'm willing to take a crack at it, sure." The men cheered encouragements. "But how about this for a proposition; how about each side takes one of these city boys here?"

"These boys here?"

"It would be nice and neighborly now, wouldn't it?"

The farmers looked skeptical. "What do they know about huskin'? Any of 'em ever tried it?"

"Don't know that," Carlin said. "But I do know that these boys have come out here to find a home and it would be mighty Christian of you to give them a proper introduction to what it's like."

"But it'd throw the sides all off!" They looked at Carlin sideways, not sure what they thought about this stranger butting into their fun.

"They'd just be fallin' all over everybody."

"Maybe they wouldn't like it. Besides, you don't know."

Carlin put up his hands. "You can do what you want. It's your husking bee."

Emma watched Carlin closely. She didn't understand him, not yet, but he had thrown himself in on the side of the children too often for it to be a mistake. It was obvious that he was drawn to them, and yet one part of himself he kept back, observing, judging.

"It's hard work. It wouldn't be much fun for 'em."

"You're probably right," Carlin said.

Tip turned to Bud. "What do you say, Bud?"

It took Bud a little longer. He grimaced and hitched up his belt. "Okay," he said finally. "We're each takin' one, right? I'll take the big kid over there." He pointed to Bruce, who brightened considerably, clapped Tom on the back before striding over to join his teammates.

Tip motioned to Liverpool. "How about you, kid? You think you can keep up with your friend there?"

Liverpool spat on his hands and rubbed them together. "Keep up with him? Why I'm going to leave that boy in the dust."

The judge raised his hand. "Awright boys, now crib your corn!" The hand came down and the men fell at it.

To Emma's eye it was an oddly thrilling sight, the teams of men bending, grabbing, tearing, tossing the yellow ears of corn high into the air like twirling batons, looping them, rattling them against the side of the crib. Each man had his own style; one as nimble and casual as a magician practicing sleight of hand; another dogged and mechanical, not wasting a single motion; another, elbows flailing, shoulders jerking like a man in a fit. When they started to flag, Tip and Bud would exhort them, "Come on, fellers, don't let these donkeys beat you! Let's pick it up!" and they would go at it with renewed energy, a rain of corn beating against the crib.

Emma watched anxiously, praying that Liverpool and Bruce would do all right, or at least not embarrass themselves. A couple of times she even found herself shouting out, "Good, Bruce!" and "There you go, Liverpool!" Liverpool was a quick study, mimicking the moves of the man next to him, falling easily into the rhythm of the work. It was harder for Bruce, who persisted by sheer brute force, his face set in a grimace. Every once in a while one of the two boys would look up to see how the other was doing, then fall back at his work with three times the effort.

As the minutes passed a great pile of husks rose behind the furiously working men, and Emma's eyes found a new focus. Surrounded by teammates, his sleeves rolled up, face shining with sweat, Carlin kept pace. More than kept pace; he laughed and shouted back and forth with the others, even managed to keep an eye on Liverpool, joking, offering encouragement. Carlin was playful, almost boyish, and full of pleasure. The other men took to him easily, and when they shouted back at him, Carlin would throw back his head and laugh, not because of the wit of it all, not because the jokes were so great, but out of good nature and exuberance.

The piles of corn shrank away. The pace began to pick up. Tom shouted out for Bruce, Patches for Liverpool, the cheerful woman pulled off her bonnet and squeezed Emma by the shoulders. "That Jeems, does he look like a man with the shakes? Does he?" Tony and Ben clung to Emma's skirts, their faces filled with awe. These wild, rough people were the ones they were expected to live with?

Liverpool held his team's last ear of corn aloft as the other side worked on frantically. Emma tried not to smile, but couldn't help it; the boy was a crowd pleaser to the last. "Anybody here says I ain't been a farmer all my life?" Liverpool dropped the last ear into the crib, and there was a great hurrah. Carlin lifted Liverpool on his shoulders. Across the rail that separated the two sides, Bruce stood up, staring. Even from the porch Emma could see that his knuckles were bleeding from the rough cobs.

Far more awesome than the husking bee, from the children's point of view, was the supper that followed. Beef and pork, ham and sweet potatoes, buttered beets, stewed apples, and pies of every kind. The children ate quickly, stared and ate some more. Tom kept snagging apples when he thought no one was watching and slipping them under his jacket. No one was looking, and he put more apples under his jacket and more again, till he was bulging like a badly stuffed Santa Claus and finally had to sit glumly in the corner, defeated by so much abundance. A large, beaming woman hugged Patches to her bosom and stuffed him with peach cobbler.

Liverpool, in contrast to the others, decided to play the gallant young gentleman, eating slowly, smiling, polite, complimenting the farm women on their cooking: What a fine

ham, what delicious sweet potatoes, how much he was looking forward to the pumpkin pie. Why, one of the principal
reasons he'd come west was all he'd heard about the pumpkin pie.

With such a build-up, it was inevitable that a great wedge
of pie was brought and set down in front of him.

Raising his fork, Liverpool smiled at the farm women. He
took his first bite. He blinked, without chewing. He began to
chew slowly, his face expressionless. He gulped. He tried
another bite, stared down at his plate as if he'd been betrayed.

"Miss Symns?" he whispered.

"Yes, Liverpool."

"Is this pumpkin pie?"

"Is something wrong?"

"Is it pumpkin pie?"

"You mean to tell me that you've never had pumpkin pie
before?"

"No, miss."

Emma stared at Liverpool. "Why, Liverpool."

"You taste it, miss."

Using her fork, Emma took a tiny bite of Liverpool's pie.
"Yes, Liverpool, that's pumpkin."

Liverpool frowned. "Don't you think it tastes kind of . . .
odd?"

Reverend Archibold was constantly at Emma's side. Emma
nodded and smiled at his stories, looked occasionally over at
the far corner where Carlin was drinking corn whiskey with
the other men.

After dinner the fiddler and the caller led them, lanterns
swinging, down to the barn for the hoedown, Emma following behind with her brood. Once inside the barn, the children scattered, some going to look at the horses in their

stalls, J.P. and Sarah settling down to play with the barn cats. Tom sat down in a nest of harnesses and began munching on one of his many apples.

The caller was a giant of a man, with sloping shoulders and receding chin. His shirt kept coming out of his pants and he kept tucking it back in. He was a toe tapper, and he leaned over the fiddler, a man about half his size, listening and twitching with a blissful look on his face, until the two of them had a rousing rhythm going between them. Every once in a while he would lean over and take a swig from his own private jug; then he would go back to his toe tapping, the gleam in his eye getting ever brighter till some internal voice told him it was time to start.

"All right, now, folks, let's make your sets. Come on, find your honey, find your sweet, get that gal out on her feet."

Couples started to come forward, one at a time, with a lot of blushing and looking back over their shoulders at their friends. Three or four of the young bucks who had been such demons at cornhusking were now transformed into awkward, tongue-tied boys afraid to ask the girl they wanted.

"They wish to ask, and they do not ask," Sarah observed.

"What a bunch of farmers!" J.P. said.

"Shh!" Emma said.

"But these people don't know how to dance, really, Miss Symns. I mean, look at 'em, they've got no carriage . . ."

"Carriage?" The voice behind them was highly amused. Emma, Sarah, and J.P. turned. It was Frank Carlin. "Did you say carriage? Since when were you such an expert on dancing, J.P.?"

For a moment there was panic on J.P.'s face, but then Carlin winked at her and she brightened.

"They don't look so bad to me," Carlin said. He glanced at Emma. "Looks like fun, don't you think?"

"It does," Emma said.

"Not too complicated," Carlin said.

"No."

Someone nudged Emma from behind. She turned and saw that it was Sarah. "Yes, Sarah?"

Sarah was embarrassed. She mumbled something that Emma couldn't make out. "What is it?"

"Oh, it does not matter," Sarah said.

Emma looked back at Carlin, aware that there was color in her face. "I hadn't realized, Mr. Carlin, that among your other achievements you were such an expert at husking corn."

Carlin smiled. "It's no more than a hobby, really."

Sarah whispered to J.P., "Come, J.P., let's go."

"What for?" J.P. said.

Sarah sighed in frustration. "They want to be . . . I think . . . alone," she said in her soft German accent. "Come on!" The two children walked off, Sarah looking back over her shoulder at Emma and Carlin once she thought she was out of range.

Carlin and Emma stood side by side without speaking, watching the dancers. The dancers whirled and turned, swinging from arm to arm, men's and women's faces flushed, following the caller's rhymes. "Swing her, boys, and do it right, swing the girls till the middle of the night . . ."

It was Carlin who spoke first. "I thought you were fine this afternoon, Miss Symns."

"You were watching me."

"I guess I was. I liked the way you spoke."

"I get that from my uncle," Emma said.

"Well, if you do, then he must be a fine preacher." Carlin's face had a rosy glow—perhaps because he'd been drinking, Emma thought. "How many children did you place?"

"Ten," Emma said.

"Not bad."

"You're surprised?"

"No, I'm not surprised. I'm glad for you . . . glad for them."

"Come now, Mr. Carlin. Aren't you a little surprised that I could handle them, as you put it?"

"I stand corrected," Carlin said.

They fell silent again. Through the forest of dancers, Emma saw J.P. and Sarah watching them from the other side of the room.

"I saw that you had a little walk with J.P. this afternoon," Emma said.

"Yes. I met J.P. down the track. We had a little conversation."

"What did you talk about?"

"Oh, you know the kinds of things you talk about with boys. This and that."

"You seem to like children, Mr. Carlin."

"I prefer ladies," he said.

Emma blushed furiously. One of the dancers reeled out of control and staggered into them. Carlin caught him and gave him a gentle push back out onto the dance floor. He grinned. "Music sure does carry people away, doesn't it?"

Again they turned their attention to the dancers. Energy had reached its highest pitch, everyone seemed to have gone into a mad whirl. Emma watched, envious of the easy linking of arms between man and woman, the carefree physical play.

Tip was prancing higher than all the others, befitting his victor's station, grinning at the fiddler, the fiddler grinning back and playing a little faster, Tip lifting his knees even more vigorously, smiling over his shoulder at Emma, clapping his hands, grabbing the caller's jug, having a swig and passing it around.

"Were you an only child, Miss Symns?"

"Yes," Emma said. "And you?"

"No, there were quite a few of us. Six."

"And what did your father do?"

"My father worked in the customs house. It wasn't what he wanted. His dream was to be a sailor, a captain. . . . He used to talk about it to us. The man wanted to go to sea. Had all the books on it. Pictures. But he never did it. Spent his life thirty feet from the water, looking through people's luggage. Funny, wasn't it? The ocean was right out there, he could smell it all the time, thirty feet away."

"But he could never get there?"

"Because of us. Because there were children to feed. He never really complained about it, never said anything, he raised us, he was a good father, I think, but it killed him, Miss Symns."

"Do you think he was a failure?"

"He thought he was," Carlin said.

"And you?"

"What about me?"

"You're not going to let children ruin your life."

"I wasn't talking about myself, Miss Symns. I was telling you about my father."

"Of course. I'm sorry."

Carlin was silent now, staring out over the dancers, frowning.

Emma *was* sorry and she tried to make up for it. "I never actually had a chance to hear about your work."

"My work? I take pictures."

"But this trip?"

A slow smile broke out across Carlin's face. He was like a boy, Emma thought. "Oh, this trip. Well . . ."

The first dance ended and Tip came bounding over to where they were standing. He was breathing hard and grinning. He nodded to Emma, looked at Carlin for a second, then looked back at Emma. "How about the next set, Miss Symns? The fiddler's just warmin' up."

Emma was speechless for a second. "Why . . . I don't know, Tip. I'm afraid that I wouldn't be much good. I've never . . . you know . . ."

"You could learn," Tip said. "She could learn, couldn't she, Mr. Carlin?"

"I'm sure she could," Carlin said. "And I'll bet you couldn't find a better teacher than old Tip here."

"That's right," Tip said. "It's no time to come down with Methodist feet. How about it?"

Emma looked at Carlin in mute appeal. He was no help. "Go on," Carlin said. "It'll be fun."

She turned back to Tip. "I'd be happy to, Tip," she said.

Emma was not adequately prepared. Tip danced her off her feet, tossing her, swinging her one way and then, without warning, swinging her the other. He was young, he was victorious, a cornhusking, high-stepping champion, and out to impress this woman from New York, which he did, if only by the violence of his swings and turns. Emma tried to listen to the caller and to watch the other dancers, but doing both only increased her confusion—she was always allemanding when she should have been sashaying, promenading instead of buckling up.

Out of breath and ducking through a tunnel of hands, she looked over at Tip. He grinned at her triumphantly and then, when Emma was spun into the middle for the Birdie in the Cage, he shouted encouragement. "You're going fine, Miss Symns! What a lady! Real good!" Emma looked over at Carlin, who stood on the sidelines, watching her and smiling. One of Emma's combs had come loose, a lock of hair had fallen down over her ear. Emma thought she must look like one of those awful women in Carlin's pictures.

The dance finally ended and Tip stood in front of her, beaming, hands on hips, making himself as presentable as he knew how.

"How about the next one, Miss Symns? That one was to just warm you up."

"No, thank you, Tip," Emma said. She brushed the hair back from her face. "I need to check on the children."

"Aww, come on, Miss Symns. They can take care of themselves. I always heard that city kids was so tough."

"I need to check on them, Tip."

"Well, it ain't like they're yours now, is it?"

"No, Tip, it is like they're mine. For the time being. Thank you for the dance. It was very, . . ." She searched for the word. "Educational."

Emma turned and left him standing. She moved through the barn, saying a word to one child and then the other, keeping count so that she knew they were all still there.

Patches was off patting and talking to the horses in their stalls. A group of children were lined up on the benches listening to Liverpool and Bruce argue about which was the best oyster bar on the Bowery. One of the country boys was trying to badger Sarah into a dance. Tony and Ben chased the barn cats among the bales of hay. Tom sat munching doggedly on one of his apples. Reverend Archibold, surrounded by country women, was digging into a plate heaped with pie.

Emma said goodbye to Mouse, who was heading home with his new family. Mouse excused himself to say goodbye a second time to the other children. One after the other they wished him well, all except Bruce, who feigned indifference, at least until Mouse was walking away; Bruce turned and gave a backward glance that seemed to Emma to carry all the passion of one child's jealousy for another.

Emma's mind was still filled with her conversation with

Carlin; his complimenting her, his concession, the story about his father. She had judged him too quickly at first, she felt, and wrongly.

Emma spied Annie sitting in a far corner. She took a few steps toward her and then stopped. Annie was sitting with the same birdlike country woman who had shown such interest in her in the afternoon. There was something in Annie's lap and when the little girl lifted it up Emma could see that it was a cornhusk doll. It was a beautiful doll with a painted wooden head and soft corn-silk hair and a bright calico dress. Annie was fascinated by it, couldn't take her eyes off it. Annie held the doll close to her face, smoothing down the corn-silk hair, not aware at all of the country woman's hand running through her own hair. The woman's husband stood in a group of corn-whiskey drinkers near the barn door, and every so often he would look past them in the direction of his wife, his mouth set and hard.

"Miss Symns?"

Emma turned. Carlin stood, leaning against one of the tables.

"Yes, Mr. Carlin?" Emma said. It sounded as if Carlin had had a bit more to drink.

"Now that Mr. Tip has taught you, perhaps you could teach me," he said.

"To dance?"

"That's right. To dance."

Emma smiled. "Well, I suppose that I could try. . . ."

Try they did. They found themselves headed in the wrong direction on the allemandes and the sashays about half the time, to the great confusion of their fellow dancers. Carlin didn't seem to mind. He smiled at Emma constantly.

Carlin's mood would not countenance any serious conversation. Their arms linked together on a promenade, Emma tried him.

"I would like to know about your work now, Mr. Carlin."

"My work? Why?"

"I like to know what people do. I like to know about their intentions."

"I'm going out west, Miss Symns, what does it matter?"

"I think it does matter. If you're taking pictures, it matters what sort of pictures you're taking."

Carlin laughed. "I think you're onto me, Miss Symns, there's no doubt about it. But let's just have fun now, eh? A little fun wouldn't hurt our intentions, would it?"

They danced some more. They didn't talk. They did laugh, a fair amount, at nothing in particular, it seemed, perhaps at themselves and their dancing. Emma thought to herself that it was quite a bit of fun.

The young country boy had succeeded in getting Sarah to dance and as she passed Emma on a promenade round she gave Emma a grave, appraising look, the kind of look, Emma thought, that intimates that I know something that you don't. Emma shot a haughty look right back. Emma wasn't going to admit that a fourteen-year-old knew more about men than she did.

The reel ended, and, almost before Emma had a chance to thank Carlin for the dance, Tip had her under the arm and was whirling her off into the next one. Tip had become intent; his eyes burning. Emma just wished he would stop. She was tired. There were the children. She had had enough vigor to last her the week. Annie had fallen asleep in the corner with her doll. She knew she should be getting these children to bed, they were traveling on the train in the morning. It would be so much more pleasant for everyone if they were rested. . . .

"Anything wrong, Miss Symns?" Tip said.

"No, no. I'm sorry," Emma smiled.

"Do I bore you, Miss Symns?"

Emma looked at him, startled. "Bored? Why, no, Tip, not at all."

The caller had grown hoarse. "The whip held high, the reins a bit slack, promenade home on the same old track."

Emma and Tip crossed hands and paraded around. The country woman sat next to the sleeping Annie, her hand resting on the child's shoulder. She should speak to the woman, Emma thought. It wasn't too late, if there was a chance for a home. . . .

"It's that other feller, isn't it?" Tip said.

"Other fellow? I don't understand."

"The likeness man, Mr. Carlin, whatever his name is."

"Mr. Carlin means nothing to me," Emma said.

"Give each other another swing, partners by the pigeon wing . . ."

Another man linked arms with Emma, swung her around, then they all joined hands and circled, Tip glowering at her from the other side of the circle. "Pass those girls, side by side, turn 'em round you and make it wide . . ."

Tip was by her side again. "Tip, please . . ."

"I like you, Miss Symns, I like you a lot. I've never met anyone like you. You're a woman of substance, a serious woman, and I know you think I'm just a boy. . . ."

"That's not true, Tip!"

"No, it is true. I can tell it in your voice, you think I'm nothing but a kid, with all my country ways and cornhuskin' and stuff, you think that's all there is to me. But you're wrong, Miss Symns. I'm a serious man, or I will be. I'm learnin'. That's all you can ask, right? I've studied logic out of books."

"I should get back to the children, Tip."

"It's him, isn't it?"

"It has nothing to do with Mr. Carlin."

"You can't tell me it's not so 'cause I know it's so. That

slicker. I'm disappointed in you, Miss Symns. I thought you woulda seen through him. He's all surface, all glib and such. He's not serious like you or me."

Now she was angry. Why was it that men found it so hard to believe that women had no other interests in life besides smoothing their ruffled masculine feathers?

"Promenade out with that pretty little girl, invite her back for another whirl!"

"I think I've had enough, Tip. Thank you." Emma walked off.

The woman lifted her hand from Annie's shoulder as Emma walked toward her. "You're not takin' her away just yet?" the woman said. "She's doin' just fine. Children, they can sleep just about anywhere."

"No, we're not going just yet," Emma said. "You like Annie, don't you?"

"Yes, miss, she's a sweet girl and awful smart, too. She knows her ciphers better than I do."

"But I'm sure there's a lot you could teach her," Emma said. "Annie needs a home."

"I know, miss."

"You'd like her to come home with you, wouldn't you?"

The woman lowered her eyes, looking away. "What I'd like isn't always . . ."

"Isn't always what?" Emma said. "You want to take her, I know you do. You'd be good for her. I don't see why your husband . . ."

The woman shook her head. "You mustn't blame him, miss. Hank is a good man, a God-fearing man, he treats me well." The woman picked up Annie's doll, fondling it, staring at the carved wooden face. "Last winter our daughter died. This was her doll. That little girl was everything to Hank, he worshiped that child. She went everywhere with him. He says there's no way we can replace her, that we'd be blaspheming her memory. . . ." The woman looked up into Emma's face. "He says that if God wanted us to have more children he would have given 'em to us."

Emma looked away, toward the bright whirl of dancers, the toe-tapping fiddler.

The woman's voice became angry. "Children die all the time here. You can't make a shrine of every dead child. . . . Hank was angry when I told him that I was going to give Martha's doll to Annie. . . . He forbid me. . . . But I don't care. I want her to have it. Dolls are to play with. And that's all. That's all they are." The woman put the doll back into the lap of the sleeping child. "I've talked too much, Miss Symns. I should go and find my husband."

Emma took her hand, trying to find some word, but was interrupted by the sudden outbreak of shouting behind them.

Tip and Carlin stood chest to chest in the middle of the barn, barking insults at one another.

"You ain't good enough to kiss her foot, you slicker."

"Now listen to me, bub, you just keep your hands off me."

"What do you know about how to treat a woman? Huh? Huh?" He poked Carlin in the chest with a finger.

"How about if I treat you to a broken nose, Mr. Tippecanoe?"

With horror Emma realized that it was her they were fighting about. The crowd was egging them on. Several of the children had squeezed their way to the front. The caller was trying to break it up, but nobody was paying him any mind now; even the fiddler, fiddle hanging at his side, was bobbing up and down on tiptoe trying to get a better look.

The whole thing was intolerable to Emma. She strode across the room to Reverend Archibold. "Reverend! Reverend, it is time for me to take these children back to the train."

"But Miss Symns, there's room here, the women have

brought quilts for the children. You don't have to sleep in that boxcar. . . ."

"Thank you, but we would like to go back to the train."

He looked at her. "I guess you've made up your mind."

"I have."

"I'll go hitch up the wagon. It'll just take a couple of minutes."

Emma moved quickly. She shook Annie awake. "Annie, Annie dear, we're leaving now."

The shouts grew even louder. Carlin had his fists raised in front of his face. Oh my goodness, Emma thought, he looks ludicrous. It was an embarrassment, she was embarrassed for him. He was better than that, she thought, it made her angry . . . and she did not want him to get hurt.

"Patches! Come over here, please. We're going now. Liverpool! Liverpool, I want you to help me round up the other children. We're leaving in just a minute."

"But Miss Symns, they're gonna have a row."

"You heard me, Liverpool." He looked at her; he wasn't quite sure about the new tone in her voice. He went off to gather the other children.

"Miss Symns! Miss Symns!" It was Tip, waving for her to come over. She did not move. She was mortified. "You're the only one who can settle this. You choose!"

Emma turned away, walked to the nest of harnesses where Tom had made himself a bed. "Tom . . . Tom, wake up. . . ." She shook him, trying to ignore the chorus of voices behind her.

"Come on, rube."

"Give it to the slicker, Tip!"

"Outside! Outside!" Everybody was shouting now, and with a rush they all grabbed lanterns and headed out of doors, sweeping the two combatants with them.

Face burning, Emma rounded up the last of her charges. They said goodbye to their hosts, women hugging the sleepy children goodbye. Reverend Archibold came in to say that the wagon was hitched up.

Emma herded the children out ahead of her, up the slope, across the wet grass toward the wagon. She saw the circle of lanterns off in the direction of the smokehouse, tried not to look. She heard the loud male voices and then stopped in her tracks. The sound of anger was gone.

The voices were still at full volume, but friendly now. Bottles were being passed, a couple of men were staggering a bit. There was a good deal of back patting. Tip was being held back by his friends, as he turned to explain to them, very loudly, that he didn't really want to fight, he respected the city feller, he really did. A few paces off, Carlin shrugged, his palms skyward as if to indicate that he hadn't started anything, and then the two men were shoved toward one another for a conciliatory handshake.

One or two of the men saw Emma and the children and waved. Reverend Archibold smiled and waved back. "I'm glad to see that it worked out peacefully," he said to Emma.

"Yes," Emma said.

The note in her voice made Reverend Archibold look at her in surprise. "You are glad, aren't you?"

"Of course I am," she said. Of course she was glad, yet at the same time, though she would have rather died than tell Reverend Archibold, what she felt most of all was disappointment, disappointment in Carlin, disappointment in the way her evening had ended.

Reverend Archibold chuckled to himself. "I'll tell you, Miss Symns, out in this part of the country, people love to push and shove. But they really don't mean anything by it. Good folks." He reached down to grab Ben under the arms. "Here we go, son, up on the wagon."

The plodding horse managed to find every rut in the dark road. The wagon lurched and creaked. Liverpool and Jane and Bruce sat at the back of the wagon, giggling and whispering, their feet dangling over the edge, while most of the younger children were asleep. The minister talked softly about his growing up in Massachusetts, his conversion and his call, his lonely life in the backwoods, but Emma didn't really hear. She was lost with her own thoughts.

A rushing sound filled the air above her. She stared up into the dark sky and could just make out the heavy forms of flocks of wild fowl cutting and honking their way above the trees.

She heard someone cackle in the back of the wagon. She turned. "Shh!" A child's head lifted for a second, then plopped down again.

No one spoke the rest of the way. She and the minister carried the smaller children to the boxcar and covered them with blankets, the older ones staggered sleepily to their covers on their own. Emma tucked the cornhusk doll next to Annie's cheek.

Emma walked Reverend Archibold back to his wagon. He didn't mount right away, but stood alongside the wagon, picking pieces of dried mud from the front wheel.

"I admire you, Miss Symns," he said. "I really do. You are doing the Lord's work. Most of the time it's powerful hard to know what the Lord's work is, so I guess you're fortunate."

The horse stomped its heavy foot on the dew-laden grass, shook its head. Emma felt cold, she ached with exhaustion. She, more than anything, wanted to go to sleep, but Reverend Archibold was determined to go on.

"You will find homes for these children, good homes. I know you will. And you will be blessed for your work." He reached out and took her hand. She felt a sudden alarm. Was he blessing her? "But sooner or later, Miss Symns, you'll have to sit down and think about yourself. It can be a very lonesome country out here, Miss Symns, for all of us."

She gently removed her hand.

He looked down. "It makes us all act a little silly sometimes."

"Good night, Reverend."

He climbed up into the wagon, flicked the reins.

"Good night, Miss Symns."

Emma, not able to sleep, sat in the open boxcar door, looking out across the moonlit tracks and the still depot. She was thinking about men. She thought about Tip and the lonely Reverend Archibold and Carlin, and her conclusion was that, however sympathetic or surprising, crude or disappointing they managed to make themselves, at bottom Emma's problem was that she didn't understand them.

Emma was continuing along this pessimistic line when she was shaken from her reverie by the crunching of boots near the depot. A man emerged, staggering from the shadows, hefting great unwieldy objects under both arms.

As he came out into the moonlight and neared the train Emma saw that the man was Carlin, and that he was carrying his tripod and two black cases.

Emma straightened up, silently. Had he seen her? No, she didn't think so. Should she call out to him? Perhaps if she moved, changed her position, he would see her. There was something almost forlorn about him as he moved unsteadily toward the passenger car.

"Mr. Carlin?" she said softly.

Carlin stopped, put his burdens down, and was still for a second, as if he didn't know where the voice had come from. Then he spied her.

"Miss Symns?"

She said nothing, but he picked up his tripod and his case and came over.

"Well, how do you like that?" he said.

"Shh! The children are sleeping," she said.

"Well, how do you like that?" he said in an exaggerated whisper.

"You don't have to be quite that quiet, Mr. Carlin," she said. He leaned his tripod against the side of the boxcar. "I'm glad to see that you're all right . . . that you weren't hurt."

"Oh, the fight," he said. "I would have knocked that whippersnapper's head off."

"You've had more to drink," Emma said.

"You're an observant woman, Miss Symns. Yes, I have, I confess." Leaning against the boxcar, he stretched his arms toward the sky. "I confess, I confess!" Emma didn't say anything; this seemed to quiet him. "It's a beautiful night, isn't it?"

"It is."

"I like you, Miss Symns. I like talking to you." He put one hand over her hand, and with his free arm encircled her waist. Emma stiffened.

"I enjoy talking to you too, Mr. Carlin," she said.

"I liked dancing with you, too," he said. He held her more tightly.

For a long moment, neither of them spoke. Then a child cried, somewhere in the boxcar behind them.

"Excuse me, Mr. Carlin. It's one of the children."

"The children are fine," he said. "Forget about them for a moment."

"Excuse me, please." She turned to rise, but he held her by the wrist.

"No," he said.

"Mr. Carlin," Emma said sharply, her eyes widening with anger.

"You can't use the children like that, Miss Symns."

That stopped Emma for a second. "Using the children? I don't understand."

"You called me over, didn't you, Miss Symns? You didn't have to do that. But you did. Nothing wrong with that . . ."

"What are you implying, Mr. Carlin?"

"I'm not implying anything."

"I think you are."

"All right, I am. I'm implying something and you know perfectly well what it is." He stared at her, his face filled with exasperation. "You're a kidnapper. Miss Symns."

"I beg your pardon."

"A kidnapper. You have kidnapped a boxcar of orphans and gotten away with it."

"Why don't we continue this discussion in the morning, Mr. Carlin?"

"I don't intend to keep you," he said. "I just wanted you to know that I know what you're up to even if no one else does." Emma didn't say anything, and Carlin took that as license to press his point. "You think you're going to be able to let go of these children? You need them, Miss Symns. I know women."

"Good for you, Mr. Carlin."

"You're going to have to let them go, all of them, sooner or later. That's not going to be very easy. Like some of these farmers would say, Miss Symns, you've picked a hard row to hoe."

"It's time I went to sleep, Mr. Carlin. Some members of this hard row get up pretty early."

"I know, I know," he said, in a suddenly discouraged tone. He looked up at her, very earnest now. "You were good with them today, Miss Symns, really good." He turned, grabbing both of her arms, stared at her again. "Miss Symns," he said with an awful intensity.

"Yes, Mr. Carlin?" Emma was terrified. His face was only inches from hers.

"Miss Symns . . ." She thought that certainly he was going

to kiss her, but he didn't. He laughed softly, let her arms drop, then shook his head, "Oh, Miss Symns," he said, and with that, he picked up his tripod and his cases, turned, and staggered off into the night.

*T*he next day was, as Mr. Carlin would have put it, a hard row to hoe. Trying to keep seventeen children profitably occupied and content in a thirty-foot boxcar from dawn to bedtime was more than any one woman could manage. As the day wore on, the bickering grew more and more petty, the rough-housing rougher, Bruce accidentally knocking Tony's head against the stove. Emma had never been quite so aware of both the number and variety of small tortures that children inflict on one another; finger bending, tying together of shoelaces, hair pulling, headlocks, and knuckle rubs were all practiced at one point or another during the day.

There were plenty of stops for water and wood and changes of crew, stops of a few minutes in dreary little towns where everyone rushed out to buy rolls and sandwiches in the lunchroom and rushed back when the bell sounded.

These stops only increased Emma's difficulties. Bruce and Tom took advantage of these brief interludes to pester the passengers for pennies, while Emma had her hands full trying to keep the remainder of the restless children from wandering off. The major tumult of the day came when Patches, at the midafternoon lunchroom stop, got the notion into his head that it would be a great joke to rush in and shout "Allaboard!" which he did, creating total havoc among the already rushed diners—drinks were overturned, hard rolls trampled, and Patches had to be rescued from irate passengers.

During these stops, Carlin made a point of coming over and speaking to Emma, but he confined himself to pleasantries. There was no mention of their midnight conversation. Carlin remarked that she looked strained and tired, was everything all right? Emma stiffened and said, yes, of course, everything was fine. Emma found these wary exchanges frustrating—she would have liked for them to have a serious discussion, to clear the air. It wasn't like Emma to leave such things unresolved—but each time they were on the verge of mentioning something substantial they were cut off by Annie tugging on Emma's elbow or Ben tumbling headlong across the tracks during a game of tag.

In the evening, after the baskets of bread and fruit were passed around and the new oil lamps Emma had bought were lit, Emma tried to teach them hymns. She thought somehow that it would be soothing, if not for them, then at least for her. It turned out to be soothing for neither.

The girls tried their best, Annie and Sarah and Jane, and some of the others sang for a while and then dropped out, but there was a trio of boys, Liverpool and Bruce and Tom, who made it perfectly apparent that they regarded hymn singing as sissy stuff. They huddled together like conspirators, giggling and whispering, ignoring Emma's angry looks.

Bruce pulled a long piece of straw out of one of the mattresses and tickled Sarah on the neck with it. Sarah turned and swatted at him.

Emma glared at the three boys. Bruce folded his hands in his lap. The three of them tried their best to appear innocent. Emma continued to fix her eyes upon them as she and the girls sang on.

> *Just as I am, without one plea,*
> *But that Thy Blood was shed for me . . .*

The three boys put their heads together, whispering back and forth, glancing up every second or so to look at Emma. Then, suddenly, they straightened up, sober-faced and reformed, and began to sing.

For a moment Emma thought she was witnessing a miracle. Though they still looked less cherubic, they sang lustily and loudly. Emma began to smile and, as she did, she realized, suddenly, that whatever they were singing, it wasn't the words to the hymn.

Emma reached out and touched Annie's shoulder. Annie stopped singing and then so did the other girls. The boys' chorus rang out clearly.

"Just as I am, without one flea . . ."

Liverpool and Bruce looked up, saw Emma glowering at them, and realized that they were in trouble. Tom, however, less alert, eyes closed, made the mistake of completing the verse.

"Now that Miss Symns's done scrubbing me . . ."

Tom's voice trailed off as he realized that he was singing solo. He looked up, utterly stricken, and pushed himself back against the bench.

It was a moment or two before Emma could bring herself to speak. When she did, it was in a perfectly low, even tone.

"You don't have to stop, Tom. Perhaps you have other verses you'd like to sing. Bruce? Liverpool? Go ahead." All of the children were silent. J.P., sitting on the bench with her knees up, swung her legs to the floor, pushed back her newsboy cap. The only sound was the oil lamps shaking with the movement of the train. "You've come all this way, supposedly to better yourselves, but if this is the way you choose to behave, all right, fine. If it's beneath you to learn to sing hymns, well, then, I'll stop. I'm quite happy to leave you to your own amusements. Quite happy." She looked at the seventeen somber faces.

There was a long moment of silence before Liverpool spoke. "It's just that you're tired, Miss Symns."

That was the last straw. Emma almost screamed back at him: "I know that I'm tired!" Her voice shook with emotion. "I'm very tired of all of you right now, if you don't mind, and I'd like to be left alone!"

It would have been a wonderful line for Emma to have walked out on, but unfortunately there was nowhere to go. Emma rose, trembling with anger, turned, nearly knocked the dipper out of the tub of water that sat on the potbellied stove, and strode to the far end of the boxcar.

Emma sat down on the bench, ignoring the stares of the silent children. She reached across to her bag, picked out her copy of *Retribution* by Mrs. E.D.E.N. Southworth, and opened it. She stared at the page before her. The swaying of the train made it impossible to read. She snapped the book shut again.

She could hear the children rustling about timidly. Even their attempts at being considerate Emma found irritating now; the tiptoeing, the murmuring and whispering, the sidelong glances.

Emma would have given anything for a moment of privacy, of stillness. She thought longingly of her room, how the light would spill across her bed as she lay reading, hour after undisturbed hour. . . . Carlin had said that it would be hard for her to let these children go, but at the moment Emma felt as if it wouldn't be hard at all. What she felt now was the burden, the bone weariness.

She leaned back against the slats of the boxcar and closed her eyes. What else had Carlin said? She couldn't remember; she was too tired to concentrate. What she did remember was that he had almost kissed her and then hadn't. She wondered why not. She wondered what it would have been like. He had had something to drink, but he wasn't a brute, not really, even with all his posturing. He had a gentleness, she had seen that in him almost right away. It would have been a bit awkward physically, with her sitting in the boxcar door and him standing down below, but then—Emma let herself think it—she could have slipped down to the ground, he wouldn't have let her fall, he would have gathered her in. . . .

Emma looked up. J.P. stood by the stove, only a few feet away, watching her.

"Yes, J.P.?"

"I didn't want to disturb your reading, Miss Symns." J.P.'s right fist was clenched tight.

"You're not," Emma said. "What is it, J.P.?"

"I found this." J.P. held out the clenched fist and opened it. In the child's open palm lay Emma's locket.

Emma reached out and took the locket, stared at it, then raised her eyes gravely to J.P.

"You found it," Emma said. J.P. pulled down on the ever-present newsboy cap. "Where?"

"On the floor," J.P. said. A smile flashed across the child's face and then vanished. "I lose things myself, you know how things just fall out some times, that must have been what happened."

Emma looked down at the oval picture of her mother. "Perhaps so," she said.

J.P. hitched up her baggy trousers. "It was lucky then, right? That it fell out inside the boxcar here, otherwise it would have been lost forever."

"It was lucky, J.P.," Emma said softly. J.P.'s mouth parted, then closed. "Yes?"

"I just wanted to say that it's all right. Your being tired of us if you want. Kids do a lot of dumb stuff, stuff they don't even mean a lot of the time."

"I know, J.P.," Emma said. "Thank you."

The child's words were transparent enough, but Emma felt a sudden welling up of gratitude. Emma smiled, gazing at J.P.'s troubled, almost delicate features. What a handsome boy, Emma thought, what a kind, good boy.

Self-conscious now, J.P. reached up and touched the newsboy cap, then turned away, walking across the rocking floor of the boxcar like a sailor across the pitching deck of a ship.

Up ahead in the passenger car, Carlin leaned back against his cushioned seat, resting his head on his hands. Down several rows, an expert in botanic medicine named Dr. Tansy, a traveling salesman, and a dainty woman Carlin would have sworn was a professional cardsharp were engaged in a game of vingt-et-un. Otherwise the car was dark and everyone asleep.

Carlin struck a match, picked up the daguerreotype with the broken case, held it close to the flame, examining it. He frowned. The image of the actress was badly scratched when J.P. had dropped it, but that wasn't why Carlin was frowning. He was frowning because he hated the picture. This was exactly the kind of picture he didn't want to take any more, studio shots of vain variety actresses. That was all behind him now. The match flickered and went out.

Carlin heard the doctor's excited voice up ahead, exclaiming over his sudden run of luck. The woman cardsharp was shaking her pretty little bewigged head sadly. The train rattled on. Carlin peered out the window, feeling morose, seeing nothing.

Carlin lit another match, held the picture up a second time, moving it a little to the left, then to the right. It wasn't that bad. Scratched as it was, what there was left of it was clear as a bell, down to the hair on the woman's head. Let some high-flown painter try to do that. . . . Besides, the woman was attractive, Carlin remembered the afternoon. She'd been rather charmed, too. . . .

The match burned Carlin's hand, and he threw it down, stomped on it with his heel. He sucked on his fingers. That's what I get for thinking about women, Carlin thought. He stared at the lady cardsharp, draped in swatches of material and bits of fur. . . .

He thought, then, about Miss Symns. There was something to Miss Symns, he liked her. Not much like the women he'd been with, but maybe she wasn't all that different, after all. He couldn't figure out whether or not she was flirting with him. One moment she was shooting him glances, the next she was demanding to be left alone. Carlin felt sudden remorse for his behavior of the night before. He had stepped over the bounds, said things he shouldn't have. She had been pretty contrary herself; she could have made it easier for him. . . .

He was going to charm her, damn it, he'd made up his mind. By the time they reached Cleveland, well, maybe he'd better make it Chicago. He'd charmed the others, he'd charm her. She wasn't such a special case. But how? There she was, back in that boxcar with all those children, he couldn't even get to her, not even on lunchroom stops. . . . Unless he went clambering across the tops of the cars, popped his head in, upside down, holding a bouquet of wild flowers. Now, what woman would resist that?

The doctor was cackling, overcome with delight at his good fortune and swelling with unwarranted confidence. The lady cardsharp lured him on, letting him get a little bit ahead of the game before she made her move. It irritated Carlin: couldn't the doctor, this master of botanic medicine, see what was coming? How come nobody ever sees?

Easiest thing in the world, Carlin thought, seeing through other people's hopes. But never your own. Carlin was a man who prided himself on delivering what he promised. The general, a hero of the Mexican War, a man among men, wouldn't have asked him to come on this survey team if he hadn't thought Carlin could do something. The general wanted authentic information, information he could trust and verify, the kind of information you could begin to make plans from, plans for railroads and settlements. That was what Carlin was going to give the general, though God only knew how he was going to mercurialize plates in the snows of the Rocky Mountains, but that he'd have to work out when he got there.

But he also had his own private dreams that he'd certainly never tell the general about, or anybody else for that matter.

He was going to come back with other pictures. Pictures that would be of no use to the general or the surveyors or the planners back in Washington, he was going to get pictures of the Indians, the mountains, the sodbusters and the railroad men, trappers and gold hunters. He was going to record a changing country, fix it, pin it to a silver and copper plate like a butterfly to a board, so that anybody could look at it and say, that's just the way it was. Nobody seemed to have much time to look at anything now, there was a lot of hurry in the country, but he, Frank Carlin, he was making it his business to take the time to look; if Americans were picking up a lot of cinders in the eye, he was making it his business to perform the Great American Eyewash.

It was sweet to think about. Sweet to think about how one great and good work might vindicate all the squanderings of emotion and energy, with women, yes, and with others, the wrong directions—Carlin had been, at one point or another, a gambler, a canal man, a printer—all the waste and failures of half a lifetime.

Still he was afraid, because there was a part of him, the harsher, always honest, critical part of him, that kept insisting that he could not know what would come next. No one knew. Not the little street Arab who'd busted into his equipment, asleep now, no doubt, back in the boxcar, dreaming about finding some open-hearted farm couple looking for a stranger's child to be their own, not the cackling doctor who thought he was on the verge of making the biggest killing in vingt-et-un ever seen on any Ohio Railroad, and not even himself, going off to hook up with a bunch of soldiers and surveyors, heading into the mountains with his precious plates loaded on pack mules.

No one knew about the future, no one knew whether their work was going to be good or bad, and it scared him. Right then, suddenly, in the darkness of the hurtling railroad car, it was scaring him to death and he wanted someone to talk to. He wanted to talk to that woman, that Miss Symns, she might know if there were any consolations, she was a smart woman . . . she would have things to say at least, she could sit in the seat beside him and they could talk on into the night.

Carlin sat, his forehead against the glass, feeling the train rock and rumble as it shot on into the darkness, listening to the clicking of the wheels on rail. Carlin watched the cardplayers and waited for the lady cardsharp to drop the ace on the ever-optimistic Dr. Tansy.

* * *

The engineer stood alone, shifting his weight from one foot to the other to stay awake, staring down the clear track. The fireman, a boy of nineteen, was propped up in the corner, asleep.

The engineer liked driving at night, he could really open up with no danger of cows on the track or farmers with their wagons. It was just him and the clouds of gray wood smoke spinning back over his head, the sparks shooting off like fireflies in the cool night air. It was then that he had the feeling that he could fly if he wanted to, just pull the lever back and lift the train right off its wooden ties and take off into the western sky.

He looked at the steam gauge. It was starting to flicker. He nudged the fireman with his foot. The boy rolled over, but showed no other sign of waking. Aiming at the ribs, the engineer gave him more of a boot. Scarcely bothering to open his eyes, the fireman lurched to his feet and stumbled back to the tender.

The rush of night air and a sudden shower of sparks that pricked at his bare arms finally made him open his eyes. He quickly filled his arms with wood and staggered back from the tender. Every American boy's dream, working on the railroad—his body was covered with tiny burns, anyone who'd seen him would have taken him for a beekeeper.

The young fireman stared down the track. He let the wood slip from his arms, clatter to the floor of the engine.

"Look out, Ira! Ira! The track!"

The moonlight lit up a fallen oak tree.

The engineer yanked the throttle, and with his free hand reached for the train whistle. The harsh, high sound cut into the night air.

There was a great lurch as the train was thrown into reverse.

In the passenger car, Carlin was knocked into the aisle. Cards and coins went flying, there was a great tangle of arms and elbows, suitcases burst open, a babble of angry, sleepy, frightened voices drowned out by the screeching sound as the train, wheels locked, slid a hundred feet. The broken daguerreotype case spun across the floor like a slippery bar of soap.

In the boxcar, children tumbled and rolled across the floor. The lamp above Emma broke away and crashed on the bench beside her. A pool of burning oil spread quickly, setting fire to Emma's skirt. Sarah screamed. Emma started to run, but the flame clung to her skirt, she twisted, but the flame twisted with her. Liverpool grabbed a blanket and ran at Emma, knocking her against the wall of the boxcar, wrapping the blanket around her legs, smothering the flames. Patches, Bruce, Tony, and the other children grabbed blankets and beat at the burning oil, smothering it, stomping it with their feet. They stomped on their smoking blankets.

The whistle sounded again. The train had stopped.

Shaken, Emma leaned against the wall of the boxcar, staring at Liverpool.

"I'm sorry, miss, I didn't mean to push you like that."

"I know," Emma said. She picked up a smoldering blanket. "Let me get this blanket outside," she said. "Here, someone help me with the door."

Bruce and John yanked the door open for her. Together they stared out.

Several of the passengers stood just outside the track, with lanterns. In the flickering light Carlin, the doctor, the engineer, fireman, and brakeman strained together to roll the tree to the edge of the track. With one great heave, the five men rolled the tree over and down the embankment.

Carlin picked up his jacket, dusted it off, and headed back to the passenger car. Just as he was about to pull himself up, he paused for a second and looked back toward the boxcar. He saw Emma, then stepped back and walked slowly toward her. "Are you all right, Miss Symns?" There was concern in his voice.

"Yes, I'm fine, Mr. Carlin," Emma said. She pulled back the charred edge of her skirt.

"No one was hurt back there?"

"No one," Emma said. He stood for a second, contemplating, looking up at her. "Is there something you need, Mr. Carlin?"

"No, no," he said. "Goodnight, Miss Symns."

"Goodnight," Emma said.

Carlin walked slowly back to the passenger car, swung up the steps, and disappeared.

In the morning Emma had on a new, bright print dress from her trunk that the children hadn't seen before. In spite of all its wrinkles, the dress made Emma look younger. Sarah and Jane murmured their approval. She dipped a washcloth in a pan of hot water, aware that all the children were watching her.

Emma scrubbed her face hard, deliberately, rinsed, and checked her reflection in the mirror. She turned to face the staring faces.

"An awfully quiet bunch this morning, aren't you?" Emma twisted the washcloth in her hands. "Sometimes it can be difficult to find the right words. No matter how grown-up you think you are. You saved my life last night. I want to say thank you." None of the children spoke. Emma smiled. "I guess it goes to prove that in a pinch there's nothing like a New York fire laddy."

Emma folded her washcloth, put her soap on top of it. Sarah stood up.

"Miss?"

"Yes, Sarah."

"Excuse me, miss. I was wondering."

"Wondering about what?"

"If I could borrow a bit of your soap."

"Of course." Emma handed Sarah the soap. "And here, you take the towel too. And the mirror if you want."

Sarah smelled the soap, dipped it in the water, then smelled it again before rubbing it on her face. She smiled at Emma before going back to her washing.

Emma sat on the bench, brushing her hair, watching Sarah wash. When Sarah was finished she came over and set the soap and towel on the bench. She stood without speaking, then reached out with an open hand, almost touching Emma's hair, yet still holding back.

"Miss?"

"Yes, Sarah?"

"Your hair . . . it curls very much, doesn't it?"

"I suppose."

"My mother had hair that curled," Sarah said.

Emma looked at her. "So did mine, Sarah, so did mine."

The train slowed as they pulled into the town of Lavalle, Ohio. Emma watched the children; Patches puffed out his cheeks, Annie held her doll tight, Bruce had fallen back into his sullen pout. The train came to a slow, screeching stop. Liverpool started to open the door.

"Just hold it a second, Liverpool," Emma said.

"What's that, ma'am?"

"Don't open the door just yet."

"But, Miss Symns, they're waiting for us."

"I know, Liverpool, and they can wait a bit longer. I think it's important for us all to have a talk."

"Talk? Talk about what, Miss Symns?"

"I want to know why you are all so nervous," Emma asked.

"Nervous? Us, nervous? I'm not nervous, are you, Tom?"

"Come now," Emma said. "Look at Patches over there, puffing up his cheeks. John, biting his nails . . . Liverpool, with that little quiver in his voice. . . ." That got a decent laugh. Even Liverpool grinned sheepishly. "You are nervous, and I think I know why."

"Why, Miss Symns?"

"You're nervous because you weren't placed in homes at the last town. You're wondering what it was, what was wrong with you, why Mouse and the others were chosen and not you, and you're wondering if you're going to be turned down again. So I'm going to tell you. There's nothing wrong with you . . . though maybe some of you could learn how to handle a knife and fork and, John, you could comb your hair once in a while." The children laughed, more easily this time. "And I'm also going to tell you right now what's going to happen out there." Their faces turned somber in a second. J.P. stood alert, her half-folded blanket in her hands.

"Some of you are going to be placed in homes here, fine homes, but probably most of you won't be, not here, not today. For most of you this is going to be a day of disappointment. And what we will do, the rest of us, we will go on to the next town and the town after that. Do any of you remember the letter I read you?"

"I do, Miss Symns," Tony said.

"Me too," Ben said.

"Where was it from?"

"Uhh . . . Rock something . . ." Patches couldn't quite get it.

"Rock Springs!" Willy said.

"Illinois," said John.

"Nobody asked for the state, stupid," Tom said.

"That's right," Emma said. "Rock Springs, Illinois. And do you remember what it said?"

"That they lost all their children and . . ."

Ben couldn't keep himself from butting in. "And the lady was getting a room ready."

"That's right," Emma said. "And that they would welcome any children who need homes." They were all silent for a moment. "We are going to find places for all of you. I promise it. I'm not turning back and none of you is going to turn back. What does it mean if you aren't chosen today? That somebody was looking for a boy that reminds them of Uncle Jethro and you don't. That someone wants a girl to cook and you can't. . . . I'm sure there are decent, kind people out there; they wouldn't have answered our circular if they weren't. I want you to talk to them in a courteous way, to answer their questions, and not pout and shuffle. . . ."

"You want us to be nice, Miss Symns?" Annie asked.

"That's right, Annie, I want you to be nice. If you're brave enough for that . . . and I know you're brave enough, I know that from last night." Emma scanned the children's faces. "Right now, I don't want to let any of you go. Whoever is chosen or not chosen today, I want you to know, I choose you all."

Tony jumped up. "Hey, that's it, Miss Symns! We can take over the train!"

"Yeah, we'll go on on our own!"

"I'm the engineer," Liverpool said.

"No, I want to be the engineer, you're not old enough," Bruce said.

"We'll go out west and live with the Indians," Patches said.

Emma smiled. "No, I don't think we can take over the train. But I want you to realize that right now we are all a family. Very odd, a little makeshift, and not as well-behaved as we should be, but a family. And just the same as in any other kind of family, people have to leave, they have to go on to other kinds of lives. And when they do, we're going to wish them well. But chosen or not, we belong to each other." Emma paused for a second and smiled. "Enough lecturing for one morning. You know what I think we all need?"

"What's that, Miss Symns?" Patches said.

"A treat."

They all started up at once. "A treat? In this ol' place? Where are we going to find a treat, Miss Symns?"

"We'll have to see."

"What kind of treat?"

"I don't know."

"How much can we spend?"

"A reasonable amount."

"What's a reasonable amount?"

"We'll have to see," Emma said.

"A nickel?"

"Ten cents?"

"We'll just have to see," Emma said. "Liverpool, will you open the door, please?"

They were in luck, because at the end of the main street of the small town stood a general store. Emma and the children marched down the main street, the mayor of Lavalle huffing alongside, explaining to Emma that everyone was already at the church, no, he wouldn't want to deny the children a treat, for pete's sake, but people had been waiting for almost an hour.

Two men sat on the front porch of the store. One of the men was tall and lank, in trousers that were too short, and he sat on a box carving away at a stick with a knife. The other man was larger, with a wide, hunched back that made him look like a turtle. He was smoking a pipe and he had on a black wool hat that was without a band and had no shape at all in the brim. As the children neared the store, he took out his pipe to stare. A couple of hounds came out from under the porch where they'd been sleeping, stretched, and loped down to meet the parade.

The lanky man stopped his whittling and stood up as the crowd of children mounted the steps. He pointed at Liverpool with his knife. "Can I help you folks?"

"Yes, sir," Liverpool said. "We're looking for a treat."

"Well, you came to the right place if it's a treat you're lookin' for. Come on in." He nodded.

"Good afternoon," Emma said.

The turtle-shaped man said nothing, drew short puffs on his pipe, and exhanged glances with the mayor.

The storekeeper led them inside. Every bit of the tiny store was filled, shelves stuffed to overflowing with bolts of gingham and calico, woolens and bonnets, the floor jammed with tubs, harnesses, coils of rope, barrels of salt, flour, and whiskey, pitchforks and ox yokes.

The lanky storekeeper clapped his hands together, making the most of this windfall business. "So what is it you boys and girls are lookin' for? Candy? Rock or gumdrop? Right over here by the counter . . ."

The children had their own ideas. They spilled over the store, trying on hats and boots, holding up overalls to their chins to show the others what they'd look like, tumbling over ropes, getting tangled in harnesses. Annie wandered about in a bonnet three times too big that covered her eyes, bumping into people. Patches squatted on a saddle, as happy as if he'd just tamed the wildest horse in the West. Liverpool and Willy tried to figure out how to break into a barrel of molasses. Emma did her best to see that no one got his eye poked out by the handle of a spade or pitchfork. The mayor kept looking anxiously at his watch. The turtle-shaped man said nothing, puffs of smoke rising from his pipe in shorter and shorter intervals.

Gradually the mayhem subsided, and most of the children settled for some candy or apples or nuts, though Sarah found a ribbon she wanted and it had to be explained to Patches, at some length, that the cost of a saddle was not what Emma had meant by a reasonable amount.

Emma remained calm and was really quite happy. She felt a surge of new confidence. She reassured the mayor and occasionally shouted out a word of warning when one of the children was about to bring a whole shelf of gingham down on his head, but mostly she just let them go; it was her party, after all, let the others wait. Emma was not going to be ruffled.

Other children's faces began to appear at the door of the store. A pigtailed girl and a red-headed boy leaned forward, peering in.

Bruce stuck out his tongue.

The red-headed boy stuck out his.

"Bruce!" Emma said.

Bruce turned around and stuck another piece of candy into his mouth. Liverpool waited until Emma wasn't looking, then spun and thumbed his nose at the faces at the door.

Emma stood up to speak with the proprietor. She was surrounded by children tugging at her. Annie still stumbled around in her oversized bonnet. The proprietor bent over a pad of paper, trying to add up the bill.

Liverpool got up, stretched, looked at the row of faces at the door. He picked up a piece of rock candy, held it up for them to see. He looked at Emma. She was too busy to keep track of everybody. He walked to the door. Bruce followed him, then Tom.

Stepping outside, Liverpool offered his handful of candy. "Any of you fellers like a gumdrop?"

The redhead waved his hand scornfully. "Naw, I don't need none of your gumdrops. Might get something." The pigtailed girl giggled.

"You guys sure do eat a lot of candy," one of the country boys said.

"Watch out you don't break a tooth," said another.

"How come you're so special?"

"Dunno," Liverpool said. "Just comes natural."

"I heard you was orphans," the redhead said.

"What of it?" Bruce said. Patches had come up to join them.

"You lose your maw?" a dumpling-shaped boy at the back shouted out.

"How'd you lose your maw? She run after the soldiers in the Mexican War?" another boy said. The redhead laughed.

Liverpool never took his eyes off the redhead. "No, that wasn't what happened."

"It must be nice, though," the redhead said, "to have a church lady pay for everything. You must be good little orphans."

"Good enough to make you eat dirt," Liverpool said.

"Yeah? You think so. You could try."

"I could try," Liverpool said.

Emma stood at the door. She stared at the two bands of children. "What's going on here? Liverpool?"

"Nothin'. They were just tellin' us about chickens and eggs and stuff like that."

"We never met no kids from New York before, miss," the girl in pigtails said.

Emma's brow wrinkled for a second, and then she decided to let it go. "All right, everybody," she said. "We're going to the church."

As Emma led them down the stairs, the redhead came up to Liverpool. "You want to see if you can make anybody eat dirt, I'll give you your try. We're gonna be down behind the feedstore. If you can get away from your church lady . . ."

"Liverpool!"

"Coming, Miss Symns."

The children were led off down the road, some of the local citizens falling in behind them. The church, shining white in the sunny afternoon, was at the end of the street. It was a small parade, buckboards and carriages taking up the rear, raising clouds of dust. Liverpool turned to look back just once at the redhead standing on the porch of the general store.

Inside the passenger car, Dr. Tansy looked out the window at the children's parade heading down the street.

"Say, Carlin, look at that, it's the Children's Crusade."

"Play your card, Dr. Tansy," Carlin said.

Dr. Tansy squinted at his cards, rolling his cigar in his mouth. Not bad, not bad. As he did whenever he had a good hand, he began to sing, "Wild roved an Indian girl, bright Alfarata, where sweep the waters of the blue Juanita . . ."

"Dr. Tansy. . . ."

Dr. Tansy chuckled. "I dunno what's the good of it, spreading street Arabs and pickpockets over the frontier. It won't be safe anywhere. Maybe they'll get their fingers bit off in mink traps."

"Don't tip your cards, Dr. Tansy. You make it too easy."

Dr. Tansy pulled his cards to his chest, suddenly looking as sober as an owl. He turned his head sharply. There was an odd click at the door. Dr. Tansy put his cards face down, stood up, and tiptoed to the door. He yanked it open and J.P. fell into the passenger car.

Dr. Tansy lifted J.P. up by the collar. "Well, what do you know? I think we've got ourselves a strayed pilgrim."

J.P. looked at Carlin for some aid. Carlin stared at her, shook his head slowly. "Don't look at me," Carlin said. "Aren't you supposed to be with the others?"

"Don't feel like it."

"Oh you don't," Carlin said.

"We'd better send him back to the lady," Dr. Tansy said. "What's your name, son?"

"J.P."

"What do you think, Carlin? Shouldn't we send the boy back?"

"Probably we should," Carlin said.

"Tell me something, J.P., can you cut a cigar?"

"Yes, sir!" J.P. perked right up. Dr. Tansy looked dubious. "And I can polish boots, empty spittoons."

"You're a real all-around fellow, aren't you, J.P.? Dr. Tansy, what do you say we make the boy useful?"

"Useful? Boys? Never did see how you could use a boy for much."

"I don't know if that's necessarily true, Dr. Tansy," Carlin said. "You never know where a boy might come in handy."

"Just as long as he doesn't step out of line. Kids like these can steal the spectacles right off your face while you're wearing 'em." Dr. Tansy stared at J.P. J.P. didn't say anything. "I don't like kids much. I tried a couple myself and it just didn't work out."

"Stop showing me your cards, Dr. Tansy."

Dr. Tansy lifted his cards quickly. J.P. leaned back against the plush seat across the aisle. Carlin winked at her. She settled back happily.

Sitting at the table at the back of the Methodist church Emma knew that she was the real gambler, she, niece of a renowned Episcopal clergyman, and not the cigar-smoking males passing a few stale hours with a handful of cards back in the passenger car. Emma was gambling with lives.

Standing in front of the table was John, the boy from Albany, whose face she had washed, whose hair she had cut, was it only days before? Now he was going off with a family—a Quaker couple and their young daughter—and what Emma was gambling on was not the information she was writing down so carefully on her forms, but that the quietness she saw in the three faces promised kindness, that in those erect, strong postures there was care.

Eleven children had been chosen in a little over three hours. Two boys went to a wealthy farmer, one to a tinner, one to a physician, one to a born-again ox driver. With some Emma was taking bigger chances than with others.

The ox driver was exactly the kind of man her uncle would have abhorred. Her uncle was a strict Episcopalian, and evangelicals and religious enthusiasts were his particular terror.

The ox driver, a man of little learning but evident good will, was, as one of the local women whispered to Emma, a religious rounder, one of those individuals who would get religion at every meeting and in a few weeks manage to get rid of it. A six-footer with a voice like a senator, after every regeneration he would go about behind his oxen singing, "I'll never turn back, any more, any more . . ."

The ox driver chose a little boy named Isaac, or rather, as he put it, "The spirit brought him to me, miss, I know it in my heart." The man and the boy laughed and swapped stories and the man was gentle with the boy, that was what Emma saw most of all, and he was patient. She wasn't going to deny that man that child no matter what his manners were, no matter how many times he fell from grace. He could raise a child, she was sure of it.

The unadorned little church swarmed with children and rough farmers. She wondered what her uncle would have thought of this scene. The church was without a single ornament, without a single bit of stained glass, without one musical instrument, the pulpit was a plain white pine box.

When Emma was a child, the most exciting part of any

week had been going to hear her uncle preach. He would be high up in the pulpit, the pulpit beautifully carved with a great eagle clutching muskets and swords, and her uncle's stern words came down to his congregation very literally from on high, till their heads would bow in deference to the authority of those words, and then the big organ would begin to play.

Yet Emma, at the age of twenty-eight, had stepped out from under her uncle's authority, even as she was carrying on his work; she had left him white and ill, lying on a stationmaster's couch in Albany, and she was carrying her little intruders into plain Methodist churches that had neither musical instruments, carvings of eagles nor, from her uncle's view, a proper understanding of authority.

There was still enough of her uncle in Emma that her prejudice was that these would be plain people; it turned out that perhaps they weren't plain at all. They had injected something of the spirit of the camp revival into the choosing of children. There was a small, large-hipped woman in charge of refreshments who, whenever she would come through with a plate of cakes, would sing out, "There's a spirit blowing through us today. You can feel it blow, can't you, Miss Symns?" As if to furnish physical proof of her statement, the cakes would slip and slide about her plate as she swayed across the crowded church.

There may not have been any musical instruments, but that was only because the people themselves were the instruments on which the spirit played, they were the rough tuning forks of the Lord, and if the spirit led them to take a child, they would take a child. Her uncle might have found it all a little too democratic and excessively zealous, but these people were not prosaic; if anything they were the most poetic of people, and whether it was good poetry or bad would have been presumptuous for Emma to judge.

* * *

A hard-looking farmer leaned forward, his hairy-backed hands resting on his knees, grilling the twelve-year-old boy named Willy.

"Poor boy, are ya?"

"Yes, sir. Anything wrong with that?"

"I guess not," the farmer admitted.

"Franklin, Webster, and Clay were all poor boys too," Willy kept on.

"I suppose you're right."

"Vanderbilt. Astor. Commodore Perry."

"I get your drift, son. You don't have to drive your point into the ground. But have you ever worked?"

"Yes, sir. I've tried everything."

The farmer looked skeptical. He straightened up and scratched his head with one of his hairy hands. "You ever planted?"

"No, but I could do it."

"How do you know that?" the farmer said.

"Lord bless you children, Lord bless . . ." The broad-hipped woman with the cakes came swirling by, and Willy reached up and nabbed a small corncake. He took a bite and chewed carefully, keeping his eye on the farmer. He waited until he had swallowed before he answered the farmer's question.

"Well, sir, I have been a newsboy and when that got slack, I have smashed baggage. I have sold nuts, peddled, and worked on the canal. When I was a newsboy and sold papers I was at the top of my profession. I had a good stand of my own."

"Then why did you quit?" the farmer asked.

"It would not do, sir."

"Would not do? Why not?"

Willy looked away. "It didn't do. I fell into bad habits."

"What do you mean?"

"The boys that I fell in company with . . . I contracted their habits. You know what my name was?"

"No, son, I don't."

"Quick-Fingers Willy."

"Quick-Fingers Willy. And how did you get such a name?"

"I used to climb up on houses to steal the lead from around the chimneys and then take it away to some junk shop and sell it."

"And what did you do with the money?"

"I usually would buy a ticket for the pit of the Chatham Street Theater and something to eat with the remainder."

"There must have been a lot of chimneys falling down in your neighborhood."

"There were, sir."

"But you want to make a new life and you're not afraid of work, I take it?"

"No, sir."

"Well, now, Willy, there's a problem."

"You don't want to take an ex-thief."

"No, son. I think you'll be over that part of your life. It's your name. Willy. Or Quick-Fingers Willy, whatever. I've got two boys, a Robert and a Willy, and that was before you got here. So how would it be if we called you Andy?"

"Andy, sir?"

"That's right."

Willy looked at the man with the hairy hands. "Andy. Always liked Andy, sir. A clean, upstanding name. Like Andy Jackson, Old Hickory. It would suit me fine, sir!"

"All right then, Andy, you're coming home with me."

Emma stood up and shook hands with John and his new family. As she did, she was suddenly aware of Sarah standing close by with a well-dressed gentleman.

Emma turned and smiled. "Sarah . . ." Emma began, and then she saw the terror in Sarah's eyes.

The man held an application in his hand. He had brass buttons on his jacket. Emma took the application from the man and read it over. She looked up. The man was smiling sadly at her. "Is your wife with you, Mr. Dunlap?"

Mr. Dunlap's sad smile became more engaging. "I'm afraid not. She's not well. I told her I'd find a girl to help out around the house."

Emma looked again at the application, ran her finger along the paper's edge. Sarah stood taut, her face frozen.

"I hope I got it right," Mr. Dunlap said. "My wife usually does these things. I think she'll be so pleased with Sarah. Before she became ill my wife was a musician in Cincinnati . . . and Sarah tells me she's interested in music. They could play the concertina together."

Emma looked up from the application. "Everything seems to be in order. I wonder if you'll excuse us for a moment, Mr. Dunlap?"

Emma took Sarah aside. "What is it, Sarah?"

"Oh, please, miss. No. Don't let him take me."

"Why, Sarah."

"He'll use me, miss."

"Sarah, what do you mean?"

"You know, miss, you know."

Emma flushed deeply. "How can you know that, Sarah? Did he say anything?"

"He didn't have to say anything. It's not his words, miss. I know the way a man looks at you."

"All right, Sarah."

"You're not going to . . ."

Emma didn't say anything. She returned to the table. I'm sorry, Mr. Dunlap. Sarah is not being placed out here."

"She's not being placed out? Why not?"

"Other arrangements have been made."

Mr. Dunlap turned his sad smile to the people around him. The broad-hipped woman with the cakes had stopped to watch, her lips pursed in sympathy.

"Miss Symns, my wife is sick, she needs help. She is an educated woman, she would be good for Sarah, and Sarah would be a help to her. If you could visit her, Miss Symns, shut up, confined to her bed, deprived of any human nourishment . . ."

"I am not moved," Emma said.

The woman with the plate of cakes drew in her breath in shock. The well-dressed man looked down for a second, the sad smile had disappeared. He stared at Emma. "You don't have any faith in people, do you, Miss Symns? I'm entitled to a child, the same as these people. Why should they get a child and not me? On what basis? What gives you the right to play God with people's lives?"

"I am not God, Mr. Dunlap, neither am I playing. Now if you'll excuse me, I have other people to attend to."

"There's not an ounce of human sympathy in you, is there? You've never been married—you don't know what it's like to see someone you're close to suffer, month after month. . . . You're a crippled, suspicious, ironic woman, Miss Symns. May the Lord defend us from people like you." He started to go, then stopped and turned back. He was trembling. He stood for a moment, trying to gather up his dignity. He tried to smile his meek smile.

"If I've offended you, Miss Symns, I'm sorry. I've not meant to slight your society. If I could make some financial contribution . . ."

"That will be enough, Mr. Dunlap. Please leave us alone. Or shall I call someone to remove you?"

Without another word, Mr. Dunlap turned and left, the woman with the plate of cakes stepping quickly out of his way.

Emma looked across the church. More children had been chosen than she realized, but there couldn't have been that many. She checked her list. Eight had been taken, but where were J.P., Liverpool, Bruce, Tom, and Patches?

The feedstore wasn't hard to find. Liverpool led the gang of them, Bruce, Tom, and Patches, marching down the main street till they stood in front of a two-story wood-frame building, bins of grain and farm implements, plows and threshing machines on the first floor and on the second, bags of flour stacked to the rafters.

At a nod from Liverpool, they marched around the building. Liverpool raised his hand and they halted. Scattered out across a grassy meadow that sloped down to a stream were the country children, playing a game.

The big red-headed boy had a ball, all wrapped in twine, in his hand, and the girl in pigtails had a bat. There was a home base marked by a flour sack and another base, marked by a rock, out in a grassy spot beyond the redhead.

"What's this?" Liverpool whispered.

"One o'cat," Bruce answered.

The big redhead was pitching to the girl in pigtails. She swung and missed, the ball rolled through the legs of the pudgy eight-year-old catcher and bounced back against the base of the feedstore, four or five feet from Liverpool. The boy turned and walked back to retrieve the ball. He stopped in his tracks when he saw the city boys bunched together.

Out on the field the other country boys seemed to perk up, alert as deer caught in an open pasture.

Liverpool bent down, picked up the ball, and underhanded it back to the catcher.

The redhead shouted, "Come on, Monk, get the ball back."

Monk obediently tossed the ball back to the redhead. The girl in pigtails had dropped her bat to stare at Liverpool.

"Come on, Hattie, pick up the bat," the redhead commanded. "Let's play."

Liverpool didn't move.

The city children watched silently as the redhead lofted a soft pitch, too high, that the girl watched go by. On the next pitch she swung, bounced the ball back to the redhead. The boy picked it up, held it for a second as the girl ran toward the rock, then ran after her. When he was about five feet away he tossed it at her legs. She jumped, but not high enough, and the ball bounced off her calico skirt. She ran laughing toward the other children. The redhead retrieved the ball, picked it up, and stared at Liverpool.

"What are you lookin' for?" the redhead asked.

"What do you think?"

The redhead laughed. "You gonna make me eat dirt, is that it?" Liverpool didn't say anything. Patches was fidgeting. Liverpool gave him an irritated look. "And when are you going to try?"

"I wouldn't want to interrupt your game," Liverpool said.

"You wouldn't be interrupting for long," the redhead said.

"Whatever game it is," Bruce said.

"What do you mean, whatever game it is? It's one o' cat."

"Oh," Bruce said. "I was wonderin' if maybe it was stink base that I used to play." He turned and winked at Tom.

"Any rules to this game?" Liverpool said.

The redhead was fuming. "Sure, there are rules. But it seems to me that if you can't hit, the rules aren't going to make much of a difference."

"Then how about your letting me take a turn?" Liverpool said.

"It's all right with me," the redhead said. "It all right with you, Monk?"

"All right with me, Duwayne."

Duwayne turned and appealed to his fielders. "All right with you if the city boy takes a turn?"

"All right with us, Duwayne," came back the chorus.

Patches whispered to Liverpool. "You ever played this here game?"

Duwayne overheard him. "That's right," Duwayne said. "You ever played this game?"

"Sure," Liverpool said. "I was the champion of Dutch Hill. Got so good everybody refused to play with me, it was so discouragin' for 'em." Bruce, Tom, and Patches regarded him dubiously, but that didn't disturb Liverpool. "Give me that . . ." Liverpool pointed at the bat. "That stick there." The girl named Hattie handed Liverpool the bat. Liverpool looked back at his supporters. Patches sighed and looked out toward the trees.

Liverpool banged the bat on the ground, then lifted it high off his shoulder. Hattie snickered.

"Look at him, he's hittin' cross-handed." The other country children laughed. Liverpool looked down at his hands, then switched them around. Duwayne rubbed the ball between his hands.

Duwayne reared back, leg high in the air, poised for a second as if to gather all his strength.

It occurred to Liverpool, as Duwayne went into his windup, that perhaps he was really in over his head, that this time his bragging had gotten him into something he didn't understand at all, but the instant that Duwayne released the ball it suddenly became all too familiar.

Liverpool and his old Dutch Hill friends had been in a fight once with the Dead Rabbit Gang, when, in a surprise attack, the Dead Rabbit Gang had leaped over a barricade of wooden crates and started throwing rocks at short range.

Now, just as then, there was no time to think, no time for worry about maintaining dignity, there was only the ball flying at him like a vengeful gray bird, the terror at the pit of his stomach, and the instinct of self-preservation.

Liverpool ducked away, and then, as the ball blurred past

and he realized that he was safe, he took a half-hearted swing, in a feeble gesture at saving his pride, much too late.

The ball thunked against the feedstore wall and bounded halfway back to Duwayne.

Duwayne grinned. His teammates shouted their support.

"Good throw!"

"He's got a swing like a barn door, Duwayne. He can't hit nothin'!"

"Hey, Liverpool," Bruce whispered. "Let me do it!"

"No!"

"Liverpool, you never played in your life. Give me that bat."

"No!" Liverpool whispered more furiously.

Duwayne, rubbing up the ball, looked down at Liverpool and smiled. "What's wrong, orphan boy?" Duwayne said. Liverpool ignored him, bent over, dusted his palms in the dirt, spat into them, and took up the bat again. Duwayne didn't like being ignored. "Didn't your father ever teach you to hit, orphan boy?"

Liverpool's eyes flickered. For a second he straightened up as if he was going out after Duwayne, but he didn't. He tightened his grip on the bat, checked to be sure he wasn't hitting cross-handed, planted his feet firmly, lifted the bat high.

"Keep your eye on the ball, Liverpool," Tom said.

"Come on, Liverpool, stand up there now, don't back down," Bruce said.

Liverpool did not look back at them.

The pitch came hurtling in, about level with the top of Liverpool's head. He wasn't sure whether or not his eyes were open when he swung, but he swung hard and there was the magical sound of the ball hitting the bat. When Liverpool looked up he didn't see the ball at first, saw only the gangly boy staggering backward toward the creek like a drunk. The ball hit behind him and bounded into a patch of raspberry bushes. Bruce, Tom, and Patches were shouting at Liverpool, and that brought him out of his daze.

"The base, Liverpool, touch base!" Liverpool started running, out toward the rock.

Duwayne stood waving his arms. His teammates raced back toward the raspberry bushes.

Liverpool touched the rock, skittered past. Now what? Bruce and Patches and Tom were shouting to him. "Come back, Liverpool. Come back!"

Liverpool put his head down and came running back. He felt as if he were covering five yards with every stride. Let those bumpkins with their mothers and doting sisters and clean clothes and faithful pets try to find that ball, he'd hit the next one farther; let those boys with fathers and baby brothers and ponies to ride tell him he hit cross-handed, he'd knock it over the trees next time.

Liverpool looked back. One of the kids had somehow retrieved the ball from under the raspberry bushes. Duwayne screamed for the ball.

The throw came in. Duwayne had the ball in his hand, he had Liverpool dead to rights, but Liverpool was coming anyway.

Duwayne pounded the ball in his hand, skipping up, closer, till he was maybe eight feet away from the barreling Liverpool. Duwayne whipped the ball at Liverpool's head, but Liverpool had his hands raised and the ball bounced off his elbow.

Liverpool never hesitated. Without once breaking stride he swerved and leaped on Duwayne, knocking the bigger boy down on his back. The two boys rolled over and over in the dust.

Country boys came thundering in from every direction; Monk from behind the plate, angry boys with their arms scratched and bloody from the raspberry bushes.

At the start, Bruce, older and stronger, was a regular Samson, dumping one and all on their heads, tearing Hattie off Tom's back, shoving somebody away from Patches; but soon there were too many of them, clinging to Bruce's legs and waist like rats to a terrier. The smaller ones circled around the outside, jumping up and down and cheering on the bigger ones. Monk disappeared around the side of the feedstore, only to reappear minutes later with his two big brothers.

Surrounded and outnumbered, the streeters fought the good fight. Bruce roared and shoved and pushed, lurching forward and back with two country boys clinging to each leg. Every time he knocked one away, another would fly onto his back, and they were hitting him hard because he was the biggest. They were hurting him, and he was crying out in pain and rage. "Tom! Tom, help me!"

Tom was in no position to help anyone; he lay on his back, kicking away four outraged, briar-scratched boys. Patches was getting his head banged against the wall of the feedstore by Monk and his brothers, while Liverpool was still locked in combat with Duwayne. Hattie, pigtails flying, circled the two adversaries, her bat raised, waiting to get a swing at Liverpool.

Liverpool realized that it was time for a strategic move. He twisted away from Duwayne, dodged the swinging bat, and made a dash for the steps of the feedstore.

Tom, lying on his back, looked up in dismay. "Liverpool! You can't! Lily-livered! Lily-liver-rr-ed!"

Two leaps and Liverpool was up the steps. Duwayne and Hattie stumbled after him. Liverpool pulled the heavy wooden door shut behind him, fixed the latch. He heard Duwayne yanking and pounding on the door from the other side.

Liverpool raced past the plows and threshers, looked frantically to the left and right, saw the wooden stairs and ran up them to the second floor. The bags of flour were stacked almost to the roof. The air was thick with the smell of the freshly ground grain. Swallows fluttered uneasily in the rafters.

Liverpool pried open the wooden window.

The battling children were right below him. They had gotten Bruce down on the ground now. He tried to rise up on one knee, but there were three kids around his neck, hanging from him, bending him back down. There was blood on his face. "Tom! Damn it, Tom, where are you?" he shouted. Tom was still being held down, a big boy sitting on his chest. Patches pulled away from Monk and his brothers for a second, but then was tripped and sent sprawling. But closest of all, the closest of targets, were Duwayne and the pigtailed girl, still working on the door directly below him.

The bag of flour was too heavy to carry. Liverpool reached into his pocket and pulled out a knife, quickly slit open the top of the bag. Some flour ran out onto the floor; he scooped out more with his hands.

Liverpool dragged the bag between his legs to the window, then tumbled it out, shoving it with his knee to give it a little distance.

It made a turn and a half in the air, spewing flour, before the half-filled bag exploded over Bruce and his tormentors. The flour rose in great billowing clouds, the battlers sat stunned, sprawled out on the ground.

Quickly Liverpool opened a second bag of flour and dragged it to the window. Like fools, they had all run to the door, instead of away from it; they were shouting angrily up at Liverpool and they wanted to get at him. Liverpool tumbled out the bag. It hit with the sound of a dull bomb, spewing whiteness everywhere.

Children coughed and staggered through the haze like

drunkards, like Napoleon's troops at Waterloo, covered with white flour. They were like ghosts or snowmen. Even if they had still wanted to hit somebody, they couldn't have; there was no way now of telling which powdery figure was a country boy and which a city one, which an orphan and which a boy with two parents and eight living uncles. One flour-covered child stumbled up to another, his fist raised. "No, it's me, Monk! I'm your brother!"

From around the corner of the building came a small army of adults, including Miss Symns, the mayor, and the lanky owner of the general store.

"What in Sam Hill are you kids up to!" the mayor bellowed.

The country boys took to their heels, while their camouflages still held, scattering out toward the trees and the stream.

Emma stared in dismay as a snow-white Bruce, Tom, and Patches got to their feet and limped toward her.

Emma didn't say a word, but began wiping the flour from their eyes, brushing their clothes. None of the three uttered a sound until, as Emma brushed the last traces of flour from around Patches's mouth and the corners of his eyes, he began to cry.

The mayor and the owner of the general store marched around the feedstore and up the steps, climbed the stairs to the second floor. The afternoon light poured in through the open window. The swallows fluttered in the rafters. There was a powdery path of footprints leading to the ladder at the far end of the loft.

*I*t took nearly an hour to wash the boys clean, to erase all the marks of their floury-white shame. Emma offered to pay the feedstore owner for the broken bags of flour, but the man refused. Emma felt it was her obligation to lecture the four boys; she tried to impress upon them that Christian forbearance was the only answer to those who were hostile to them or found them strange. It was not a long lecture. Emma's heart wasn't in it. Liverpool, who had slipped back to the train ahead of the others, felt himself victorious, and nothing that Emma said could change that. Bruce, on the other hand, looked angry and bitter. The others hadn't protected him, he said; if the others had just watched his back he could have held those country boys off all afternoon.

There were only nine of them now. The afternoon at the church had been a great success, eight children placed, Timmy and Eileen with a blacksmith and his wife, Jane, the crossing girl, with the school mistress. John, Isaac, Willy . . . with dismay Emma looked across the boxcar. It felt empty to her.

Early the next morning, somewhere east of Cleveland, the train came to a stop. The conductor, resplendent even at that early hour in his buff vest and blue cutaway with shiny brass buttons, came back to tell Emma that there had been an accident a couple of miles ahead and they would have to wait until the track was cleared.

The brakeman was appointed to take the handcar and ride ahead to see how things were. Carlin persuaded the crew to let him go along, and so the two of them, Carlin and the young brakeman, went flying down the track, pumping the tandem till they disappeared from view.

There were cornfields as far as the eye could see where the train had stopped. A morning mist lay over the harvested ground as if over a lake. A rusted sign on the nearest fence advertised a remedy for ague. The children walked up and down the length of the train, talking with passengers. Tom managed to cadge some fruit from a Mormon lady. Liverpool and Tony went back to examine the stock car full of cattle that had been hooked on during the night: they poked their fingers through the slats and then gave little yelps depending on how close the irritated animals came to snapping their fingers off. Bruce stood off by himself, leaning against a fence post, gnawing at the remains of an apple.

Emma knelt outside the boxcar, sewing up a tear in Annie's dress. Annie stood patiently, holding onto Emma's shoulder. Emma found the small hand comforting, the quick movements of the needle pleasurable, and it was during this state of lulled inattention that Emma heard the two children's voices whispering inside the boxcar.

"You're not?"

"No, I'm not."

"How can you not be . . ." It was Sarah.

"I'm just not, that's all." And J.P.

"You do not try, J.P. You don't even go with us to meet these people. So how will they choose you?"

"I've got other plans," J.P. said.

"You say."

"I do too."

"What plans?"

"Can't tell."

"Why not?"

"Secret."

"Oh. So you do not want to tell me?" There was a long silence. Emma frowned, tying off the last stitch in Annie's dress.

"You promise not to tell?" Emma heard J.P. whisper finally.

"I promise."

"Hope to die?"

"Yes, I hope to die."

"Mr. Carlin's promised to take me out west."

"No he has not," Sarah said.

"He did!" J.P. said. "I'm going to help him. He's going to take pictures in the Rocky Mountains with a general . . . to look for a place to make a railroad . . . and I'm going to be his assistant . . . an apprentice kind of . . ."

"You're making a joke, J.P. . . ."

"I'm not joking. He promised me. Yesterday, while you were all trying to be nice to farmers."

Annie looked up at Emma. "Miss Symns?"

"Yes, Annie?"

"Are you done sewing my dress?"

"Yes, Annie."

"Thank you, Miss Symns." Annie ran off to join the boys who were teasing the cattle.

Emma was too stunned and angry to think. She walked to

the front of the train, past the knots of passengers. The engineer and the fireman, standing together on the track, turned when they heard Emma approach.

"They're coming back now, miss," the engineer said. He pointed down the rails to where a wavering dark mark grew thicker. Emma could see that it was the handcar. The two small figures seesawed back and forth, their shirttails flying. One of the figures raised a hand and waved.

The engineer turned to the fireman. "Looks like she's all clear, I guess. We'd better get the fire up." He smiled at Emma. "You can start gettin' your boys and girls back in the train, miss. It won't be long."

The engineer and the fireman turned and walked back toward the locomotive, but Emma waited. The handcar sped down the tracks toward her, Carlin pumping away, having the time of his life. The handcar slowed as it neared the train, and Carlin jumped off and waved to his partner the brakeman. Carlin walked along the tracks, kicked at the bunches of dry weeds, his face flushed with exertion and excitement, his arms swinging loose at his sides like a man without a worry in the world. When he saw Emma, he smiled, surprised, and waved.

Emma stared at him. Didn't he understand about children? Didn't he know that you don't make promises to children unless you can keep them? The irresponsibility, the carelessness of it. . . . She would have to speak to him, but not now, now she was too angry for words. She turned and waved for her children to get back to the train.

It took another three hours to reach Cleveland. The children were excited about seeing Cleveland because it was, as Patches put it, "a real city," and maybe they'd see a firehouse, a concert saloon, an oyster bar, something. Liverpool had heard from Willy about Lake Erie, and he sure wanted to see that. Emma tried to keep them from building up their hopes. They would only be in the depot, it probably wouldn't be more than an hour stop at most, and, besides, their goal now was Rock Springs—Rock Springs, Illinois, still a good two and a half days farther out, where people were waiting for them.

The idea of Cleveland, however, had caught the children's fancy. Even Bruce, who had been sullen all day, began to come out of his funk, laughing with Liverpool. Sure, he'd go for a walk with Liverpool to have a look at this Lake Erie, why not?

When the train ground to a halt, Bruce was the first one up, yanking at the boxcar door. "Come on, Liverpool, let's see what's here." He yanked at the door again, and this time it flew open. Bruce put his hand on the side of the car, preparing to jump down, when the commotion in front of the depot made him stop and look up.

There, standing in the middle of the dingy railroad yard, surrounded by porters, was the grandest-looking bunch of people Bruce had ever seen. The women were done up in extraordinary scarves, capes, and bits of Irish lace, the men in fine high hats and velvet vests in all the sunset hues. To Bruce their gestures seemed larger than life, their clothes brighter than clothes had ever been. They stood in an island of great worn trunks, shiny brass horns and drums, with a pack of dogs of various origins that tangled their leashes in spite of the efforts of their young keeper.

In all of this, there was no mistaking the leader. Standing slightly aloof from the island, his silver-headed cane raised to instruct others about the loading of the trunks, was a silver-haired man of about fifty, whose cream-colored cape draped artfully over his cream-colored suit. The splendor of his appearance took Bruce's breath away.

It was an extraordinary outfit—and what was even more extraordinary about it was that, in the sooty railroad yard, it remained spotless. This marvelous effect wasn't as mysterious as it seemed. In fact the wearer of the outfit never touched anything, but confined himself to directing all the others with his silver-headed cane, letting them do all the toting, heaving, and wrestling with luggage.

It was standing room only in the boxcar door.

"Look, Miss Symns!" Patches said. "Actors! Real actors!"

The silver-haired gentleman courteously acknowledged their presence with a flourish of his silver-headed cane, then went on with the conducting of the packing of dogs, drums, tubas, and trunks. Carlin and Dr. Tansy had emerged from the passenger car to watch the spectacle.

The children barraged Emma with questions.

"Who are they, Miss Symns? Can't we find out?" "Are they going to do a show, Miss Symns? Can't we help 'em, Miss Symns?" "Maybe they'll sign their names!" "Let's go help 'em, huh, Miss Symns?"

"Children, please! We're going to stay in the boxcar. It's only a brief stop, I don't want to lose you. Ben, don't fall out . . . Ben!"

As Emma reached out for Ben, J.P. moved past her on the other side and leapt to the ground. Carlin walked toward them.

"J.P.!" Emma demanded. "Where do you think you are going?"

"Don't worry, Miss Symns, I'll be fine. If I ride up with them, it won't hurt anything, will it? You'll know where I am. It's the same train, right?"

"If I let you ride up front, J.P., how can I say no to the others?"

"I don't know, Miss Symns, but please, I'll be real good, I promise, cross my heart. . . ."

Carlin put a hand on J.P.'s shoulder. "I'll keep an eye on J.P., Miss Symns," he said.

"You and I need to have a talk, Mr. Carlin," Emma said.

Her tone made the smile disappear momentarily from

Carlin's face. "Of course, Miss Symns, if something . . ." J.P. took Carlin's hand, and his smile reappeared. "Any time," he said. "But I can take this rascal off your hands for a few miles, it would be no trouble at all." He grabbed J.P. playfully by the back of the neck. J.P. winced.

"That's right, Miss Symns," J.P. said.

"Mr. Carlin, these children are my responsibility."

The actors strolled toward the passenger car. Bruce, transfixed, couldn't take his eyes off the silver-haired man.

"I know they're your responsibility," Carlin said. "I wouldn't think of asking you to abdicate your responsibility." He looked at her, questioning. "Is something wrong, Miss Symns?" He smiled again. "It doesn't have to always be so serious, does it?" J.P. was grinning victoriously. "But we will talk, Miss Symns," he said. "I'm counting on it."

Carlin put his arm over J.P.'s shoulder, and the two of them headed toward the passenger car.

The sight of the actors disappearing into the train suddenly shook Bruce out of his trance. He jumped down and ran after them.

"Bruce!" Emma shouted.

Bruce turned back for a second, stumbling, gesturing with his hands, too frustrated and in too much of a hurry to use words, then dashed up into the passenger car.

The remaining children loosed a chorus of complaints. "Miss Symns, how come they get to ride up front and we don't?" "It's not fair!" "How come, Miss Symns?"

"Close the door, please," Emma said.

"Well, I sure don't think it's fair." "Me neither." "They just took off and you let 'em get away with it . . ."

"I asked you to close the door!"

A crowd got on the train in Cleveland. There was heated competition for good seats among the new passengers, who included two women teachers from a female academy, a saw-mill owner and his wife, a newspaper editor from Indiana, and a downstate farmer and his family. All the elbowing, pushing, and shoving came to a pause, however, as the actors paraded through the car.

The sawmill owner pulled his valise out of the aisle to let them pass. The newspaper editor took off his hat to one of the actresses. Dr. Tansy held back as long as he could and then he couldn't any longer. As the silver-haired gentleman was lowering himself into his seat, Dr. Tansy suddenly stuck out a finger at him and blurted: "Edward Whitcomb? Aren't you Edward Whitcomb?"

The silver-haired gentleman looked up and smiled as if this sort of thing happened all the time. "It would be an affectation on my part to pretend otherwise," he said.

Dr. Tansy beamed. *"The Idiot Witness.* Philadelphia. Eighteen fifty-one. October, I think."

"I believe it was November fifth that we opened, if I remember correctly," Mr. Whitcomb said graciously. He turned to the elderly woman next to him. She wore a little hat that dripped lace, and although she was heavily made up, her face seemed almost girlish. He addressed her in the most gallant way. "Can you remember, dear?"

She smiled a bright, young smile. "Yes, I think it was November."

Dr. Tansy, still beaming, extended his hand. "You were brilliant, sir. Oh, my, it was a great triumph. It is a pleasure to meet you. My name is Dr. Tansy, botanic medicine."

Mr. Whitcomb's smile dimmed only for a second. "Botanic medicine, how very interesting. Meg, this is Dr. Tansy. Doctor Tansy, my wife." Mrs. Whitcomb tilted her head demurely. "Meg is also a member of our troupe. We met during the run of *The Idiot Witness* as a matter of fact . . . or was it *Slasher and Crasher,* dear?"

"I believe it was *Slasher and Crasher,* dear," Mrs. Whitcomb said.

Dr. Tansy felt he had to share his good fortune. "Mr. and Mrs. Whitcomb, I'd like you to meet a young picture-taker friend of mine, Mr. Frank Carlin. He's from New York, a daguerreotypist."

Mrs. Whitcomb smiled demurely. "Oh, how nice. As you probably know, we actors are always interested in pictures."

"I do know," Carlin said. He smiled, though perhaps not cordially enough. J.P. looked up at him.

As if to make up for his lack of cordiality, Mrs. Whitcomb smiled back at Carlin very prettily.

"Looks like you're touring quite a show here," Carlin said politely.

Mr. Whitcomb leaned across his wife. "Indeed, we are!" he said, "I've been in the theater for nearly fifty years, Mr. Carlin, and never have I been in anything to equal it."

"Is that right?" Carlin said.

Mr. Whitcomb's voice took on a thrilling tone. "I consider it an honor to be involved with a play that's not tawdry, not one of your claptrap melodramas or leering, outdated farces, but a play unparalleled in the American theater, a play that addresses itself to the most urgent issues that concern us today . . ."

Carlin was becoming irritated. Mr. Whitcomb may have considered it an honor not to be doing claptrap melodrama, but he was not above using the old melodramatic actor's trick of saving the crucial bit of information until last.

"And what is the name of this play, Mr. Whitcomb?" Carlin asked, his hand on J.P.'s shoulder.

Mr. Whitcomb raised his silver-headed cane. The two women teachers listened intently. Bruce, squatting against the door, watched Mr. Whitcomb's every move. "The play, Mr. Carlin, is our own dramatization of *Uncle Tom's Cabin.*"

"We're doing a matinee tomorrow in Toledo," piped up a gawky girl sitting a couple of rows forward.

"We have been doing this play for nearly a year now, Mr. Carlin, in tiny hamlets and thriving metropolises, and the responses have been the most heartening I've ever encountered in the theater."

"I thought *Uncle Tom's Cabin* was playing in New York," Carlin said.

"That's right," the gawky girl tossed in.

"There are a number of productions," Mr. Whitcomb said a little coldly.

"We ran into two other troupes in the Pittsburgh train station last week. Can you imagine that? Three Simon Legrees all in the same first-class coach," the gawky girl said.

"This play," Mr. Whitcomb said, controlling his temper, "is the essential event in the American theater. It is a play that must be brought to America and all Americans."

"And Edward Whitcomb's the man who's going to bring it to 'em, isn't that right?" The speaker was an elderly, but extraordinarily limber, actor, who swiveled around in his seat to address them. He spoke to Carlin and J.P. in low, confidential tones. "You've got to see it to believe it . . . the death of Little Eva . . . gets 'em every time. There are not many things you can count on these days, but when a kid expires on stage, you can't miss. Right, Edward?"

Mr. Whitcomb smiled, not wanting to identify with his fellow-actor's more cynical view. "This is Asa Drew," Mr. Whitcomb explained. "He plays Uncle Tom in our production, and with a remarkable spirit, too."

"Mr. Whitcomb is too kind," Asa Drew said, not really bothering to acknowledge the compliment. "That's Little Eva up there."

He pointed to a little, curly-headed blond girl, sitting by herself sucking on a stick of taffy. Absorbed in her sticky candy, pausing to lick at her fingers, noticing no one, she seemed a picture of glowing, if slightly self-satisfied, good health.

Asa Drew ended up treating the passengers to almost an hour of anecdotes. Taking a discreet sip now and then from a concealed bottle, he held forth with a never-ending supply of stories: escaping from creditors through the trapdoor in the stage, traveling by wagon, barge, and horseback, performing on riverboats and in Texas gambling houses, bringing art to the untutored.

"On stage once with forty Creek Indians," Asa Drew said, leaning across the aisle. J.P. smiled. Talking made the gaunt old actor expansive, and J.P., sitting across the aisle next to Carlin, was an ideal, attentive audience. Asa Drew leaned back, stretching his long arms. "*Pizarro.* That was the play. Just happened to be these Indians walking down the street, and our manager, he figured he could use 'em for the Peruvian Army. He had a lot of smart ideas, that manager. Right around two, four . . . act two, scene four, that is, the Indians break out in this war dance and those of us on the stage, we were in it, nothing else to do. . . . How many actors you know have got a Creek war dance in their repertoire?" The actor took another swig from his bottle. "Dancer. That's how I started out. Comic songs, some of 'em a little blue, to tell you the truth. That was my first love, dancing. I'm a song-and-dance man, down deep. Then I got rheumatism real bad playing in Pittsburgh. It was the dampness. Never play in Pittsburgh if you can help it." He winked at J.P.

J.P. looked back at him, straight-faced. "Do you know 'Pierre de Bon Bon'?"

Asa Drew was genuinely startled. "Do I know 'Pierre de Bon Bon'? Do you realize whom you're addressing?" He rose unsteadily from his seat; neither the alcohol nor the swaying train were a help to him. "Every artist has a specialty, some favorite. . . ."

A red-haired actress who'd been playing with Dr. Tansy's fingertips looked up at Asa and spoke sharply. "Asa! Asa, you've been drinking. Get back in your seat. Asa. . . . You're going to bruise your hip again, Asa!"

Asa Drew was not to be deterred. His hands extended for a second like a diver, his face beaming, he gave a little kick with his left foot, then just brushed the floor with it coming back, and began to sing in a growly, seductive voice.

> *I'm Pierre de Bon Bon de Paree, de Paree,*
> *I drink the eau de vie, eau de vie . . .*

Step and brush, step and brush, nothing excessive, nothing straining, not a young man's dance, but with control, very professional. J.P. watched his feet, remembering, kick, brush, step, cross-step.

J.P. stepped out into the aisle and without missing a beat fell in step. She had it all, kick and brush, the roll of the eyes, step, cross-step, a little wiggle, a suggestive sweep of the fingers. The passengers craned to see.

> *When I ride out each day in my little coupé*
> *I tell you I'm something to see . . .*

The sawmill owner poked his wife to have a look. Having J.P. as a partner, Asa Drew outdid himself. He kicked and wiggled, putting on a little of the Frenchified airs. They were moving together, he and the boy—this boy was not an amateur.

> *And I care not what others may say*
> *I love my Rosalie*

A little wiggle, bump, sweep around with the hands, nice and slow. . . . The two women teachers blushed.

Little Rose, charming Rose . . .

and kick into the finale . . .

I'm in love with my Rosalie . . .

The two of them swept down into their bow. Everyone in the car, with the exception of the taffy-sucking Little Eva, applauded.

Gulping for air, Asa Drew plumped down in his seat. He regarded J.P. with a suspicious eye.

"Now where'd you learn to do that?"

"Just learned it." J.P glanced back at Carlin, embarrassed. Carlin watched her with one eyebrow raised.

"You don't just learn that, young feller," Asa Drew said. "How many young fellers your age can dance like that? It's rare, that's what I'm saying. You gotta be taught and they don't teach dances like that in Sunday schools."

"My mother taught me."

"Your mother!"

"My mother was an actress."

"What was her name, son? Maybe some of us know her. After all, taken all together we've trod a few boards."

They were all looking at her. J.P.'s heart was pounding. What if they did know her? What if by some wild outside chance they knew where she was?

"What's her name, son?"

"Lucy Watkins," J.P. said.

The actors and actresses looked from one to another. "I knew a Harry Watkins once. In Houston it was," offered a young, soft-faced actor with wild dark hair. "Maybe it's some relation." J.P. shook her head.

"Wait a minute now," Mr. Whitcomb said, leaning forward on his silver-headed cane. "There was a Lillian Watkins from Philadelphia. Did opera . . "

"*Lucy* Watkins," J.P. said. She shut her eyes and repeated, "*Lucy* Watkins."

"If we haven't made her acquaintance, perhaps we will," Mr. Whitcomb said. "Is she acting in New York now?"

"No, she's not," J.P. said. Carlin was looking at her, considering. It made J.P. very uncomfortable.

"I see," Mr. Whitcomb said.

"She's done a lot of acting out west," J.P. said. "San Francisco, you've heard of San Francisco?"

"Why, of course," Mr. Whitcomb said.

"That's probably why you haven't heard of her," J.P. said. "She's on tour now."

"Where is that, son?"

It took J.P. a second to deal with the question. "Where?" Mr. Whitcomb nodded. "In Europe," J.P. said. "She's very popular there. When she comes back I'll be living with her again."

Everyone looked very concerned and a little puzzled. Dr. Tansy's brows were knit with skepticism. J.P. stood up. Again she glanced at Carlin. She was afraid of what he had thought, afraid that she had given herself away. "Excuse me, won't you? I have to use the convenience." With all the dignity of a veteran trouper, J.P made her exit.

"So who's the boy?" Asa Drew asked Carlin. "He travelin' with you?"

"No. No. Not me." Carlin said.

"Orphan," Dr. Tansy interjected. Mrs. Whitcomb clucked sympathetically. "Oh, you think that's something. Him. He's an orphan too." Dr. Tansy pointed to Bruce squatting near the door.

"You too?" the gawky child actress said.

"Poor boy!" said Mrs. Whitcomb.

"I'm not really an orphan," Bruce said. "Just that me and my old man don't get on real good. . . ."

Dr. Tansy advised Mrs. Whitcomb. "I wouldn't expend myself if I were you, ma'am. It's not as if orphans were rare as hen's teeth, particularly on this train. They've got another ten or so of 'em in the boxcar behind."

"Oh, dear!" said Mrs. Whitcomb, unable to contain herself.

Mr. Whitcomb was dismayed. "A boxcar of orphans? There must be some explanation. What is it, son?"

Bruce gulped at being asked a question by the great man. "Well, sir, we're being taken . . or some of us are. . . . We're going to work, you see. . . ." Bruce's eyes started to water, he suddenly felt very, very young, and self-conscious.

"Work for whom, son?" Mr. Whitcomb asked patiently.

"For anybody. Anybody'd have us. Farmers, I guess . . . and we'd grow up out here . . . and we'd be somebody . . . we wouldn't be mean any more . . . or get in trouble . . ."

Mr. Whitcomb reached out with his silver-headed cane and tapped Bruce on the shoulder, a gracious gesture that served simultaneously as a benediction, a bestowal of knighthood, and a sign that Bruce needn't go on with the struggle to speak, since it was Mr. Whitcomb's turn.

"Son, you needn't speak any more . . . words aren't necessary. There are moments when heart can speak to heart. You think that we don't understand what it means to strike out for the unknown, to seek one's fortune among strangers? No, if there's anyone who understands orphans, it's actors, because actors are orphans themselves. . . ."

A groan rose up from some anonymous source.

"Oh, now, Edward," Mrs. Whitcomb said.

"No, it's true. Still homeless children, still believing that the world is capable of splendors, that the world can be astonishing. . . ." He carved invisible castles in the air with his silver-headed cane. "Still seeking a home, if only in the hearts of our audience. Mrs. Whitcomb and I were never blessed with a child of our own, and this company is the only family we have. . . ." He smiled with the full warmth of paternal affection at Bruce. "We have no place, so we can't offer you a home, we manufacture no goods, so we can't offer you a job. . . . All we have to offer is our affections, our good wishes . . . and if the others agree, a bit of our performance."

"Hey, Edward . . ." The actors perked right up.

"Not another benefit, Edward, come on."

"At the next depot when we stop for wood and water," Mr. Whitcomb said, "we will offer up our humble play for these orphans."

"We can't do the *whole* play, Edward, a train's got a schedule."

Mr. Whitcomb lifted his silver-headed cane, silencing his critics. "We'll do selected scenes."

"We're not doing this full dress, are we?"

"Full dress," Mr. Whitcomb insisted.

"Couldn't we just give a reading?"

"We're going to have to get in blackface, Edward?"

"A real actor never compromises his performance," Mr. Whitcomb said. The train seemed to be slowing to a stop, as if on cue from Mr. Whitcomb.

The actors groaned and grumbled as if they had been frequent victims of Mr. Whitcomb's high standards and generous gestures.

The train screeched to a stop. Mr. Whitcomb stood up and Bruce stood up too, in tribute to the presence of the great man.

"Mr. Whitcomb, we're going to have to dig out all our stuff. That takes time."

Mr. Whitcomb wasn't hearing any more criticism. Mr. Whitcomb winked at Bruce and poked him lightly in the ribs with his silver-headed cane. "Remember, son, there are no small performances, only small performers." With that, he shrugged off his cream-colored cape, tossed it on the seat, then tossed his silver-headed cane lightly on top of it and strode toward the door of the car.

It wasn't much of a stop, really, a small stone depot at the crossing of two rail lines and a wide dirt road—the only people around being a corpulent station agent and a woman selling milk. At the top of the hill were an old hotel, a tavern, and a large stable. Over the door of the tavern hung a sign: ENTERTAINMENT FOR MAN AND BEAST. The old stage stop had clearly been there for years, but now, alone at the top of the hill, it looked a little forlorn, like a relic of an earlier decade.

Mr. Whitcomb walked back and announced to Emma that he and his troupe would be proud to do a brief performance for her and the orphans. Emma, taken utterly by surprise, tried briefly to protest, but Mr. Whitcomb didn't believe she meant it, and besides all of the children overruled her.

The conductor warned Mr. Whitcomb that they only had an hour, the train would be pulling out as soon as they picked up passengers from the southbound train, which was due in at ten after four. Mr. Whitcomb assured the conductor that they would perform their little piece with a rapidity without parallel. Both the fireman and the brakeman said they'd certainly enjoy seeing a bit of acting.

Out came the trunks and the musical instruments. Asa Drew and one of the boy actors named Harvey untangled the so-called bloodhounds and ran them up the hill to get them some water at the stable.

The actors used the passenger car to get into makeup and costume, and it was impossible to keep the children out. They stared, fascinated, as the actors transformed themselves, one after the other. Asa Drew, with powder on his hair, some picturesquely tattered overalls, and black grease paint rubbed methodically over every inch of his face, neck, and hands, became the faithful Tom. The young soft-faced actor, whose name was Chauncey, used a little grease to slick back his unruly locks and a pencil to darken his brow. With the addition of jangly boots and a great leather whip he evolved into the ferocious Simon Legree.

Bruce was fascinated with Mr. Whitcomb and couldn't tear himself away, falling all over himself and the actor like a puppy. While never losing his courteous air, Mr. Whitcomb turned to Bruce mildly irritated: "Yes, son?"

"I wonder, sir, if there's anything I can do for you."

"Something you can do for me? Why, son, we're doing something for you, right now. . . . I just hope you'll enjoy it."

"But, Mr. Whitcomb!" There was an urgency in Bruce's voice that made Whitcomb stop for a second. Bruce faltered. "Mr. Whitcomb . . . I just wondered if there was anything you needed."

"Well, let's see. . . . There's a tavern up there, isn't there? If you could bring me a draught of ale, it would be awfully nice."

"Ale, sir?"

"Beer, whatever they have, something cold. Here, son, let me give you something." He handed Bruce a couple of coins.

Bruce brightened. "Yes, sir!" And he was off.

Annie sat on the arm of one of the seats, talking to the gawky girl actress whose name was Sally Ann and who played Topsy. Sally Ann stared into the mirror as she rubbed the black grease paint fiercely into her cheeks.

"You're an orphan, huh?"

"I guess," Annie said.

"You guess? You don't know?" Sally Ann said. "There's worse things, though. They're going to find you a nice home, some big old farm lady to make you beaten biscuits and pie. I'd rather be you, let me tell you."

"I bet you wouldn't," Annie said, hugging her cornhusk doll.

Sally Ann looked up from smearing grease paint in the corners of her nostrils. "Bet I would." Sally Ann looked quickly around the passenger car. "Maybe I should run off with you."

"You wouldn't like it," Annie said.

"How do you know?" Sally Ann said. "You think this is so wonderful? It ain't. They pick on a person all the time. Shout at you when you miss one silly line. Play favorites too." She flicked a grease-painted finger in the direction of Little Eva, who at the moment was the focus of Liverpool's swaggering attentions.

"You mean her?" Annie said.

"That's right. Little Eva! She's no actress, not really. She's well-drilled, that's all. You should have seen me when I was Little Eva. I made them cry, really cry . . . they had to lead ladies out of the theater at every performance, it was too much for them. I had a voice, I had presence, I had it all, but then I got breasts and I couldn't play Little Eva any more."

"It was 'cause of your breasts?" Annie said, looking dubiously at Sally Ann's chest.

"That's right," Sally Ann said bitterly.

"Little Eva can't have breasts?"

"That's what they say. So now I'm Topsy." Sally Ann, her face shining black, bent her head to one side to tie a bit of colored rag in her hair. "Now I do comedy. I'm funny, you'll see. But people used to cry over me. Now I've got breasts and I'm a comic figure."

Mr. Whitcomb stood in the door. "Come on, now, everybody, hurry it up. Time rushes on!"

* * *

Grim-faced, Emma waited as the actors rushed about hauling their props up to the depot platform, the excited children at their heels. She watched J.P. and Carlin talking to Asa Drew. The actor was in blackface now, and he bent over so that J.P. could feel the grease paint. J.P. showed them her smudged fingers and the three of them laughed. Emma waited, and finally her chance came—Drew took J.P. over to look at the dogs and Carlin stood alone.

"Mr. Carlin?"

He turned. "Yes, Miss Symns?"

"I think it's time we had a talk."

"Of course," he said.

"Not here," Emma said. Mr. Whitcomb rushed past, waving directions to his actors.

"That's all right with me," Carlin said. He regarded her skeptically. "You don't want to see the play?"

"I think this is more important, Mr. Carlin." Now he was starting to look interested. "Perhaps we could take a walk," Emma said.

J.P. looked up from scratching the ears of one of the dogs to see Miss Symns and Carlin pick their way across the tracks and head up the dirt road. J.P. felt her heart leap. Maybe, just maybe, they were going to talk about her; maybe Carlin was going to ask Miss Symns if he could take J.P. out west as his assistant. Scarcely aware that Mr. Whitcomb had mounted the steps of the depot and was announcing the start of the play, J.P. crossed her fingers in her pockets and watched as Miss Symns and Carlin moved slowly up the hill.

The streeters watched with mouths agape as Eliza leaped from one ice floe to the next, the bloodhounds howling in pursuit. There was no ice, of course, just the wooden slats of the platform, and the dogs weren't bloodhounds, just a pack of well-fed and somewhat spoiled mongrels. The only thing they were in pursuit of was the bit of raw meat that Eliza artfully concealed in her hand, except for the one or two blotches of blood that dripped to the depot platform as she made her escape.

Still, the illusion held. When Eliza made her final leap to the far shore, the streeters let go with whistles and a mighty cheer. The audience of children, train passengers, and the tavern crowd that had drifted down to have a look, all applauded till their hands hurt. Sarah was the only silent one, overcome by the performance.

Mr. Whitcomb stood just off the stage area, beaming at the response his entertainment was creating.

At the top of the hill, coming out of the tavern door, was Bruce, his hands cupped tenderly around a mug of beer.

Mr. Whitcomb patted his hair, smoothed out his vest, preparing himself for his entrance.

Down the hill Bruce came, rushing one moment, anxious to deliver his favor, then braking the next, afraid of spilling the beer in the grass. He came up behind Mr. Whitcomb just as the actor was pulling in his belly.

"Mr. Whitcomb?"

Mr. Whitcomb turned. "Yes?"

"I've brought your beer, sir."

"Beer?"

"You asked me to get you a beer."

"Well, thank you, son," the actor said vaguely, adjusting his collar.

"Mr. Whitcomb, sir." Exasperated, Bruce reached out and grabbed Mr. Whitcomb by the coat. This assault on his costume made the actor turn savagely, knocking the boy's hand away.

"I said thank you, now what do you expect? To be kissed and dandled upon the knee?"

Bruce stepped back, still balancing the mug.

Even as the applause was dying, Mr. Whitcomb recovered, fixed his tie, and walked into the bare dirt arena with the genial ease of a great man.

Bruce stood with the mug of beer in his hand. Tom came up to him.

"Hey, Bruce, is that for me?"

"No."

"Come on, Bruce, just a swallow." Tom reached for the mug, and Bruce whacked him in the head with his free hand. Beer sloshed to the ground.

"No," Bruce said.

They watched the actors for a moment in silence. Mr. Whitcomb played Mr. St. Clair, Little Eva's father, and he played wonderfully, every gesture carved out of the air spoke of strength, kindness, patience.

"Hey, Bruce, you savin' that for me?" This time it was Liverpool. Bruce didn't say anything. Liverpool reached out for the mug, and this time Bruce let it go. Ducking down so no one would see, Liverpool took a deep swallow.

"Hey, save some for me!" Tom hissed.

Liverpool handed the half-full mug to Tom, who quickly finished it off. Tom wiped his mouth with the back of his hand.

"Thanks, Bruce."

"Yeah. Thanks, Bruce. That was big of ya."

Stone-faced, Bruce looked at the two of them. "Come on," he said.

"Come on?" Tom said. "Where we goin'?"

Bruce walked off several paces. "Just come on."

"I'm staying here," Liverpool said. "I want to see the play."

Tom looked from Bruce to Liverpool and back again. He trotted after Bruce.

Mr. St. Clair had just given Topsy to Ophelia, the old-maid cousin from the North. Tony and Ben grinned and nudged one another at Ophelia's attempts at interviewing her.

"Who was your mother?"

Topsy grinned. "Never had a mother."

Ophelia looked astonished. One of the bloodhounds started moaning back in the audience, and Asa Drew patted it to calm it down.

"Never had any mother? What do you mean? Where were you born?"

Topsy took her time answering, playing to the gallery of streeters. "Never was born."

Patches giggled, wiped his nose, looked up at Sarah, and grinned.

"You mustn't answer me that way," Ophelia said. "Tell me where you were born and who your mother and father were."

Topsy rolled her eyes in the direction of Patches. "Never was born, tell you' never had no father, no mother, no nothin'. I was raised by a speculator . . ."

The streeters burst loose into whistling, hooting, and applause. Topsy just couldn't contain herself any longer. She slapped herself on her knees, leaped up, and ran out into the children, accepting their cheers and claps on the back. Mr. Whitcomb confined himself to looking very stern indeed, and it was Asa Drew and Mrs. Whitcomb who pried Topsy from her admirers and got her back on the stage.

J.P. stared up the dirt road at Emma and Carlin. He's going to ask her about me, she thought. He is, I know it. . . .

They walked side by side, silent at first, falling into stride. The trees at the top of the hill blazed red and orange. Blackbirds sat in the road and flew up as Emma and Carlin advanced toward them, only to settle farther on.

Finally Emma decided to plunge right in. "Mr. Carlin, yesterday I heard something that disturbed me very much." She waited for him to acknowledge that he knew what she was talking about, but he didn't. "I overheard J.P. talking with Sarah in the boxcar. He told Sarah why he'd been ducking all the placings-out. Do you know why?"

"No, why?"

"Because J.P. has a plan, a secret plan."

Carlin walked along, head down, kicking at the stones in the road. A blackbird sang mightily somewhere ahead of them. "You know how children talk. Children always have secret plans."

"J.P. said that you had promised to take him out west with you. As your apprentice."

Carlin turned, his mouth agape. "I what?"

"J.P. said that you promised to take him out west with you. That's not true?"

"Of course it's not true."

"Somehow he got this idea in his head. How do you think that happened?"

"How do I know? Boys get all kinds of things in their heads. You're not saying that I. . . ."

"You could have let him think. . . ."

"Oh now, Miss Symns!" Carlin bent down and picked up a rock, pitched it at the blackbirds sitting in the road ahead of them. The birds scattered and flapped away.

"You like the child," Emma said. "I see the two of you talking together."

"That's right, I talk to the boy. I like him. But you're not going to take me to task for being decent to a child, are you?"

"You can't toy with children's affections, Mr. Carlin. When you tell them things, they remember them. Things that may not mean very much to you can mean a great deal to them. If you are leaving in another day. . . ."

"Two days, Miss Symns."

"In another two days, whatever, and never expect to see the child again, you have no right to build up hopes. Trust is a fragile thing. These children have been cheated so many times, Mr. Carlin . . ."

"I do not care how many times they've been cheated, Miss Symns, I did not . . ."

"Oh, so you're indifferent . . ."

"No, I am not indifferent! The only reason I met that child in the first place was because I caught him breaking into my equipment. He nearly wrecked the stuff. I could have killed him on the spot, but I decided to be decent, charitable. . . ."

"He broke into your equipment?"

"That's right."

"You didn't tell me."

"No, I didn't tell you. J.P. made me promise not to tell. He was afraid you'd send him back. But there, now I've done it, betrayed a child's confidence. I'm just as bad as you say I am."

Emma stared at him. She was dismayed, angry at herself for again being so ready to think ill of him.

"I'm sorry, Mr. Carlin," she said.

In the heat of their discussion they had come to the top of the hill. Emma and Carlin stood in front of the stable and the now empty tavern, looking back down the slope at the crowd gathered in front of the depot. The actors parading back and forth on the depot platform seemed tiny and bright as tin soldiers.

"Miss Symns," Carlin said, almost hesitantly. "I thought that there might be some other reason why you'd asked me to go for a walk."

"Mr. Carlin, please . . ."

"Isn't it time to speak plainly, Miss Symns? There's no time to do anything else. I've grown very fond of you, Miss

Symns. . . ." He stopped for a second. "I think you're a very admirable person."

"Please stop thinking I'm admirable, Mr. Carlin."

"But you are."

"Mr. Carlin, you've met me on a train, under rather unusual circumstances. Perhaps you're a bit bored, there's no one to talk to . . . I can scarcely blame you . . . so you've taken a passing fancy to me."

"I'm not letting it pass, Miss Symns."

"Oh, Mr. Carlin, you don't know what you're saying."

He smiled. "So what are we going to do then?" he asked.

"We could go back and watch the play," Emma said.

"I can't stand actors," Carlin said.

Emma laughed a little. "You have very definite opinions, Mr. Carlin."

"What would you like to do?" he said.

"We could go in and look at the horses," she said. "Do you like horses, Mr. Carlin?"

"More than I like actors," he said. Their eyes met for a moment, and then he yanked open the door to the stable.

"It's about the most sorrowful excuse for a deathbed scene you ever saw, isn't it? Look at her, Annie. All she does is roll her eyes around and shake her hands a little."

"She has a lot of lines," Annie said.

"That's right," Topsy said. "That's about all you can say for her, she knows her lines." Hands on hips, Topsy stood beside Annie, delivering a running critique of Little Eva's death. "I mean, look at that! It's an imitation, that's all it is! You've got to feel it—that's what I did."

"Shhh!" Annie said, without looking up.

Topsy gave Annie a skeptical stare and shrugged.

Cattle bells jangled in a nearby pasture; a dog stood on the tracks and barked; the surrounding hills were bright with fall colors; yet no one heard or saw anything but the child dying on her bed. Little Eva had them all in the hollow of her hand, all except J.P., who kept glancing up toward the hilltop.

"Papa," Little Eva said in her tremulous voice. "Isn't there a way to have slaves made free? If I should die, won't you think of me, and do it for my sake?"

Mr. Whitcomb shook his head sadly. The audience was so still that the wind rustling the stand of poplar on the far side of the tracks went through them like a shiver. "Oh, child, don't talk to me so! You are all I have on earth!"

Little Eva pulled herself up, the sheets falling from her shoulders, draping her.

"You see?" Topsy said. "She's got no grasp. You can't rush like that. . . . It's a question of timing . . ."

"Shhh!" Annie said.

"Papa, those poor creatures love their children as much as you do me." She looked at Uncle Tom, at the black-faced Asa Drew, singer of blue songs, rheumatic vaudeville dancer, who was wringing his hands in grief. "Tom loves his children." She turned her fevered face back to her father, reached up and took his hand. "Oh, do something for them!"

Mr. St. Clair patted her hand. "There, there, darling, I will do everything you wish."

The audience stood silent, transfixed by Little Eva's power to reunite parents and children through her death; the dying child seemed to loom from her bed, fluttering like a great white butterfly against the stone depot wall. J.P. stared up the hill, shielding her eyes from the afternoon sun. Carlin and Miss Symns had disappeared into the stable.

The stable was dark and still, the only light the shafts of late-afternoon sun gleaming through the narrow windows, the only sounds the occasional clop of a hoof and the soft cooing of birds high above in the rafters.

"Why is it you don't like actors?" Emma said.

"Their vanity, I guess. They all take themselves so seriously."

"But you don't take yourself seriously?" Emma said.

Carlin smiled. "Oh, I think I take myself quite seriously, Miss Symns," he said.

Emma moved a step or two ahead of him, her long skirt picking up bits of straw as it brushed the floor. "Tell me about your trip. You're leaving in two days. For where?"

"I catch the stage in Springfield. That will take me to St. Louis."

"Where you meet the general," Emma said.

Carlin smiled, picking up a bridle from one of the pegs on one of the stalls. "You know about that?"

"I overheard J.P. talking to Sarah. I told you."

"And what else did you hear?" Carlin said.

"That you're going into the mountains with a general. To search out possible routes for a railroad."

"Well, at least J.P. got that right," Carlin said.

"And you're taking the pictures." Horses moved uneasily in their stalls. "That's very exciting," Emma said.

"It is."

"And very important work, too."

"I think so." A barn cat slunk quickly by them.

"Have you been planning this for a long time?"

"It took me two years of scheming to get this appointment," Carlin said. He put the bridle back on its peg.

"How long will you be gone?" Emma said.

"I don't know. It could be a year. It could be longer. Miss Symns . . ." He reached out, caught her by the arm.

Emma pulled gently away, reached up and patted the soft muzzle of one of the horses. "You're a nice man, I enjoy talking to you, you mean well, I know that, Mr. Carlin . . ."

"But?" he said.

"I didn't say but," she said, turning back to face him.

"Then don't."

"This is impossible, Mr. Carlin."

"How do you know? I'm very drawn to you, Miss Symns. I admire you, I enjoy talking to you, too. I respect your courage, your seriousness, but also I'm attracted to you and I want you to admit that you're attracted to me. I know you are."

"I don't know how much attraction could count for, Mr. Carlin."

"What does count, then?"

"Our intentions, perhaps," she said.

He was still for a second, then reached out and took her by the waist. "Don't pull back," he said. "Unless you mean it. Unless that's your intention."

Emma stared at him, her eyes wide. She let her arms fall slowly to her side.

He took her by both arms and kissed her, then held her close to him. "Miss Symns, Miss Symns . . ." he said, almost making a lilt of it. She grasped his hands tightly, kept them there at his sides as she took a step back. She looked up at him. There were tears in her eyes. She turned and ran out of the stable.

Little Eva's death quickened. Dr. Tansy looked up to see Bruce and Tom come meandering back into the crowd to stand next to Liverpool. The onstage actors pressed around the bed.

"Do you know me, darling?"

"Dear, dear papa! Mama, please, kiss me!" Mrs. St. Clair bent down and kissed her. "Uncle Tom, now I'm happy." Little Eva sighed.

So did Topsy, in exasperation, offstage.

Uncle Tom suddenly looked out over the train.

"Look! Look! Massa, she can see things that we can't see!" Uncle Tom knelt, swinging out his bum leg.

Eva stared out before her, smiling. "I see . . . I see . . . the crystal gates, wide—wide open—love—joy—peace . . ."

Her head fell to one side, the blond curls tumbled along her white neck. The nurse reached for Little Eva's pulse.

Everyone waited for the nurse. "It is over."

"You can say that again," Topsy whispered.

"Shh!" hissed Annie, angrily.

Mr. St. Clair sobbed once, and then, his voice deep and emotional, spoke. "Eva! My darling!"

All the offstage actors had their musical instruments ready, and they struck them up, right on cue. The actors turned and took their bows. Little Eva hopped up and shook out her curls, curtsied, and held out her palms for the receiving and bestowing of blessings. Both men and women were sobbing, everyone beat their palms red. Dr. Tansy was wiping away a tear, and the farmer next to him, a man with a face as creased as salted beef, wept into his hands.

"Now this is where Little Eva goes up to Heaven on a board," Topsy said. "But since we're not in a real theater there's no way to rig the board." Mr. Whitcomb was waving for Topsy to come take her bow. "Too bad you can't see it," Topsy said. "It's a nice effect."

A long, piercing shriek of a whistle cut the air, and everyone looked up, the dogs began to howl. Half a mile down the track, smoke billowing and sparks flying, was the southbound train, coming in as if on cue.

Once the southbound came into the station there was a great rush of activity: passengers switching trains, children, full of admiration, tugging at the actors, the station agent stumbling over dogs and their leashes as he tried to transfer baggage from one train to the other.

Alone, J.P. walked down the dirt road to meet Emma.

"Hello, Miss Symns."

"Hello, J.P."

Miss Symns looked very upset, J.P. thought. "Did you have a nice walk?"

"Yes, I had a nice walk."

"You and Mr. Carlin?"

"That's right," Emma said sharply. J.P.'s bright expectancy was more than Emma could bear. The child really believed that Carlin . . . "J.P., what are you thinking?"

"Nothing."

"I know what you're thinking, J.P. I think somehow you've gotten the idea you're going out west with Mr. Carlin."

J.P. looked up at Emma, stunned. "What do you mean?" she said.

"Mr. Carlin never promised you that he would take you, and you shouldn't be telling people that he did."

"I didn't," J.P. said, her lip trembling.

"You did. I overheard you telling Sarah. Mr. Carlin's a nice man, J.P., he's been very kind and attentive to you; but in two days he's going to St. Louis. By himself. He never promised you anything, did he, J.P.?"

"No, Miss Symns." J.P. looked away to hide her tears.

Emma took J.P.'s hand. "Just so we all understand that. How was the play?"

"It was good," J.P. said.

"Come along, then, the train will be leaving in a minute."

In the rosy afterglow of the performance, Liverpool and Sarah asked Emma if they could ride up in the passenger car with the actors. Emma said that that would be fine. Topsy came back to ride in the boxcar with the rest of the children.

The engine was all stoked up and ready to go, everyone in their place. They were all set to steam right on into Glory when suddenly a voice rang out.

"Stop this train!"

Mr. Whitcomb leaned out the window of the passenger car, waving for the engineer.

The engineer looked back. "What is it, Mr. Whitcomb?"

"There's been a robbery."

Mr. Whitcomb's cream-colored cape and his silver-headed cane were missing. The conductor was in no mood for a search. He was already behind schedule, he'd made a delay for the actors, and he couldn't make another.

Mr. Whitcomb was adamant. His silver-headed cane was invaluable, an antique, given to him by Lola Montez when he was on his European tour.

"I can't run a railroad this way, Mr. Whitcomb, I'm sorry." The conductor shook his head.

"Sir, you can't know what that cane means to me. I implore you, sir. . . . I can no more go on without that cane than you can go on without this train. In the name of Humanity, sir, I beg you, just fifteen minutes. . . ."

The conductor looked down at his feet. "Awright," he said, finally, "but fifteen minutes is all you get."

Dr. Tansy was at Mr. Whitcomb's shoulder. "Mr. Whitcomb, I don't want to give advice, but if I were you, the first thing I'd check out would be those kids."

Mr. Whitcomb looked at Dr. Tansy, then at the children, who were milling about, one or two hanging out of the windows of the passenger car. "Yes, of course," he said quietly. "Of course."

Emma had just climbed down from the boxcar and, hand in hand with Annie, was approaching the men.

"Is there a problem here, Mr. Whitcomb?" Emma asked.

Mr. Whitcomb explained about the missing cape and cane, impressing on her the values of these items, and, though he wasn't casting any aspersions, children had been known to run off with things. . . .

"These children particularly," Dr. Tansy said. "These light-fingered rascals have been involved in a lot worse than this."

Emma gathered the children in front of the boxcar for a talk. Topsy and Eva listened in. Emma explained the situation as matter-of-factly as she could, but it didn't matter; the children stood silent and morose, not looking at her. They felt accused and unjustly so. When she asked if anyone had seen the cane, no one spoke.

Emma returned to Mr. Whitcomb. "They say no, Mr. Whitcomb."

"No?" Mr. Whitcomb's face hardened as he looked past her to the group of silent children. "Well, I think we'd better begin a very careful search."

For fifteen minutes, Mr. Whitcomb and the actors searched every inch of the train, turning over seats, going through luggage, searching the entire depot area. Emma had the children help too, which they did grudgingly. Dr. Tansy, wiggling a finger, motioned her over. The two of them spoke quietly for several minutes.

Emma climbed into the boxcar. Bruce and Tom were sitting together on one of the benches. When Emma pulled the door half shut behind her they looked up in surprise.

"It seems to me," Emma said, "that I have trusted you boys."

"What do you mean, Miss Symns?" Bruce said.

"Do either of you have any idea what happened to Mr. Whitcomb's possessions this afternoon?"

They shook their heads in unison. Bruce, his mouth in a pout, looked down at his nails.

"I don't know why it is stuff always gets blamed on us," he said. "Doesn't seem square with me. Just 'cause we've been in trouble once, anything goes wrong, they come lookin' for us. Other people could have taken that stuff, you know."

"That's right," Tom said. "It could have been one of them people from the other train."

"It could have been," Emma said. "Dr. Tansy saw you two leave, you know."

Tom's eyes widened for a second.

"Leave where?" Bruce said.

"You walked away from the play in the middle."

"I don't like plays," Bruce said. "I think they're boring. So does Tom. We went for a walk after. Just like you. Right, Tom?"

Tom nodded.

"You can't make us say we did something we didn't do, Miss Symns," Bruce said.

"No," Emma said. The three of them were silent. Through the slats of the boxcar they could see the bright, flitting images of the searchers.

"What are you thinking, Miss Symns?" Tom said. Tom was getting worried by the silence. "What do you want us to do?" he asked.

"Will you give me your word that you didn't take Mr. Whitcomb's cane and cape?"

Bruce looked at Tom, whose eyes were filled with torment.

"I give my word," Bruce said calmly. "How about you, Tom?"

"I . . . I give my word," Tom said faintly.

Emma straightened up. "All right, then. There's nothing more to say."

Emma climbed down from the boxcar. The two boys were alone.

The floor was lined with bars of light. Tom sat on his blanket, picking absently at the corners. Bruce moved silently to the wall of the boxcar, stared out through the slats.

Tom looked up at Bruce, stricken. Bruce looked down. Mr. Whitcomb stood only a foot or two away, close enough for Bruce to see the beads of sweat standing out on his forehead, the specks of soot that dotted the cream-colored suit. Bruce pressed silently against the slats as the disheveled man walked below him.

Nothing was found. The conductor insisted that they had delayed as long as they could, and everyone got on board. Mr. Whitcomb was the object of much sympathy, but remained inconsolable. It seemed to Carlin that Whitcomb was acting like a child, but then Whitcomb had covered himself by saying how much actors were like children. Mr. Whitcomb was as grief-stricken as Job. He had been generous, he had made a gesture, put on a free show for the orphaned children—and then to have his prize possessions disappear. . . . Well, it took the heart out of him, or at the very least, the wind. To Carlin he seemed visibly deflated.

The other passengers clucked over him, told him how noble he was, and how unfortunate it was, but you just can't trust children, unreformable, really, vicious, untrustworthy, a losing proposition; if it weren't for the sentiments of mothers, there'd be a bounty on them, and wasn't it the case that some times bad news came in small packages?

Mr. Whitcomb didn't really listen. He sat next to the window, his elderly wife whispering secret, girlish consolations to him, an old, wrinkled figure staring out into the night.

Emma slept fitfully that night. There were stops for water and wood, and once Ben cried out, frightened by his dreams about dying children. He had to be rocked back to sleep, Emma reassuring him that Little Eva wasn't really dead, it was all pretend. Two or three times, perhaps, Emma thought she heard the door to the boxcar open and close, and once she did look up to see the face of the young fireman at the boxcar door. "Just makin' sure you're all right back here," he said.

Every time she was awakened she had trouble getting back to sleep. She didn't even know for sure that Mr. Whitcomb's cape and cane had been stolen; they could just have been misplaced, picked up by accident with other baggage. But it was night, and everything appeared in its worst light. The theft meant that she was a failure, that the children had learned nothing. She shouldn't have taken the walk with Carlin, turning her back on her responsibilities. Carlin kissing her, her letting him, meant . . . oh, she didn't know. . . . She felt a terrible attraction for him, and yet he was leaving in two days. What point could there be?

In the morning the train arrived in Toledo. The troupe's advance man was at the station to meet them. The actors said goodbye to the passengers, stretched, and began to make their way from the train. Mr. Whitcomb stood on the platform, looking somewhat recovered, though he was still a little white and shaken. He ordered the other actors around with a gruff vigor, but they weren't snapping to with the same energy they had shown previously.

Asa Drew and Chauncey, the actor who had played Simon Legree, ambled back to the baggage car and yanked open the door.

"Edward! Edward! Look at this!"

Asa Drew held both arms aloft. In one hand was the cream-colored cape, and in the other, glittering in the morning light, was the silver-headed cane.

Mr. Whitcomb's eyes went as wide as a child's at his first Christmas. He couldn't speak. He stumbled to Asa Drew, lifted the cape from him and then the cane.

The cape was covered with dust from the floor of the baggage car, and Mr. Whitcomb gave it a couple of good shakes. He twirled the cane, as if to see that it still had its full powers. He beamed.

Children stood staring from the door of the boxcar, Bruce stared at Mr. Whitcomb, watched him spin his cane in the air. Bruce turned back, looking for Tom. Tom was kneeling in the corner, tying his shoes. He refused to look up.

There was a good deal of speculation about the reappearance of the lost cane and cape. The actors swore they had checked and doublechecked the car the afternoon before. Dr. Tansy, switching sides again, was saying very loudly, Didn't they all feel bad now, blaming everything on those poor, homeless children?

None of it mattered to Mr. Whitcomb. His authority had been restored, the rest could be forgotten. He returned quickly to full voice. "Into costume, everybody! Come on, now, Sally Ann, there are people waiting. . . . Costumes! Chauncey, let's water the dogs! Little Eva, your carriage is here!"

It didn't take the actors long at all to get back into costume. They fit back into their characters as easily as a hand slides into an old, familiar glove. They used the station house to change, and with Mr. Whitcomb and the advance man exhorting them, were ready in what seemed only minutes.

They came to say goodbye to the children as if nothing had happened.

"J.P.! J.P.!" Asa Drew reached out and scrunched up J.P.'s newsboy cap. "Now any time you think you want to hook up and be a team—I'm ready when you are." He winked and put her cap back on her head.

Liverpool stood alongside Little Eva's tiny carriage and said a stuttering goodbye, Topsy waved to Annie, and Tony and Ben patted the bloodhounds one last time. Bruce sat in the door of the boxcar, just watching.

"Ready?" Mr. Whitcomb said, raising his silver-headed cane.

"Ready!" the actors chorused back.

"All right then, Thespians. Let us bedazzle the citizenry of Toledo!"

The horn players bleated their first notes, the drummer set in on his thumping, and they were off. Down the main street they went, the blackface actors out front, singing and dancing, Topsy weaving in and out like some imp, then Simon Legree, glowering, jangling, snapping his whips over the happily panting bloodhounds, then Little Eva, the blond child goddess in her gently rocking black carriage, her mother and father walking patiently alongside. One after the other, heads poked out of windows, people came out of doors; the blacksmith and the storekeeper, the deacons and the farmers, the shoemaker and the justice of the peace, all came out to see what miracle was transpiring on their dry, dusty street.

*B*ruce turned it into a hard day, bullying and ragging the other children. Emma's warnings didn't help; it was as if he had the devil in him.

Bruce made Tom his special target. Bruce kept bringing up the fight with the country boys. If Tom hadn't been a coward, if Tom had shown any grit at all, it would have turned out different.

Tom took the abuse without any attempt at fighting back, but it was getting on the nerves of the other children.

"We might as well face up," Bruce said. "This whole trip is just a bust. It's all for nothin'. Nothin's gonna happen but what's already happened. Nobody's gonna take us, we're the bottom of the barrel."

"Shut up, Bruce," Liverpool said.

"We're just like all these other crazy people goin' west, we're the bummers, the ones who couldn't make it nowhere, and we think it's gotta be better somewhere else, but it's not gonna be."

Liverpool leaped across at Bruce and threw a wild punch that just missed his head. Bruce retaliated with a quick right hand that caught Liverpool in the chest. The two of them grappled, rolling on the floor.

"Bruce! Liverpool! Stop it! Stop it!" Emma reached for the struggling children, and then Patches and Tom and Sarah came to help her, pulling the two combatants apart.

J.P. stood near the stove, refusing to help. Bruce was right, she thought, nobody's going to take us, nothing's going to happen but what's already happened.

In Fort Wayne a new locomotive came on and so did a new crew. The conductor was a nervous man, small and dumpy, constantly checking his watch while the engineer, a homely, lanky young man with huge hands, paid him no mind. The engineer stood outside the train, trading jokes with the fireman, who was busy oiling the valves with his tallow pot.

The sawmill owner and the farm family disembarked, while several new passengers came on: a bearded preacher, a printer from Peoria, and a fearsome-looking riverboatman named Joe Plug, a burly fellow in a red shirt and yarn suspenders who'd been visiting his mother in Fort Wayne.

Carlin wandered out from the lunchroom and came back to the boxcar, where J.P. was sitting in the open door. He offered her half his sandwich. She refused him without a word, jumping down and running off to join Sarah at the outdoor pump.

Finally the conductor snapped his watch shut and hollered down to the engineer. "Let's get movin', Sam, we've got a schedule to keep."

The engineer tipped his hat to the conductor, and then he

and the fireman climbed up into the locomotive and they were off.

Some time after ten in the evening the train began to slow down. Some of the children awoke and peered out the door into the dark countryside. "What is it, Miss Symns?"

"Not another accident, it can't be."

"There ain't no town here, Miss Symns, look. . . ."

The train shuddered and came to a full stop. When J.P. and Liverpool leaned way out the door, the first thing they could see was the lanterns bobbing far down the track, moving toward them. After a moment a man on horseback and a horse-drawn wagon bearing two men came into view.

The men got down from the wagon and trudged toward the engine. The engineer came down to meet them. As the men spoke, the children whispered among themselves: Were they outlaws? Bandits? Was it a robbery? Annie hid her cornhusk doll under her straw mattress just in case.

The men spoke in low, harsh accents. The two men speaking with the engineer had full beards and the lantern light flickering made their faces seem glittering, hard, as carved as the faces of Old Testament prophets. The horseman stayed back, away from the light, the big animal snorting and moving uneasily on the wood ties.

The two men walked back to their wagon and returned carrying a pine box about four feet long. The engineer led them back to the baggage car. The conductor watched from the step of the passenger car, his face impassive.

As they passed the boxcar, the engineer looked up at Emma. "Don't worry, miss," he said. "We'll be moving again in a minute. We're just putting on a little freight."

The baggage-car door was opened and the pine box put aboard. The engineer and the two men talked briefly, and then the two men trudged back to their wagon and the engineer back to the engine. The horseman and the wagon rode off into the darkness.

The engineer watched them go, then climbed back up into the engine. As he did, J.P. suddenly jumped out of the box-car.

"J.P.!" Emma shouted after her. "What are you doing?" J.P. dashed toward the baggage car without looking back. "Get back in here!"

J.P. struggled with the baggage-car door. "I'm going to sleep back here."

"J.P.!"

"I want to sleep by myself once, is that all right? I'm not hurting anybody."

"No, J.P.," Emma said.

"You can't stop me, Miss Symns." Grabbing the corner of the door, J.P. scrambled up into the car.

The train shuddered, slipped forward, shuddered again, and began to move. All Emma could see of J.P. was the spritelike face, peering around the edge of the door.

"I'm not hurting anybody, Miss Symns. . . ." J.P. shouted out at her, and then the baggage-car door slammed shut.

Emma took a deep breath and leaned against the slats of the boxcar. She would talk to the child again in the morning.

J.P. was alone in the dark baggage car. It had been a long time since she'd spent any time alone. The baggage car smelled of leather and of sawdust, and, very faintly, of dogs. It was a little frightening too.

J.P. groped her way through the car and found an old blanket that she folded up to use as a pillow. She slid several trunks around until she had made herself a nest, and then she lay down.

She was just as glad. Just as glad that that Carlin didn't want her to go with him. Who would want to be working with a bunch of smelly chemicals all day anyway and him always carrying on about his precious equipment. . . . She hoped that a pack mule with all his plates would slip and crash into some canyon, that would serve him right. . . .

As she slipped closer to sleep, her mind began to move back to the afternoon with the actors, their gestures, their bright costumes, bits of their songs . . . *I drink the eau de vie.* . . . She had been crazy to get up and sing with Asa Drew, what had she been thinking. She didn't want to have anything to do with actors either, with their fake tears and their embraces and their protests of love . . . her mother's admirers with their bouquets and their high black hats. . . . Oh, so you're her daughter, I can see you're going to be a beauty, too . . . and their soft hands reaching out toward her. She thought of Lizzie the Dove's hands and then the long stained fingers of the blind beggar. She didn't want that, didn't, didn't. They were never going to get her back, never. . . .

The only sound was the steady click of the rails beneath her. She was moving west, moving away, away from actors, to some wilderness where there were no theaters, no orchestras, away from her mother's crying, away from the arguing voices, the soft-handed, high-hatted men standing in the half-closed door, not letting her mother shut that door, not letting J.P. ever sleep. . . . J.P. was going away, into some wilderness, where there was stillness.

J.P. fell asleep and dreamed. She dreamed of her mother. Her mother was on stage in a play and it wasn't in America, but someplace foreign, the painted scenery was of impossibly blue lakes and high mountains. Her mother was radiant in the play, weeping and laughing and dancing. She had the audience enraptured.

When the curtain swept down, the applause was thunderous. The audience rose to its feet, and when her mother

stepped out they wouldn't let her go. Young men in cutaways brought bouquet after bouquet from the wings. Her
mother's face was shining. She looked out over the audience,
her eyes searching, and when she saw J.P. she stretched out
a hand, gesturing for J.P. to come join her. J.P. pushed her
way through the crowd, and suddenly she noticed it wasn't
just a theater crowd—there were people there in dark
ragged clothes. Bruce was there, and sweaty, soot-covered
men blocking her way. J.P. struggled and pushed forward,
led on by her mother's gesturing, till she finally stood just
below the stage.

Her mother bent toward her, beckoning her prettily. J.P.
reached up, she could just reach the stage with her fingertips, but she couldn't get a hold, not a real one, and she kept
falling back. Her mother became angry and began to stamp
her little slippered feet on the stage floor, still gesturing, but
impatient now. The elegant young men stood beside her
mother, waiting with their bouquets of flowers tied with red
ribbons. J.P. tried to claw her way up, but she couldn't, she
kept slipping back, again and again. Her mother's face was
hard and pinched now, she stamped her feet, stamped
harder, and J.P. was crying.

J.P. woke with a start. There was a sound in the baggage
car, the sound of something moving. J.P. lay very still. She
heard the sound again. It wasn't the sound of a rat, no, it
was the sound of something heavier.

She heard it a third time. This time J.P. moved quickly
and silently among the trunks. She knelt beside the pine box
that the bearded men had brought aboard the train. Her
heart was pounding. She put her ear to the box. She heard
breathing.

J.P. sat silently for a second. In the darkness she could
make out a small white sign: THIS SIDE UP: HANDLE WITH
CARE. There was something alive inside. An animal. It made

her angry. It was terrible to nail up an animal like that, there weren't even any air holes, it was a wretched, mean thing to do.

She knocked softly on the box with her fist. The sound of breathing stopped, J.P. knocked again; there was only stillness, the click of the rails.

J.P. felt along the dirty floor of the car with her hands, patting over the leather bags and wooden trunks till her fingertips found the handle of a hoe. Using the sharp edge as a wedge, J.P. worked away at the pine box, prying under one of the boards. Finally she pulled the board free with her hands and stared into the eyes of a man curled tight inside the box.

"Who are you?" he hissed at her.

"Who are you?" J.P. moved back, grabbing the hoe.

Using his hands, the man painfully began to work his way out of the box, squirming like a butterfly out of a wood cocoon, or Lazarus out of the grave. He was black.

"What side you workin' fo'?"

J.P. held up the hoe in a swinging position. "I'm not working for any side."

"You mighty little fo' an abolitionist," the man said.

"What's an abolitionist?" J.P. said.

The man stretched out, grimacing as he felt the lower part of his back. He was a tall man, almost six feet tall, in overalls, no shoes, with a scraggly few days' growth of beard on his chin. He scrutinized J.P.

"You're just a young boy, ain't ya?"

"Anything wrong with that?"

"No. Just that you should look what you're doing with that hoe. You ain't careful you're likely to bang somebody back of the head." J.P. lowered the hoe a bit. "Not much more than a pup," the man murmured. "What's your name, pup?"

"J.P. What's yours?"

"My name's Ned."

"Where you coming from, Ned?"

"Now, what does that matter, where I come from? Why would you want to know that?"

"No reason," J.P. said. "Where you going then?"

Ned sat down on one of the trunks. He didn't trust J.P., not quite yet. "Same direction as you, I guess," Ned said.

"You're going west," J.P. said.

Ned looked at her, frowning. "What do you mean, west? I'm going north."

"No, you're not, you're going west."

"No, I'm not. I'm going north. I'm going to Canada, what are you talking about?" Ned pushed himself up from the trunk he was leaning on and went to the railway-car door. He peered out through the slats into the night. "That's not north?"

"Nope," J.P. said, putting down the hoe. "Going from Toledo to Danville."

Ned pondered for a minute. "Huh. If you're lyin' to me . . ."

"I'm not lyin'," J.P. said.

"Well, there's a reason, I know there is. They'll put me on another train, I know they will. . . . I been on so many trains, you wouldn't believe it." He peered out into the night. "It's all right . . . they wouldn't be trickin' me. . . . Ain't no way to be runnin' an Underground Railroad, though, you gotta say it." He looked back at J.P. "It's all part of the plan you see. . . . As long as we're movin' it's part of the plan. . . . But what are you doin' back here?"

"I got tired of the others," J.P. said.

"What others is that?"

"We're all orphans," J.P. said. "They're placing us out on farms and places like that. They think it'll make us better citizens. But they're all no-good kids, anyway, and I just couldn't stand 'em any more."

"I can see that," Ned said. He arched his back, feeling with his hand. "Oww, I got a crick back there. Anybody in charge of you orphans?"

"There's a lady in charge of us."

"Sure don't sound like you like that lady."

"She's all right. She's a little churchy, but she's all right. She means to do right, you know what I mean? Just that I don't know that I should trust her."

"What do you mean, you can't trust her?"

"She says she's gonna find us homes. And she doesn't know, really. . . ."

"If she says she will, she will," Ned said firmly.

"Oh, come on, you don't know any more than she does!"

"You believe in her, that's all I'm sayin'. That's the only chance you've got, young man."

"But how can I know?"

"The only chance you've got!" Ned said. The car swayed. Ned stumbled and then regained his balance. "If we can't believe in people, we all stuck. You take me now, J.P., I ran away. Did it all on my own, nobody tol' me to do it, made the break to freedom. But for me to make it all the way, I need other folks, all kind of folks, black ones and white ones, green ones if I got to, folks I never laid my eyes on in my life. I been hidin' in the brakes at nighttime and people's barns in the daytime, bumpin' along in the back of some wagon with all kinds of octoroons, mulattos, runaways of very kind of color, not knowin' which way we was headed. Only thing I could do was trust, young man, that's my point, I had to believe, that's what kept me from breakin' down. . . . So when the people say, Get off here and go hide in them woods and it's the middle of the night and the slave hunters are back there somewhere, why I do it, and I wait in them woods listenin' to the crickets singin' and hearin' every lull in the wind and waitin' for that lantern swingin', comin' toward me . . . trustin' that it's the right somebody hangin' onto that lantern. . . . That's where you end up trustin' to some odd-lookin' folks, deacons and whiskey drinkers, hunters, and some strange-talkin' farmer folk. . . ."

"Hmm," J.P. said skeptically.

"If I can get in a box and have 'em nail me up like I was dead and trust that they're gonna ship me to Canada, well, that's puttin' yourself in people's hands." J.P. scratched her neck, looking sour. "You ain't gonna give up now, are you?"

"Did I say I was givin' up?"

"You're gonna find a home, same as me," Ned said.

"Mmm," J.P. said.

"There you go again, mm-ing and mmm-ing. You ever hear the story about the two frogs in the pail of milk?"

"No," J.P. said.

"Well, I'm goin' to tell it to you then. Seems there was these two frogs that fell into a pail of milk and they been swimmin' and swimmin' for hours and there don't seem to be no way to get out, the lip of the pail is higher than they can reach with their webbed feet and things are lookin' bad. They're both powerful tired, they feel like their legs are about to drop off, and one of 'em—he's sorta your mmm-ing type frog—he says he just can't make it any more, he just can't, and without no more talk, he sinks right to the bottom of the pail. Now the other one, he's just as tired as the first, but he keeps goin' on anyhow, just keeps on keepin' on, till he's about knocked out. And when he wakes up next morning, there he is, sitting on a pad of butter."

J.P. smiled in the darkness.

"Now ain't that a good story?" Ned said. "Huh?" Ned pulled his arms back, stretching like a rooster. "Lord, but it's nice to have some room to move around in."

"It is a nice story," J.P. said. "It is."

"You don't happen to have anything to eat on you, do you, J.P.?"

"No," J.P. said.

Ned draped himself across a pair of trunks. "Well, don't worry about it none. It's nice to jus' stretch out for a little while."

They both fell silent, the only sound the clicking of the rails. An hour could have passed, or even two. J.P. was almost asleep when she realized that the clicking of the rails sounded wrong. She didn't know what it was at first, and then she realized that the time between the clicks was growing, the train was slowing down. She sat upright and looked around wildly. It was still night. Ned sat already poised and alert.

"What is it, Ned?"

"I dunno, but I figure Lazarus done raised himself up a bit early." Ned went to the slats of the car and peered out. J.P. was quickly at his side.

"I don't see any stop," J.P. said.

"That's 'cause there ain't no stop," Ned said. His voice was light and humorous, as if the whole thing sort of tickled him. "Well, now, son, I better be cozyin' down in my pine box again. I'm trustin' in you, son, to hammer me back in real good. You can do that?"

"Sure," J.P. said, her voice a little frightened.

Ned folded himself back into the box, tucked his head in just as the train whistle screeched. There was the scream of the brakes. J.P. picked up the loose board. Her hands were trembling.

Ned grinned at her. 'It's okay, son, it's okay. You come up to Canada sometime and I'll take you for a ride on a moose."

J.P. fitted the board in place, fumbled in the dark to fit the nails in the nail holes. With the back of the hoe she hammered the nails back in place, hammering quickly, afraid that someone would hear her.

The train had come to a complete halt.

J.P. went to the door and looked out. There was a group of men on horseback on the tracks, lanterns at their side. One of the men rode down the track, the horse picking its way gingerly. The engineer leaned out to greet him. The two men talked. In the light from the lantern J.P. could see a badge shining on the horseman's chest.

J.P. jumped down, shut the baggage car door behind her, and walked slowly toward the orphan car. She was greeted with jeers. "Too dark for ya, J.P.?" "Kinda skeery?" "Bad dreams, J.P.?" "Not too good for us any more, J.P.?" J.P. ignored them, plopped down on her blanket, and said nothing.

The sheriff climbed into the passenger car. Another of his men came back and poked his head into the orphan car.

"Well, I can't believe it's true," he said. He was a lean young man with a puppy-dog manner, and a big country smile that split his face a little sideways. "They tol' me there was a load of orphans back here and damn if it isn't true . . . 'scuse my language, miss."

Emma was in her duster, which she had pulled around her in her most haughty manner. "May I ask why you're disturbing us?" Emma said.

"Oh, we're just lookin' through the train, miss. The sheriff's received a complaint. . . . Sorry for waking you up like this." He looked inside the boxcar, his face curious. "Say, you fixed it up real nice." He beamed at a very grouchy-looking Patches. "Say, now, how you kids likin' it out here in the West?" No one spoke. Liverpool and Bruce rolled over and tried to go back to sleep. Ben was picking his nose sleepily, staring at the deputy. "You don't have to all pipe up at once," the man said.

The sheriff jumped down from the passenger car, landing heavily, jangling like a bag of loose change. He walked back toward them. J.P. stood up, taking her blanket with her, and clung to the boxcar door.

The young deputy wasn't to be discouraged. "Well, I suppose it would be hard for you, getting used to it, I mean. It's not the big city, that's for sure. I read in some magazine where they got them big clipper ships now. Boy, I'd like to see one of them. And the Latting Observatory where you can go up on a steam elevator. My Uncle Robert, he'd love that, 'cause he says there's nothing he hates more than going up the stairs. . . ."

The sheriff looked up at the orphans. Two of his men stood just back of him with lanterns. One of the men had a shotgun under his arm. "Mornin', miss," the sheriff said. "Let's go, Emmett."

"I'll be with you in a minute, sheriff."

The sheriff and the two older deputies walked to the baggage car. J.P. watched them, holding herself back. The sheriff stood aside and let his two men pull open the baggage-car door.

"Any of you ever ride on a steam elevator?"

"I did," Tony said.

"Me too," said Ben.

"You did, huh?" Emmett tousled Ben's hair. "How'd you like it?"

"Good," Tony said. Ben nodded.

"I tell you, I know how you kids must feel. My dad, he died when I was little and I had to pretty much raise myself, though my Uncle Robert he helped me out some, he really did . . . but it was a hard time anyway."

Most of the children were rolling themselves back into their blankets, sleepily paying half attention to the deputy. The deputy, however, was as wide awake as if it was the middle of the morning—there was a kind of excitement in his voice. It made Emma feel that there was something wrong. She looked back toward the baggage car.

"Emmett, get back here!"

"Be there in a second, sheriff!" the deputy shouted back.

"I'll tell you young folks something. If you want to make something of yourself, and you ain't got nobody to help you, this is the country to do it in. The people out here, you meet them halfway, they'll open their hearts to you. Honest. No lyin'."

The deputy noticed J.P. and Emma staring back toward the baggage car, and he looked back too. The sheriff stood outside while his two other deputies searched inside the car; their lanterns shone eerily out through the slats.

The deputy tousled Ben's hair again and looked up at Emma. "Now, miss, I don't know what you'd think of this. . . . My sister, she lost a baby in childbirth last year and they've been tryin', but you know how it goes. I don't know what your procedure is, but I'll bet you a bottom dollar she'd take one of your kids."

There was the sound of breaking wood and then a shout.

J.P. leaped out of the boxcar and ran. Emma started to go after her, but the deputy suddenly stepped out in front of the door, his hands held out in warning.

"Now, just take it easy, miss. It's nothin' for you to be gettin' mixed up in."

The shouts of two, three men rose together. The deputy may have been able to hold back Emma, but the children started jumping out of the boxcar like rats, slipping by Emmett on every side. Emmett finally realized it was a hopeless effort and he gave it up, turned, helped Emma down, and went loping after the children. Heads poked out of the passenger car. "What's the ruckus?" "We're tryin' to sleep up here." "Hey, we got a fight back there?" Passengers hustled down, half-dressed, to see what was going on.

The passengers, adults and children, stood in a semicircle, in front of the baggage car. Thrust forward in the doorway, held by each arm by a deputy, was a gaunt black man with a stubble of white beard. One of the deputies held a crowbar.

Pieces of the shattered pine box lay on the floor behind them. The sheriff came forward and bent down to hand the lanterns to one of the passengers, then jumped to the ground. "Well, that's all for tonight," he said. "You can all go back to bed."

"You can't take him!" J.P. said.

"What's that, young feller?"

"You can't take him!"

"Young man's right," said the burly riverboatman, pulling his yarn suspenders. "It's a free state."

"That's right, it's a free state," J.P. said.

"He belong to you, son?"

"No."

"Well, he's a runaway. And he's goin' back to his owner."

"But you can't. . . . There's no slavery here . . . this is Indiana, right? A free state. . . . Right, Miss Symns?"

Emma could only stare at the face of the sheriff.

The sheriff answered. "There's a law, I'm afraid, young man. It's called the Fugitive Slave Act. Any runaway slave that's caught, free state or not, goes back to his owner."

The two deputies were trying to get themselves and Ned down from the baggage car, at the same time without letting go of his arms, and it was about as awkward as a potato-sack race. They finally all tumbled out, one of the deputies landing on his knees.

J.P. went up to Ned, put her hands on his arms above the deputies' hands.

The first gray streaks of dawn had appeared on the eastern horizon. A couple of heads still peered out of the windows of the train, eyes shielded from the harsh glare of the lanterns, but most of the passengers who'd come out to take a look began to drift back toward the passenger car. Carlin and Joe Plug and a few others held their ground.

"Let the man go, sheriff, what's it to you?" Carlin said.

The sheriff pulled up his belt. "I enforce the laws, that's all there is to it."

"Don't you already got enough laws to worry about, sheriff? Let him go," said Joe Plug.

"The slave people payin' you off, sheriff?" It was the young fireman. The engineer stood next to him, his face taut, saying nothing. He tugged on the fireman's arm, but that wasn't about to stop the young man. "What did they give you, sheriff?"

The sheriff scratched his neck, as if considering what to do. "Now, young man, I'm going to let that pass. But you listen to me, you railroad people, there are laws here, and they apply to everybody. . . . You too, Sam—we've been keepin' our eyes on you. . . . You run your train through my town, you're goin' to abide by those laws or you're goin' to end up in a heap of trouble."

"I've got a sporting proposition for you, sheriff." The voice rose clear and taunting in the night air. All faces turned toward Carlin. "How about we all go in, all the passengers that want to, we make a little collection, I'll bet you we could raise double the reward." The sheriff snuffled. "I mean there are rewards, aren't there, sheriff? And somebody gets them, just that we don't know who. So you could give it to whomever you wanted. . . . Give it to your local missionary society, whatever." One or two of the crowd laughed.

The sheriff's face reddened. "This here slave is goin' back," he said.

J.P. pressed against Ned, staring at the crowd, looking from face to face. Carlin angry; the engineer silent now, holding back his young fireman; Joe Plug belligerent and pulling on his yarn suspenders; the two lady teachers from the female academy huddled by the steps of the passenger car, whispering; Emma standing guard over her children.

No one moved. Didn't any of them see? Were they too tired or too afraid, what? These were the same people who had cried at *Uncle Tom's Cabin,* who had wept and applauded when the slaves were freed, how could they not understand? Just because it wasn't acted out for them? J.P. was not Little Eva, she wasn't blond or dying or rich, no, J.P. was a dirty city kid who couldn't even admit that she was a girl, hiding under her newsboy cap, and she had only learned one way to get free of anything.

J.P. spun and kicked one of the deputies in the shins. "Run, Ned, run," she shouted. She pivoted smartly and hit the second deputy in the crotch with her fist.

The man bellowed in outrage, staggered back a step, and then, from a half-squatting position, let go with a sweeping uppercut. J.P. tried to duck, but the man's fist caught her under the right eye and suddenly she was down on her back in the dirt.

J.P., stunned, was staring at her attacker, afraid that he would hit her again, when she saw Carlin move. He took two quick steps and then threw himself at the deputy, the force of his rush tumbling the two of them to the ground, J.P. rolling to avoid being crushed by the falling men.

Everything began to happen at once. The sheriff tried to move to help his deputy, but Joe Plug stepped up and wrapped his massive arms around the sheriff's middle, jerked him off the ground, lifting him like a bag of flour, squeezing agonizing groans out of him. The young deputy pulled his pistol, and, as he did, the fireman crouched down to pick up the crowbar.

Ned stood stock-still, uncertain whether to run or join in the fight.

Dr. Tansy stared in disbelief, "What's going on here? Carlin, what the hell are you doing?"

The engineer grabbed Ned by the arm. "You're coming

with me," he said. He reached over and slapped his young fireman on the shoulder. "Billyboy, put that thing down and let's get the steam up, we're movin' this train out of here."

The fireman let his crowbar drop, and the three of them raced toward the front of the train.

The young deputy was frantic. He ducked and darted, gun in hand, afraid to shoot into the tumbling, twisting fighters, and finally, in frustration, fired a shot into the air. This had the opposite effect from the one he had intended: instead of stopping anyone from fighting, the shot seemed to galvanize the bearded preacher who had stayed clear of the conflict until then.

He picked up the crowbar and started running at the young deputy. The deputy dropped his gun and ran down the track with the bearded preacher in hot pursuit, swinging the crowbar over his head like Moses with his staff.

Emma tried to herd the children back toward the boxcar, holding the crying J.P. by one arm. The passengers were divided; half ran back toward the car, half leapt out of it and ran toward the fighters. The train whistle pierced the air. Clouds of smoke were billowing out of the stack.

Carlin and the deputy were on their feet now, their hands at each other's throats. J.P. pulled away from Emma, grabbed up a lantern, and ran and swung it at the back of the deputy's legs. The man let out a shout and fell over backward. "J.P.!" Emma shouted. Emma ran back, grabbed J.P. by the arm, and dragged her toward the boxcar.

The whistle sounded again. The engineer leaned out, waved for people to get on board. The other passengers and the children started running for the train.

The preacher had chased the deputy almost out of sight down the tracks. Carlin had the other deputy down on the ground, and Joe Plug still had the sheriff elevated a foot in the air. Joe Plug, the sheriff gasping in his arms, staggered toward Carlin. With a great shout, the boatman dumped the sheriff on top of the deputy and then secured the pile by throwing himself on top of the two of them.

The whistle sounded a third time. Joe Plug shouted to Carlin to make a run for it. "Go on, get on the train, I got 'em! Preacher! Let 'em go!" Sprawled across the two lawmen, the boatman held them fast.

The train made a jolt forward. Down the tracks, the preacher stopped, looked back at the train, dropped his crowbar, and came running.

There was a sprint now for the slow-moving train, Carlin in the lead, the preacher behind. There were heads at every window of the train, urging the runners onward. Joe Plug staggered up from his flesh pile of lawmen and started running too.

Carlin and then the preacher were pulled up into the boxcar by Emma and the children. Joe Plug, slower on his thick boatman's legs, seemed to be losing ground for a moment, with the sheriff and his two deputies only paces behind. The children leaned out of the car, waving and exhorting the boatman forward.

Holding onto the door by one hand, Carlin leaned far out of the boxcar, reaching down as far as he could. The gasping Joe Plug summoned up one last burst, caught Carlin's hand, and struggled up.

The train began to pick up speed. The sheriff and the older deputy had fallen far behind, but the young deputy kept gaining on the train, running alongside. When he tried to climb on, a kick from the preacher sent him sprawling in the dirt. The three lawmen headed for their horses.

Bedlam reigned inside the train. Debate raged back and forth, the two teachers from the female academy on the side of antislavery, the printer from Peoria and Dr. Tansy arguing for abiding by the laws of the land.

The journalist was in a state of high excitement. He kept

putting his head out the window and then pulling it back in just long enough to scribble notes on a pad—"Incredible! Passenger revolt! Outlaw train! Runaway slave! My God!" And then out the window his head would go again.

The conductor was distraught. He ranted, to no one in particular. "Damn him! Damn that Sam! We're all going to be arrested now. We deserve it. I have nothing to do with this! I wash my hands of the whole thing! I am not the conductor." With that, he sank down into a seat, folded his arms, and tried to ignore what was going on around him.

The journalist pulled his head in. "They're coming after us! The lawmen are after us!"

The train was gathering speed, but not fast enough. Ned crouched near the door of the boxcar, holding the sobbing J.P close to his chest, watching the horsemen move up. His fingers moved absently across the child's back, comforting.

Joe Plug sat on the floor, gasping like a fish out of water. Patches stared at the boatman with complete awe. Sarah and Annie clung to one another.

"Look at that, Mr. Carlin, they're gainin' on us!" Liverpool tried to lean out the door, but Carlin caught him and pushed him back. Emma saw blood on the back of Carlin's hand.

Emma felt sick with fear. Behind her the preacher paced up and down the car, raving, but she couldn't hear what he was saying. All she could focus on now was protecting the children. She reached out and held Ben to her.

Sparks from the smokestack flew past the boxcar door like fireflies. The three lawmen were driving their horses to the limit and kept pace with the train. The sheriff shouted out to his deputies. The older deputy pulled his rifle out of its sheath, resting the butt against his thigh, and looked back at the sheriff. The sheriff waved him on.

"Get down, all of you!" Carlin shouted. "Get away from the door!"

– 245 –

Carlin pushed Liverpool to the floor. Ned pulled J.P. down behind the stove.

The deputy fired a shot straight up, into the air. That further outraged the preacher, who strode to the boxcar door. "Ransomed sinners! The day of vengeance will come!"

The deputy rested his rifle in the saddle. The sheriff was still waving and shouting at him when the train whistle sounded.

The preacher leaned out and looked down the track. "Yes, Lord!" he said. He turned back to the rest of them, huddled on the floor and behind benches. "The Lord takes care of his own," he said.

This time there was no way Emma could keep the children from thronging to the open door, and they all did.

A quarter of a mile ahead, the track cut a path through a tangle of underbrush and scrub timber. Even as the train neared the narrow pass the horses of the two deputies began to shy off, but the sheriff stubbornly whipped his mount onward, until he had drawn even with the train. As the train thundered through, the sheriff drove his horse into the tangle of vines and branches. The horse struggled, still trying to obey its commands, lunging forward until, a foreleg snared, it stumbled and pitched the sheriff into the briars.

The train, under full steam now, sounded its whistle in triumph.

The children piled on Carlin and Ned and Joe Plug and the preacher, all trying to talk at once.

"I heard the bullet, Mr. Carlin," Tony said. "I heard it whiz right by . . ."

"Me too, I heard the bullet too," Ben echoed.

"Mr. Plug, you are the strongest man I ever saw. I'll bet you could've squeezed them bones right in two," Patches said admiringly.

"Never gave the bloody police the slip in a train before," Liverpool said.

"I woulda helped you, Mr. Carlin, I woulda licked that man if Miss Symns hadn'ta held me back." Tom said.

The children shouted over one another for attention; all except J.P, who sat by herself on one of the benches, still sobbing softly. It was Emma who first noticed.

"J.P., are you all right?"

J.P. looked up, tried to stifle her sobs, but couldn't entirely. Emma's mirror lay across her legs. Carlin took Ben off his lap and stood up.

"It's all over, J.P., we've left them behind. . . . They're gone." Carlin shook J.P. by the shoulder. "Hey, now . . . that man didn't hit you that hard did he?"

J.P. picked up Emma's mirror and stared at the reflection of her puffy eye. "It just looks so terrible!" J.P. said.

"You can't be worrying about how it looks, J.P.," Carlin said. "You handled yourself like a real man out there."

"But I'm not a man!" J.P. sobbed. "I'm just a girl!"

"A what?" Carlin said. Bruce laughed.

"A girl. I'm a girl."

"Oh, J.P.!" Emma said. The children all stared at J.P., but she refused to look back at any of them, instead gazing at the mirror and the reflection of her bruised face.

"Now doesn't that just beat everything, Patches?" Liverpool said. "J.P.'s a bloody faker." Emma quickly hushed them both, and the only sound then was the rocking of the car. Emma saw J.P. glance quickly at Carlin, in mute appeal.

It was Ned who finally spoke, glaring at Liverpool and then at Bruce. "You think that's so funny? If she says she's a girl, she's a girl. That's all there is to it. This here child's the one that got me out of the hands of that jailer . . . so you all leave off gawkin' at my friend. You want something to look at, you go look out the door, 'cause I'm sure there'll be something comin' down the track. We ain't out of this thing yet."

"Sarah!" Emma said. "Patches! Children, come now, let's settle down. You all need some rest. Tony, you help Sarah straighten the blankets." The children slowly returned to their straw mattresses, casting occasional sidelong glances back at J.P. Carlin stood in front of Emma. Emma looked up at him. "You will speak to the child?" she said softly.

"Of course I will," he said. They looked at one another, wordless for a moment.

"What's going to happen next?" she said.

"I don't know," he said. "We started it. I expect somebody else is going to try and finish it."

When the train came to a halt again the prairie was ablaze with a fierce, bright morning sun. There was not a building in sight; a dry coulee meandered its way toward a grove of cottonwoods.

A number of the exhausted passengers stumbled out into the sunlight. As the engineer strode past, tight-lipped and serious, one or two of the most quarrelsome tried to grab him by the arm, demanding explanations, but he pulled quickly free of them.

The engineer and Carlin and Ned walked a distance from the train, stood talking quietly at the edge of the coulee.

The passengers lined up along the car, squinting into the sun, one or two shivering in the early morning cold, and speculated on the conversation among the three figures standing by the coulee.

"It's the craziest thing I ever saw," said Dr. Tansy. "That engineer's just gone loco. His job is gone once the railroad hears about this, you can bet on that."

"He's a brave young man, if you ask me," said one of the teachers.

"What do you reckon they're sayin'?"

"You know what they've done," said the printer. "They're tryin' to give that slave an escape route. I don't see how he'll make it, though, no way. They got people all through this country."

"They should have given him some food," said one of the teachers.

"They should have given him a gun, that's what they should have given him," said Joe Plug.

The engineer was pointing to the north, toward the cottonwood grove. The printer saw the engineer pointing and spat contemptuously. "They're all in on it, aren't they?" said the printer. "Lawbreakers, all of 'em. Well, I guess now we know where they're sendin' him."

Joe Plug turned on the printer. "You may know, but if I hear you tell anybody, I'll make it a point to come back and find you and pull out your tongue, mister."

The printer stared at Joe Plug, decided that the boatman probably meant what he said, and kept quiet.

Several of the children peered out from the door of the boxcar. J.P. stood fingering her bruised eye. Tom poked at Bruce. "Look, Bruce, he's gonna be free, he's gonna make it. . . ."

"He hasn't made it yet," Bruce grumbled, turning away and flopping back down on his straw mattress.

At the edge of the coulee, Ned turned and shook hands with Carlin and the engineer, then raised his hand toward the train. J.P. raised her hand in return, and then Joe Plug, the two women teachers, and finally, reluctantly, Dr. Tansy did the same.

Then, as naturally as a man would slip into a pool of water, Ned bent down and slid over the edge of the coulee and vanished. Several seconds later there was a shout from the boxcar. Tom had spotted him, trotting through the tan-

gle and brush of the dry bottom, and then Ned disappeared
for good.

Carlin and the engineer walked back toward the train.
The passengers looked uneasily at one another. Dr. Tansy
cleared his throat and banged his pipe against the side of the
passenger car.

"The whole thing's foolishness," the printer said. "Plumb
foolishness. And besides, it's cold out here, I'm goin' back
in."

Ten miles east of Danville there were a dozen armed
horsemen and a couple of wagons gathered around the water tank, waiting for the train to come in. As the train eased
to a stop, a strong-looking man of sixty with a mane of wavy
white hair hitched up his belt and walked toward the locomotive. He wore a sheriff's badge.

The distraught conductor was the first one off the train.
He staggered out into the bright morning sun with his hands
raised as if he thought they'd shoot him. The sheriff waved
for him to put his hands down.

"Let's just keep it calm, here, conductor, I just need to talk
to your engineer for a piece."

The engineer and the fireman climbed down from their
locomotive, eying the armed horsemen. Two or three of the
horses began to stamp their hooves as the engineer and the
fireman walked toward them. The sheriff faced his men.
"Now, you boys just keep these guns where they belong, I
don't want nobody shootin' his foot off." He took off his
hat and scratched at his wavy white hair. "Hello, Sam," he
said.

"Hello, sheriff," the lanky engineer said. "What you doin'
way out here in the country?"

"Well, we heard there was a little trouble. We're just tryin'
to figure out what it was." The sheriff rubbed his nose, look-

ing off across the clearing to the row of trees that ran along a small, twisting stream.

"What kind of trouble?" the engineer said.

"What we got over the telegraph was that there was a slave on the train, and when the sheriff from the county over here tried to take him off, some of you boys got in his way."

"Rubbed his face in the mud is what we did!" the young fireman muttered.

The sheriff ignored the remark, narrowing his eyes at the young engineer. "Is that what you boys did?" The engineer didn't say anything. "Mighty puzzling. Tell me this, Sam, you had a slave on this train?"

"Yes, sir."

"And he's not on the train now?"

"No, sir."

"And do you know where he got off the train?"

"No, sir."

"Mighty puzzling." The sheriff turned slowly, his hands on his hips, and faced the passengers that had crowded together on the steps of the train. "Any of you people know where that slave might have got off?"

No one spoke. The wind rustled through the trees down by the stream. The printer fidgeted and looked pained, but Joe Plug glared steadily at him.

"It's a mystery, I tell yuh," the sheriff said. He picked at a scab on the back of his hand. "Sam, I'm afraid you'll have to be comin' with us. We're not goin' to have any trouble, are we? 'Cause if we are, we'll have to put on the cuffs."

"You've got no trouble from me, sheriff, long as you give me time to shut down my locomotive."

"Oh, we got time, Sam, don't worry about that. You can ride in the wagon with the deputies there. There'll be plenty of lawyers up in Danville happy to represent yuh, so don't worry about that. If there were any others out here that were involved, well, that's none of my business, they didn't put it on the telegraph, but I'm going to tell you something, Sam, you can just bless your stars that you got yourself arrested in the right county."

"What about us, sheriff?" shouted out one of the passengers.

The sheriff looked back at them. "Folks, I hate to do this to you, slow down your trip this way, but we're arrestin' your engineer. I reckon it'll be a couple of hours before they can get another crew out here, so anybody that wants to ride into town with us and make other connections is welcome. Otherwise, sit tight, and they'll have another crew out here sometime this afternoon."

One or two of the passengers tried to protest. Laws had to be enforced, but things had reached a pretty sorry state of affairs when that interfered with the running of the railroad. Emma decided that she and the children would stay with the train. The other passengers were leery about being stranded out in the country, and all of them except for Carlin, Joe Plug, and the preacher elected to take the wagons into Danville.

There was a great flurry of activity as the passengers lugged their baggage out of the baggage car and onto the two wagons. Joe Plug was fuming, ready to fight this bunch of lawmen too, any bunch of lawmen, but the engineer, as cheerful and full of jokes as ever, calmed him down. It was bound to happen, sooner or later, the engineer said, those were the chances you took. They'd gotten a man free, that was the point, and, anyway, if there was going to be a trial he had a better chance in Danville than a lot of places.

The children looked on in awe. Patches wanted to know if they were going to hang the engineer, and why he didn't run, or fight. Emma tried to explain about living in a society of law and how sometimes people had to abide by laws even when they were unjust. Patches was skeptical. As the engineer walked off with the sheriff, Bruce said, "They wouldn't take me like that. They'd have to shoot me first."

The children stood and waved as the caravan of horses and wagons rumbled off down the road. The engineer waved back grinning, turned to say something to the sheriff, then pointed out across the open field where a quail was flying low, heading for safety.

*T*hey all stood and watched till the horses and wagons disappeared from view. Bruce spat, then kicked at the ground. Carlin broke the silence. "I've never seen such a sad bunch of faces," he said. "What are you all looking so glum for?"

"They are going to put him in jail!" Sarah said.

"You think so?"

"They arrested him. The sheriff took him off!" Liverpool said.

"I'm disappointed. Really I am," Carlin said. "Do any of you know where we are?"

"Illinois," Sarah said.

"That's right," Carlin said. "And do you know what there are more of in Illinois than in any state in the Union?" The children were silent. "Well, I'll tell you. Abolitionists. That's right. There are more abolitionists in Illinois than you can shake a stick at. When our friend the engineer gets in front of a jury of twelve, it's a good bet seven or eight of them are going to be abolitionists. . . . I'd be surprised if he spends a single night in jail—very surprised." One or two of them didn't look convinced; Bruce was still sullen. J.P. looked skeptically at Carlin.

Carlin went on. "If you ask me, though I know you didn't, you should be proud of yourselves. There's a man free somewhere north of here, and maybe he wouldn't be if it weren't for you. You should be proud of this train."

"So? So what if we are?" Bruce said.

"So maybe you'd like to have your picture taken," Carlin said.

"You'll take our picture?"

"Sure. It'll be my going-away present to all of you."

The words stuck in Emma's heart. She stared at Carlin. He smiled back.

"Emma," he said," I want you in the picture, too."

The children loved the idea of the picture. Their spirits rose instantly. Sarah ran back to brush her hair, and Annie followed her. Tony washed Ben's face and they generally got themselves spruced up. They lined up in front of the box-car, J.P. turning sideways to hide her black eye. They squeezed in when Carlin told them to squeeze in, and though it took a while to get Ben to stop fidgeting—he insisted that Patches was poking him—eventually they were all perfectly still, as gravely still as any choirmaster could ever want, holding until Carlin told them that was it, and then they let out a whoop.

They crowded around the mercury bath, scarcely giving Carlin enough room to work, badgering him with questions about what he was doing. Carlin answered every question patiently, thoroughly. After the plate was mercurialized and washed, then dried over the alcohol lamp, Carlin held it high to keep them from getting their fingers on it. Carlin let the children decide on a case. After a fierce debate, they chose one that had a harp embossed on the outside and purple silk lining on the inside. Carlin complimented them on their choice; that was his favorite too.

Carlin handed the finished daguerreotype to Emma.

They all pressed around, pointing out how one looked and the other. Didn't J.P.'s shiner show up pretty good, Liverpool said. And wasn't Liverpool's grin weird, like a skunk eating sand, Patches said. And after they had all had their look and tossed all the barbs they could think of, they went running off toward the woods, and there was nothing Emma could do to stop them. There was no reason to stop them, not really. They had all disappeared in a matter of minutes, all except J.P., who meandered to the far end of the clearing and sat with her back against a tree, looking back from time to time at Carlin.

Emma stayed behind. Carlin was busy repacking his equipment, hefting the mercury bath under one arm. Emma offered to help, but he said no, he could handle it fine himself. Emma stood watching him, fingering the harp-embossed case.

The preacher had stretched out in the passenger car to take a nap. Joe Plug had wandered off into the trees with the children. Except for J.P. sitting at the edge of the clearing, Emma and Carlin were quite alone.

"It was awfully nice of you, Mr. Carlin, to go to all that trouble."

Carlin looked at her, hefting the odiferous box of chemicals and walking past her. The fumes of iodine and bromine made Emma cover her nose and mouth with a hand. He set the box down near the passenger car.

"It's not so much trouble," Carlin said. "Taking pictures is my business. That's why they call me the likeness man."

"It was very nice of you," she said, "to speak to the children like that." Carlin looked down, silent for a moment. "You're quite sure that the engineer will be all right?"

"I don't know if I'd say quite sure."

"But you told the children . . ." Emma said.

"I know I told the children," Carlin said. "And maybe what I told them was right. Maybe he will get a jury full of abolitionists. I don't know . . . you don't know how these things are going to turn out."

"But how could you lie to those children, Mr. Carlin?"

"Lying? Is that what I was doing? What was I supposed to say? The man was a hero. Am I supposed to tell those children they might take him off and lynch him?"

"I don't see how you could give them reassurances when there weren't any."

"Everybody needs reassurances, Miss Symns, everybody."

Emma fell silent. A kingbird clamored in a nearby tree. Carlin went back to putting away his equipment. She felt dismayed that she never seemed able to say the right thing to him, that she was constantly disagreeing, contantly judging him. It depressed her. As she watched him snapping down the legs of his tripod in the bright autumn sunlight, she felt enormously drawn to him. There was so little time, she thought, and she was letting it slip away.

Suddenly he turned back to her and smiled. "You know what I would like, Miss Symns?"

"What's that?"

"I'd like to take a walk with you. Just you. No children along. And we wouldn't even talk about children, about what we should have said to them, or shouldn't have said to them. How does that sound to you?"

Emma stood up. There was no mistaking her look: her face was shining. "It sounds wonderful, Mr. Carlin."

"And do you think we'd find things to talk about?"

"I think we might," Emma said. "And when could we take this walk?"

"I think maybe there's time now, Miss Symns. Before the new crew shows up. What do you think?"

"I think now would be an excellent time," Emma said.

As Carlin leaned his tripod against the passenger car, there was a shout from across the clearing.

"Miss Symns! Look, Miss Symns! Look what I brought you!"

Annie ran across the clearing, waving her treasure aloft. It was a nosegay she had made out of mullen stock and corn-husk twisted with grass, and she insisted on putting it on Emma's blouse. Patches was a minute behind her, walking carefully with his hands full.

"Look here, Miss Symns!" Patches held up a handful of acorns. "Illinois filberts!"

"I believe they're called acorns, Patches," Emma said.

"We found 'em along the road," Patches said. "There are lots more, if you want 'em." Patches suddenly eyed the two of them. "Where are you two going?"

"Mr. Carlin and I were going for a walk."

"What for?" Annie said.

"We thought we'd look for some of those Illinois filberts."

"We can show you where they are," Patches said.

"Mr. Carlin and I were going for a walk by ourselves," Emma said.

Annie wrinkled up her nose. "By yourselves?"

"But how can you find the filberts if we're not along?" Patches said.

"I don't think we could," Carlin said, smiling. He reached down and took Annie's hand, then put his arm around Emma's waist. "So I think you two should come along and show us."

Tom only waded in the stream up to his knees, but he still found it numbing cold. Bruce grinned back at him, edging farther and farther out toward the fastest part, flaunting his courage.

"Watch this now, Tom." Bruce slid down into the water,

letting the stream carry him, then reached up, twisting, catching hold of an overhead branch. The water tugged at his body.

"Look out, Bruce, it'll pull you in."

"Ain't you a fraidy-cat," Bruce said. "Come on, you try it."

"Naw."

"Sissy."

"Naw, I'm just not a swimmer, I told you that. It's too cold anyway." A raft of sticks and grass swirled by. Recent rains had filled the stream to the top of its banks with fast-running water. Tom stood, kneedeep, bunched, his teeth chattering. Bruce grinned broadly, letting Tom know that the cold didn't bother *him*.

"I thought you were my pal, Tom," Bruce said.

"You know I'm your pal," Tom said.

"You sure been acting pretty funny for a pal then," Bruce said. "I woulda never thought it of you, Tom. I woulda never believed it if somebody had told me."

"They would have found the stuff anyway, Bruce. What could we have done with it? A dumb old cane. . . ."

"That's not the point. The point is that you caved in . . . a regular old Faint Heart, Old Knock-Knees. We do something like that together, and then without talking to me you turn everything back."

"I didn't turn it back."

"What do you mean, you didn't turn it back? You put it out where they can't miss it. . . . Didn't you?" Bruce let go of the branch and let the water carry him downstream on his back for eight or ten feet before he hit a bar. Dripping, he walked to the bank, crawled out, and made his way toward his clothes.

"When we made friends, I thought you had some grit. I didn't know you were such an old lady. Miss Symns looks at you cross-eyed and you fall into a fit."

Tom was smarting, but he said nothing. He came out of the water, picked his way gingerly in his bare feet over the twiggy grass. He bent down and dried the bottom part of his legs with his shirt.

"So who's your friend, Tom, Miss Symns or me?"

"You are, Bruce."

"Don't think I don't know why you're acting like this, I got eyes. Your big idea now is you want to act right so Miss Symns'll get you a nice cozy place on one of these farms, right? Your big ambition now is, you want to be somebody's hand." Bruce laughed. "Old Tom is *re*formed."

Bright leaves fell into the stream and spun slowly once, twice, and then whirled downstream. Tom's face burned as he got into his clothes.

"You all *re*formed, Tom?" Bruce pulled the word out so it sounded real dirty. He started walking up along the bank. "I'll tell you, Tom, you're a coward, clear to the core."

Tom hurried after Bruce, tugging up his trousers. Bruce didn't bother to wait. He'd found a short stick and was whipping at a stand of milkweed, sending tufts of down swirling into the air. A squirrel clattered up a tree ahead of them.

They stood at a narrow wooden bridge. Bruce leaned back against the rail, his elbows resting on it.

"We were goin' to be a team, remember? Like Ali Baba and his Forty Thieves, like Jack Sheppard, nobody was goin' to tell us when to go to bed and when to get up, what we had to eat for breakfast, nobody was goin' to boss us. We were goin' to live by our wits. But I guess you ain't got the sand for that no more, is that right?" Bruce clapped Tom on the shoulder. "It's all right. You want to be somebody's hand, that's all right."

Tom leaned his elbows on the rail, stared down into the water. Right below, in a still part of the stream, there were minnows. When Bruce pushed himself away from the rail, his shadow passed over the water and the minnows fled under the bridge. As Tom watched them disappear, he thought, Afraid of shadows. That's what Bruce thinks of me, afraid as a minnow.

Bruce put one foot up on the split rail of the bridge. Tom looked fearfully at him. "What are you doing?"

"Give me a hand up here," Bruce said. Tom didn't move. "Get over here."

Tom obeyed. Bruce used Tom's shoulder to push himself up, taking Tom's hand to get his balance. He stood erect on the rail.

"Now let go."

Tom was too afraid to do anything but obey.

Bruce wavered for a second, one arm windmilling slowly in the air, then found his balance again, paused. He swung his left foot out, placed it in front of his right. There was only a tremor. Then he put his right in front of his left. Tom walked alongside, afraid for Bruce, but then he saw that he didn't need to be afraid and he stopped a third of the way across and let Bruce go. Bruce was the cock of the walk, the daredevil, the toughest kid on the Bowery, even if he was out in God-knows-where, Illinois, walking across a rickety rail bridge. Bruce had grit, Bruce wouldn't end up as anybody's hand.

When he reached the far end Bruce raised his arms and leaped to the ground. He was grinning.

"Let's see you do it, Tom boy."

"Me?"

"Yeah, you. You're my pal, right? Prove to me you got some sand . . . my old pal, Tom." Bruce sauntered back across the bridge, laughing and easy now, his face flushed with his conquest of the bridge. "You can do it, Tom boy."

"Sure, I can," Tom said. His voice couldn't quite hide his

shakiness, but he wasn't going to let Bruce down, not again. Bruce was the only one who'd ever stuck up for him. He took a deep breath. He wasn't going to let Bruce down.

"I'll give you a hand up," Bruce said. "It's a cinch, honest. You just keep your eyes on the rail." Bruce's hand was extended, waiting.

Tom took the hand, lifted his leg, set his foot solidly on the rail. Bruce began to lift, slowly, steadily. Halfway up Tom got the shakes and went into a crouch, jumping down. Bruce didn't say anything.

"I just need a fresh start," Tom said.

They started again, Bruce steady as a rock, lifting, lifting, until Tom stood on the rail, one foot placed in front of the other. He waited; his heart was beating too fast.

"Don't you look swell?" Bruce said. "Ain't you one o' those guys in the circus?"

Tom laughed nervously. "Come on, Bruce, don't make me laugh."

"Awright. . . . You tell me when you want me to let go."

Tom's heart was still thumping a mile a minute. He looked quickly down at the water; he didn't see the minnows. His heart was beating like a minnow, like a bunch of minnows in his chest. Bruce was right. He would only look at the rail.

"Awright," Tom said. "Let go."

Bruce let go of Tom's hand.

Tom heard the wind rustle through the trees. A red oak leaf fluttered across in front of him, brushed the rail, fell. Tom refused to let his eyes follow it. He would keep his eyes on the rail.

His first step was wobbly. Oh, but he wanted to jump down onto the bridge, to call it off. Bruce couldn't get too mad, he'd make fun of him sure, he'd rag him for a while, sure. . . . No, not this time. He couldn't let Bruce down. Not this time.

He took his next step. Tom could hear insects in the dry grass on the far bank. He could hear the water running, fast, beneath him. He mustn't look at the water. He would only look at the rail right in front of his feet.

Bruce was walking alongside him. Bruce was talking, about dogs or something, how wouldn't it be great if they had a big dog to hunt with . . . Tom couldn't quite understand.

The rail creaked for a second. Tom teetered, but found his balance. He was doing better. He took two more steps, three more. He'd come a long way now, he must have. . . . He wanted to know how far he'd come. The insects singing on the far bank seemed to be singing right in his ear. He had to know how much farther.

Tom looked up and saw the long rail still in front of him. The trees on the far bank threw their dark shadows out toward him. It was a long way and the rail only seemed to get narrower, or were his eyes fooling him. . . .

His right foot came down on the edge of the rail, and he lurched outward toward the river. He flailed with his arms, trying to claw his way back, he was falling, head downward. For a second, Tom saw Bruce's face at the rail, it was upside down, everything was backward, but it was the terror on Bruce's face that scared Tom, because Bruce was never afraid. . . . The slap of the water stunned Tom, the sudden cold took his breath away, and then there was water closing over his head for the first time.

The swift, full river took Tom quickly downstream. Bruce shouted from the bridge for Tom to paddle, all the time knowing it wouldn't help. Tom couldn't swim, but why couldn't he get his feet down, it wasn't that deep.

It took time for Bruce to race to the end of the bridge. He pushed his way through the briars and underbrush and ran along the shore, branches clawing at his face. For a second he saw Tom's head above water, and then Tom bobbed under and came up again. Bruce shouted at him, ran faster, trying to keep Tom in sight, but the stream was moving faster than he could run through the clinging underbrush, having to dodge trees, and then Bruce tripped on a rock and went sprawling headlong. He landed on his chest, it took his breath away. He lay there, gasping for air, and when he finally pushed himself up and looked down the river he could see only the sun rippling on the fast-moving current.

By the time Emma and Carlin returned from their walk with Annie and Patches, the new railroad crew had arrived and was ready to go. Joe Plug was playing a game of catch with Sarah and Liverpool, Tony and Ben and J.P. sat on the grass watching, and there was a new passenger, a farmer in a thick woolen suit with his cardboard suitcase clutched tightly in his hand.

The new engineer, a gaunt, jittery man, glared at Emma, but she paid him no mind. She was tired and happy; no one was going to disturb the contentment she felt. The trees down by the creek glistened in the falling sun, and the air throbbed with choruses of insects.

Patches and Annie quickly made up a new game, the object of which was to see how far out of the boxcar door they could jump. First J.P. and then the other children joined in, jumping, then rolling and somersaulting in the grass.

Bruce came into the clearing. He watched the children rolling and laughing on the grass, then walked through them without a word, hopped up into the boxcar, and went to sit on his blanket.

The new conductor waved at Emma. "All right, miss, if you've got all your children together, we'll be taking off now."

"All right, J.P., Annie, come on now," Emma said. She

stood, her arms at her side, looking at Carlin. He was smiling. He reached out and touched her cheek.

"You got a little sun today," he said.

"You go back to your car now, Mr. Carlin," she said softly.

Patches tugged at her arm. "Miss Symns? Miss Symns! Tom isn't here."

Emma looked down at Patches. "Well, where is he?"

"I don't know. He's not here."

She stared at Bruce, who was gnawing away at some sweetmeat he had hidden under his pillow.

"Where's Tom, Bruce?"

Bruce looked sleepy and vaguely cross. "Dunno."

Emma felt as if her reserves of patience were at low ebb. "You don't know? I thought the two of you did everything together. Didn't you go off with him a couple of hours ago?"

"Oh, yeah, for a while; but then I dunno where he went." Bruce stared at Tony, who was shouting as he jumped out the boxcar door. "Hey, Tony, shut up for a while, would you?"

"Bruce, the train is leaving! Would you please go find him for me!"

"I don't know where he is, Miss Symns. I'm not his nurse, am I?"

Emma turned to the other children. "Have any of you seen Tom?"

"No, Miss Symns."

"No, Miss Symns."

"Tony, come over here!" Emma shouted. Tony untangled himself from his somersault. "Tony, have you seen Tom?"

"No. I thought he was with Bruce."

"I don't know where Tom is, honest, Miss Symns. . . ." Bruce's voice was choked and desperate.

Carlin regarded Bruce for a moment. His voice was grave. "Miss Symns, why don't I take Bruce for a while? We'll go look for the boy."

The conductor, standing behind the group of children, said, "Mister, this train is pulling out of here."

Carlin ignored him. "Not quite yet. We should look before it gets dark," Carlin said. "I'll get a couple of the men here to help us."

Emma watched as Carlin went to Joe Plug and the other men. They talked soberly for several minutes before Carlin turned back.

"All right. Bruce, you're going to show us where you saw Tom last."

Bruce looked down at his shoes, then back at Carlin. He seemed miserable.

Emma stayed with the children. They had become suddenly quiet, sensing that there was something seriously wrong. The sound of katydids pulsed in the dusky air. An hour passed. Emma wanted something to happen, anything.

Finally the men appeared at the edge of the wood, dark figures moving slowly out of the shadows. Emma started forward, thinking that she saw Tom with them, but then she realized that no, he wasn't.

Carlin went directly to Emma. "It's getting too dark," he said. "We'll have to bring out torches. There's a store up the road. The man has a couple of hounds. They could make it easier."

"Make it easier?" Emma said. "I don't understand how dogs could make it easier."

"Bloodhounds," Carlin said. "They'll pick up any scent that's there. The man promises."

"That's the truth," the farmer said. "Them is real good animals."

Carlin reached out and squeezed her hand. "We'll hurry."

The men walked up to the store to get torches and lanterns. Frost had started to appear on the ground. The train loomed in the dark, like a heavy, resting beast. Sarah had taken her blanket from the boxcar and laid it on the ground.

She and Annie sat on it, their arms around one another to keep warm.

The older children were quiet, but the younger ones had questions that they had to ask. "Do you think he was captured by Indians?" "Got bitten by a snake, I'll bet." Ben was sure that Tom had fallen into a bear pit, and though Tony told him that was ridiculous, that there weren't even any bears out here any more, Ben wasn't convinced. He'd seen a picture once where there was a pit with sharp stakes at the bottom and it was all covered over with branches and then grass and sticks so it looked all natural and that would be just the sort of thing that Tom wouldn't be keeping his eye out for. . . .

A ghostly procession of lanterns moved down the road toward them. Bruce watched them come, his hand tightening on Patches's shoulder.

A broad-shouldered man with a limp led the way, being pulled by three panting hounds on leashes. There was the storekeeper and the storekeeper's wife, who had fixed a couple of baskets of food for the children. She brought her baskets around to all the children, regarding them pitifully, murmuring, "God bless you, child, God bless you, I'm going to pray for you all . . ." To their great surprise, she did pray for them, kneeling down in front of a startled Patches just as he was reaching for a chicken leg. "God bless these children and keep them from harm. Watch over them, Lord, In Thy Name we pray. Amen."

Carlin sent Bruce into the boxcar to find a piece of Tom's clothing. Bruce came back with a shirt of Tom's and handed it to Carlin. The men were all silent. Insects bounced fiercely off the glass of the bright lanterns. The man with the limp rubbed the shirt in the muzzles of the hounds.

The storekeeper stood watching, wide-eyed, scratching his long white neck. Over his shoulder he had a heavy, dark net.

"What's that for?" Liverpool asked.

The storekeeper looked down at the boy. "Oh, this? This is just in case, son." He looked at the hounds, fingered the small knots of the net. "It's for dragging the stream."

The procession set off for the river: passengers, farmers, Carlin, and the three oldest boys—Bruce, Liverpool, and Tony. They were led by the eager, baying hounds that yanked their handler behind them like a rag doll.

Emma stayed with the rest of the children. After an hour she insisted that they go to bed or at least go into the boxcar and lie down.

A thin mist descended, through which Emma could see the night sky and the tops of the trees and traces of dim, grotesque forms moving in the scattered underbrush.

From time to time she could hear Liverpool's or Tony's voices calling out Tom's name, calling one of their own. Emma found her uncle's Bible and just held it, too tense to read. The katydids came to a sudden stop, and in that hush Emma heard herself muttering, "Dear God, save him, please save him. . . ."

An hour passed, more. Emma got up and went to look in on the boxcar. J.P. was propped up on one elbow, sleepily touching the swelling around her eye. The other children were asleep.

Emma went back to her blanket, sat down, wrapped herself in it. She felt the anger rise up in her; she couldn't help it. Of course it was Tom who would run off and get himself lost, he was the weakest of all the children, no more sense of responsibility than a baby, he was probably in some farmer's kitchen now, eating corn dodgers. . . . She resented that the two of them—he and Bruce—had caused her nothing but trouble. . . . Her heart almost stopped as she realized what she was thinking. Shame, shame on her. The boy could be lying hurt, with a broken leg, helpless, what was wrong with her, she was responsible for that boy, for all of them, she had taken on that responsibility, and though all of them were going to be taken from her, it wasn't supposed to be like this, not like this. . . .

In the quiet Emma could hear the hounds baying across the creek. Night animals began to call, one answering the other; the night had begun to stir.

A figure stood at the edge of the mists. Emma stood up. The figure walked closer and Emma saw that it was Bruce.

"Bruce! Bruce, have they found him?"

"No, ma'am."

"I don't understand. . . . They haven't given up?"

"No, Miss Symns." His breathing was irregular with anguish. "I need to talk to you, Miss Symns. Please. . . ."

"Of course," Emma said, more stiffly than she meant to, stiffly because she was suddenly frightened.

The big, awkward boy stood with his hands shoved deep in his pockets. "Couldn't we talk someplace else?"

"I have to stay near the children, Bruce," Emma said.

"But not right here," Bruce said.

"We can walk to the front of the train if you'd like," Emma said.

Bruce followed her dutifully. When they stood on the tracks in front of the train, Emma turned to him. Her voice came hollow and remote. "So what happened, Bruce?"

His face went weak, the corners of his mouth turning down as if he was about to cry. "We were only playing, miss."

"Who was playing?"

"Me and Tom. We were just playing a game. I didn't mean nothing. . . ."

"What were you playing, Bruce?"

"We were walking on the rail of the bridge. I had already done it, it wasn't so hard. I did it easy, and Tom would've too, but he looked up, I told him to keep his eye on the rail.

. . . That was why he fell, 'cause he looked up. . . ." Emma shut her eyes. Her heart was closed to this boy. "Miss Symns . . ."

"Go on, Bruce. Just go on."

"I ran after him, but the water was so fast, Miss Symns, it swept him right along. I ran on the bank, I tried to catch up, but I couldn't . . ."

"What happened to him, Bruce?"

"I don't know, I don't know. The water took him."

"Did he drown?"

"Please, listen to me, Miss Symns . . ."

"Say it, Bruce, say it. Say that he drowned!"

"No, Miss Symns." His voice was a terrified moan.

"Can't you talk, child? Why can't you speak? Why didn't you tell anyone?"

"I was scared, Miss Symns."

Emma stared down the long tracks, the rails gleaming in the moonlight, then looked quickly back at Bruce. He had known, for six or even eight hours he had known, and he hadn't said anything. Emma felt her stomach turn with revulsion. "Did you bully him into it, Bruce?"

"No, miss."

"You didn't bully him? Tom never did anything unless you told him. He wouldn't have walked two steps on that rail unless you'd been ragging him . . . or did you push him, Bruce?"

"No, Miss Symns, no. He looked up, I told him not to. . . . You've got to believe me. I know you can't think any good of me, miss . . . I know. Nobody's ever set much store by me, and I know I'm mean sometimes, but I don't want to be. . . ."

His blubbering made Emma furious. It was intolerable that at such a time he could only feel sorry for himself.

"Do you understand what you've done, Bruce?"

"We were only playin', miss . . ."

She slapped him across the face. He stepped back, the tears welling quickly to his eyes. The corners of his mouth went down and he reached up and put a hand to his great, soft, round face. He began to cry.

Emma stood trembling with dismay. She couldn't have done that, she was horrified. That couldn't have come out of her. Dear God, forgive me, forgive my cruelty, open my heart to this boy, dear Jesus, only Your love is great enough to forgive us both. . . .

She stared at the blubbering boy. It was with despair that she realized how little emotion she felt for this unhappy child, this wretched child, with what coldness and clarity she viewed him; the baggy overalls, the hulking shoulders, the collar folded under on one side of his neck. Emma reached out automatically to fix it, pulling it out so it was right, and when she did the boy moved toward her, crying out, and she lifted her arms to him and held him. Dear Lord, bless this poor child, forgive our weakness, we are all children, Lord, forgive us that, take us into Your mercy. . . .

She stood, letting him cry, and in one corner of her mind she was thinking that someone should go down and tell the others that they could stop their search.

Liverpool and Tony had been sent up to the boxcar to get their sleep, and within the next hour most of the farmers gave up the search too. There wasn't much chance of finding Tom tonight.

Only four men kept up the search. Carlin, the man with the hounds, Joe Plug, and the backwoods preacher. The hounds were exhausted and discouraged; as one trace after the other came to nothing they began to whine and complain, moaning to their handler. The backwoods preacher still wandered silently in and out of the woods, pushing aside

the underbrush, now and then stopping with a jerk to listen
to some night sound.

Carlin had moved farther downstream, away from the
others. It had gotten steadily colder for the last hour.
Around him were the hooting and cries of owls and wildcats.
The thing he had to do was to keep looking. To look, no
matter what he might fear.

The moon had come out and shone on the rippling surface of the water. The surface gleamed and winked, seemed
as shiny and impenetrable as molten lead. The trees came
down to the river, and, where some of the bank had fallen
away, the exposed roots reached down into the water. When
Carlin let his eye follow one of the gnarled roots down, he
could suddenly see beneath the surface. It was a simple trick
of refocusing his sight.

He followed the twisted root down into the dark water
and then suddenly he saw, waving in the fast-moving water,
a cloth sleeve tangled in with the root, and then he saw the
boy's arm.

Carlin lowered himself clumsily into the stream and untangled the limp body. It was hard to stand in the fast-moving current, and he fell back into the water a couple of
times. He finally carried the body up onto the shore, stumbling under the weight of the heavy, wet limbs. Carlin laid
the dead boy there on the grass. He stared at the pale, limp
body, the wet clothes twisted up around it; one of the boy's
shoes was gone. Insects hummed in the night. Carlin did not
want to look very long. He did not want to look at all.

Carlin carried the body back. The storekeeper's wife, who
had been sleeping on the steps of the passenger car, woke
up and began to cry. The exhausted hounds hobbled to
their feet and sniffed in the direction of the body. The storekeeper scratched at his white neck and offered to spend the

night building a coffin. Emma, rigid as a statue, stood to one side.

Bruce lay asleep on the ground outside the boxcar. The talk did not wake him. When the others left, Emma found a blanket and covered the sleeping boy.

Emma and Carlin were alone. Carlin's photographic equipment stood beside the train. Carlin walked to it, wiped away the beads of dew.

"I hope your equipment will be all right," Emma said.

"It's pretty sturdy stuff," Carlin said.

"Bruce told me what happened. They were playing on the bridge. Tom fell. Bruce was afraid to tell me. When he did tell me, I didn't believe him . . . I didn't trust him. I was awful."

"You're not always going to be right with children; no one is," Carlin said.

Emma looked up at him, her voice suddenly full of need. "Mr. Carlin, what am I going to tell those children in the morning?"

He didn't say anything right away. "You'll know then, I suppose," he said.

From the woods came the cries of a rabbit or a bird being carried off by some animal, the cries long and drawn out like the cries of a child, growing fainter and fainter and then disappearing altogether.

"We had such a wonderful walk," Emma said. "With the trees and the leaves and the way the sun was on the water. . . ."

"I know," Carlin said.

"And I can't help but thinking that while we were out walking, that boy was drowning, he was choking for air . . ."

Carlin took her in his arms, held his hand over her mouth. Her eyes were shut tight, she was crying. "Don't," he said. "You can't think that way."

* * *

In the morning Emma gathered the children. They grouped sleepily in front of the train. Emma was very tired and her hands were shaking. "Where's Patches?" They all shrugged. "Somebody go and get him up. Right away!"

They all waited silently until Tony returned, dragging Patches behind him. Patches rubbed his eyes and tried with little success to shove his shirt into his pants.

Emma told them as calmly and completely as she knew how that Tom had died, that he had fallen in the river and he had drowned and that it was an accident.

"What's an accident?" Ben asked.

"An accident is when nobody meant it," Tony said.

"Didn't he swim? I would have swimmed . . ."

"Does that mean he went to Heaven?" Annie asked.

"Yes, I think so," Emma said.

"Is he there *now*?" Ben asked. Tony blushed for his brother. Sarah was upset, touching her face distractedly, trying not to cry. Patches watched Sarah, and only seemed bewildered. Liverpool stared grimly at Bruce as if he knew, even if the others didn't.

"Liverpool," Emma said. "The woman up at the store said that she was going to make breakfast for all of us. I want you to go up there and see if you can help her."

They buried Tom across the road from the country store. There was a small, fenced-in plot there with three other fresh graves. Ten or eleven of the local farmers came to pay their condolences, passing the story of the boy's death around in hushed tones. The backwoods preacher conducted the brief service, the pages of his Bible rippled by the prairie wind as he stood over the grave. Annie and Ben had picked flowers to put on the grave, and they held their bouquets with somber faces as the preacher preached about dying in alien corn, being buried in strange ground. Patches whispered questions to Sarah, but she only poked him to be quiet. Bruce stood away from the others, his head to one side, picking at the corner of his eye as if the wind had blown some speck in it. Tony stood behind his brother Ben, holding him by the shoulders until Ben finally shrugged irritably, and Tony took his hands away as they listened to the promises of peace and a Heavenly Rest and how they would all rise together one day.

As the children were getting back into the boxcar, Bruce caught Emma by the arm. "What is it, Bruce?"

"They don't want me to ride with 'em."

"Did anyone say that?"

"No, but I know it."

"Bruce, this is nonsense!"

"It's the way they look at me. Please, miss . . ."

Emma stared at Bruce. It wasn't something to argue. Emma went to Carlin and asked him if Bruce could ride up in the passenger car and if Carlin would look after him. Carlin said of course he would.

The train set off again. The passenger car was not very full. Only the preacher, Joe Plug, and a couple of farmers remained. Carlin invited Bruce to sit next to him, but Bruce said no.

Carlin settled back in his cushioned seat and shut his eyes for a moment. He felt exhausted and confused, as if everything were spinning. He was supposed to be leaving, it was only a matter of hours now, catching the St. Louis train at Springfield, but he felt as if he couldn't, not yet, he and Emma were just coming to something, they just needed time, it was too soon to make a break. . . .

Carlin opened his eyes. Bruce sat up ahead a few rows, staring out the window. Carlin watched the boy, who huddled, his arms folded tight to his body, like someone fighting the cold. As the conductor came lurching down the aisle, heartily greeting all the passengers, Bruce never once looked at him. The boy was in a lot more agony than Carlin was. There was a cheap little book with bent edges lying on the seat next to Carlin. He picked it up, turned it over, then stood and walked down the aisle.

"Hello, Bruce."

"Hello." Bruce glanced at him without turning his head.

"Bruce, I found this on the seat next to me. Somebody must have forgotten it." Carlin held up the book. "Let's see here . . . it's called *The Yankee Among the Mermaids and Other Waggeries and Vagaries.* Probably humorous, don't you think?" Bruce didn't reply. "Thought you might like to have a look at it."

"No."

Carlin thumbed through the badly printed book. "It has some pictures in it."

"Not interested in pictures."

"What are you interested in, Bruce? What could I do for you?"

Bruce's lip was trembling. "Nothing," he said.

"You hungry? You didn't eat anything all morning, did you?" Bruce didn't say anything, just stared out the window at the farmers and their teams working slowly up and down their fields.

"Well, Bruce," Carlin said, "it can get to be a very long trip. I'll just leave the book here. In case you change your mind." Carlin let the book drop on the cushioned seat. As he walked back down the aisle, he sensed Bruce's eyes watching him.

At Danville, an elderly German couple got on. The woman was straight-backed and proper, and she carried a basket. The man moved heavily; he had a massive head with a great shock of white hair. They took a seat across from Bruce.

Once the train started they spoke to one another in German, she speaking more quickly and severely, he nodding and replying with a word or two. She brought out sandwiches, liverwurst and sausages with mustard and pickles. The strong, rich smells quickly filled the car. The old man ate with loud, crunching bites. Bruce, who hadn't eaten for a day, darted one quick envious glance in their direction, and the woman caught his look. Bruce leaned his head against the glass, stared out again across the fields.

They spoke to one another in German, whispering, looking in his direction. The woman reached down in her basket, and unwrapped a piece of heavy chocolate cake. She offered it across the aisle.

"*Bitte* . . . would you like . . . *ein bisschen Torte?*"

Bruce turned and shook his head. "No, thanks," he said.

The old man leaned forward. "*Sprechen Sie Deutsch?*"

Bruce smiled.

"He asked if you speak German," Carlin said.

"No, I don't," Bruce said.

The woman held up the piece of cake. "*Ein bisschen Torte?*" Again Bruce shook his head, but this time the woman thrust the piece of cake at him, Bruce catching it the best he could. The woman smiled. "*Ja, ja.*"

Bruce stared at the frosting that had gotten on his thumb. Slowly he raised his hand and licked off the frosting.

"*Ja, ja,*" the woman said. "You travel by yourself?"

Bruce moved the piece of cake from his left hand to his right.

"No, I'm traveling with some other kids," Bruce said.

The woman nodded and smiled, and then she and her husband conferred in German. Bruce's reply had thrown them into some confusion. The woman looked around the car timidly, as if expecting to see other children, though she knew perfectly well that there weren't any others, and it was then that she spied Carlin.

"This boy, is he with you?"

"No, no," Carlin said. "Not with me." Carlin stood up and walked forward. He sat down in the seat behind the German couple. He tried to speak very precisely, the woman following his every movement. "With the lady with the orphans. They are looking for homes."

"*Ja? Ja?*" The woman looked alarmed.

Bruce took his first bite of cake, wiping the crumbs from the side of his mouth.

Carlin explained as best he could. The woman listened carefully, translating for her husband. Carlin told them about the children and their journey. The woman frowned, very serious. She wanted to know why Bruce was so sad, such a nice boy. . . .

She came back and sat in the seat next to Carlin so they could speak more privately. They spoke in low tones, the train rocked back and forth, and Bruce, only a few feet away, never looked up from his piece of cake, as Carlin told the old couple about Tom's death.

"The boy drowned . . . his friend . . ." The woman murmured. "He thinks it is his fault." She clucked softly. "Such a nice boy."

"No," Carlin said. "Not just a nice boy. Before, when he lived in New York, he was a thief. . . ."

The woman frowned. "He was very poor. He had no other way. . . ." Her husband leaned across, wanting to understand. "*Der Dieb,*" she said. "A thief." He looked across the aisle and stared at Bruce for a long time. "*Ein schönes Gesicht,*" the old man said.

The German couple had been to visit his brother and now they were going home. They had two boys, both grown now with families all their own, very busy, so there were just the two of them in the house . . . this boy, he seemed very nice to them. . . .

Bruce sat, the cake finished, staring out the window. The old man smiled at him, nodding. Bruce was still uncertain. The old man suddenly stood up and moved clumsily past his wife. He leaned over and patted Bruce on the cheek. *"Du hast ein schönes Gesicht,"* the old man said. "Can you say that? *Ja?"*

Bruce looked startled. "I dunno."

"Du hast . . ."

"Du hast," Bruce said.

"Ein schönes Gesicht!" the old man said.

"Shyness Gesicht," Bruce said.

"Ein *schönes Gesicht!"*

"Ein schönes Gesicht," Bruce said.

"You have a good face," the woman said.

The old man nodded approvingly. *"Ja, ja."*

The woman reached across and patted the boy on the hand. "You will come home with us. It will be nice, yes?" The man nodded again.

"Ein schönes Gesicht," Bruce murmured.

"You see? You will learn. You will see," the woman said.

The train stopped to let off the German couple and to take on water and wood. Carlin took Bruce and the German couple and Emma to one side, and, with Carlin doing the translating, the couple was interviewed.

Would they see that Bruce was sent to a school for part of the year? *Ja, ja,* there was a nice log schoolhouse, only a mile away, he and his sons, they built it a few years ago, and they had a new schoolmaster, an Irishman named O'Neill, liked to sing too much, but he was very good with boys, *ja.* And would there be work for Bruce? *Ja, ja,* they had five cows still, and in the spring there was corn to be planted, and they wanted to repair the barn during the winter, with all their boys grown it would be a help to have a big, strong boy like Bruce. . . .

As they talked, Emma saw the fear in Bruce's eyes.

"So we pass the examination?" the old woman said.

"Everything seems very good," Emma said. "You'll just excuse me for one moment."

"Thank you very much," the woman said.

Emma took Bruce aside. "Tell me what's wrong, Bruce."

"I don't know, Miss Symns."

"You don't want to go with them?"

"I don't know. . . ."

Emma stared up at the laboring horses. "You're the only one who can decide."

"I know, Miss Symns, I know." Bruce looked around, looked at the kids gawking at him, at Patches sitting cross-legged on the ground, frowning. "But they don't understand, Miss Symns. They don't understand what I did."

"I think they understand."

"But I don't know what Mr. Carlin told them. I don't know if it's right. Did he tell them, Miss Symns?"

"Yes, Mr. Carlin told them."

"And they still want me?"

"Yes, they want you."

Bruce took a deep breath, bewildered. The old woman was smiling at him.

"You don't have to go if you don't want to, Bruce," Emma said.

"I'm scared, Miss Symns."

"I know."

"Do you want me to go with them or . . ."

Emma didn't say anything.

"I'm going to go with them. I am. They do know, don't they?"

"They know. Go get your things, Bruce."

Bruce ran to the boxcar. It took him about two minutes before he reappeared, all his things stuffed under one arm. He jumped down from the boxcar door and stood awkwardly, staring at the other children. Bruce started an anxious smile that faded. He rubbed his chin. Finally Liverpool came forward and shook Bruce's hand, and then Patches and the others did the same, figuring that Liverpool knew best.

Emma stood and watched as Bruce and the old German couple walked up the hill, the boy taking the old woman's bag after they had gone a hundred feet or so. When he did, he turned and waved to Emma and Carlin and the children. They all waved back.

Emma turned to Carlin.

"Bloomington is up ahead, isn't it?"

"That's right."

"With connections for Springfield and St. Louis," Emma said.

Carlin's face was a blank.

"You're aware of that?"

"I haven't thought about much else," Carlin said.

"Do you know what I would like?" Emma said.

"What would you like, Emma?"

"I would like to ride up in the passenger car with you. If you don't mind."

"I don't mind at all. What about this gang of yours?" He nodded toward the children.

"I think the children will take care of themselves," Emma said.

Emma patted down her dress and smiled and craned her neck to look out the windows.

"It's quite lovely riding up here, isn't it?"

"I suppose," Carlin said.

"Windows are quite a luxury," Emma said.

Carlin looked thoughtful for a moment, saying nothing.

"That old couple, they did understand, didn't they?" he asked. "About Bruce? You felt that they did?"

"I don't know that they understood completely," Emma said. "But you can love something before you understand it."

"Emma . . ."

"Yes?"

"What if I don't get off?"

"If you don't get off? What are you talking about?"

"If I stayed on the train. If I went with you to the end. Until all the children are placed." Emma was silent. "Is that so unthinkable?"

"No, it's not," she said. She placed her hand in his. "It's not unthinkable at all. There have even been moments when I've thought that I could make you come with me, if I just put my mind to it. Women still have the power to do those things."

"Then?" he said.

"It would be wrong," Emma said.

"Wrong? Since when did you start deciding what's right and wrong for me?"

"You'd miss your survey."

"That's right," he said.

"What would you do?" she said, her eyes faltering.

"Maybe I'd open another daguerre parlor in New York. Or it wouldn't have to be New York; it could be Philadelphia, or even Cincinnati, or what about St. Louis . . . but maybe you wouldn't like St. Louis. I made a good living that way before. It wouldn't take me long to get set up. . . ."

"You can't. I won't let you."

"It's not that important, Emma."

"It is that important. Your father lived his whole life thirty feet from the sea and never went out on it . . . and you told me what it did to him. I'm not going to be responsible for doing that to you."

Carlin slouched down in his seat, frowning. "So what is supposed to happen, Emma? Am I supposed to just forget about this?"

"I would hope not."

"Then what?"

"Really, Mr. Carlin, sometimes you do overdo the barbarian."

He snorted, "Well, it's all well and good to call me a barbarian, but what do people do?"

She was smiling. "I have no intention of spelling it out to you."

He stared at her, silent for a moment. "But I'll be gone a year, maybe more . . ."

"And do you expect to meet someone?" Emma asked.

"Don't be ridiculous." He scrutinized her for a moment. "Do you expect to meet someone?"

"No," Emma said.

Carlin straightened up in his seat. "I don't want to let you go."

"I don't want to let you go either," Emma said.

"What if I made you a promise?"

"What kind of promise?"

"That when I finish with the survey, I would come back for you. If I made that promise . . . would you believe me?"

"I would rely on it with all my heart," Emma said.

When the trained stopped in Bloomington, Emma told the children that Carlin was leaving. She was sure that they would all want to thank him for his kindnesses to them, to wish him well with his very important work. The loafers around the depot drifted over to listen, curious. The children listened to her soberly. Her hands shook slightly, as she spoke, but her face was glowing; the children did not miss either fact.

J.P. was the only child who did not come up to say good-bye. While Carlin spoke to the other children, J.P. stood back of the train, pitching rocks down the track. Carlin finally looked over the heads of the other children.

"J.P.!" he shouted. She winged a rock off a rail far down the track. "Hey, J.P.!" His face became very determined. "Excuse me," he said. He picked up his tripod and camera and walked after her.

"Are you going to help me or not, J.P.?" She looked up at him, juggling a stone in her hand. "Take this." He handed her the tripod. "And this." He gave her the coating box. "I'll take the rest. And be careful, will you? There are chemicals in there."

Carlin walked back and picked up the rest of his photographic equipment. J.P. followed him, her arms full, managing as best she could. Carlin shouted up to the fireman. "How much time till you take off?"

"Half-hour, somethin' like that," the fireman shouted back.

"Okay, let's go," Carlin said. He and J.P. marched down through the prairie grass, carrying their equipment. A bobwhite flew up in front of them.

"Where are we going?" J.P. said.

"Where do you think?" They were walking toward a grove of cottonwoods.

"I dunno."

"I made you a promise, J.P."

"What?"

"*What. What.* That I was going to take your picture. By yourself."

* * *

Emma had given them all the time that she could, but there was no more time. The stationmaster said the train was leaving in fifteen minutes, children or no children.

She moved slowly down the slope toward them, her full skirt rustling through the long, dry grass. The man and the child stood near the cottonwoods. Emma saw the man reach out and offer a small velvet case to the child, saw the child take it, then throw it away. The child turned and tried to run, but the man lunged forward, caught her by the wrist. The child struggled to get free.

Emma, feeling like an intruder, stopped a dozen feet away. She could hear the train steaming and hissing up the hill behind her.

"J.P.," Emma said.

J.P. twisted around, her face flushed.

"J.P., we're going to leave now," Emma said gently.

"I'm trying to go, but he won't let me," J.P. said.

Carlin let go of her wrist. J.P. stared down at the ground, breathing hard, unable to move. Emma glanced at Carlin, their eyes met.

"Say your goodbyes to Mr. Carlin," Emma said.

J.P. never lifted her eyes from the ground. "I hope you have . . . a nice trip. . . . I hope you take lots of nice pictures. . . ." Tears welled up in her eyes. "I hope that you . . ."

Carlin took a step toward her, and she stepped back, looked at him, then turned and ran up the hill.

"J.P.!" Carlin shouted after her. "Come back here! J.P.!" She did not stop. Carlin turned to Emma. "Should I go after her?" he asked.

"She'll be all right," Emma said.

Carlin bent to one knee and picked up the daguerreotype that J.P. had dropped in the grass. He handed it to Emma. "If you could give it to her. She may want it later on." Emma opened the case and looked down at the picture. J.P.'s accusing little face stared fixedly back at her.

Emma closed the lid of the daguerreotype case and looked up at him. "She just needs time," Emma said.

A lock of hair blew across Emma's face. Birds were flying low over the grass, and clouds had moved up on the horizon.

"It looks like a storm coming," Carlin said. "I hope that you'll . . ."

"We'll be fine," Emma said. "We just telegraphed ahead to the people in Rock Springs. They sent the message back that they're all waiting for us. It's only a few hours away. The children are very excited."

"I'm coming back for you," he said. "I promise. I promise."

"I know," Emma said.

Carlin reached out and took her hand. She stepped up close to him. He brushed the lock of hair from her face, then held her, caressed her, his hands moving slowly up and down her back.

When he looked up he could see J.P., halfway up the grassy hill, staring at them. She looked as if she had stopped crying. Farther up the hill, gathered by the locomotive, the other children were watching too. One of the train men was waving for her to come up.

Carlin stepped back. "You should get back to them," he said.

"You're not coming up?"

"I have to collect my equipment. You should go ahead."

"Don't be silly," she said. "You can't carry it by yourself."

"It will take a while," he said.

"I can wait," she cried.

Without another word, Carlin gathered up his equipment. Emma carried the tripod in her arms, Carlin carried the rest—the camera, the mercury bath, the coating box. They began walking up the hill, side by side. When J.P. saw them coming, she turned and ran the rest of the way to the train.

The breeze across the prairie had grown stronger, pushing the grass into great, whispering waves.

"It almost sounds like the sea," Carlin said. Emma smiled. "What are you smiling about?"

"Spoken like the true son of a sailor," Emma said.

The Bloomington depot at that moment was not a place anyone would have chosen for an intimate farewell. As Emma and Carlin came back up the hill a crew had just finished uncoupling the passenger car from the locomotive and replacing it, amid great commotion and unsolicited advice from children and bystanders, with two livestock cars full of hogs. To top it all off, the engineer was raising a ruckus with anybody who would listen, marching up and down the platform.

It was not a run the engineer wanted to make. He kept looking up at the fast-moving clouds on the horizon and muttering that he didn't see why he had to take a two-bit train that didn't carry anything more than hogs and children, take it when there was a storm coming on. He kicked at the great iron wheels of the train—they couldn't even get him the right gauge, he complained bitterly.

The fireman and the brakeman tried to jolly him out of his foul humor, but the engineer was not about to be appeased. "The Lord doesn't want me to make this run."

"Now how do you know that?" the brakeman asked skeptically.

"I'm old enough to tell these things in my bones," the engineer insisted.

The fireman looked apologetically at Emma and Carlin. "Don't mind him, miss, he's got this religious streak that passes over him sometimes, but he'll be all right in a minute."

The engineer stomped off and went around behind the depot. When he came back a couple of minutes later, he seemed calmer, and, even from where Carlin stood, his breath a bit fragrant with whiskey.

"All right everybody!" the engineer shouted. "All aboard!" He yanked himself up into the locomotive, muttering as he went. "What kind of run can it be, anyway? They won't even give me a conductor. . . ."

Carlin stood beside the boxcar, reaching up, holding Emma's hand. The loafers around the station were pointing and chuckling, but Carlin paid them no mind. Steam from the engine swirled down around him, and then the fireman leaned out and waved for Carlin to move away from the train. Carlin ignored him too. Neither he nor Emma spoke.

The train whistle sounded, and a moment later the cars made their first lurch forward. Carlin walked alongside the train, still holding Emma's hand, then walked faster, beginning to run as the train picked up speed. Carlin was laughing up at her as their hands parted. He continued to run, slapping at the hog cars as they moved past him, then gave the last car a final shove as if he were the force propelling them on to their destination.

Emma stood in the boxcar door waving at him. Carlin stood on the tracks, waving, as the smoke from the smokestack trailed back toward him. Emma stood watching until she couldn't see him any more.

She turned back and saw that all the children were silently watching her. There were tears at the corners of her eyes, there was no way for her to hide them. She reached up and touched her eyelids with her fingers.

"Are you all right, Miss Symns?" Sarah said.

Emma smiled, leaned forward, and kissed Sarah on the forehead. "I couldn't be finer," she said.

As the afternoon wore on, long columns of mist and light began to rise and fall, shifting on the horizon.

The eerie light began to make the children silent and uneasy. Annie sat in a far corner comforting her cornhusk doll. Tony and Ben and J.P. played a game of cards, while Emma braided Sarah's hair. Patches and Liverpool sat in the open door like sentinels, their feet hanging out, staring fixedly at the coming storm. Both held out their open palms.

"I felt it," Patches said.

"No, you didn't," Liverpool said.

"Yes I did."

"Patches, you lie."

"There, I felt another one," Patches said. Liverpool looked at him in disgust, and that made Patches silent for several minutes. "So what if no one takes us?" Patches said.

"They're going to take us. They're going to take everybody. You heard the letter."

"But what if they think I'm too skinny?"

"Well, then I guess they'll have to fatten you up."

"You're sure?"

"Patches, you saw Miss Symns telegraph to the people same as I did. They're waiting for us up there right now."

"You're sure?"

"Course I'm sure. What's wrong with you, Patches?"

Patches stood up. "Miss Symns?"

Emma looked up from braiding Sarah's hair. "Yes, Patches?"

"Are they all waiting for us. Really?"

"Yes, Patches, they are."

Patches stared at her, unconvinced. "Could you read us the letter again?"

"Of course. If you'll just get it from my bag—it's there, by the stove."

Patches dutifully found the well-thumbed letter in Emma's bag and returned it to her. "Read it, Miss Symns, read it."

Emma dropped Sarah's braids and held up the letter in the fading light. Suddenly Liverpool turned.

"Miss Symns? Look. It's started to rain." He held out his wet palm, thrusting it toward her.

It was as if the rain and the night came together. The storm hit with a fury, announcing itself with long rolls of thunder, and then the lightning began to hit, again and again, until it seemed to be leaping out of the ground. The rain came in sheets, and the train was slowed to a crawl.

A bolt of lightning struck a huge elm only twenty yards from the rails, splitting it with a mighty crack. The light flashed through the slats of the boxcar, illumining the children huddled against the walls with stunned faces. Ben started to cry and his brother Tony held him, his own eyes wide with fear. Annie's fingers were clutched around the cornhusk doll.

Even though they were only inching along, the car had begun to shake. The children looked at one another and at Emma as the train shuddered to a halt.

After a few minutes there was a knock at the door of the boxcar. When Emma pulled the door open the brakeman stood below her on the ground, his coat pulled tight around him, water streaming down his face. He held a pair of lanterns in his left hand.

"It will be a couple of minutes, miss. We're havin' a little trouble with the rails up ahead here. . . . It's a question of the gauge, you see. . . . We just want to make sure everything's riding all right back here."

"We're riding fine," Emma said. "Will we be very late? There are people waiting for these children."

"I know, miss, I know." He wiped the rain from his face. "The ride may be a little rough, but we're going to get you through. Illinois River's up ahead here, and if it ain't too high and the trestle ain't washed out, we're gonna highball it right on through and then we'll be settin' pretty. So just hang on, children, hang on. I gotta go check on the animals. Good night, miss."

The brakeman turned and slogged back through the mud to examine the hog cars. He bent low to look under the train. Even from the boxcar, Emma and the children could hear the restless pigs grunting and squealing.

Apparently satisfied by his inspection, the brakeman hung a bulls-eye lantern on the side of each of the livestock cars and then came running back to the locomotive, pulling the collar of his coat up to protect his head from the merciless rain.

The brakeman hadn't been lying about their highballing it. The train began by picking up speed and then kept going faster and faster, the cars rattling and shaking even more than they had before. A basket of food fell off one of the benches, apples went rolling across the floor. The lanterns swung wildly from the ceiling. The children gritted their teeth and held on.

Liverpool, braced between the two benches, looked up at Emma. "This ain't right, miss, it can't be . . ."

Liverpool pushed himself up suddenly and a lurch threw him back for a second, but he caught his balance and stumbled to the door. When he threw it open, a gust of rain splattered into the car. Patches and J.P. shouted at him.

Liverpool paid no attention. Holding onto the door with one hand, he poked his head out and pointed down the train. "It's the river, Miss Symns, we're coming onto the river."

"Liverpool, get back in here!" Emma said.

Before he had a chance to obey, the train rocked to one side and the door slammed shut, taking Liverpool with it, flinging him, still holding tight, like a rag doll. Then, just as quickly, the train rocked to the other side. The door slid back, dragging Liverpool along on his knees. He stared out into the driving rain.

"Liverpool!" Emma lunged across the shaking floor at Liverpool and tried to pull him back.

"No, miss, no. Look yourself."

They were well out on the trestle now. As Emma looked out all she could see was the dark swirling water far beneath them.

"No, miss, there, back there!" Liverpool pointed back down the track.

Emma looked back. The bulls-eye lanterns on the hog cars behind them swung wildly, throwing an eerie, flickering light. With horror, Emma realized why—the wheels of the livestock cars were no longer on the rails, but were bouncing and hitting directly on the ties.

Emma tried to scream ahead to the locomotive, but the driving rain and then the screech of the train whistle drowned out her voice.

The wind tore at her hair. "Get back, Liverpool, get back!" Emma said.

She felt sick and dizzy. Bracing herself, she covered her eyes with her hand for a second, trying to regain her equilibrium, but she still felt as if she were sliding, as if everything was giving way. When she took her hand away, the feeling was still there. She wiped the rain from her face. She staggered. Then, looking down through the gaps in the trestle at the swollen river, she realized that she wasn't dizzy—things were moving, the entire trestle, weakened by the rushing water and the jarring of the derailed cars, was swaying back and forth. She could hear the timbers creaking beneath the train.

There was a quick series of loud cracks, like shots from a rifle. At first Emma, staring out dumbly into the night, didn't understand. She didn't understand until she stared back, beyond the last car, where the long timbers that supported the trestle pitched slowly into the river. They went over like a row of matchsticks, or dominoes, one after the other, down into the swirling waters, a fan of falling timbers, opening faster and faster. The collapsing timbers gained on the speeding train until they caught up, and the timbers gave way under the last livestock car.

There was the rending of metal and the splintering of wood. The entire train shuddered and then the thirty-foot car broke off as if it were no more than a toy, tumbling down into the darkness, its twisting fall marked only by the dot of light that was the bulls-eye lantern, darting and flickering like a frantic insect. When the car hit the water there was a sudden spilling of light, then flames, as the lantern broke and burning oil caught the straw on fire, then the wooden slats. The trapped animals screamed inside the flaming, floating car.

As the locomotive struggled to move forward, the train shook, another timber fell away into the darkness.

Emma turned back to the children, slamming the boxcar door behind her. "Hold on . . . Patches . . . Tony. Annie, grab hold of the benches. Get down, Liverpool. Quick!"

Again there was a sharp crack, louder than any before, directly beneath them. The front of the boxcar rose up, lurched to the left. Again there was the rending of metal and wood. Patches slid across the floor, screaming, grabbing for a hold. Blankets, baskets, and children flew through the air.

Emma tried to move. Her ribs hurt; it hurt even to

breathe. For a moment she didn't know where she was. She blinked, trying to focus her eyes. Somehow she had managed to hold on to the handle of the door and ended up getting knocked against the wall.

The children stared at her, huddled at the back of the boxcar. The boxcar was still pitched at a terrible angle. Annie and Ben were crying; Sarah grimaced, holding her arm.

Emma heard the creaking of timbers, then felt the car move, a little to the left, then back, as if they were floating. Somehow, on something, they had found balance.

"Shh!" Emma said. "Ben! Stop crying!" Her ribs made it painful for her even to talk. "This minute! Listen to me, all of you. I don't want any of you to move. Do you hear me? Is everyone all right?"

"Yes, Miss Symns," came back the frightened chorus. Ben was still sniffling.

"Ben?"

"Yes Miss Symns," he said.

As Emma tried to stand she felt the car move and she went back down to her knees. Maybe they were balanced, but not on very much, and maybe not for very long. Emma stayed there, her head down, wanting to pray, but not being able to, not being able to think, until she heard the shouts of someone outside.

She reached up and carefully opened the boxcar door. Rain swept in, blinding her momentarily. She wiped the water from her eyes and stared down. Below in the river she could see the two livestock cars flaming as they floated downstream. The screams of the dying, trapped animals, sounded, at such a distance, like the honking of geese.

"Miss! Miss! Down here!"

Emma stared through the darkness. There, on the ties ahead, holding a lantern, was the brakeman, bending forward, then straightening up, trying to keep his balance in the wind and rain. Farther ahead on the rails and still intact sat the now silent locomotive.

"Are you all right, miss?"

The sound of a human voice seemed to clear her mind. Looking down, she could see now that the boxcar had found a fulcrum on an unsteady surface of twisted rail, ties, and still-standing timbers of the trestle. The back of the car swung out over empty space. She closed her eyes; she couldn't look any more.

"Was anybody hurt, miss?"

"No, we're all fine." Emma shouted back.

"We've got to get you out of there, miss. I don't know how long any of this trestle is going to last. You hand the children down to me."

"But we can't even move in here," Emma shouted back. It's too unsteady!"

"I know the balance ain't the greatest, miss," the brakeman shouted back. "But it's only going to get worse. There's no other choice."

"But where's the engineer? Can't he do something?"

"He's in no shape to help. We've got to hurry, miss."

Emma turned back to the children. They stared silently at her. "Children." Emma summoned up her strongest voice. "Children, we're going to be all right. As long as we stay sensible and calm. We're going to get out, all of us. I want you one at a time to crawl up to me. Along the wall to your right. Don't make any sudden movements, don't rush. When you reach me, I'll let you down."

For a moment no one spoke. Finally Liverpool had a question. "What are you lettin' us down into, Miss Symns?"

"It's a drop of about five or six feet to the ties. The track is still firm, at least for now. It's not that far. The brakeman will be there to catch you. Who wants to go first?"

There were no volunteers. Annie began to whimper, then covered her mouth, trying to stop her crying. A gust of wind rocked the boxcar softly, the timbers creaked beneath them.

"I'll be first," J.P. said.

"Come on then," Emma said.

On her hands and knees, J.P. moved along the wall. Once or twice the boxcar seemed to shift, and when it did, J.P. waited, motionless, before moving forward again. "Slowly, J.P., slowly. That's right." Emma reached out and pulled J.P. up to her, held her for a second.

"How'd I do, Miss Symns?" J.P. whispered.

Emma held her away, a smile flickered across her face. "Fine, J.P., just fine."

J.P. pulled her newsboy cap down with both hands, pulled at her belt, and then swung her legs over the side. She hesitated for just a second, puffing up her cheeks, then dropped. When she hit the ties, the brakeman was there to gather her up.

They came, one after the other, Ben and Tony and Annie, then Patches and Sarah and Liverpool. The process was excruciatingly slow. Ben, afraid to make the jump, clung shivering to Emma, and had to be held and comforted for several long minutes before he would make the short drop into the brakeman's arms. They inched forward, crawling on all fours, even as the car shuddered and creaked.

Finally there was only Liverpool left, scuttling up along the wall, moving too quickly, too confidently. Emma had to warn him, but then he, too, made it, springing out, arms spread wide, bouncing up from the ties, victorious. The children were all out.

Emma realized that her hands were perspiring, even in the rain and the cold. She looked back at the dim, now empty interior of the boxcar. Everything was in shambles; blankets strewn everywhere, baskets and bags overturned,

small, odd children's treasures and a shattered daguerreotype scattered across the floor. This had been their home,
she thought.

"Come on, Miss Symns, what are you doing up there?"

Emma looked down at the small band of children below
on the ties, waiting for her.

Leaving the boxcar was not a graceful matter for Emma.
She swung her legs over the side, adjusted her skirts, wiggled forward, adjusted her skirts again as the car swayed
precipitously out to the left.

"Hurry, Miss Symns, please!"

Emma twisted around, supporting herself on her arms,
and slowly slid down, dangling for a second until she felt
their hands on her. She dropped to the ties. The children
crowded around, patting and congratulating her. Emma
stared up at the boxcar, yawning over the edge of the destroyed trestle.

The brakeman put a comforting hand on Emma's back.
"Let's get off of here," he said. "There's no time to waste.
You follow me. And be careful where you step." He laughed
ironically, pointing down to the nails and twisted spikes embedded in the ties. "The company did that to discourage pe-
destrians. Leave it to the company. Let's go."

They moved slowly, single-file, down the trestle toward
the silent locomotive. The ties were about a pace apart, and
the smaller children linked hands with the larger to make
their way from one to the other. Through the gaps, they
could see the black, rushing water. Far downriver now, the
burning livestock cars had broken into small flaming islands
that lit up the night.

Emma turned and saw Annie standing alone, apart from
the others, looking back at the dark, swaying boxcar that
moaned and creaked in the wind.

"Annie!" Emma shouted. "What are you doing?"

Annie never looked at her, but began to leap from tie to tie, back toward the boxcar.

Emma ran after her, stumbling for a second on the rough wood, catching herself, the splinters cutting into her hands. "Annie!" Emma righted herself. The little girl hopped from tie to tie. Emma ran again, caught her by the skirt, and Annie fell forward with a cry, sprawling across a gap in the trestle.

Emma pulled the child to her, shook her. "Annie! Annie! What are you doing?"

The child was crying. "My doll, Miss Symns. I forgot it. I can't leave it. I promised the lady that I'd take care of her."

"No dolls now, Annie. There's not time. She'll be all right. Someone will find her. But later, Annie."

Overhead, the precariously balanced boxcar seemed to float higher, rising above the trestle like an opening jaw, the tortured metal and wood underpinning groaning in the wind.

Emma carried the crying child back down the tracks.

"You've got to get these boys and girls off this bridge, miss. There's some blankets and lanterns up in the locomotive I can give you."

"We've got to walk all that way?" Patches was incredulous. "How come we can't ride up in the engine?"

"This engine isn't going anywhere. Not for a while. When the cars went, the locomotive threw one of her connecting rods." He turned to Emma, "Come on, you can help me."

Emma set Annie down next to Sarah and climbed up after the brakeman into the locomotive.

The engineer sat, bent over like a man who was trying to cough but couldn't. His hands were covering his ears. The corpulent fireman, sober and white-faced now, stood behind him, comforting him with tiny pats on the shoulder. The engineer jerked up to stare at Emma and the brakeman. The muscles in his face were contorted with pain.

"I'm going to give these children some of our blankets and a couple of lanterns," the brakeman said. "I'm going to get them off the bridge.

The engineer didn't say anything.

"It was the hogs' screaming that got to him, miss," the fireman said softly. "He couldn't stand that."

The engineer watched silently as the brakeman gathered up blankets and lanterns and handed some of them to Emma. Slowly he let his hands drop to his lap.

"The children are all right?" he said.

"Yes," Emma said. "They're safe."

The engineer turned and stared out at the river. "The swine of the Gehedrene . . ."

"What swine is that?" the fireman said.

"Christ cast out the spirits, cast them into the swine . . . and they rushed down to be drowned. . . ." He looked back quickly at Emma. "The children were saved."

"Nobody's been saved till they're off of this damn trestle," the brakeman said. "Come on, miss."

The engineer batted at the throttle. "Useless," he said. "Useless."

Emma and the brakeman climbed down from the locomotive, handed the blankets and lanterns to the children.

"This will help some," the brakeman said. "I wish I could help you more, but the man up there's in a pretty poor condition."

"But what can you do?" Emma said.

"We'll do what we can. Me and the fireman, I guess we'll see if we can fix up some makeshift connecting rod and try to get her to move."

"But you can't stay, the bridge isn't going to last," Emma said.

"Oh, I know. We'll be keeping our eyes open, I can promise you that. But you got to get the children here off."

Sarah pulled a blanket around her and Annie. Patches stood, teeth chattering, staring at the brakeman.

"But what do I do when I get them off?" Emma said. "I don't even know where we are."

"Search me, miss."

"What about Rock Springs?" Liverpool said.

"What's that, son?" the brakeman asked.

"How far is Rock Springs?"

"A good ten miles."

Liverpool pulled at Emma's sleeve. "We could walk it, Miss Symns. We can do it."

"Now, I wouldn't be so sure, son," the brakeman said. "It's a good piece, and on a night like this, don't look like there's goin' to be any break in the rain. You got some small ones with you too, don't forget that—it would be a strain. . . ."

"You aren't talking about us, are you?" Ben piped up. "I'm not too small."

"Me either," Annie said.

"I don't know, seems to me it would be a mighty miserable walk. . . ."

"But there are people waiting for us," Patches said. "If we don't show up they'll all think we're dead or somethin' and they'll go home. They'll think we decided not to come, that we don't want homes, that we were just foolin' . . ."

"Yeah," Tony said. "The next time I go to sleep, I want it to be in a house."

The brakeman frowned, looking down through the rain at the traces of fire, far down the river now. "You wouldn't get lost?" he said.

"We'd just follow the tracks, they'd take us right there," Liverpool said.

The brakeman turned and smiled slowly at Emma.

"You've got a smart bunch of children here," he said. "Do you think you could do it?"

"I think they've made up their minds," Emma said.

"Well, then. . . ." The brakeman hitched up his belt. "You better get movin'. All you'll get from standing here is wet."

The children all said their goodbyes to the brakeman, who became bluff and short suddenly, hurrying them along. "Be careful on those ties, now, there's spikes in some of 'em. Watch your step. Help each other. Here, I got an extra corn-cake in my pocket, you take it. You'll be hungry soon enough."

As they walked past the locomotive the engineer staggered to the steps of the disabled locomotive to watch them go. "It was a miracle . . . the children were saved . . . a miracle."

The brakeman never looked up at the engineer, but stood silently in the rain, watching the chain of the children and Emma, their hands linked, laboring from tie to tie. They moved slowly, stopping only to steady themselves to a sudden gust of wind, then moved ahead again. The rails and twisted spikes embedded in the ties caught at their clothing. Two or three times they could feel the trestle creak beneath them.

Patches, stumbling, smashed his lantern against the trestle and the light went out. He never made a sound, but stayed down on all fours, trembling.

"Get up, Patches!" Sarah said.

"No."

"You've got to, come on, get up!"

"No."

Emma came back, leaned over and touched his shoulder. "Patches, what's wrong?"

He looked up at her. "I was just thinking, miss. . . . I couldn't help it."

"Thinking about what?"

The bridge swayed in the wind. "About Tom. About Tom falling into the water and drowning. How it must have been like this."

Emma was silent for a second. She wiped the rain from Patches's face. "It's not the same, Patches." He didn't say anything, stared down through the trestle at the surging river. "It's not the same because I've got your hand. And Sarah will take your other hand. We won't let you go. Come on now."

Patches took her extended hand and pulled himself up. Sarah squeezed his other hand.

"All right, children, let's get moving. Come on," Emma said.

They set out again. The dark forms of uprooted trees swept silently beneath them.

Finally there was the feel of cinders and wet earth. With a confusion of whoops and hollers, they pulled one another up onto the bank.

Suddenly, Liverpool pushed away from the others, looking back at the river. "Look, Miss Symns, look, it's going over!"

They all turned back in time to see the boxcar twisting in the wind, its angle higher, impossibly higher, until it finally broke free. In the seconds it took for the car to tumble to the river, Sarah screamed. The boxcar hit the water and the stove inside exploded and everything went up, brighter than any of the other fires on the river, tongues of flames licking up at the darkness, illuminating even the locomotive thirty feet overhead on the trestle. The fire glowed so fiercely that, for a minute, it seemed as though neither the driving rain nor the rushing water could extinguish it.

None of the children moved. They stood close together, Annie biting on the edge of her blanket, watching. The river broke the car in two, swirling the burning fragments of what had been their home, swirling them away, and it grew darker.

They could not see one another's faces any longer. "All right," Emma said, "we're going now. There's nothing more to look at."

The muddy ground made for treacherous footing, but for more than an hour they kept up a steady pace. Liverpool kept the banter flying back and forth through the darkness. "Who's afraid of the dark? You, Patches?" "Not me," Patches would sing back. "Who's afraid of the rain? You, Tony?" "Not me," Tony would shout. "I love the rain." "Hurry up now, Annie, if you don't keep up the goblins'll get you. . . ."

After the banter started to falter, Sarah started them singing. They sang "Jacob's Ladder" and "Hard Times Come Again No More." Sometimes there was only one voice singing, and then a second would come in, a few yards ahead or behind in the dark, then all the voices joined in on the parts they knew, until finally they were too tired to banter or to sing, too tired to do anything but concentrate on putting one foot in front of the other.

Sometime after the second hour of walking it stopped raining. Their clothes were soaked through and everyone was shivering. The mud had worked itself into their shoes and Emma could tell where everyone was by the squishing sounds. The lanterns swung more slowly now.

Emma heard a cry behind her. Ben had slipped and fallen in the mud. Tony rushed over to help him, but Ben, tired and cranky, wouldn't let his brother touch him. Ben stood there, wiping the mud from his pants, trying to shake it from his hands, crying silently.

When Emma reached out for him, he didn't resist. She lifted him into her arms. The wet little boy was heavy. His face was hot; she hoped he didn't have a fever. When they got in she would make sure he got a warm bath. . . . She would, or someone else would . . . she was going to give them up finally.

It was pitch black. It had stopped raining, but there were clouds and no moon. Once she heard a dog bark, far off. There was nothing to see but the rails, leading them onward.

She lost track of how long they'd been walking. How many miles had the brakeman said? What if he'd been wrong? It seemed as though they'd been walking . . . no, she couldn't be sure.

Emma's muscles quivered with fatigue. The sleeping child grew heavier and heavier. Emma wanted to stop and rest, but she was afraid to even think about it, because if they stopped, they would sleep, they would never move again. . . . The children shambled ahead of her in a ragged line.

Emma felt so tired she could scarcely think. She stopped from time to time, her legs powerless and clumsy. The trees began to appear like a ladder . . . Jacob's Ladder, that's what they'd been singing. She was climbing. She hugged the sleeping Ben to her, he was hot and perspiring, oh, he had a cold, she was sure of it, she would have to find him a hot bath . . .

The muscles in her arms had begun to knot painfully, hurting so steadily that finally her mind began to drift free. . . . She remembered Carlin, how he had held her arms, run his fingers down them, soothed them; and for a moment she felt that he was almost there, beside her, lifting her up, helping her, steadying the ladder as she climbed, but then she stumbled on the cinders and it woke her. The boy clung more tightly to her neck, hanging like a stone. The stubborn dreamlike figures of the orphans drifted ahead of her, down the track.

The darkness became soft. Emma could make out the shape of low bushes, dripping from the rain, and dark, heavy birds flying across in front of them, not making a sound. The sky before them began to turn gray, began to take on more colors, and then one of the children shouted.

They all stopped and turned back. A fierce red light shone far down the track, its rays streaking across the rails. For one terrible moment, Emma, startled and exhausted, was afraid, as if the light rushing at them were some far-off train, bearing down on them with silent vengeance. Then, in the moment it took to become awake, she knew that it was the sun. She saw it lift softly off the horizon, off the rails. The children smiled at one another in the dull red light, too tired to speak. The last lanterns were tossed to the side of the roadbed. The corncake was broken up and passed around, and then they went on, the light at their backs silently pushing them forward, warming them, drying their wet clothes.

Ben woke up on Emma's shoulder grumpy and bewildered about where he was, but after a few minutes he insisted on getting down and walking. Annie was limping with a blister, but she refused to let Emma look.

Suddenly J.P. went running down the track. On the horizon was a dark clump of buildings.

For the last two miles, they hobbled and ran, stopping to pick up the blankets they kept dropping in their haste. They were woozy, delirious. Sarah started to giggle and couldn't stop, every time she caught anyone's eye, she started again.

Tony tried to point out the buildings to his brother. "Look, Ben . . ."

Ben rubbed his runny nose. "I can see myself. Just leave me alone."

Ducks flapped up from a small pond. As the buildings drew closer, the children became silent again.

The town was completely still. At the railway station there were some freight cars shunted off the main line. The station was locked, and when they looked inside the windows they could see no one.

There were four or five stores, a stable, and a blacksmith's

shop. The streets had dried quickly in the cool wind. A dog
came up and sniffed at the children. Some chickens
scratched in the weeds around the station. If anyone had
been waiting, they had given it up a while ago.

Liverpool ran ahead to look in the windows of the stores.
He peered in the windows at rows of tea canisters, bolts of
calico. There was no sign of any one.

Annie stood in the middle of the street, looking bewildered. The children wandered up and down the street, looking in the windows, trying the doors. Around the corner of
each building was the prairie, the grass blowing endlessly.

It was J.P. who heard the singing first. "Miss Symns!" she
shouted. They all straightened up, Tony shoved the dog
away; they all heard it, coming from the end of the street,
coming from the church.

They ran, Annie limping, Patches dropping his blanket,
having to stop and retrieve it once again.

Buggies and wagons were lined up outside the church.
The horses raised their heads as the children ran toward
them, a roan mare whinnied. The singing came from the
church in waves. "Let the cir-cle be unbro-ken . . ."

The children stopped. Liverpool brushed back his hair.
Tony wiped the dried mud from Ben's pants. Emma turned
to take J.P.'s hand but J.P. pulled it away. Annie looked as if
she were ready to bolt. Emma saw the hesitancy in their
faces. They were suddenly as shy as wild animals.

"Now," Emma said. "I see. After all we've come through
this is what frightens you? Is that right?" They were all looking at her uncertainly. "Is that right, Patches?"

"No, Miss Symns," Patches said, his voice little more than a
whisper.

"Wipe your nose, please, Ben," Emma said. Ben did, and
then finally took his brother Tony's hand. "All right, then,
let's go."

Emma opened the door of the church. "In the sky, Lord

. . ." An old woman in the back pew turned, squinting fiercely at the sudden intrusion of light. Emma felt J.P. pull back in fear. Everyone in the church turned, the song dying away except for the few singers in the front who couldn't see what was going on. They murmured, whispered to one another. A young farm woman took the arm of her husband, a startled widening in her eyes. A gray-haired woman gave a thin, gasping cry. A round, older man wiped his hand across his forehead, staring at them intently. He gestured for them to come in.

The children held back, clinging to Emma, pressing close to her for this one last moment, it seemed as if they all had a hand on her.

The minister strode down the center aisle toward them, smiling. He walked straight to Emma, leaned forward, and said something softly to her, but she didn't hear him. She couldn't speak or utter a sound, her throat felt thick and dead. She let the minister take her under the arm and lead her into the church. The children trailed her, staying close. People leaned out of the pews and patted the children, timidly, tentatively; a giant bearded farmer stepped out and clasped Liverpool's hand in his two mammoth hands and pumped it up and down.

The minister stood with Emma in the midst of the church and he raised his arms, singing out in a strong tenor, "Let the circle be unbroken . . ." and the congregation picked up the song again, singing more strongly than ever, the gray-haired woman's soprano floating high above all the others as the tears streamed down her face. The children sang out too, their voices sweet and light, like a balm.

A man picked up Ben and put him on his shoulders. Tony followed them up the aisle, reaching to hold Ben's hand and steady his brother. The bearded farmer had his arm around Liverpool's shoulder. An older man took off his coat and threw it over Patches's damp shirt. Two young girls shared a hymnal with Sarah. The gray-haired woman, without interrupting her singing, swept Annie up in her shawl, rocked her back and forth.

The young farm couple stepped out of their pew to make room for J.P. J.P., moving uncertainly, stepped in next to them. They smiled at her, J.P. didn't smile back. The man reached over and took off her newsboy cap. J.P. panicked, grabbing for the cap, but the man held it away from her. He took her reaching hands gently in his. "Not in here."— Emma saw him mouth the words. He pressed the cap back into J.P.'s hands. The woman leaned over and began to whisper to her, running her hands softly over J.P.'s hair. J.P. looked from one to the other of them. The man held out a hymnal, J.P. took it. The man pointed out the line to her, and then he began to sing. J.P. watched him, then turned and set the newsboy cap down on the pew behind her.

Emma watched them being taken in, saw the hands reaching out to touch her children, to hold them, the hands that would bear them away to a new life; and the hands were kind. The plan could work, there would be more trips, more placings-out, she could go back and tell Brace and her Uncle Edward and the others. . . .

Emma looked down, letting her mind form a picture on the bare plank floor, the picture that Carlin had taken of her and the children. She let it enlarge until it took in a tripod and then the man behind it. The words of the song swept over her, she looked up again, opening her mouth, trying to clear her throat, taking another breath, regaining control, and then finally singing, letting her voice blend with the others.

"Let the circle be unbroken, by-and-by, Lord,
    by-and-by . . .